Manx on her mot... Helens and brought up on Merseyside. After studying modern languages at university, she trained as a translator and secretary, going on to win the 'Secretary of the Year' award. She is an experienced author of business and self-help books, including BLUFF YOUR WAY AS A TOP SECRETARY, COPING SUCCESSFULLY WITH MIGRAINE and YOU AND YOUR TENANCY. Her other novels, ACROSS THE WATER and A FAR TOMORROW, are also available from Headline.

Sue Dyson now lives in Gloucestershire.

One Golden Summer

Sue Dyson

HEADLINE

First published in 1996
by HEADLINE BOOK PUBLISHING

First published in paperback in 1997
by HEADLINE BOOK PUBLISHING

A HEADLINE paperback

10 9 8 7 6 5 4 3 2 1

ISBN 0 7472 5450 8

Typeset by
Letterpart Limited, Reigate, Surrey

Printed and bound in Great Britain by
Cox & Wyman Ltd, Reading, Berks

HEADLINE BOOK PUBLISHING
A division of Hodder Headline PLC
338 Euston Road
London NW1 3BH

One Golden
Summer

Prelude

St Helens, Lancashire – Spring, 1931

'Dum – *dee* – dum . . .'

   '. . . *Dee* – dum – dee . . .'

   '. . . Dum – *dee* – dum . . .'

   '. . . dee-dum-dum . . .'

   '. . . dum-dee-dum, di-dum-di-dum . . .'

   '. . . DAA-DAA!'

The two girls giggled as they danced and pirouetted and sang, all the way from the Tivoli Cinema to the end of the street. The taller girl was about twelve years old, rather tall and gangly, with bony knees showing beneath an outgrown skirt and mouse-brown hair tied in frizzy bunches which stuck out on either side of her face. Her companion was eleven but looked younger, a petite girl whose apparent fragility was belied by bright, sea-grey eyes, an elfin chin and a mouth which was accustomed to smiling.

'Come on, Jenny, let's try the dance again.' The elder girl hitched up her skirt and spun round on one foot. Jenny wondered how Mae managed it without falling over, but then everyone knew that Mae Corlett danced like a gazelle.

Jenny panted and bent over, hands on knees, shaking her mass of shiny black hair.

'Let me get my breath back!'

But Mae Corlett was too excited to wait. She was already trying out the new steps, dodging out of the way of Saturday morning shoppers as they struggled along the street with their baskets of groceries.

1

'One-two-*three*, one-*two*-three, one-two-*three* . . . come on, Jen!'

'Aw, Mae, you know I can't dance for toffee.'

'And I can't sing like you, but who cares? Come *on*, I'll lead and you can be the lady.'

Jenny Fisher could hardly sing for laughing. But with her arm about her best friend's waist and the spring sun cutting through the factory smog, she could almost believe she really was a big Hollywood star. On Saturday afternoons she was no longer little Jenny Fisher, the coal-miner's daughter, but Mademoiselle Jennifer, the greatest singer ever to grace the silver screen . . .

'We'll be stars one day, just you see,' declared Mae as they tapped and spun over the paving stones and into Jubilee Street.

'Not if your dad catches us, we won't,' said Jenny, nodding to the far end of the street where John Corlett's corner shop stood.

Mae bit her lip.

'Better not let him see us,' she said. They bent double to sneak past the shop-front, fingers to lips, trying hard not to giggle.

'What did you tell him?'

'I said we were at your Auntie Jane's.'

'We'll catch it if he finds out you went to the flicks.'

'But he won't, will he?'

Safely past the shop, they straightened up.

'Did he see us?'

'Shouldn't think so, he was too busy weighing out spuds.'

Jenny looked back at the shop door, jangling from an incessant stream of shoppers. Saturday was the busiest day of the week, and John Corlett was a widower, with only his daughter to help him run the business.

'Shouldn't you be getting back, to serve in the shop?'

Mae hesitated then wrinkled her nose with its light sprinkling of freckles.

'Let's go back to your house first. P'raps your mam'll make us a jam butty.'

'Oh, all right then.' Jenny knew how much Mae liked

coming back to her house; the Fisher kids had a mam *and* a dad, unlike Mae. Besides, Mr Corlett was Manx and a bit stern, nothing like big smiling Dan Fisher.

It couldn't have been a nicer day, thought Jenny, as they skipped along together. They'd been to see *The King of Jazz* at the pictures, they knew all the songs and all the dances, they'd pretended to be all the famous film stars, and one day they would be – only better.

It wasn't until they rounded the corner into Gas Street that Jenny saw the pit ambulance. The big, beetle-black van was crawling slowly down the street, drawing closer and closer to number forty-two. Women were coming out on to their doorsteps, eyes wide and fixed on the ambulance, willing it to stop anywhere but outside their house.

Mae stopped in mid-dance and put her hand on Jenny's arm.

'It's stopping . . . outside your house!'

Jenny froze in her tracks. No, it couldn't be. Not outside number forty-two. Dad was safe at the pit, he'd be back at six and Mam would scrub the dirt off his back at the kitchen sink. Then he'd have his tea, and a bit of a sleep in front of the fire. No, she wouldn't believe it, she couldn't.

'It *is*,' whispered Mae. 'Oh, Jenny.'

'Dad! Dad, Dad, Dad . . .' Jenny started running, hurtling down the sloping street towards her house, forgetting everything and everyone but the huddle of people gathering around the ambulance. The back doors were opening, two men in pit clothes sliding out something covered in a blanket.

Somebody caught her by the shoulders and tried to hold her back, but she shook free and walked on trembling legs towards the stretcher. Something lay very still underneath the red blanket. From one corner a bootless foot protruded at an unnatural angle, covered in smears of a darker, brownish-crimson.

'No! Dad!'

As she stretched out her fingers to touch her dad's cold flesh, Mrs Pateman from number forty-four took her hand and pushed it away.

3

'There's bin an accident at pit, love, best not touch.'

'I want me dad, I want me dad, I want . . .'

Mae was by her side now, but Jenny was following the stretcher towards the still, ramrod-straight figure of her mother. Dot Fisher was standing at the front door, her face chalk-white, her eyes as hard and expressionless as glass. The newborn baby in her arms was bawling, a grizzling toddler pulling at her skirt, but she paid them no attention.

'Mam,' gasped Jenny. 'Mam, what's happened?'

If she had expected tenderness from her mother, she was quickly disappointed. Dot's eyes flickered towards Jenny with a look of indifference – no, hostility.

'He's gone,' she spat.

'Wh-what?'

'Your precious dad's dead, Jenny. Is that what you wanted to 'ear? Dead an' gone an' left us all to starve.'

Jenny did not follow the stretcher into the house. She sensed that she was being excluded, that she was not wanted here, any more than the squalling baby or the whimpering tot. The front door slammed with a resounding crash.

Sympathetic voices spoke to her, soothing hands tried to pull her away, but she heard and felt nothing. She was numb all over.

'Jenny.'

Mae's voice was the only one to penetrate the veil of silence. Jenny looked round at her. The Manx girl's eyes were bright, too bright, as though she was holding back tears.

'Mae. It's me dad, he . . .'

'I know.' She put her arm round Jenny's shoulders. 'There's nothing you can do.'

'I want . . . I want to see him.' Jenny started to shake, the numbness turning to cold and shock. 'I want me dad.'

Mae shook her head.

'Not now,' she said. 'Not yet. Come on, Jenny, come back to the shop with me. Dad'll know what's best.'

She drew Jenny gently away, through the gaggle of onlookers. Pitying voices murmured in hushed tones about

4

'them poor kids' and wondered 'what'll become of 'em now?' Jenny craned her head back over her shoulder towards the front door of number forty-two, still obstinately closed against her.

'I can't leave Dad,' she said. But Dad had left her, and how could life ever be the same again?

Chapter 1

January, 1938

Jenny Fisher glanced round the shop. It was Saturday night at Corlett's store, the busiest time of the week. Mr Corlett had left her in charge while he was in the store-room and Eddie the shop boy was measuring tea out into blue paper bags. No one would notice, and in any case where was the harm? She always put the money back in the till, soon as she had it.

'There you are, Mrs O'Brien. That's sevenpence exactly.'

Jenny leant over the counter and slipped something extra into the shopping basket, along with the three pounds of potatoes and the pathetically small cube of margarine. Seven pennies tinkled on to the polished shop counter; even with the clandestine gift of half a loaf of yesterday's bread, it was sevenpence more than Molly O'Brien could afford.

Mrs O'Brien took a peek into the basket.

'I don't know as I should . . .'

''Course you should.'

'You're a good girl, Jenny Fisher. Your dad'd be proud of you, God rest his soul.'

The hand which briefly clasped Jenny's was cold and much too bony, with veins that stood out against the translucent skin like blue string. The O'Briens had twelve children and Col's lungs were so weakened from labouring at the chemical works that he was rarely well enough to work. Molly O'Brien was accustomed to making ends meet by going without herself.

In the seven years since Dad had died in the pit accident,

the Fishers had come perilously close to that kind of poverty too, especially in the dark days when Dot had sought comfort in drink. Mr Corlett said God helped those who helped themselves, but Jenny couldn't just stand back and let the O'Briens starve.

'I'll pay you back Monday,' promised Molly O'Brien, tucking her empty purse into her basket.

'When you can manage, eh? Oh, Mr Quigley, your usual, is it?'

Jenny's heart pounded a little too quickly as she reached down a packet of ten Woodbines. Yet it was nothing really – just helping folk get by when they'd no money to feed their kids. On the other hand, Mr Corlett had been very kind, giving her Mae's old job – and there was precious little work for young girls in St Helens. What's more, she knew John Corlett disapproved of giving "tick".

The shop was busy, and the last hour passed quickly. It would be ten o'clock soon, and her elder brother Tom would call for her on his way back from a swift half at The Feathers.

Just before ten, when Jenny was bagging up the last of the "specky" apples, Eddie the shop boy came across from slicing roast mutton, his fingers leaving greasy smears as he wiped them on his apron.

'Coming to pictures with me on Monday then?' His pudgy face split into a suggestive grin.

Jenny decided to ignore him. At sixteen, Eddie Timms was a smelly, unlovable pest but he was harmless enough; sooner or later he'd get the message and leave her alone.

Eddie sidled a bit closer. It was cold in the shop, but he was pungent with stale sweat.

'Well?'

'Well, what?'

'It's a George Formby.'

'No, ta.'

'You'll be sorry if you don't.'

'I doubt it.'

Jenny turned to walk back across the shop, and found herself wedged between Eddie and the counter.

'Stop mucking about, will you? I've got these apples to bag up.'

'Give us a kiss then.'

'You what!'

'Give us a kiss and I'll let you by.'

Jenny wasn't sure whether to laugh or be sick. She gave Eddie an impatient shove and he reluctantly slid off sideways.

'You ought to be nice to me,' he whined.

She turned to look at him over her shoulder as she weighed up the apples and dropped them into two-pound bags.

'Why's that then?'

'I know things.'

'What things?'

'About you. About what you've been getting up to when old man Corlett's not lookin'.'

Jenny's heart turned a somersault. She stayed bent over the barrel of apples, praying that Mr Corlett wouldn't choose this moment to come down and lock up the shop for the night.

'I don't know what you're talking about.'

'I've been watching you. You've been givin' stuff away, haven't you?'

'Don't talk rubbish.'

'I saw you put that bread into Molly O'Brien's basket. You know what that is, don't you? It's *stealing*.'

'It is *not*! I always put the money back.'

Eddie sneered.

'I bet old man Corlett would love to know you've been nickin' food off him.'

Jenny sprang up and swivelled round to glare right into Eddie's face.

'You wouldn't dare!'

He smirked, revelling in his new-found power.

'Coming to the pictures with me then?'

'Drop dead!'

He shrugged.

'Please yourself. But if you know what's good for you . . .'

9

Jenny raised her hand in a sudden reflex. She might well have smacked him across the face with it, but at that moment the shop door jangled and a tall young man stepped in, taking off his cap and slipping it into his pocket. The yellowish light gleamed on his dark cropped hair, shiny with brilliantine. Tom Fisher was twenty-one years old, and – despite Dot's entreaties – a collier like his father. His body was slender but strong beneath his worn brown jacket and trousers.

'What the bally 'eck is going on here, then?'

'Tom!' Jenny swung round to face her elder brother. 'Me and Eddie were just . . .'

'It's all right, sis.' Tom's eyes flicked from Eddie to Jenny and back again, taking it all in. He had the same pale grey eyes and near-black hair as Jenny; as small children they'd been inseparable. 'I can work it out for myself. You!' He jabbed his thumb at Eddie. 'Get away from her.'

Eddie laughed nervously.

'I weren't doin' owt . . .'

'Stay away from my sister. You hear?'

Eddie scowled at Tom, but moved across to the other end of the counter where he started tidying up a pyramid of cocoa tins.

'Right,' said Tom. 'You ready for the off then?'

'Almost,' said Jenny. 'I just have to wait for Mr Corlett to come and lock up.' And pay me, she told herself. She'd keep a shilling back and on Monday morning, slip it into the takings to cover what she'd given away.

'I'll wait with you then.'

'There's no need . . .'

'It's pitch black an' comin' on to snow. I'm not havin' you walk home on your own.'

'Oh, all right then.'

Jenny went across to turn the shop sign to "Closed". When she was little, she'd hated it when Tom came over all protective. But since Mam had married that thug Ivan Price, she'd been glad of all the allies she could get. Tonight, though, she couldn't help worrying that Eddie was about to say something spiteful that would make Tom ask

10

questions. And what if he carried out his threat and told Mr Corlett, before she'd had a chance to replace the money?

Tom hoisted himself up on to the counter and sat on the end.

'You all right then, Jen?'

She nodded.

''Course I am.'

'I'm surprised you can stand workin' in this place.' Tom glared at Eddie, making him flinch.

'I'm fine, honestly. Eddie doesn't mean any harm.' She caught sight of her brother's bandaged hand. 'You've hurt yourself.'

'It's only a bruise, don't take on. I did it down pit this afternoon. One o' manhauler cars broke loose an' knocked over a coal tub. Be right as rain in the mornin'.'

John Corlett came down from the flat above, entering the shop through the stock-room at the back. The arms of his brown coat were sprinkled here and there with white, from carrying sacks of flour. Jenny saw how tired he looked, and felt a twinge of guilt.

She patted her hair, took off her overall and smoothed her dress; Eddie snapped to attention like a toy soldier. Tom slid off the counter and flicked his cap across it.

'How're you doin', Mr Corlett?'

'Oh, middling fair, middling fair.' If anything, ten years of living in St Helens had only served to broaden John Corlett's Manx accent. 'Here's the key, Jenny. You lock up while I count the takings. Busy night, was it?'

She thought of the three half-loaves of stale bread she'd given away, and the money she had to pay back. Three stale loaves at fourpence each, a shilling exactly. Maybe she could put in one-and-six, if she could find a way of hiding the money from Ivan?

'We sold all the apples, and the carrots.'

'That's good.' Mr Corlett counted out sixpences and shillings, sliding them towards himself across the counter and into little calico money bags. 'Ten-and-six, eleven, eleven-and-six. Did you sell any of the corned beef?'

11

'Only two slices.'

He tut-tutted and shook his head as he counted out the last of the takings.

'That'll never do, it won't keep past Wednesday. I'll have to mark it down. Here you are, Jenny – fifteen-and-six.'

'Thank you, Mr Corlett.'

Jenny took the ten-shilling note and handful of change, and put them carefully into her purse. It was nice to feel the weight of the money, *her* money, if only for a little while. She dithered.

'Mr Corlett, I was just wondering . . .'

'Hmm?' He glanced up at her through little round spectacles perched on the end of his nose. He looked so preoccupied and sad.

'I was wondering if you'd heard from Mae?'

At that, Mr Corlett's face tensed, then looked even sadder.

'Not recently. No.'

'Oh. I'm sorry, I . . .'

'It's well past ten. You get off home and I'll see you on Monday morning.'

It was only a five-minute walk from Mr Corlett's shop to the top end of Gas Street. Jenny was fit enough, but she had to walk quickly to keep up with her elder brother's long strides.

'You'll tell me if that Eddie bothers you again?'

'I suppose.'

'An' if you've got any sense, you'll not go askin' daft questions about Mae, neither. It hit her dad hard, her leavin' home like that.'

It had hit Jenny hard too. These last few years had been a real struggle for the Fishers, and Mae's friendship had been the one thing that had given Jenny faith in the future. First Mam had taken to the drink to escape Dan Fisher's death and Jenny had had to become a second mother to Billy and Daisy. She'd badly needed a friend, someone to tell all her darkest fears to, and Mae had always been there. And when Mam had met and given in to Ivan Price, who wouldn't

12

leave her alone till she married him, Mae had been there to reassure Jenny that everything would be all right.

But Mae wasn't here any more. Four months ago she'd upped and left St Helens, won a contest to become a chorus-girl with a dance band. Mam said she'd broken Mr Corlett's heart.

Tom and Jenny turned down the alleyway which ran behind Gas Street. A light was on in the back kitchen of number forty-two, and a pair of miner's iron-shod clogs sat defiantly on the back steps.

'Ivan's home,' said Jenny quietly.

Tom pushed her forward, though he seemed no keener to go in than she was.

'Best get in. No point in hangin' around out here.'

Ivan Price was standing at the stone sink, stripped to the waist, his back to the door. Dot was washing him with water from a huge enamel jug, raising it to shoulder height to send the water cascading down over his shoulders and back, leaving greyish streaks where the last of the coal dust had been. She greeted Tom's arrival with a smile that lit up her prematurely lined face.

'Tom, love, there's a bit of pie in oven – I kept it warm for you. Jenny, fetch the pie and a couple of plates. Nancy, cut a slice off that loaf.'

Jenny's fifteen-year-old sister Nancy pulled a face as she threw down her magazine.

'I've been workin' all day up the bottle-works. Why do *I* have to do it?'

'Oh, give it here.' Jenny took the knife and cut a couple of inch-thick slices from a day-old loaf. It was pointless reminding Nancy that she too had been on her feet, from eight in the morning until ten at night. 'A fine wife *you'll* make somebody, Nancy Fisher!'

Tom threw Ivan a look of distaste as he took off his jacket and put it over the back of a chair. 'Evening, Ivan.'

He straightened up and turned around, taking the towel from Dot's hand and using it to swab the water from his powerful body. His eyes were a piercing blue beneath low brows and thick, wiry black hair. He didn't bother to smile.

13

His eyes flicked from Tom to Jenny, lingering too long. Ivan always made Jenny feel uncomfortable; she sometimes wondered if he meant to. She'd often felt he was the sort of man who liked to wield power over people.

'So you're back then?' The voice was harsh and heavy, the accent straight from the Welsh valleys. 'What time do you call this, girl?'

'Mr Corlett didn't lock up till gone ten. Tom waited so he could walk home with me.'

Ivan's mouth curled into something between a smile and a sneer.

'What's that, Tom – frightened to walk home on your own now are you, boy? Why don't you tell your mam how you banged your hand down the pit today, an' had to have a bandage put on it.' He laughed humourlessly. 'You're a soft bugger! You should let me harden you up a bit.'

Tom glowered. He wasn't a violent man but Ivan awoke feelings of violence within him, feelings he had to struggle to suppress. Ivan was his overman at the pit as well as his stepfather; it could cost Tom his job if he fell out with him. But there were times . . . Scraping back his chair on the bare wooden floor, he sat down at the table and turned his attention to the plate of pie Jenny was handing him.

Jenny didn't bother eating, she wasn't hungry any more. Ivan was enough to put anyone off their food.

'You feeling all right, Mam? You look tired.'

Dot rubbed her hand over her swelling stomach. She was quite small for five months gone, thought Jenny.

'Right as rain.'

'Have you been eating properly, like the doctor told you?'

'I had summat at tea-time with Billy and Daisy.' Jenny was sure it was a lie. 'Check up on them, will you? Billy's taken to reading under the bedclothes – he'll ruin his eyes.'

Jenny got up from the table, pushing her supper across to Tom for him to finish off.

'I'll go up now.'

'No, she won't,' cut in Ivan, who was buttoning up his shirt. Tufts of black curly hair were visible through the open neck. He was like an animal, thought Jenny. A big, hairy, uncouth animal. He held out his bear's-paw of a hand. 'First she's got something to give to her *dad.*'

He emphasised the word with relish, knowing how much it revolted Jenny. Too late, she remembered that she had meant to keep a shilling back, to pay off her debt to Mr Corlett.

'Well?'

With the greatest reluctance, Jenny picked up her handbag and took out her purse. Inside lay the precious ten-shilling note, the two florins, the shilling and the shiny sixpence. Her money. *Hers.* She'd earned it, why should she have to give it to Ivan Price who wasn't her father and never would be?

'I'm waiting, girl. Don't try my patience.'

There was a wide leather belt around Ivan's thick waist; Jenny watched him fingering the brass buckle lovingly. With cold, unresponsive fingers she opened the purse and upturned it on the table top.

The halfpenny and the three farthings she picked up and dropped back into her purse, following them surreptitiously with the shilling. She looked up into Ivan's face, praying that she could lie convincingly.

'Fourteen-and-six,' she said flatly, handing over that amount and no more.

'Don't you lie to me, girl.'

'I'm not, I . . .'

'D'you want a good thrashin'? Give me that purse.'

He took it from her, emptied it on to the table. In desperation, Jenny watched Ivan scoop out every last coin and put them into his pocket, even the three farthings. She stared at him, aghast.

'My money! I . . .'

'*Your* money, is it?' Ivan laughed sarcastically. 'Well, seein' as I'm such a good da to you . . .' He flung the three farthings at her. 'Don't you say I don't give you nothin'.'

Jenny crouched down and picked up the three farthings, scratching them up off the floor with her fingernails. Ivan stood over her, watching her with obvious satisfaction.

'Don't you think you ought to thank your *da?*'

Jenny looked across the back kitchen. Nancy had picked up her magazine and Dot was darning socks, but they were both watching her, waiting to see who would win the trial of strength. Tom's eyes were fixed on Ivan, but he said and did nothing. Anger stirred within Jenny; she longed to scream at Ivan, tell him what she really thought of him.

Dot's nerve broke.

'Say thank you, Jenny. Your dad's a good man, takes care of us all. He puts a roof over your head, remember that.'

Jenny got slowly to her feet. Even at full stretch she was a foot shorter than Ivan. It was impossible not to feel intimidated by him.

'Thank you.' The words stuck in her throat.

But Ivan wouldn't let go that easily, not when he was winning.

'Thank you, *Dad*.'

For her mother's sake, Jenny knew she must give in – this time. Besides, Mam was right. If not for Ivan Price the whole family might be out on the street by now, and Dot no more than a drink-sodden wreck. Jenny told herself that there must be some good in the man after all.

'Dad,' she said, almost inaudibly, and slipped the three farthings into her purse. She promised herself that next time would be different. But in the meantime, how was she going to pay back the money to Mr Corlett?

Mr Corlett seemed not to have noticed the missing bread, and things were better at number forty-two over the next week. There was a good demand for coal so Ivan was hardly at home, there was a new Ronald Coleman film showing at the Savoy Picture House, and – best of all – Jenny received a letter from Mae.

She read it out to Daisy and Billy as they ate their breakfast doorsteps of bread and jam.

Dear Jen,
The band's on the move again. Guess where we are now? Glasgow! The dancing and stuff is hard work but

16

much better than working in the shop. Wish you could be here too.

Is Dad still angry with me? He didn't answer my last letter. You can write to me care of this address, but we move on next week, I'm not sure where. There's a rumour it might be Cornwall! Might be able to pay you a visit if we get a few days off.

Chin up, and write soon. Missing you loads.

Love,

Mae XXX.

Billy licked the last of the jam off the spoon.

'Where's Glasgow?'

'In Scotland.'

'Where's Scotland?'

Billy's eight-year-old brain had only the vaguest grasp of geography. His younger sister Daisy bounced on her chair.

'I know, I know – it's in Liverpool!'

Jenny laughed so much she almost choked on her tea.

'Don't be silly, that's Scotland *Road*! Scotland is a long way away, miles and miles up north.'

'When's Mae comin' 'ome then?'

'I don't know. I don't even know if she *is* coming home. It all depends . . .'

Nancy walked into the kitchen, hitching up her stockings. She looked small and skinny wearing Jenny's cast-off skirt and well-worn blouse.

'What depends on what?'

'I was just telling Billy and Daisy about Mae. I've had a letter from her – she might come and see us sometime, if she gets the time off.'

'Oh.' Nancy sniffed. 'I'm surprised she'd dare show her face. Leaving her dad like that, all on his own.' She cut a slice of bread and lathered it with marge. 'There's no jam left!'

'Billy had the last of it, I'll see if Mam'll give me the money to get some more. Anyway, you can't have marge *and* jam.'

'Why not?'

'You know why not. We can't afford it.' And the reason we can't afford it, thought Jenny, is that Ivan Price hardly gives Mam enough housekeeping to keep body and soul together. She wondered what he did with the rest of his money – and Jenny's and Tom's. Everyone knew that overmen were on a good wage.

Still chewing, Nancy spoke through a mouthful of bread. 'You'll plait my hair for me, won't you, Jenny?'

'Well . . . I mustn't be late for work.'

'*Please*. If I don't tie it back, the foreman'll send me home. An' it looks nice plaited.'

'Oh, all right then. But hold still or the brush will pull.'

Nancy chattered on as Jenny fixed her long brown hair. 'Where's Mam?'

'In bed. I told her to have a lie-in and I'd fix Ivan's snap for him. So don't you go waking her up, she needs the rest.'

Daisy piped up: 'Is Mam really goin' to have another baby?'

'Yes.'

'Will it be a baby brother or a baby sister?'

Jenny smiled.

'We'll just have to wait and see. There, Nancy, you're all done. Help me clear away these breakfast things or we'll both be late for work.'

By running all the way to Mr Corlett's shop, Jenny just managed to get there on time, diving into her cap and overall moments before John came down to open the shop.

'Good morning, Mr Corlett.'

'What? Oh – good morning, Jenny.'

If he seemed distracted, at least Eddie was more cheerful than usual. He even whistled as he humped the huge sacks of potatoes into the shop from the stock-room, and made up orders to take out to his delivery bike.

Business was always a bit slow on Mondays, what with housewives doing their weekly wash and the need to economise after the weekend. Short-time working and lay-offs made things tight for a lot of people.

It was just after three o'clock when Jenny heard the little

girl crying. She was standing outside the shop window, her face pressed up against the glass and her cheeks stained with tears. She couldn't have been more than six years old. Curious, Jenny went outside.

'What's the matter?'

The little girl wiped a grimy hand across her eyes.

'I – lost – it. I – lost – it.' The words were punctuated by sobs. Jenny crouched down so that she and the little girl were eye-to-eye. This close to the child, you couldn't help but notice the reek of poverty that surrounded the tiny, fragile body.

'What's your name?'

'D-Dora. Dora O'Brien.'

The penny dropped. Jenny knew she'd seen the child before – she was one of the O'Brien brood, from the slums down Canal Terrace.

'What is it you've lost?'

'The money. Me mam gave me thruppence. I dropped it, an' it went down the gutter.' Tears glistened at the corners of Dora's swollen eyes. 'Me mam'll kill me.'

Jenny knew that that thruppence had probably represented the only meal the O'Briens would get that day. She'd have replaced it from her own money, but her purse was empty, thanks to Ivan Price.

'Come with me, it'll be all right. But don't say anything.' Jenny put her finger to her lips.

The little girl shook her head very gravely, the blonde curls dancing about her dirt-smeared face.

One small loaf of bread . . . no one would notice that it had gone. Jenny checked that Eddie and Mr Corlett were out of the shop. One loaf. Not stale, it was true, but how could there be any stale bread to give on a Monday? Just as soon as she was paid, Jenny would replace the money. What else could she do? She had to do something to help the child . . .

'Here. Take this.'

'Miss?' The eyes grew even larger in the small white face.

'Shh. Run home quickly now, and don't drop it.'

The door clattered noisily shut behind the child. There

were a few seconds of silence, and Jenny heard the ferocious thumping of her heart inside her chest. The running figure of Dora O'Brien turned to a brownish blur in the distance.

'So Eddie was right after all.'

Mr Corlett's voice froze Jenny to the spot.

'Why, Jenny? Why have you been stealing from me?'

Stealing? The thought seared right though her like a thunderbolt. White-faced, she spun round.

'Mr Corlett – I wouldn't steal from you!'

John Corlett's expression was more sad than angry, and that only made things worse.

'I've just watched you give away a loaf of my fresh bread.'

Jenny's mouth opened and closed. Suddenly all the reasons she had given to herself seemed like flimsy excuses.

'I . . . I'm not a thief, Mr Corlett, I swear I'm not. It's not like that. I was going to put the money back, only Ivan . . .'

John Corlett just kept on looking at her, his face full of sorrowing disappointment.

'Oh, Jenny.'

'The O'Briens are starving. The baby died last winter for lack of food . . .'

The grocer's expression hardened a little. Jenny knew it wasn't that he didn't understand suffering, only that there was too much of it, and once you became involved with other people's misery it could drag you under.

'The Public Assistance Board looks after people like the O'Briens. This shop is not a charity, Jenny.'

She hung her head, suddenly not proud any more but profoundly ashamed. How could she have been so utterly, criminally, stupid?

'No, Mr Corlett.'

'Eddie tells me this has been going on for weeks.'

Jenny raised her head a fraction. Her shame at being found out was only matched by her contempt for Eddie.

'Three weeks, Mr Corlett. But I swear, until today I've given away nothing but a few half-loaves of stale bread and

20

I put the money in on a Monday. But then Ivan took all my wages . . .'

John Corlett sighed. Sorrow had aged him. First his wife, then his daughter, and now Jenny; everything and everyone deserted him in the end.

'Listen to me, Jenny. I know you're a good girl at heart and you meant well, but you've let me down badly.'

'It'll never happen again, Mr Corlett, I promise. I'm so very, very sorry.'

'I know.' He laid a weary hand on her shoulder. 'The thing is, Jenny, I was meaning to have a word with you anyway. Business is very bad just now, the shop isn't doing at all well, what with the big Co-op so close, and I just can't afford to pay both you and Eddie. I was thinking of letting him go, but now . . .'

A coldness was spreading through Jenny's body. She didn't want to listen.

'I'll give you a good reference, Jenny.'

'Mr Corlett!'

He put up his hand for silence.

'There's nothing else I can do. I'm giving you a week's notice as from today.'

Chapter 2

The walk back from Mr Corlett's shop to the house in Gas Street was the longest of Jenny Fisher's life.

It was a chill February day, with a weak sun that did nothing to warm the frozen pavements, and a yellowish smog hanging low over the distant clocktower of Beecham's factory.

Oh, why, why, why? Why had she done it? Why hadn't she seen that it was wrong, no matter how well-intentioned? If she hadn't been such a fool, perhaps Mr Corlett would have kept her on, or sacked Eddie instead of her.

Mrs McCarthy waved to her from the doorstep of number thirty-nine, and called across the street.

'Your mam keepin' well, is she, love?'

'Yes, thanks.'

'Well, you just tell me if there's owt she needs.' The woman paused in her carpet-beating, and straightened up. 'You're home early today.'

'Yes,' said Jenny, and turned down the passageway to the back of number forty-two. She wasn't going to let on to anyone what had happened to her until she'd told Mam.

The back door was ajar, the passageway festooned with washing and a few wisps of steam coming from the copper in the wash-house. Dot was mangling the last of the clothes and putting them into the washing basket. She looked up in surprise at Jenny.

'What are you doing here?'

Jenny didn't answer, but gently took the handle of the mangle.

'Let me do that.' She began pumping the handle round and round, imagining it wasn't a bed-sheet but Eddie's pudgy little body emerging, squashed flat, from between the rollers.

'Something's happened, hasn't it?' demanded Dot, folding her red arms over her pregnant stomach.

Jenny could have wept for shame.

'Yes.'

'Well? Are you going to tell me or do I have to guess?'

Jenny took a pillowcase and fed it into the mangle.

'I've got the sack. A week's notice.'

Dot stared, open-mouthed, her high colour draining to a greyish-pink.

'The sack? No!'

'Mr Corlett's shop isn't doing very well, he can't afford to keep me on.'

Dot shook her head, coming to terms with this new and very unwelcome development.

'But, Jenny, you were doing so well. And how will you get another job?'

Jenny had been thinking the very same thing. Unemployment in St Helens was high, especially so for women. She hadn't a hope of getting into Beecham's or Pilkington's, and the thought of picking coal with the pit brow lasses filled her with dread. Still, it was her own fault, and she'd have to find a way of sorting it all out.

'Mam.'

'What?'

'Mam, there's something else. You remember when . . . when Dad died, and we had no money and no food?'

Dot's expression was wary, unwilling to look back over something which she had consigned to the dim and distant past.

'What about it?'

'That man in the butcher's, you know, Pearson's – he used to slip you a few bones and offcuts under the counter, remember?'

'What's that got to do with anything?'

Jenny had hoped her mam would understand. Now she

24

wasn't so sure. Perhaps she should have taken Mr Corlett's advice and kept it to herself.

'Mam . . . Mr Corlett caught me giving a loaf of bread to one of the O'Brien kids – I was going to pay him back for it soon as I had the money . . .'

Dot stared at her in horror.

'You *stole*? From John Corlett? Oh, Jenny, how could you?'

'I don't know, I didn't think . . . it didn't seem like stealing. And I only gave away the odd bit of stale bread.'

Dot sank down on to the old chair she kept by the copper.

'Oh, Jenny. Nancy I could understand, she hasn't the brains she was born with, but *you*?'

'I'm sorry, Mam, really I am.' Jenny took her mother's work-roughened hands in hers. 'Mr Corlett's giving me a good reference, I'll get another job somehow.'

She looked at her mother for reassurance, but Dot got to her feet and started jabbing at the load of whites boiling in the copper.

'Mam?'

'What?'

'I said . . .'

'I heard what you said. And now you'll have to say it all again, won't you?'

Heavy footsteps sounded behind her in the yard. Jenny didn't need to turn round to know that it was Ivan, back from the day shift at the pit.

'What's going on here then? Back from the shop already?'

Dot picked up the wooden tongs and started lifting the whites out of the copper, dropping them one by one into the dolly-tub. She glanced up at Jenny, and the briefest flicker of sympathy crossed her face then was gone.

'Jenny has something to tell you.'

'Oh, yes?' Ivan folded his arms. His eyes glittered in a coal-blackened, sweat-streaked face, like the eyes of a pantomime devil. 'Well, let's have it then, and I hope it's good.'

'I . . . I've lost my job.' Jenny appealed silently to her mother not to divulge the whole, shameful truth. 'Mr Corlett . . . Mr Corlett says business is bad and he can't afford to pay me and Eddie, so he's given me notice.'

Ivan's eyes narrowed.

'You stupid little bitch!' He gave her a light shove and she stumbled back against the wash-house wall. As he struck her she noticed the stink of beer on his breath.

'Ivan, please don't,' Dot intervened, softly and ineffectually. He took not the slightest notice of her, far too engrossed in venting his anger on Jenny.

'You stupid, brainless little bitch! That's fifteen-and-six a week gone, with seven mouths to feed an' another on the way . . .'

'I know. I know, I'm sorry.'

'Sorry? Is that the best you can say for yourself, girl?'

'Just leave me alone. I said I'm sorry. Leave me alone!'

Jenny stumbled out of Ivan's way, her eyes burning with unshed tears, and ran up the yard to the back kitchen, slamming the door behind her. Somewhere at the bottom of the yard she heard her mam's voice, soothing, urging: 'Leave her be, Ivan. Let her go.' Jenny stood with her back to the door and let the tears stream down her face. What was she going to do? What *could* she possibly do to make everything all right?

She filled the kettle and dragged it on to the top of the cooking range with shaking hands. Perhaps a cup of tea would make things better, like Dad used to say it did when she was a little girl and had scraped her knee in the yard. She remembered those days as vividly as if they were yesterday. Dad would pull her on to his knee and give her milky tea to drink from a saucer. Then he'd sing to her until she smiled again: songs like *You Are My Sunshine*, and *Let Me Call You Sweetheart*. He'd been a lovely singer, had Dan Fisher.

The dirty plates were still on the table from breakfast. Jenny began clearing them away in a kind of automatic daze, vaguely aware that Ivan would be angrier still if a meal wasn't waiting for him when he'd had a wash.

She was up to her arms in the sink when the door opened. She hoped it might be Mam, or Tom, or even Nancy back from the bottle-works; but in her heart she knew it was Ivan Price.

'You'll not back-chat me like that again,' he said very quietly and very angrily, closing the door behind him.

Jenny didn't turn round. If she didn't face him, he couldn't see how afraid of him she was.

'I've said I'm sorry.'

'Oh, and you reckon that makes everything right, do you?' Ivan seized Jenny by the shoulders and forcibly swung her round. Wet soapsuds trickled and dropped from her fingers on to the kitchen floor. 'Let me tell you, little Miss High an' Mighty, while you're in my house you'll do as I say and you'll earn your keep.'

'I told you, I'll get another job.'

Ivan sneered through his shiny coal-dust mask.

'Oh, really? How?'

'Somehow.'

'A daft little bitch like you? You should count yourself lucky I don't give you a good hidin'.'

Jenny glared back at him with a defiance she scarcely felt. Inside she was trembling, and Ivan was much too close for comfort, pushing her up against the sink, his hands gripping her by the shoulders.

'The kettle's boiling. I have to . . .'

'You'll do what *I* say. When *I* say.'

To Jenny's horror, she felt his right hand slip down from her shoulder to her breast, leaving a damp, dirty trail of coal dust. She cried out and tried to wriggle free as he squeezed her breast very hard through her dress.

'Don't do that, you're hurting me!'

Ivan smiled, in the way that only he could. There was a whole world of sadistic pleasure in that smile.

'Listen to me, girl. If you can't get a job, you'll make yourself useful in other ways, understand?'

Jenny didn't want to understand.

'N-No. Let me go . . .'

He laughed.

'Don't give me that. You bitches all love it! Listen to me, girl. If you can't earn money, you'll earn your keep *this* way. And you want to please your *da*, don't you, Jenny?'

He was really hurting her now, one hand squeezing her breast while the other travelled down her belly, pulling up the skirt of her dress and trying to force her legs apart.

The kettle was just within reach. As they struggled, Jenny fumbled for it with her free hand, managing to knock it off the range and on to the floor. Ivan let out a stream of Welsh curses as a fine spray of boiling water fell across his bare forearm, and Jenny sprang clear.

'You little . . .' Ivan swore as he turned on the tap and swabbed his arm with cold water.

'Keep your hands off me!'

He wrapped a wet teatowel round his arm and took a couple of slow steps towards Jenny. The smile returned, and Jenny's heart sank into the pit of her stomach.

'Don't think you've heard the last of this, girl.'

Chapter 3

'You haven't heard the last of this, my girl. An' don't you think you can go blabbin' to your mam, neither, or you'll feel worse than the weight of my hand.'

Jenny knew how to keep her mouth shut. The difficult thing was keeping out of Ivan Price's way.

Every night before she fell asleep, Jenny's last thought was of his coal-black, leering face, and his voice rasping in her head. Had it really happened? Had he really tried to do *that* to her? She felt sick when she thought about it, but could hardly think about anything else.

Not having a job any more made it harder than ever to avoid Ivan. At least he was at the pit most of the day, but Mam expected her to have his dinner on the table when he got home, and once or twice she'd even sent Jenny up to the colliery gates with Ivan's snap-tin. It wasn't that Jenny minded doing her share in the house, or looking after the kids, but how could she explain to Mam that she yearned to be a million miles away from her stepfather? Mam was so determined that they were all going to be one big, happy family. So desperate to be happy she wouldn't let herself see the truth.

Jenny spent days trudging the streets of St Helens, desperately looking for a job. She must have visited every shop in town, every factory, every office; Beecham's, Pilkington's, the bottle-works, the hospital. She even stood outside the brickworks and the colliery gates, envious now of the pit brow lasses with their filthy clothes and cut, infected hands. Everywhere the answer was the same: No work today, try tomorrow. And every night she had to face

Ivan Price's sneering face across the kitchen table.

'No job yet then, girl? We'll have to find somethin' *useful* for you to do.'

Just when she had almost given up hope, temporary salvation came in the unlikely form of The Feathers, the ale-house on the corner of Tannery Row. The landlord, Denny Finch, called out to Jenny as she was passing the pub one afternoon.

'Heard tha's lookin' for a job, lass.'

'That's right, Mr Finch.'

'Our Aggie's been took ill. Few hours' cleanin' suit thee? Start at six tomorrow mornin'.'

'Thank you, Mr Finch!'

'Just till our Aggie's on her feet again.' Denny Finch tipped his cap back on his curly ginger head. 'It's 'ard work, mind. Think you're up to it?'

'You won't regret it, Mr Finch, honest you won't.'

She was there at a quarter to six the next morning, firmly resolved that she would make a success of this meagre chance. Over the next two hours, she discovered just how backbreaking the work could be: sluicing out the toilet, washing out the spittoons, scrubbing down the bare wooden floors until they were white and dry as bleached bone. But no matter how her back ached and her knuckles bled, this was a job and she was hanging on to it for grim death.

'Tha's a good worker, Jenny,' observed Denny Finch as he paid her at the end of the week. 'Clean an' respectable. Fancy a night or two serving behind the bar?'

And so it was that she found herself working as a barmaid at The Feathers. She'd hardly have dared go into a pub before, only to the off-sales to fetch a jug of ale, and then not willingly: memories of Dot's long weeks sunk in drink were still painful even now. If Dot hadn't discovered the gin bottle in the weeks after Dad's accident, maybe she would never have lost her mind enough to fall for Ivan Price . . .

But The Feathers wasn't like the gin palaces Dot had frequented. It was a friendly place, hardly luxurious but warm and full of smoke and chatter. Jenny found herself enjoying the company, and the chance to get away from all her worries for a few hours.

'Pint o' Greenall's best, lass.' A jolly, round-faced man pushed a fistful of coppers across the bar-top.

'That's sixpence, thank you.'

'Like it here, do you?'

Jenny took a moment from polishing glasses.

'Yes, I do. I didn't think I would.'

'Your mam not like you workin' in an ale-house?'

'Well . . .'

The man sipped at his beer reflectively.

'Must say – an' don't take me wrong, lass – I'd not 'ave my own daughter workin' in a pub. There's a lot of, you know, *men's* talk. It's not right for a decent lass. No offence meant.'

'None taken.' Beggars can't be choosers, thought Jenny to herself, and there's a lot worse things a girl can do than work behind a bar. She turned to the next customer; 'Now, Mr Pearson, what can I get you?'

'Half of mild'll do me, the missus'll crown me if I fetch up drunk on t'doorstep.'

This caused much merriment in the bar. Everyone knew that George Pearson lived in awe of his domineering wife, who had been an army nurse in the Great War and never let him forget it.

'What's that, George? Lettin' your Emily lead you by the nose? It's time someone showed her who's boss!'

That deep-throated growl made Jenny slop some of the beer on to the bar-top. Ivan! What was he doing here? He never drank at The Feathers; that was one of the reasons Jenny had taken the job.

'Sorry, Mr Pearson, I'll just top it up for you.' She wiped up the mess with a rag and refilled George's glass.

Ivan pushed his way through the throng to the bar.

'Wastin' good beer, Jenny? Denny Finch won't like that. Can't think why he took you on. You always were cack-handed.'

'Now, Ivan . . .' hazarded George Pearson. Ivan rounded on him.

31

'If you know what's good for you, you'll keep yer nose out of other folks' business.'

Jenny made a special effort to be civil.

'Can I get you something?'

She knew as soon as the words left her mouth that it had been the wrong thing to say. Ivan's freshly scrubbed face creased into a parody of a smile.

'That's what I like to hear.' He winked at the man standing next to him. 'Obliging girl, is our Jenny.'

It was obvious what Ivan meant. Was it obvious to other people too? Jenny felt her cheeks begin to burn. Her lips were parched. She flicked her tongue nervously across them.

'Did you want a drink or what?'

Ivan leant his elbows comfortably on the bar-top.

'Seein' as you're offering, a pint'd be very nice. On the 'ouse, of course.'

'I can't do that!'

'No?' The look in Ivan's eyes told Jenny that he knew; knew what she'd done at Corlett's and was revelling in the knowledge of her imperfection. 'I'd heard you were a very generous sort of girl, Jenny. Very . . . giving.'

'Was that a pint or a half?'

'Give me a pint of bitter.' Ivan scowled as he reached into his waistcoat pocket and took out a shilling, slapping it down on the counter. 'And don't worry, I'm payin'. I always pay what I owe, see, and I always take what I'm due.'

Much to Jenny's relief, Ivan left her alone after that. He didn't come into The Feathers again. Perhaps he'd given up trying to intimidate her; perhaps it had only been the drink talking . . .

Cleaning out the pub on a Sunday morning was the worst job of the week. It meant getting up at half-past five and spending three hours scrubbing the place from top to bottom, but Jenny didn't mind. Denny Finch paid her wages on time, and there was no sign of his wife Aggie's coming back to work, so perhaps the job might even turn into a permanent one.

Before walking back to Gas Street, Jenny took the precaution of slipping a shilling into her shoe. It was the only way she could be sure of keeping anything for herself. The rest of the money, she would hand over when Ivan demanded it.

This morning the back door of number forty-two was unlocked, and the house was empty. She called out: 'Mam? Nancy?'

No one replied. Good. Mam and the kids would have gone to her Auntie Jane's, Tom would be out somewhere with his friends, and Ivan – the hypocrite – would be at Chapel in the centre of town. She'd have a good hour to wash and change her clothes. A whole hour of peace.

There was still some warm water left in the kettle. Jenny poured it into a bowl and carried it upstairs, setting it on the washstand with her flannel and a cake of soap. Then she took a change of underwear from the drawer and started to get undressed quickly; it was cold in the unheated bedroom, so cold that her breath misted in the air.

She took off her right shoe carefully and made sure that the shilling was still in the toe. Later on she'd find a better place to hide it. Her dress was good quality but old and shabby now; it had been second-hand when she bought it. She hummed to herself as she dreamed of swathing herself in satins and silks, like Ginger Rogers or Hedy Lamarr. One day, when she and Mae were both rich and famous . . .

A sound brought her back to reality. A leering face was reflected in the washstand-mirror in front of her.

She gasped and turned round, hastily pulling up the bodice of her dress to cover her brassiere.

'What are you doing in here? Can't you see I'm getting undressed?'

'Oh, I can see all right,' leered Ivan. 'I can see a lot from here. Why don't I come closer so I can get an even better view?'

He stepped into the room. He was a wall of muscle underneath his black Sunday suit and high stiff collar.

'What's wrong, Jenny? Aren't you pleased to see me?'

'I . . . thought you were at Chapel.'

'Thought I'd give it a miss today, girl. There's a lot to be said for nourishin' the soul, but a man has to have his home comforts too, if you get my meanin'.'

Jenny got his meaning only too well. She stepped backwards but there was nowhere to go. Ivan had blocked the doorway and now he was shutting the door behind him, cutting off her only avenue of escape.

'I told you . . . keep away from me.'

'And I told you, girl, you'll do what I say, when I say. It's about time I taught you a lesson . . .'

Ivan seized hold of her with such sudden violence that Jenny had no chance to struggle, not even the chance to cry out. He was inhumanly strong, his hands tearing at her clothes, ripping the dress from her body.

At last she found her voice, but all she could do was repeat the same terrified syllable over and over again.

'No, no, no . . .'

'Shut it, bitch! Shut it if you know what's good for you!'

Ivan struck her across the face with his fist, so hard that she flew sideways and crumpled to her knees on the old, cracked lino. Dizzy from the blow, she stared down at the faded rose-patterns; they seemed to be turning into sneering faces.

She heard a scream as Ivan grabbed her by the hair, and supposed it must have been her own voice though it sounded very different, like the sound a frightened animal might make. He banged her head on the floor, once, twice, so that she almost lost consciousness; but she forced herself to focus on the pain and, rolling over, kicked out at Ivan's belly with her stockinged feet.

'Bastard! You bastard, I won't let you . . .'

'Fight me, would you? Defy your dad, would you? You little hellcat, I'll shut your mouth for you!'

Dragging her up by the hair, he threw her backwards on to the bed. Her flailing hands tried to scratch at him, but his snarling face was out of reach. He held her down, ripped the last of the dress from her so that she was naked

34

except for her underwear and stockings. She knew what was going to happen to her; it was something that only happened to other girls, bad girls, girls who were no better than they ought to be.

'You love it, don't you? All you bitches want is a real man . . .'

He was on top of her now and fumbling at the buttons on his trousers, the other hand stopping her mouth. Jenny writhed with all her strength, punching and kicking with every last ounce of resistance she could muster. At last she found some hidden reserve and, biting into the flesh of Ivan's palm, momentarily freed her mouth from his suffocating grasp.

'No, no, help me, help me, please . . .'

It was useless, she knew it. Ivan had forced her back on to the bed. In a moment it would be too late. But a ferocious hammering and shouting made him stop in his tracks.

'What the . . .?'

The hammering kept on. Somebody was thumping on the front door, and shouting up: 'What's going on in there?'

Ivan threw Jenny a look of purest hatred as he flung her sideways and got up off the bed. She lay there, panting and shaking, as he ran down the stairs two at a time and opened the front door.

A few moments later she heard him talking to Mr Pateman from next door.

'. . . nothin's wrong, Jenny took a fall down the stairs.'

'Are you sure? It didn't sound . . .'

'Sure? 'Course I'm sure. You know how clumsy she is.'

'Shall I fetch doctor?'

'*Diw*, no! No need for that. I've put her to bed and she'll be fine. Like I said, stupid girl just took a tumble down the stairs. She'll be right as rain in the mornin', just you see.'

Jenny got unsteadily off the bed and reached for her dressing gown, slipped it on and walked slowly and dizzily down the stairs. Mr Pateman's eyes opened very wide when he saw her, and when she touched her aching forehead her hand came away with a smear of blood on it. Ivan glared and pushed her behind him, back into the house.

'Get back to bed, girl, 'tisn't decent lettin' folk see you half-undressed.'

'You all right, Jenny?' asked Mrs Pateman, who had joined her husband on the doorstep. Jenny glanced at Ivan. His expression was more expressive than a thousand words.

'I'm . . . fine. Really.'

If only Mam and the kids hadn't chosen that very moment to get off the trolley-bus from Peasley Cross. Jenny would never forget her mother's expression as she pushed through the little huddle of neighbours and saw her daughter's battered face.

'Jenny? Ivan? What's happened?'

Mr and Mrs Pateman cut in.

'She fell down t'stairs, see . . .'

'. . . lass must have cut her head when she fell . . .'

Dot listened to all the explanations and seemed to take them in. But a look passed between her and her daughter, a look which shocked Jenny to the core.

It seemed very much like jealousy.

It wasn't too difficult to hide the bruises on her body, but the lump on Jenny's forehead came up like a duck-egg. Over the next few days it turned all colours of the rainbow: black, purple, magenta, yellow. Dot's eyes seemed to be watching Jenny at every moment, yet she said nothing about what had happened. Not one word.

If she couldn't tell anyone about what Ivan had tried to do, there was only one alternative: to retreat into a fantasy world that would let her forget, if only for a short while. She had the small amount of money she'd managed to save from cleaning and serving at The Feathers, but she couldn't afford to go dancing like she used to. Then some of her old schoolfriends suggested a trip to the pictures.

As they all squashed on to a bench in Victoria Park, they discussed the possibilities.

'How about *The Lady Vanishes*?' suggested Gloria Moffat, puffing very importantly on a cigarette. Gloria had a job on the make-up counter at Woolworth's, and thought it important to look glamorous. 'It's on at the Sutton Bug.'

Alice the office clerk shook her head.

'There's a Gracie Fields on at Thatto Heath, if you can scrape up the 'bus fare.'

'Which one?' demanded Ethel, who worked as a packer at Beecham's.

'*We're Going to Be Rich.*'

'Fat chance!' laughed Gloria. 'The only one of us lot that's ever going to be rich is Mae Corlett.'

'Chorus-girls don't get rich,' scoffed Ethel.

'No, but they marry millionaires and film stars, don't they? And then they get to be big stars too, and go to Hollywood. I bet Mae's got her eye on one right now . . .'

'Tell you what us lasses need,' announced Alice, 'summat really *glamorous*. 'Specially some of us,' she added with a glance at Jenny's swollen face. No one had mentioned it, but news travelled fast and people had their own ideas about what had been happening at forty-two Gas Street.

'Such as?'

'*Mad about Music* – Deanna Durbin's latest.'

Jenny sighed. She loved Deanna Durbin films. Well, to be honest she loved all films, especially anything with singing in it. When she and Mae used to go to the flicks together, every Saturday morning, they'd learn the songs off by heart and sing and dance them all the way back to Gas Street.

'It doesn't matter which,' said Jenny, 'I can't go. Can't afford it.'

'We'll have a whip-round,' suggested Alice.

Jenny shook her head.

'I'm not taking your money,' she said firmly.

'Tell you what then.' Gloria sprang off the bench and put out her cigarette under the heel of her shoe. 'We'll sneak you in through the side doors, like when we were kids and Mae's dad wouldn't pay for her to go, 'cause . . . what was it?'

Ethel laughed as she tried to impersonate Mr Corlett's slow Manx drawl.

' "'Cause I'll not have a girl of your age watching that romantic drivel." ' She cocked her head on one side reflectively. 'Wonder what he makes of her cavorting around the stage in a load of sequins and not much else!'

'I shouldn't think he's any too pleased,' volunteered Jenny, who knew the Corletts better than most. 'But he's a nice man,' she added.

'Don't know how you can say that when he gave you the push from his shop,' said Gloria bluntly. 'Still, never mind. Let's go up the Rialto on Saturday. We'll sneak Jenny in through the side doors when no one's looking. What do you say to that?'

Going to the pictures with the girls was more fun than Jenny had thought it would be, almost as much fun as it had been when she was little. It was surprisingly easy to forget her troubles.

'Wait here,' whispered Gloria, pulling up the collar of her coat and taking a peek round the corner. 'Good, no coppers. Now listen, Jenny. We'll go and pay, and once we're inside and it's dark, I'll open the side door for you. Got that?'

Jenny stifled a giggle. It was the first time she'd felt like laughing in ages.

'Right you are.'

Her heart was racing, but this time with excitement, not fear. This was a child's game and it was good to be a child again. Being a grown woman had so far brought her nothing but trouble.

She waited. It seemed like ages. Couples strolled past arm in arm and gave her odd looks, but she just smiled back. Through the side door of the cinema she could hear the boom of the speakers as the newsreel started up. She pressed her ear against the door, and could just make out something about Adolf Hitler threatening to take over Austria. A couple of minutes later, the door grated open a tiny fraction, and she heard Gloria's dramatic stage-whisper: 'You there, Jenny?'

'Of course I am.'

'Sorry you had to wait, that usherette's a nosy old bag. Ready?'

'Ready.'

In the split second that the door opened a few more inches, Jenny slipped soundlessly into the auditorium. A young man and his girlfriend, sitting right next to the door, saw exactly what was going on but the youth put his finger to his lips and grinned.

Sneaking along the back of the rows, Gloria and Jenny circumnavigated the usherette and slid into the seats alongside Alice and Ethel. The magic surrounded and engulfed Jenny instantly. It was impossible not to feel it, she thought to herself; tingling right through your bones and making you believe things – such *wonderful* things; making you believe that anything could be possible. Time rolled back and she was fifteen again, and she and Mae Corlett were going to be Gracie Fields and Greta Garbo and Ginger Rogers, all rolled into one . . .

Three hundred faces lifted simultaneously, bathed in flickering light, as the film began. Deanna Durbin smiled out from the centre of the screen, hardly more than a kid herself and slim as a lath, with those dark, bubbling curls and a voice that soared with such effortless power that it seemed not to be a part of her body at all. She was wearing a dark tailored costume, nipped in at the waist, a tiny feathered hat and lipstick that accentuated the fullness of her perfect mouth.

'Oh, look at that 'at!'

'Never mind her, *he's* a bit of all right, i'n't 'e?'

'Shush, I'm trying to listen!'

Although Jenny didn't know the songs, she found herself memorising them automatically as she'd always done with Mae, her lips moving soundlessly to the words, her whole being alive with the happy, carefree, exhilarating music. When the film was over and she stepped out into the cold street again, a small part of this film would still be inside her. She would never forget these songs, would sing them softly to herself as she knelt down to scrub the bar-room floor at The Feathers.

Life on the screen wasn't like life outside. Perhaps that was why she wanted so much to be a part of it. It was sunshiney and happy and golden, an eternal summer where, if things ever went wrong, they always, *always* turned out right in the end.

That was how life was meant to be, and that was how she was going to make it: happy, and golden, and forever.

Chapter 4

The warm glow of certainty didn't last very long. That was the trouble with going to the pictures; the glamour and the happiness wore off all too quickly and then you felt even worse than you had in the first place.

Jenny went through the next week in a daze, doing whatever had to be done, saying as little as possible, getting by the best way she knew how. No longer feeling safe in her own family, she took refuge in her thoughts. But there was no avoiding the big decision she had to make, one that frightened her so much that she couldn't bring herself to do anything at all.

'What's up wi' you then?' she heard Ivan demand as she cleared his dinner plate one Thursday night.

She kept silent and avoided eye-contact but he seized her by the wrist, tightened his grip and twisted, just hard enough to make her gasp and look into his face.

'You'll answer me when I speak to you, girl.'

'Leave 'er be, Ivan, she's not got over her accident yet,' said Dot wearily. She was sitting by the range knitting baby clothes while Daisy sat cross-legged at her feet, winding wool. God help that baby, thought Jenny bitterly. God help all of us now Ivan Price has his hobnail boots under our table.

'I said, what's got into you?'

'Nothing.' Jenny glared back at Ivan, snatched her wrist away and went on with wiping down the oilcloth on the table. When she'd finished, she wrung the cloth out under the tap and dried her hands. 'All right if I go now, Mam? I'll be late for The Feathers.'

41

Dot looked up from her knitting.

'I'm not sure you ought to be workin' there.'

'Why not?'

Dot focused on the regular click-clack of her knitting needles.

'When's Aggie Finch comin' back to work?'

'I don't know. I haven't seen her. Why?'

'It's just . . .'

Ivan overruled Dot with a wave of his hand.

'Let the girl go. God knows she brings home little enough. Not saltin' it away somewhere, are you, Jenny?'

She shrank from Ivan's question. Did he know, or was he guessing?

'I've nowt but what I give you,' she retorted. 'Now, can I go?'

All that evening at The Feathers Jenny wondered what Dot had meant about Aggie. It was true Jenny hadn't seen her in a while, but Denny said she was in bed upstairs, under doctor's orders, and she had no reason to think that wasn't true. Denny had been kind to her ever since she'd lost her job at Corlett's.

It was hard to concentrate on serving behind the bar. She longed to go somewhere quiet, and just think. Should she tell, and get it over with, or keep her mouth shut and let her Mam go on playing happy families? The question gnawed and corroded inside her until the pain of indecision became almost physical. As she walked home in the dark that night, she realised that it was no longer a question of whether she would tell Dot what had happened, just a matter of how and when.

This wasn't a film. She wished it was – films had happy endings. But this was real life: cold and dreary and cuttingly painful. She had to tell Mam what Ivan had tried to do to her; had to make her see the truth before it was too late.

The following morning, when she got back from cleaning at The Feathers, Jenny found Dot on her knees in the kitchen, blackleading the range.

'I'll do that if you like, Mam?' Jenny took a clean apron from the hook behind the kitchen door, and put it on. 'Why don't you have a nice sit down?'

'Aye. All right then, I won't say I don't need it.' Dot hauled herself on to a chair. She looked washed-out, thought Jenny; washed-out and wary. 'Summat wrong, is there?'

Jenny took the rag and started rubbing it over the cast-iron range, buffing it with all her strength. Telling Mam was going to be harder than she'd thought.

'Ivan's on day turn then?'

'You know he is. He'll not be back till after six.'

'Where's Billy and Daisy?'

'Playing ball in the street.'

'And Nancy?'

'She's gone on an errand to the Co-op. What is this?'

Jenny let her breath out in a soft sigh of relief. It was best that there was no one else around to hear what she had to say.

'Mam – there's something I have to tell you. I should have told you before but I was too afraid.'

Dot leant forward in her chair, her body tensing.

'Go on.'

'It's about falling down the stairs.' Jenny fingered the yellowing bruises on her arms. 'I didn't.'

In an agony of suspense, she turned her head to look at her mother's face. Dot's expression was calm, unsurprised.

'Do you understand what I'm saying? Mam, I'm frightened he's going to hurt me again, and I won't be able to get away.' Jenny's words ended in a dry sob. She despised herself for being so weak, but the need for love and understanding was overwhelming. 'Mam?'

Dot's face softened and she reached out a hand to pat her daughter's shoulder.

'I knew all along,' she said.

'You . . .?'

'I knew you couldn't have fallen down the stairs, it didn't make any sense. Then Ivan kept dropping hints . . .'

'Ivan! He admitted it?'

'Jenny lass, I tried to warn you about Denny Finch, but you wouldn't have it. Now Aggie may put up with him knocking her about, that's her business, but I'll not have him hittin' my daughter . . .'

'Denny! Denny Finch?' Jenny stared in amazement at her mother. She almost laughed out loud. 'You think *Denny Finch* did this to me?'

''Course he did, but you don't have to worry about him doing it again. Ivan'll go round an' sort him out for you.'

'Mam! Mam, listen to me.' Still on her knees, Jenny took Dot's hands in hers, willing her to comprehend. 'Denny didn't do this to me, it was Ivan! Don't you understand?'

Dot's indulgent half-smile faded from her face, and she snatched her hands free. They had contracted into claws.

'What!'

'Ivan, Mam, he hit me. He . . . he tried to . . .'

'Don't you tell lies about Ivan, he's a good man, better than we deserve. He's been like a father to you . . .'

Desperation flooded Jenny's soul. It had taken all the strength she had to tell the truth and now Mam didn't believe a word of it, but thought she was lying. There was no going back.

'He tried to . . .' She swallowed down the tide of acrid-tasting saliva. Tears were gathering at the corners of her eyes. 'Oh Mam, Mam, he's been mucking about with me . . . he hit me because I wouldn't let him have his way. Please believe me, please!'

Dot's quiet voice trembled with rage and loathing.

'You little liar!'

The sting of her mother's slap made Jenny clap her hand to her cheek.

'Mam, it's true, I swear it!' There was nothing for it but to frame the truth in words no one could misunderstand. 'Ivan tried to rape me.'

'Take that back before I . . .'

'I can't.'

'Take it back *this minute*.'

'No. Don't ask me to do that, please don't.'

'How *dare* you tell such filthy lies?'

44

'It's the truth, Mam. I wouldn't lie to you, I couldn't! I've *never* lied to you.'

Jenny scrambled to her feet, holding out her hands imploringly. She was sobbing openly now, her shoulders heaving with the effort of trying to control herself, her vision obscured by a mist of tears. The pain of not being believed was far, far harder to bear than the pain of Ivan's fists.

The more the blackness of despair overwhelmed her, the less control Jenny had over her words.

'Oh, Mam, why can't it be like when Dad was alive? Why did you have to marry Ivan? Dad would never have done what he did . . .'

Dot's eyes were blazing now. She dragged Jenny to her feet and spat out her reply.

'Ivan Price *is* your father now.'

The words hit Jenny like a blow in the stomach.

'Never!'

Still weeping, she turned aside, but Dot hadn't finished with her.

'Ivan was right about you, Jenny. I told him he was too harsh with you, that you were a good girl really, but now I know he was right all the time. You're a thief and a liar and a filthy little whore. How many men have you had, Jenny? Has one of them got you in the family way, and you thought you could blame it on Ivan?'

'No!' Deeply shocked, she backed away from her mother, advancing in fury. 'No, it's not like that at all. He touched me, he tried to make me . . .'

'Shut up!' Dot silenced her by seizing a handful of her hair. It hurt, but not as much as her mam's rejection. 'I've done with you, Jenny. You've lied to me and tried to ruin the little bit of happiness I've got, but I won't have it, do you hear?'

She half pushed, half kicked Jenny along the passageway to the front door, wrenching it open with her left hand whilst the right held Jenny fast by her hair.

'Mam . . . please don't, you're hurting me!'

'Get out, Jenny. Get out of my house.'

'Mam! Mam, no!'

'Get out. And don't bother coming back, because you won't be welcome.'

The door slammed shut with a crash and Jenny was left standing alone on the pavement, more alone than she'd ever been in her life before.

They had buried Daniel Fisher in the cemetery on the hill, overlooking the town.

It wasn't an expensive headstone; Dan's insurance money had just covered the cost of the cheapest funeral and a plain slab, engraved with his name and the short span of his life.

The cold wind cut through Jenny's thin cardigan as she climbed the hill and pushed through the gate. She had often been here; a good deal more often than her mother, whose way of coping with her husband's death had been to try and blot him out of her memories altogether. She'd even made a bonfire of the few family photographs they'd had, as though the flames would purge her own grief and Dan Fisher's sin in daring to die.

'Hello, Dad.'

Jenny crouched down beside the grave, in the lee of the headstone. It wasn't quite so bitterly cold out of the worst of the wind, but the sky above was a swollen grey, threatening a downpour at any moment.

'I'd have brought you some flowers, only I don't have any money, see.'

She pulled a few straggly weeds out of the neatly raked gravel which covered the plot.

'Mam's thrown me out, Dad.'

The beginnings of a shuddering sob caught in her throat but she was determined not to cry again. What would crying solve? It wouldn't bring Dad back and it wouldn't make Dot Fisher see the truth.

'I told her what Ivan tried to do, but she didn't believe me. She threw me out of the house and told me never to come back. Do you think she really meant it?'

A fat raindrop escaped from the low cloud above Jenny's

head and landed on the ground at her feet.

'She loved you so much, Dad. How could she forget you?'

And more to the point, how could she replace Dad with a man like Ivan Price? Jenny thought bitterly of the leering face, the pawing hands, the brutish strength.

'I haven't forgotten you, Dad. Nor has Nancy. And I keep telling Billy and Daisy all about you.' Who'll tell them now, she wondered, now that I'm not there any more?

'What should I do now, Dad? Should I go back? Should I try and find somewhere else to stay? Maybe if I went to see Mr Corlett he'd tell me where Mae is . . .'

She laid the flat of her hand against the gravel. She could almost imagine the pulse of a distant heartbeat, warm and strong.

'I miss you, Dad.'

Curling up on her father's grave, she imagined that she was a child again, curled up on her father's lap. And when the cold, hard rain fell on her face, she felt only the warmth of Dan Fisher's love.

It was late in the afternoon when Jenny made up her mind to go back to the house on Gas Street.

After leaving the cemetery, she'd walked round and round the streets, thinking long and hard about what she ought to do. Mam had told her to get out and stay out, and never to come back, but people said harsh things when they were angry. Perhaps Mam had had a chance to think about what Jenny had said. Perhaps she would give her the benefit of the doubt. Perhaps she would even believe her.

The thought of Ivan Price made Jenny hesitate for a long time. Mam would undoubtedly have told Ivan what Jenny had said about him. Maybe even now he was stalking the streets looking for her, his belt wrapped round his fist. Hadn't he told her that, sooner or later, he always got what he wanted? She shivered at the thought of ever seeing him again.

But running away was never the answer. Hadn't she always told Billy that if someone bullied you, you should stand your ground and square up to them? On the other hand, it was easier to give advice than to take it, she thought to herself as she crossed the road and walked past Mr Corlett's shop.

The lights were on and she could see Eddie sweeping the floor, prior to locking up for the night. She couldn't go in, she just couldn't. Things could have been different if she hadn't . . . but it was no use dwelling on what might or might not have been. She walked on by, trying not to let her eyes linger on the food. She hadn't eaten since breakfast, and that had been a snatched slice of bread and jam at half-past five.

Turning into Gas Street, she made out a small, solitary figure standing close to the lamp-post. There was a cheap canvas suitcase on the ground by her legs and she was carrying something in a string bag. Jenny quickened her pace.

'Nancy – is that you, Nancy?'

The figure stepped into the pool of dingy light cast by the streetlamp.

'Nancy, what are you doing out here? You'll catch your death.'

Nancy's face looked pale and her eyes were red-rimmed and swollen, as though she had done a lot of crying. But her voice was harsh and hostile.

'Where do you think you're going, Jenny?'

'Home.'

'You can't.'

Jenny felt a sickening lurch of apprehension.

'B-But . . .'

Nancy's eyes were full of pain and accusation. Resentment too, realised Jenny; perhaps even the beginnings of hatred.

'It's all your fault, Jenny. What did you do to make Mam so angry?'

'I . . . can't tell you.' Jenny stepped closer. 'Are you all right?'

Nancy gave a loud, resentful sniff, but nodded. She drew up her head defiantly.

'You can't come home, Mam's raging mad at you and Ivan . . . you 'ave to leave and not come back.'

'But what about you and Billy and Daisy? And there's Tom's tea to cook. Who's going to look after you and Mam?'

'We'll manage, we don't need you.' Nancy's eyes were too bright, as though she was trying not to cry. 'It's all your fault. If it wasn't for you everything would be all right.'

'I *can't* leave you.' Jenny was no longer certain if it was herself she was pleading for, or the kids she'd been mother to ever since Dan Fisher died. 'At least let me come back and explain to Billy and Daisy – they won't understand.'

'Neither do I.' Nancy's voice was firmer now, and more urgent. 'You've got to go, Jenny. Now, before they see you. Look, I brought you some things, a few clothes and a bit of food.'

'Where will I go?'

'How should I know?' A spark of vindictiveness flared in Nancy's eyes. 'You should have thought about that before you . . .'

Jenny swallowed.

'Yes.'

The streetlamp's anaemic light cast shifting patterns on Nancy's face, and it was only now that Jenny realised she had been right. There *was* the faintest shadow of a new bruise on the side of her sister's cheek; a little puffiness and a shadow of darkening red. Now Jenny was beginning to understand why Nancy was so desperate for her to go. Ivan had hit her because of what she, Jenny, had done. It was Jenny he was angry with, nobody else. Once she was gone, the others would be all right.

She reached out gentle, tentative fingers to touch the bruise, but Nancy flinched and pushed her hand away.

'You stayin' won't help, Jenny.'

'Nancy . . .'

'It won't help anyone, can't you see?' She thrust the string bag of food into Jenny's hands. 'Go away, Jenny. Haven't you made enough trouble for us?'

Chapter 5

'Please let me stay, Mrs Biggs. It'd only be for a few days.'

'We've no room for you here.'

'But Mrs Biggs, Gloria said . . .'

'I don't care what she said, you'll have to find somewhere else.'

The door snapped shut, leaving Jenny standing out, on the pavement in the drizzle. It was Eastertide, but she was hardly in the mood for celebration. Mam had thrown her out, Nancy had made it clear she wasn't wanted back, and to all intents and purposes Jenny Fisher was completely homeless.

Her right stocking was wet through from the rainwater that had soaked up through the hole in her shoe, and Jenny wondered if she would ever be dry again. She had very little money on her, hardly enough for food, let alone a place to sleep. The Salvation Army had taken her in last night, but she couldn't keep going back there. She had to find a proper place to stay.

At first she had thought it would be easy. She had lots of friends in St Helens. She'd go to Gloria's or Ethel's or Alice's; one of them would be happy to take her in for a night or two. They'd understand. But her friends' mothers had been less than pleased to see Jenny; news travelled fast in a small town like St Helens, and Ivan Price had been sure to spread a few choice rumours about 'that slut Jenny Fisher'.

Now there was only Auntie Jane left to turn to. Jenny comforted herself on the long walk to Thatto Heath with the thought that at least her aunt would help her. She wouldn't have to spend a third night without a roof over her head. These last few years, Jenny had often felt closer to her mother's younger sister than she'd been to Dot herself.

Auntie Jane was very proud of her new house; it was in the middle of an estate of brand-new council houses, with its own inside toilet, and a great big garden at the back where Uncle Eric grew vegetables and flowers. No more dib-holes and trips to the bath-house for Auntie Jane, these days she was almost refined – at least that was what Mam said. There were three bedrooms in Auntie Jane's house, and only two children: plenty of room for one niece with nowhere else to go.

Jenny rang the doorbell and waited. The spotless net curtain twitched at an upstairs window. Someone was definitely at home, but they didn't come down to open the door. She rang again, in case they hadn't heard. Muffled voices were arguing somewhere at the back of the house, she couldn't quite catch what they were saying.

At last she heard footsteps, and the bolt being drawn back. The door opened a few inches and Auntie Jane appeared. She looked flushed and ill at ease.

'Jenny,' she said flatly, as though this was something she'd been expecting but not looking forward to.

'Auntie Jane, something terrible's happened. Mam's thrown me out, and Ivan . . .'

Jane put up her hand.

'I heard.'

'You'll put me up for a couple of nights, won't you? Just till it's all sorted out?'

Jane lowered her eyes, unable to look her niece in the face.

'I can't.'

'But . . .'

'You heard me, Jenny, I can't. Eddie's studying for his pit deputy's exam, he needs a room to himself. And there's our Sadie, she's at a difficult age . . .'

Jenny listened to her aunt's words with growing panic. Why was she lying to her, why was she shutting her out like some unwelcome stranger?

'I'll sleep anywhere – on the floor, I don't mind.' She touched her aunt's hand. Jane clasped it briefly, then pushed it away as though the gesture had been a mistake.

'You've heard what they're saying about you? It's all over town. About what you've been up to with men?'

Jenny was shaking now, half with cold and half with anger.

'None of it's true, Auntie, none of it! Ivan's been telling lies about me because . . . because of what he . . .' Her voice tailed off; she couldn't put into words what Ivan had tried to do to her. It made her physically sick just thinking about it.

Jane's face told her that she already knew, or at least suspected. Her eyes were hollow and dark.

'That's as maybe. But I'll not take you in,' she said. 'I daren't.'

'You're afraid of Ivan? Has he been threatening you?'

Jane's lips twitched with black humour.

'If your mam had been more afraid of him, you and she'd not be in this mess.' Jane sighed. 'She never had much sense, your mam. But she's family and I'll stick by her, no matter what.'

'I'm family too!'

'I'd like to help you, really I would. But I've told you I can't and that's an end to it.'

'Can't I at least come in for a bit? To warm up? I'm soaked through.'

Jane hesitated. Jenny could sense the emotion in her; the pull of love and obligation on the one hand and of fear and loyalty on the other. There was a fire and a sofa in Jane's front parlour, and Jenny was wet, cold and exhausted.

'Best not,' she said briskly. 'Our Geoff's on nights, he doesn't like being disturbed.' She paused. 'Look, we haven't got much, but I'll give you what I can – a few shillings to get by on. That'll see you right till something turns up.'

It's not the money, Jenny wanted to say, though Heaven alone knows how much I need it; it's the love. All I want is someone to hug me and tell me I haven't done wrong.

'Please, Auntie Jane.'

'Take it or leave it, Jenny.' Jane reached into her purse and took out two half-crowns. 'I can't do any more for you. You made your bed, now you'll have to lie in it.'

Over at The Feathers, Denny Finch was putting on a new barrel of mild when he heard footsteps coming down the cellar steps.

'That you, Aggie?'

A shadow cut across his field of vision.

'Get out way, will tha', I can't see barrel.' Turning round to give his wife an impatient shove, he realised that he had been very much mistaken. 'Ivan? What's tha doin' here then?'

'Wanted a quiet word with you, boy.' Ivan folded his arms and leaned casually against a stack of crates.

'What about?' asked Denny nervously.

Not that he needed to be told. He'd known something was up when Jenny didn't turn up for her shift. Now everyone around here had heard about Jenny Fisher and what she had or hadn't done. Though gossip was readily available on every street corner, the truth was somewhat harder to get at. And sometimes it paid to believe what you were told to believe.

'You're no fool, Denny, you know what about.' Ivan scratched his ear. 'Thing is, boy, I don't want my Dot upset, not in her condition. She needs peace an' quiet, if you get my meaning.'

'I see.'

'The last thing I want is certain people causin' trouble round here, see. Certain people who deserve to be out on the street like the filthy lying sluts they are.' Ivan paused, digesting his own words with evident relish. 'So I'm askin' you, Denny – man to man like – not to do nothin' as might be *upsettin'* to my Dot. You get my drift?'

'Aye, Ivan. I reckon I do.'

'An' if you see that little bitch, you tell 'er I've not finished with 'er yet, not by a long chalk. You tell 'er that from me, boy, understand?'

Denny understood all right. He'd known Ivan Price ever since he came to St Helens, well enough to be sure he wasn't a man you'd want to cross. It was crystal clear that any help Denny Finch offered Jenny would be repaid with an equal amount of retribution. By the time she turned up at The Feathers, around midday, he had already prepared what he was going to say.

'I'd like to help thee, Jenny, tha knows I would. Heaven knows tha's been hard done by, only . . .'

'Only what?'

Denny scratched his scalp through his ginger curls.

'Only Ivan Price dun't see it that way.'

Jenny felt cold fingers slither down her spine.

'Ivan? He's been here?'

'Aye, lass.'

'Looking for me?'

'Ivan give me a message for thee. He said . . .' Denny coughed awkwardly. 'He said as tha'd not seen last of 'im.'

Jenny felt sick to her stomach.

'And he told you not to take me in?'

'In a manner of speakin', aye.'

'Can't I at least come back to work here?'

Denny wrung out a dishcloth and swabbed down the bar-top.

'Aggie's on her feet again now, lass. I'm right sorry an' that, but it were always a temporary arrangement.'

That night there was no room for Jenny at the hostel. She spent the hours of darkness pacing the streets, utterly exhausted yet too afraid to sleep. Every shadow held a whispering, unseen menace; and in her mind every sound was the ring of Ivan's iron-shod clogs on the paving stones, never more than a few steps behind her.

In desperation she even thought about committing some crime, doing something, anything, that would get her hauled off to a nice warm dry police cell.

As dawn broke over the smoking rooftops, Jenny lay curled up under her coat in the doorway of a men's outfitters. She hadn't slept more than fleetingly all night, but at least here she was out of the rain.

A milkman was coming along the street with his horse and a float full of clanking milk churns, but Jenny couldn't afford to buy milk. She had one and thruppence-halfpenny in her coat pocket, and no idea of how long it would have to last.

The royal blue sky turned to grey, blushed with pink and yellow. The sun would be up soon and people would be walking into town, trolley-buses rattling through the streets, carrying folk to work. She couldn't bear it if someone she knew saw her like this.

'You been there all night, miss?' The policeman towered over her, dark and shiny as a bat in his oilskin cape.

'No, officer, I was just . . . I was just having a rest.'

'You got somewhere to go, have you?' His tone was not unkind.

Jenny hung her head.

'No.' She knew what she must look like, with her unwashed hair and grubby clothes. A waif, a stray, a hopeless, feckless vagrant. But she wasn't like that, she wasn't! She forced herself to look up at the policeman. 'Not yet, but I'm looking for a place.'

'If I find you here again, I'll have to take you in. Vagrancy's an offence, you know.'

'I was just . . . going.'

She got to her feet slowly and painfully, her shoulders and legs aching from being cramped and twisted into unnatural shapes. Picking up her suitcase, she began trudging up the street. Perhaps today someone would offer her a job. Perhaps . . .

But no, it was no use fantasising. She knew in her heart that no one would help her. Ivan had poisoned everything and everyone, leaving her nowhere to turn. Everyone in the whole world hated her now, everyone. Except perhaps one person . . .

John Corlett.

The thought came to her like a bright flash of light. Why hadn't she thought of him before? Mr Corlett was a good man, he gave a lot of money to the church, surely he wouldn't turn her away? But could she do it? That was the question. Could she throw herself on his mercy when she'd abused his trust before?

Her hopes were stronger than her doubts, and her step quickened as she turned into Jubilee Street. Mr Corlett's grocery store was on the corner at the far end. Even this early in the morning the windows were lit up, a bright beacon in the grey twilight. It was dry and warm in there, not drizzly and cold like it was out here on the street.

He'll help me, she told herself, out of breath from walking so fast. The suitcase felt light in her hand now, no longer a dead weight of soggy canvas. He'll help me, he will, he *will*, I know it.

She was almost at the corner of the street when it hit her: the weight of memory. Light was pouring out of the shop and inside she could see Mr Corlett in his brown shopkeeper's coat, setting out rows of fresh, four-pound loaves on the wooden counter. That had been her job, just a few short weeks ago; counting out the loaves, setting them out, putting yesterday's stale bread on one side to be sold at half price . . .

He hadn't seen her yet. He was saying something to Eddie, patting him on the shoulder, sending him off out to the stock-room. There was nothing to stop her walking right up to the door and pushing it open. The doorbell would jangle and she would step inside, breathing in the scents of fresh, yeasty bread, cooked meat and apples. It would be so easy to ask for help and he wouldn't turn her away – so why didn't she?

Shame and sorrow welled up inside her so suddenly that she wasn't prepared for the sheer force of her emotions. I can't do it, she realised, I can't. Only a sheet of glass separated her from safety, but it seemed impossibly far away.

Jenny turned and ran, not knowing where she was heading. She simply ran and kept on running, the suitcase banging against her hip, her wet coat flapping about her knees. People stood and stared at her but she scarcely noticed them, didn't care what they thought of her, not any more. She didn't stop until her lungs were aching fit to burst.

Leaning against the crumbling wall of a condemned house, she fought to get her breath back; but every indrawn breath became a sob of despair and she sank slowly to the pavement, her back scraping against the wet bricks.

'Why, Mam? Why?'

There, slumped on the kerb with her head in her hands, Jenny cried her heart out; certain that her life was in ruins, and that everything wrong in the whole world was Jenny Fisher's fault.

'Jenny? Jenny Fisher?'

Through her sobs and the drumming of rain on the pavement, Jenny heard a voice; a woman's voice, calm and concerned and oddly familiar, with the touch of an Irish lilt mixed somewhere in the St Helens accent.

'It *is* you, now, isn't it? Here, take this, dry your eyes.'

Thin, cold fingers pressed a handkerchief into her hand. Surprised, she looked up through swollen, misted eyes.

'Mrs O'Brien?'

'That's right, Molly O'Brien. You remember me now, don't you?'

'Of course I do.' Jenny sniffed back her tears. She felt silly and self-indulgent. 'At the shop . . .'

'You helped us, Jenny. And when you've got nothing, you don't forget a kindness.' The thin, surprisingly strong hands reached out and helped Jenny to her feet. 'Now if you don't mind my sayin', it looks like you've a bit of trouble yourself.'

'I . . .' Jenny was baffled, tongue-tied and shamefaced. 'I'm all right, really.'

'You don't look all right to me,' commented Mrs O'Brien, stepping back to take a long, critical look. 'How long is it since you ate?'

Jenny racked her brains. 'I can't remember,' she admitted lamely.

'Then you'll come home with me for a cup o' tea and a bite?'

'But . . .' Jenny thought of the twelve ever-hungry mouths of the O'Brien children, of skinny, rickety Dora and poor Col O'Brien, most of the time too weak to do much more than draw breath. 'I can't, you need your food . . .'

'We may not have much,' said Molly firmly, 'and what we have's not fancy. But what we have, we share. Now, you are coming back with me, or do I have to drag you there with my own two hands?'

Chapter 6

'Come in now, come in, sit you down. Dora, put the kettle on. Aileen, run and fetch those broken biscuits from the larder. Mary, find a chair.'

A swarm of eager faces greeted Jenny as she stepped through the door into Molly O'Brien's back kitchen, each high-pitched voice chorusing shriller than the last.

'Who is it, Mam?'

'It's the lady from the shop, her as give me the bread . . .'

'Is she staying, Mam?'

'Why's her coat all wet through?'

Jenny knew that places like Canal Terrace existed, but knowing and seeing were two very different things. Slum clearance had passed by this part of town. The houses crowded together like blackened and chipped teeth, tiny two-up-two-downs with a single ash-pit privy between six backyards. Sodden wallpaper peeled in huge, ballooning strips from walls that ran with damp. Out of every cracked lintel oozed the reek of mould and unwashed flesh. It didn't matter how proud a mother might be; no one could keep her children properly clean with no running water in the house, and the only tap a standpipe at the end of the street.

As Jenny stood stock-still in the back kitchen, not knowing what to do or say, Molly was already marshalling her troops, organising her mini-army of junior O'Briens.

'Leave Jenny be. Wipe that jam off your face, Bernie. Annie, find the oilcloth and put it on the table.' Molly turned to Jenny with an apologetic smile.

'Take off your coat and dry yourself by the fire. Col's

only just this minute put a bit of coal on.'

Jenny blinked at the tiny fire sitting in the vast empty grate. That was probably all the coal the O'Briens could afford for a whole week. She felt immensely guilty and profoundly grateful to these people who hardly knew her.

'It's . . . very kind of you to let me come here, Mrs O'Brien. I don't know what to say.'

'You needn't say anything, love. And you'll call me Molly.'

Jenny hoped that Molly couldn't read the shock on her face, hadn't seen her flinch at the first sight of a big brown bug, scuttling up the wall above the fireplace and running across to the middle of the ceiling. As she stared at it, she realised to her horror that it wasn't alone. What she had thought at first were brown dots on the wallpaper were bugs of all shapes and sizes, dozens and dozens of them. She had to force herself not to retch.

Mr O'Brien, who had been sitting quietly in a sagging armchair, followed her gaze and nodded understandingly.

'Don't you fret about them, Jenny love, they're ugly enough but they'll do you no 'arm.'

'I'm sorry, I didn't mean to . . .'

'To be sure, it'd take more'n that to offend me. Whole street's riddled with bugs, see.' Col took a long, laborious breath and started again. 'Council man comes now and then, burns a sulphur candle, but it makes no difference.' He laughed wheezily. 'Reckon the buggers'll see me out.' His laughter ended in a coughing fit that left red-flecked sputum on the grey-white handkerchief.

'Now, now, Col,' scolded Molly, fussing around her husband and patting the cushion at his back. 'You know I won't have talk like that in this house.'

She was like an animated skeleton herself, thought Jenny, a perennial battler who simply refused to give up when any lesser woman would have gone under long ago. Jenny thought fleetingly and bitterly of her own mother. Wherever did Molly O'Brien find so much strength?

Molly stood up and folded her arms. 'Now, Jenny love, you've nowhere to stay?'

'Well . . . no.'

'Then you'll stay here with us.'

She stared blankly at Molly.

'Stay? Tonight?' After so many rejections, the possibility of help from such an unlikely source was difficult to take in.

'As many nights as you like. It's six to a bed here, mind, but at least you'll not feel the cold.' Aileen and Annie arrived with a large brown teapot, a blue paper bag of broken biscuits and the stale end of a tin-loaf. 'Put those on the table and get Jenny a plate. Quick, mind! She's 'ungry. Well, sit down, love, sit down and tuck in. We don't stand on ceremony here.'

Jenny's legs almost buckled underneath her as she sank on to the O'Briens' only good chair. Suddenly, inexplicably, the last drop of resilience seemed to have drained out of her. She wanted to eat, but she could scarcely remember how.

'Th—Thank you,' she whispered, looking up at Molly O'Brien. All at once the kindness of strangers filled her heart and she felt sadder and happier than she could ever recall feeling. Her face crumpled and the tears came again. 'Thank you, thank you . . . oh, I'm sorry, I'm so sorry, what must you think of me?'

'Sorry? What on earth would you want to be sorry for?' Molly O'Brien smiled, and putting her arm about Jenny's shoulders, did her best to soothe the hurt away.

'The worst sin of all is giving up.' That's what Dan Fisher used to say to his children. 'Just you remember that when things get bad.'

Dad would have got on well with the O'Briens, thought Jenny, Irish Catholics or not. No matter how awful their life was, no matter how little they had, the thought of throwing in the towel never seemed to cross their minds.

The squalor of Canal Terrace took some getting used to, but Jenny had never known such friendly, open people. They were always stopping her in the street to ask her how she was, or to give her things when they hardly had enough for themselves. The more often it happened, the more guilty Jenny felt at not being able to give anything in return.

One morning, over a meagre breakfast of bread and scrape, Mrs O'Brien announced cheerily that she had found Jenny a job.

'It's nothing much, mind, just a bit of cleaning.'

'A job!' Jenny's heart soared. 'But how?'

'Had a word with our Clodagh, she's an usherette at the Alhambra. Turns out they're looking for a nice young girl to clean for them, three times a week.'

Work! Work meant money, independence, a chance to win back some dignity. And yet . . . the excitement inside Jenny faltered momentarily. Jobs for women weren't easy to come by, that much she'd learnt for herself the hard way. And the O'Briens needed the money far more than she did.

'It's kind of you, but I can't,' she began.

Molly cocked her head to one side.

'Why's that then?'

'You should have the job, not me. It's not right.'

Col O'Brien took a slurp of milkless tea.

'Take the job and stop frettin'. It's a young girl's job. And besides, Molly's got her hands full, what with me an' the kids an' takin' in other folks' washing.'

'I'll give you every penny I earn.'

Molly shook her head.

'There's no need for that. Give us a shillin' or two now an' then if it makes you feel better. There,' she beamed, 'that's settled then. Just turn up at the Alhambra tomorrow afternoon, and ask for Mr Gregson.'

There was no arguing with Molly O'Brien. At two o'clock the next day, Jenny set off down Canal Terrace and headed for the centre of town. Her coat had dried out and didn't look too bad; she'd washed and ironed her dress and you couldn't tell that the hole in the sole of her right lace-up shoe was patched with a piece of cardboard. Molly had even loaned her her hat, the one she pawned every Monday and redeemed without fail on a Friday: turning up for confession without a hat on would be an unthinkable sin.

The Alhambra was near the bottom end of Bickerstaffe Street. Almost as swish as the Savoy Picture House, it was an imposing building with tall pillars and ornate scrolling above the doorway. As far as Jenny was concerned it was just about the most exciting building in St Helens – apart, of course, from the wonderful Theatre Royal. Taking a deep breath, she stepped into the foyer.

She found Mr Gregson fussing about in the auditorium, waving his arms about and arguing with the cinema organist about "repertoire". The Alhambra's manager was a sort of fey beanpole in an off-the-peg grey suit that revealed two inches of ankle. His sandy-coloured hair and skinny frame made him look like an overgrown schoolboy, though he might have been anywhere between thirty and fifty. He wore round, steel-rimmed spectacles which he was continually pushing back up to the bridge of his long, pointed nose.

'Excuse me . . . Mr Gregson . . . sir?'

He swivelled round, poking his glasses higher on his nose.

'Miss Fisher?'

'Yes, Mr Gregson.' Jenny hoped that she looked tolerably respectable, though she felt shabby and unkempt in this palace of gilded scrolling and sculpted cherubs. 'I've come about the job.'

'I see. You have experience of this kind of work?'

'Yes . . . well, sort of. I used to clean at The Feathers.'

'Indeed?'

'Before that I worked in a shop.'

'I see.'

He looked unconvinced so Jenny added, 'I *can* do the job, sir. If you take me on, I'll prove it.'

The ghost of a smile passed across Mr Gregson's face at this display of youthful confidence.

'You really want this job, don't you, Jenny?'

'Yes, Mr Gregson. I *need* this job.'

He nodded thoughtfully.

'Very well, very well.'

Jenny caught her breath.

'Sir, I . . . are you offering me a job?'

Claude the organist was waving a handful of sheet music under the manager's nose.

'Really, Simon, I must insist . . .'

Jenny hardly dared speak up again. She touched the manager lightly on the shoulder.

'Mr Gregson?'

He turned round and nodded at her.

'Seven-and-six a week, one week's trial. You can collect your mop and bucket from the store-room. Minnie will show you the ropes.'

'Mind you clean right down the side of those seats, Jenny.'

'Yes, Minnie.'

'Mr Gregson's very particular about his moquette.'

'I won't forget.'

'And while you're at it, Claude says some kid's been sick on the organ seat. You'd better give it a wash-down with carbolic.'

'Right you are, soon as I've mopped this floor.'

Working at the Alhambra wasn't nearly as hard as The Feathers, though it could be sticky work sometimes, what with all the melted ice-cream on the backs of the moquette bucket seats, and the half-sucked boiled sweets that fastened themselves to the bottom of her shoes.

Jenny worked hard, made a big effort to get on with Minnie and please Mr Gregson, and took pride in taking her seven-and-six a week back to Canal Terrace. It was only half what she'd earnt at the shop – and *that* wasn't a fortune – but at least she was finding a way to pay back some of Molly's kindness.

From time to time she caught sight of old friends and acquaintances in the happy, laughing crowds who spilled out of the cinema on a Saturday night: Gloria, Alice, even Eddie on one occasion. Every time she held her breath for a sight of Mam, or Nancy, or Tom, but they never came. If they knew where she was and what she was reduced to doing, they obviously didn't care. And at least there was no sign of Ivan Price, for all his threats.

66

She often thought of Billy and Daisy. Did they miss her? Did they ask after her, and wonder where she'd gone? If only she could have had just a few moments with them to explain . . . but with Ivan ruling the roost at forty-two Gas Street, perhaps it was better if she kept her mouth shut and let them forget all about her.

Twenty times she'd walked past the end of Gas Street, her mind made up to knock on the door of number forty-two. Twenty times she'd turned back before she got within fifty yards of the house. Surely if they'd wanted to see her, if they'd cared about her at all, they'd have made some effort to get in touch?

Perhaps Nancy had been right all along, and they really were better off without her.

A jab in the ribs jolted her back to the job in hand.

'Get a move on, Jenny, picture starts in half an hour.'

'Sorry, Minnie, I was miles away.'

'If you're not finished and cleared away in ten minutes, he'll not let you stop in for the big film.'

The best thing about being at the Alhambra was that Mr Gregson often allowed her to stand at the back and watch the Big Picture. *Gold Diggers in Paris*, Rogers and Astaire in *Swing Time*, *The Adventures of Robin Hood* with dashing Errol Flynn, gorgeous Robert Taylor and heavenly Vivien Leigh in *A Yank at Oxford* – she saw them all, drank in their glamour and yearned silently for it all to happen to her.

When she stepped out of the cinema and back into the ordinary world, she took a little of that glamour with her. And really that was the *worst* thing about being at the Alhambra: leaving the perfect world of the picture show and realising that real life wasn't like that at all.

If she hadn't been so determined not to give in, that realisation might have broken Jenny's heart.

'Nearly ready, is it?'

Dot's voice floated down the stairs to the kitchen.

'Nearly.'

'Your dad's just comin' up the road, he'll want his tea.'

Nancy Fisher peered into the saucepan on the hob. It contained an oily brown bubbling mess which was supposed to be stew but didn't look or smell very much like it. Nancy never had been that keen on cooking; what was the point of learning? Before Jenny had left, she had hardly ever had to lift a finger.

Now she was learning the hard way just how much Jenny used to do in the house: cooking, cleaning, bringing in money. And now, what with Mam being so very pregnant and tired all the time, everything that had been Jenny's job had become Nancy's. It wasn't fair, and that was the truth of it. Nancy was only fifteen and pretty with it; she should be out having fun, not scrubbing floors and peeling potatoes.

She stabbed the brown mass with a spoon. If she threw in a few potatoes it might not be too bad.

'Nancy, Nancy!'

Daisy came bounding into the kitchen, almost cannoning into her sister. As ever, Billy was hot on her heels, laughing and pulling faces.

'Will you watch where you're going!'

'Nancy, Nancy, Billy says I can't play cops an' robbers 'cause I'm only a girl.'

Nancy clenched her teeth. She was sick to the back teeth of all this bickering.

'Will you stop arguing and behave? You'll 'ave the pan off the stove, then what'll we 'ave for tea?'

Billy wrinkled his nose and stuck out his tongue.

'Poo,' he said expressively. 'It stinks like dog's poo. Do we have to eat that?'

'Yes.'

'I'm not eatin' it.'

'Neither am I,' agreed Daisy.

Nancy took the pan off the range and plonked it on to a trivet on the table.

'Then you can go without, can't you?'

'You can't cook,' declared Daisy. 'Can't, can't, can't,' she sang as she pirouetted around the kitchen.

'Shut up,' snarled Nancy. 'Will you shut up and do what you're told?'

'Jenny can cook,' said Billy in perfect innocence. 'She does tater scouse an' 'ot pot. I want Jenny. When's Jenny comin' back?'

Nancy turned flashing eyes on her little brother and sister. At that moment she could have strangled the little brats, not to mention their wretched elder sister.

'Never,' she hissed, banging down a plate on the table. 'Never, do you hear? Now sit down and eat your tea, or you can go 'ungry.'

As luck would have it, Ivan ate his plate of stew and potatoes without complaint. He even smiled at her and thanked her when she took his plate away to be washed. She knew for certain now that he'd only hit her because he was angry at the lies Jenny had told. Ever since Jenny had left he'd been nicer to her, even paid her the odd compliment when she did her hair a different way or dressed up to go out somewhere. Oh, he was strict all right, but he wasn't a bad man, not if you kept out of his way when he'd had a drink.

Nancy was standing at the sink in the back kitchen when the door opened and Ivan came in.

'All on your own then, girl?'

'Just washing up.'

He closed the door softly and came across to the sink. Now he was standing right behind her and Nancy couldn't see his face. She felt ever so slightly uncomfortable, she didn't quite know why.

'You're a good girl, Nancy. Not like your bitch sister. You know when to do as you're told, don't you?'

'I . . .' She tried to answer him, but the words wouldn't come out right. As Ivan's hands snaked around her waist and he pushed himself against her back, she started to shake.

'Please . . . please don't do that.'

'Hush, Nancy. You want to please your da, don't you?'

She heard him chuckle softly, then his hands slid upwards to cup and squeeze her breasts. Her face burned crimson. She wanted to cry out and wriggle free, but she couldn't. All the strength had gone out of her.

'Ivan . . .'

'You'll make some man a fine wife, Nancy,' said Ivan as he gave her breasts a final squeeze and let her go. 'One day soon . . . when you're ready.'

'I'm quite pleased with your work, Jenny.' Mr Gregson took off his glasses and fiddled with the earpieces. Praising staff was so much more embarrassing than telling them off. He handed her a brown envelope. 'There's sixpence extra in your pay this week.'

'Thank you, Mr Gregson.' For a fleeting moment at least, Jenny felt a glow of happiness. She'd slip the extra sixpence into Molly's purse when she wasn't looking; that would save arguments.

Later Minnie added, with an air of importance: 'Peggy's off with her legs again. Mr Gregson says you can stand in for her tonight, if you like.'

Standing in for Peggy was the highest accolade that Mr Gregson could offer. Peggy the usherette had been at the Alhambra since it opened in 1912 and was as much a fixture as the plaster angel over the proscenium arch, but lately her varicose veins had been giving her gyp and Jenny had enjoyed a few temporary promotions. True, all she had to do was tear tickets in half and show people to their seats, but it was a sign of trust and it meant a lot to her.

Just before six o'clock, she put on the red usherette's uniform and took her place at the door to the stalls.

'Tickets, please. Thanks.'

'There's a few seats in row E, halfway down on the right-hand side.'

'Sorry, sir, you can't come in without a ticket.'

'Wrong door, madam. Circle's through there to your left, and up the stairs.'

It was busy at the Alhambra tonight. They were showing the latest George Formby and he always went down well, though Minnie said he was daft as a brush and no oil-painting either. Jenny was rushed off her feet showing people to their seats, taking tickets, smiling at people in the half-darkness, proving to Mr Gregson he'd been right to take her on.

She was so busy keeping an eye on the crowds of lads and lasses that at first she didn't notice the young woman in the fashionable fox-fur jacket, hanging on the arm of a well-dressed older man as they walked in through the foyer. In fact, even when the two of them were practically face-to-face, Jenny hardly recognised her. But she could hardly fail to recognise the bright, happy voice which greeted her.

'Jenny? Aren't you even going to say hello?'

'Tickets, please, sir, madam . . . oh!'

Jenny almost dropped her handful of ticket stubs. Like her dad, Mae Corlett had never lost her Manx accent – her voice was unmistakable. And now she was grinning impishly at Jenny from underneath the wide brim of a very rakish, feather-trimmed hat. It couldn't be true, it couldn't! Jenny stood and gaped.

'What's up, Jen? Aren't you pleased to see me?'

Joyful excitement exploded inside Jenny; she wanted to jump up and down and scream and shout. Thrilled and delighted, she threw her arms round her friend and they hugged each other for dear life.

'Mae! Mae, is it really you?'

'Of course it is, who else would it be!'

'I don't believe it's you! What are you *doing* here?'

'I might ask you the same thing,' remarked Mae with a searching look.

Please don't ask, thought Jenny, at least not right here and now. I'm not sure I could bear it. And she wondered how much Mae already knew, whether she had been to see her father and if he had told her what had happened. Jenny hardly knew whether to be thrilled at seeing her, or ashamed at what she'd brought on herself.

'It's a long story,' she said evasively.

'Well, I want to hear it *all*.' Mae turned to her companion, a balding man in his fifties wearing a long cashmere coat. 'This is Jenny Fisher, my best friend, did I tell you about her?'

71

'Only about thirty times,' he replied, offering Jenny his hand with a smile. His handshake was firm and friendly. 'Sid Dukes. Pleased to meet you, Jenny, Mae's told me a lot about you.'

'All good, I promise,' giggled Mae. 'Now, we've got to have a really long chinwag . . .'

'Oi! What the 'ell's going on?' demanded a woman's voice just behind Mae.

'Stop that gabbin' lass, an' take us tickets.'

'Aye, are you goin' ter lerrus in or do we 'ave to watch George Formby out in street?'

With horror, Jenny realised that a huge, jostling queue of people had built up behind Mae and her beau.

'Oh, Mae, I'm sorry but if I don't get on . . .'

'Don't worry, Jen, I can see how busy you are. We'll meet up after the film and go somewhere for a nice long talk.' She gave her companion a sly wink. 'Come on, Sid, I can see a couple of empty seats on the back row.'

Chapter 7

'*This* is where you're staying? It's . . . enormous!'

Jenny looked up at the big red-brick villa, with its bay windows and neat front garden. Lights glowed welcomingly through the curtains at one of the upstairs windows. This was very definitely the respectable end of St Helens.

Mae led the way up the path to the front door.

'We're all staying here, all the Dukettes. Mrs Jenks is famous for her theatrical digs.'

Jenny couldn't suppress a very childish giggle.

'All the *what*?'

Mae put on a reproving, mock-schoolmarmish look.

'Sid Dukes's Dukettes, what's funny about that? I'll have you know we're very well thought of in the business.'

After the film – no doubt prompted by Mae – Mr Dukes had made his excuses and headed off towards The Black Horse, leaving Mae and Jenny to their own devices. Jenny was thrilled to see her friend again, but at least while Sid had been there it was easier to avoid Mae's barrage of awkward questions.

She reached into her handbag, took out a key and unlocked the front door.

'Come in. Mrs Jenks will be in bed by now, we can have the parlour to ourselves.'

Jenny hung back.

'I don't know if I should, it's very late . . .'

Mae took her by the elbow and steered her inside, shutting the front door very firmly behind her.

'You've been trying to avoid talking to me ever since I walked into the Alhambra,' she said firmly. 'And I'm not letting you go until I've found out what's wrong.'

'Nothing's wrong,' said Jenny.

Mae slipped off her natty little fox-fur jacket and draped it over the banister. Her adolescent gawkiness had turned into a lithe, willowy dancer's figure, which was set off beautifully by a tailored dress in soft blue jersey.

'You always were a rotten liar, Jenny Fisher.'

'I don't . . .'

'Save your breath, I'm not having any more of this. Let's make ourselves a pot of tea and sort all this out, shall we?'

It wasn't until Mae slid the long glass-headed pin out of her hat that Jenny realised the most dramatic change that had taken place in her appearance in the months since she'd last seen her. She wondered how she could possibly not have noticed it before.

'You're . . . you're blonde!'

Mae laughed out loud at the look of utter astonishment on Jenny's face. She tossed her bouncy, Jean Harlow curls and gave a mannequin's pirouette.

'What do you think? Does the platinum look suit me?'

Funnily enough, it did.

'Mae, I'd never *dare*!'

'Yes, well, you've got lovely hair already, you don't need to. I was fed up being all mousy.'

'Whatever does your dad reckon to it?'

At this Mae went uncharacteristically quiet.

'Well, you know Dad and I don't always see eye to eye.' She brightened. 'But then again, he didn't throw me out when I went round to see him at the shop, so he can't think I'm a *complete* trollop . . .'

She stopped in mid-sentence, suddenly noticing the expression on her friend's face.

'Jen – Jenny, what's the matter? You're *crying*. What's *happened* to you?'

Jenny had been so determined not to give in to weakness and spoil Mae's bubbly chatter, but so much had happened to her since they'd last seen each other, so much had changed and seemed impossible to mend. All of a sudden the tears just came welling up in her eyes and spilling over on to her cheeks. She wiped them away with the frayed sleeve of her dress.

'You don't want to know.'

'Oh, yes, I do.' Mae steered Jenny through a door into a large, comfortably furnished sitting room, dotted with easy chairs and a cosy jumble of odds and ends. 'Friends for ever, remember? You're not going home till you've told me *everything*.'

'Home? I *can't* go home. I can't ever go home, not any more.'

Mae pushed a red-and-blue sequinned outfit off the back of one of the chairs, tut-tutting about Phoebe and her untidiness.

'Sit down. We're going to get to the bottom of this.'

It was a command. Jenny obeyed. Frankly it was a relief to let somebody else take charge. Mae sat down on the floor, cross-legged at her feet.

'Right, Jen. I'll tell you what I know, and you can fill me in on the rest. Fair enough?'

'Fair enough.'

'Here.' Mae took a lace-edged hanky from her pocket and handed it to Jenny. 'Buck up. Whatever it is it can't be that bad.'

She bent one knee and rested her chin on it.

'The band's playing Warrington all next week, only we couldn't get decent digs for the singers and dancers, so I suggested to Sid – that's Mr Dukes – that we could stay in St Helens. Of course, soon as I got here, I went round to my dad's shop but you weren't there . . .'

'No,' sighed Jenny. 'What did he tell you?'

'He was a bit cagey. Said he'd had to lay you off because business was bad. I pushed a bit and he said he'd caught you giving away bread to the O'Briens.'

Jenny nodded glumly. She was still too ashamed of herself to talk about it.

'Anyway, he said he wasn't angry with you any more and wished he hadn't lost his temper. The thing is, he said he was worried about you. Said he hadn't seen you in weeks and people were saying your mam had thrown you out of the house, and wouldn't have you back no matter what. It's true, isn't it?'

'I wish it wasn't.' Jenny blew her nose on Mae's hanky. 'What did you do when you found out?'

'Went round to Gas Street, of course. But Ivan wouldn't give me the time of day, and your mam said it wasn't any of my business anyhow. So these last three days I've been tramping all over St Helens every spare moment I could get, trying to track you down. If I hadn't bumped into Minnie outside the Alhambra, I'd probably still be looking. What's going on, Jenny?'

She took a long, deep breath. They'd been best friends for years, but who could tell if Mae Corlett would believe her, any more than Mam had?

'It was Ivan,' she began. 'Only if I tell you, you won't believe me.'

'Try me.'

'He tried it on, you know . . .'

'Made a pass, you mean?'

'Worse, a lot worse.' Even the memory of it made her tremble. 'He tried to make me . . . you know . . . tried to force me, and when I wouldn't let him, he knocked me about.' She fingered the spot on her forehead where the lump had been, the memory more vivid than ever. 'I was scared that the next time he'd really hurt me, so I told Mam.'

Light was dawning on Mae.

'You told Dot what he'd done and she didn't believe you?'

'She said I was telling wicked lies about Ivan because I was jealous of her and the baby. She thinks I'm a slut and I've been with loads of men.'

'You? Oh, Jenny, how could she?'

'Then Ivan started spreading rumours about me and threatening people, and no one would help me or take me in, and I even had to sleep in a shop doorway, and . . . oh, Mae, it's the truth, I swear it's all true, every word of it!'

'I know.' Getting up, Mae perched on the arm of the chair and slipped her arm round Jenny's shoulders. 'Didn't

I say I hated that Ivan Price the minute I set eyes on him? I never understood what possessed your mam to fall for him like that.'

'She was lonely, and he was strong.'

'He's just a bully. Dad was always telling your mam so, but she wouldn't listen.'

'I know, but . . . he helped her stop drinking, and stopped the colliery throwing us out of our house. She's grateful to him. I was grateful too.'

'But, Jenny, you're Dot's daughter, you worked all hours to keep that family together when your dad died and all Dot could think of was the next bottle of gin. How could she take Ivan's word over yours?'

'I don't know. I just don't know. Sometimes I think she's jealous of me, but I don't know why.'

'You're young, you're pretty, you're not tied down . . . perhaps that's it.'

'Perhaps.'

Mae tried another tack.

'So you've been cleaning at the Alhambra?'

'It was the only work I could get.'

'Where are you staying?'

'With the O'Briens.'

'In Canal Terrace!'

'Molly took me in off the street. She was so kind to me and I hardly knew her.'

'All the same, you can't go on staying there. I won't let you! Those slums were condemned years ago, they're infested . . .'

Jenny rose to Molly O'Brien's defence.

'Molly and Col have brought up twelve kids in that house.'

'And another four died of diphtheria and starvation and God knows what. Look, Jen, why should you suffer when you've done nothing wrong?'

'I'd forgotten how bossy you are,' commented Jenny ruefully.

'Then it's time I reminded you.' Mae sprang to her feet. 'Come on.'

77

'Where to?'

'My room – upstairs.'

'What for?'

'The first thing we have to do is find you something decent to wear.'

Mae's room was upstairs, at the front of the house. It had a bay window, a dressing-table littered with Ponds powder compacts and tubes of stage make-up, a square of faded blue carpet, a double bed and a large wardrobe. After Canal Terrace, it seemed like the ultimate in luxurious decadence.

'Go on then,' urged Mae, bouncing bottom-first on to the bed. 'Choose something. Anything you like.'

Jenny tentatively opened the wardrobe doors. Amazing! She'd never seen so many clothes all at once, except in a shop window in Liverpool.

'Are these all *yours*?' She ran her fingers along the row of hanging skirts, blouses and dresses. Some of them were obviously stage costumes, silky or sequinned, or trimmed with bits of feather and lace. The rest were ordinary clothes but stylish and well-made. The smooth fabrics felt wonderful to her cracked and calloused fingertips.

'Yes – well, all except the stage clothes. They belong to the company really.'

Jenny reached in and pulled out a hanger. It held a smart powder blue costume with a fitted skirt and a jacket trimmed with black astrakhan.

'Gloria was right then,' she commented.

'Gloria Moffat? What about her?'

'She said you must have found yourself a millionaire.' Jenny stroked the soft woollen material. 'This is beautiful.'

'It was a birthday present from Sid.'

'From . . .?' Jenny thought of her brief meeting with Sid Dukes. He'd seemed all right, but he was old enough to be Mae's father. Grandfather even. Why, he was even going bald!

'Sorry, *Mr Dukes*,' Mae corrected herself half-jokingly. She smiled. A very warm smile, thought Jenny, warm and happy. 'Actually, he's given me most of my nice things. I wouldn't be able to afford them on a dancer's pay. He's not a millionaire though!'

Even in the short time she'd seen them together, Jenny had noticed the way Mae and Sid had looked at each other, the way she hung on his arm and the affectionate way he patted her hand. And it was difficult not to take stock of the double bed and the pair of men's brown brogues sticking out from under it.

'So you and Mr Dukes are . . . you know . . .?'

Mae winked.

'Let's just say he's been very kind to me.'

'Isn't he a bit . . .?'

'Old?'

'Well . . . yes.'

Mae laughed.

'I never did go for young lads, you know that. Sid's a decent man, Jenny, you'd really like him if you got to know him. Now, why don't you try on that suit?'

'Really . . . I shouldn't.'

'Go on. If you like it, it's yours.'

Jenny shook her head and slid the hanger back into the wardrobe.

'Can you imagine me scrubbing floors at the Alhambra wearing that?'

Mae slid off the bed and flung the wardrobe doors wide open.

'What about this – or this?' She pulled out armfuls of clothes; a brown sweater, two tweed skirts, day-dresses, an embroidered bolero. 'Tell you what, this grey dress isn't too fancy, and it matches your eyes. Go on, Jenny, put it on.'

'Well, all right, I'll try it on just to see what it looks like, but that's all . . .' Jenny took the dress from Mae and laid it down on the bed while she undressed. Part of her rebelled against the thought of taking 'charity', but on the other hand it was a real luxury to slip out of her shabby clothes and into the neatly pressed grey dress.

Mae fastened the buttons at the back.

'There! I knew that colour was right for you. It's an inch

79

or two too long, but I'm good with a needle and thread. I had to learn fast after Mam died . . .'

Jenny looked at herself in the dressing-table mirror. The dove grey dress mirrored the soft grey of her eyes, making them seem larger and more lustrous in her pale face. Mae was right; the dress *did* match her eyes, but it also emphasised the dullness of her hair, the pallor of her skin, the callouses and cracks in her work-roughened hands.

'I . . . don't know,' she said.

Mae turned her round to get a better look.

'Don't you like it? There are lots of others you can try.'

Jenny shook her head.

'No, it's lovely, really it is. But look at me – I'm a mess. It'd take more than a nice dress to make me look half-decent.' She began fumbling at the buttons. 'Help me out of this, Mae. I need to get back before Molly sends out a search-party.'

'You're not going back to Canal Terrace, surely?'

'Where else would I go?'

'You can stay here.'

'Here, with you and . . .?'

'Sid won't mind sleeping on the sofa downstairs.' Mae put her arm round her friend's shoulders; she felt cold and shivery to the touch. 'Look, we're playing Warrington all this week and next. Why don't you stay here with me?'

The temptation was strong. It would be so seductively easy not to go back to the O'Briens' house. She could curl up here, on Mae's carpeted floor. She'd be clean and warm and dry, instead of having to share a mildewed mattress with five of the O'Brien kids and the bugs that crawled over her face while she slept.

'Stay here, Jenny. Don't go back there tonight, it's late. You can go and explain to Molly in the morning . . .'

The brief snapshot image of two slices of stale bread and a bit of cheese, sitting waiting for her on a cracked plate, shot into Jenny's head. They'd have saved that food for her supper, gone without so that she'd have something to eat when she came in from work.

'I can't,' she said firmly, wriggling out of Mae's grey dress.

'Why not? Wouldn't you rather stay here?'

Jenny turned her eyes on Mae.

'Of course I would. But I can't just walk off and forget about the O'Briens when it suits me, can I?'

'Molly would understand, surely?'

'She might, but that's not the point. And what would I do when the Dukettes leave St Helens? It's all right for you, you'll be off on your travels, but what about me?'

Mae looked downcast.

'I hadn't thought of that,' she admitted. 'But you can't just . . . give up!'

Jenny sighed.

'I know you want to help, Mae, but I've done all right on my own so far. So I reckon it's best all round if I just carry on that way, don't you?'

'Nancy?'

At first, there was a hint of disbelief in Mae Corlett's voice. She couldn't quite believe that the distant, solitary figure really was Jenny's younger sister: spoilt, vain, cocksure Nancy Fisher. The girl was almost bent double under the weight of an immense shopping basket, which she was half carrying, half dragging along the pavement.

Then Mae called out to her: 'Nancy, wait!'

The girl paused for a moment, as though getting her breath back, glanced round briefly then went on walking. Perhaps she'd been mistaken and it wasn't Nancy at all – no, no, it had to be Nancy. She recognised the green coat and the long brown plaits. Mae ran the length of Bickerstaffe Street, cursing the slender heels on her fashionable shoes. Nancy just kept on walking, grimly dragging along the overloaded shopping basket with her two clenched hands. Poor kid, thought Mae. Poor little skinny kid, what have they done to you?

'Please, Nancy. I need to talk to you.'

She touched her on the shoulder and Nancy glared at her, then shook her off and kept on walking.

'Leave me alone.'

'It's important.'

Mae took Nancy by the shoulders and spun her round.

'Listen to me. *Please*.'

This time Nancy was forced to stop and let the basket fall to the pavement. Her palms were criss-crossed with deep red indentations from the rough straw handles.

'Just go away, will you?' The dark eyes were pleading. 'Look, you have to let me go, I mustn't be long, I promised Mam . . .'

'This won't take long, I promise. It's about Jenny.' Mae saw Nancy's expression change instantly from self-pity to anger. 'She's really sorry about what happened . . .'

'*She's* sorry!'

'. . . and all she wants is to see you all again, only she daren't go near Gas Street, 'cause your mam won't have her in the house. So she asked me to speak to you or Tom.'

'Well, you've done it, can I go now?'

'In a minute. She gave me this.' Mae opened her handbag and took out a sealed envelope. 'It's a letter to you. She's written her side of the story – you should read it.'

Mae held out the letter. Nancy stood transfixed, staring at the envelope as if she dared not touch it for fear of its exploding.

'Go on, take it.'

Nancy's hand lifted an inch or two, then fell back to her side. She was nodding her head very slowly, her face filled with a mixture of emotions: fear, anger, hope, indecision.

'Where's the harm, Nancy? Jenny just wants you to know the truth. Go on, take it and read it.'

To Mae's surprise, Nancy nodded.

'All right then, I'll take it.'

She took the envelope and turned it round and round in her hand, reading the name on it again and again: Nancy Fisher. Not Nancy Price like Mam and Ivan said, but Nancy Fisher. What she used to be.

'Aren't you going to open it? Nancy, are you listening to me?'

Almost before the words were out of Mae's mouth,

Nancy was ripping the letter savagely across, tearing it again and again, until nothing was left but a confetti of torn paper and unread inky scribbles, blowing along in the gutter.

'*Now* will you leave me alone?' she demanded, her dark eyes blazing. 'Just go away, like you did before. And this time, you can take Jenny with you!'

It was lovely having Mae's friendship again, of course it was, but in some ways her presence made Jenny's life more difficult. It was impossible to stand next to her and not make comparisons. Mae Corlett was glamorous, happy, successful, in love – but what was Jenny Fisher? Lucky to have a part-time cleaning job, a slum bed to sleep in, and her dreams of what might have been if that talent scout had spotted her instead of Mae . . .

They changed the programme at the Alhambra on Thursdays, and Jenny finished early. As she walked back towards Canal Terrace, she wondered if Mae had managed to find Nancy or Tom and speak to them. Surely once they'd read her letter they'd begin to understand about Ivan, and why she'd had to tell the truth?

This thought made her feel brighter. Once she had an ally, things would change at forty-two Gas Street, she was sure of it.

There was a hat shop near the market square. As she walked past it something in the window caught her eye. Oh, it was such a lovely hat! Not fancy like Mae's hats, it was true, but nicely made. The sort of hat that would make you feel beautiful even when you were wearing shabby clothes. It would cover her hair, too, she thought as she automatically ran her hand over her dry scalp. She used to be proud of her hair, but not now. It was weeks since it had had a proper wash in warm water, and what with all the worry and not eating properly, it had lost its dark, lustrous sheen.

She could save a little from her wages every week. Perhaps the shop would keep the hat for her until she could afford it. Oh, yes, it was a lovely hat. Dark green felt with a broad brim. Set on her head at a jaunty angle, it would make her feel that she was ten times better than she really was.

And ten times better than the O'Briens, too? The thought came to her with a jolt of guilt. How could she possibly be thinking about buying hats, when she'd come to the market to buy food with the little extra in her purse? Something nice, something a bit better than those poor kids were used to. It broke Jenny's heart every time she saw Bernie and Annie O'Brien scrabbling around the stalls for bits of bruised fruit and yellowed cabbage leaves.

It was coming to the end of the afternoon and produce was being sold off cheap. A cabbage, that's what she'd buy. Maybe a few offcuts of mutton or some pigs' trotters if she could haggle a little – and if she asked Mr Parsons nicely she was sure he'd throw in a carrot or two to go with the cabbage. A pan of soup or a good thick stew, that was what the O'Brien kids needed, and that was what they were going to have.

As she hurried up to Mr Parsons' fruit and veg stall, the crowd parted a little and she made out a familiar figure, leaning against a lamp-post. There was no mistaking Jack Inglis – he was a giant of a man, well over six feet of solid muscle, with fists like boiled hams and a flattened, lopsided nose. He was a hard man, was Jack Inglis, well-known as a boxer when he wasn't at work on his stall. A hard man, but fair. Not like Ivan Price.

It wasn't until Jenny drew closer that she realised Jack Inglis was talking to someone. And not just anyone. Her heart skipped a beat and she felt as though an iron band was tightening about her chest. She stood rooted to the spot, staring through the gap in the milling crowd at Ivan Price.

Ivan! She'd been bound to spot him somewhere, sooner or later, Jenny had known that; but she still wasn't prepared for it. It was a long time before she realised that the jingling sound in her ear was her own shaking hand, making the coins in her purse rattle together.

Ivan was deep in conversation with Jack Inglis. As she

watched, he reached into the back pocket of his trousers and, with a glance to left and right, counted notes into Jack's hand. For a moment he looked across towards the fruit and veg stall, and seemed to be looking straight at Jenny; she was sure he must have seen her, but he turned back to Jack and went on talking.

'What can I get thee, lass?'

Mr Parsons' round red face was addressing her over the top of a mound of King Edwards.

'Make tha mind up,' grunted a woman behind her. 'We've not got all day. Them onions firm, are they?'

''Course they are, missus, hard as nails. Now, lass?'

Jenny had one eye on the stall, the other on Ivan Price. He had finished his conversation with Jack Inglis and was walking slowly in her direction. She couldn't stand here and let him find her.

'I'm sorry. I've changed my mind,' she gasped. And she turned and ran, not stopping until she was absolutely sure that Ivan Price wasn't following her.

Chapter 8

Mae waited until ten-thirty the following morning before deciding that Jenny wasn't coming.

'I'll have to go,' she announced, springing up and slipping on her coat.

Sid Dukes, who was sitting at the dining table penning a band arrangement, looked up from his sheet of manuscript paper.

'Go? Where?'

'To Jenny's. She said she'd be here by now.'

Sid's face registered mild alarm.

'Canal Terrace? Hang on a mo, I'll get my coat. I'm not having you going down there on your own.'

Mae's face dimpled with pleasure as she dotted a kiss right in the middle of his bald patch.

'You're such an old sweetie. But I'll be fine. It's all right round there, really it is. They're not all cut-throats and bandits, you know.'

'I suppose not.' Sid accepted this judgement grudgingly. 'But if you're not back by twelve, I'm coming to fetch you.'

'Right you are.' Mae speared the crown of her hat with a glass-headed pin. 'See you later.'

'And don't forget, there's a rehearsal with Geoff at two. Joss wants to run through all the changes in her second number.'

'I won't forget,' Mae promised, and blew Sid a kiss as she stepped out into the hall. Wish I could though, she added silently. Lead band singer Joss Flynn was a nasty, spiteful little prima donna and everyone knew that Geoff Tait – Sid's deputy – was a bit of a tricky character. It was Sid's

87

band, of course, but he was just too nice for his own good; people were always taking advantage of him.

She walked down the street and took the bus to the other side of town. Even though it was broad daylight she felt alone and slightly afraid. Afraid of what? she wondered. This town had been her home for ten years, why should any of it frighten her? She knew every street, every back alley, every bend in the canal – it was just that there were some streets you wished you didn't know.

A mongrel dog barked and ran around her legs as she turned the corner into Canal Terrace.

'Shoo! Go away, get off.'

A gaggle of bare-legged children whistled to the dog and they ran off together in a higgledy-piggledy pack, down to the end of the street. It was gloomy and smelly in Canal Terrace. Mae had forgotten the distinctive smell of the slums.

She counted her way along the houses. Number twelve, number fourteen, number sixteen. This must be it. A cramped jumble of bricks with a zig-zag crack like a lightning bolt, right up the middle of the front wall. Damp dripped from the broken guttering with a monotonous splat, splat, splat, on to the pavement. In the normal run of things, Mae might have been tempted to turn round and walk away; still, nothing ventured, nothing gained. She knocked on the door and waited.

Jenny was sitting with Col and Molly in the back kitchen at sixteen Canal Terrace when Bernie and Kate and Annie came bounding in, falling over each other in their haste to tell the news.

'There's a lady at t'door for Jenny . . .'

'. . . in a 'at . . .'

'. . . with a feather . . .'

'. . . an' lipstick an' all. She's right pretty . . .'

'. . . she's a film star!'

Col waved his arms about as if conducting an orchestra.

'Pipe down, will you, an' let 'er get by?'

Jenny looked up to see her visitor walk in, flanked by Dora and Mikey O'Brien.

'Here she is, here she is . . .'

'. . . she says 'er name's Mae.'

Jenny's eyes met Mae's.

'Oh, Mae. Mae, I'm sorry, something happened and I forgot all about this morning.'

'Sit yourself down,' urged Molly O'Brien, wiping her hands on her apron and flicking a teatowel over the seat of a wooden stool. Mae lowered herself gingerly on to it. 'Now, you'll take a cup o' tea.' It was a statement, not an invitation. Mae nodded and smiled, trying not to flinch as something scuttled across the toe of her shoe.

'Jenny, what's wrong? Why didn't you come?'

Jenny looked down at the handkerchief wound round her fingers. It was bone-dry, but twisted so tight it was scarcely better than an old rag.

'It was Ivan.'

'He's been here?'

Jenny shook her head.

'No, not that. At least, not yet. I saw him . . . in the market.'

'Jenny 'ad a bit of a fright,' explained Molly, pouring boiling water on to the single teaspoonful of tea at the bottom of the brown earthenware pot. 'She'll be right as rain come tomorrow.'

'Did he see you?' asked Mae.

'No. At least, I don't think so, but I can't be sure. He was talking to Jack Inglis. But, Mae, I came so close to walking right into him. It'd be so easy for him to find out where I am – what if he already knows?'

Mae took Jenny's hands in hers.

'Why should he bother finding out? He's got you out of the house. That's what he wanted, isn't it?'

'It's *me* he wants, Mae. And you know what he said to Denny Finch, about coming after me. He's not going to let me get away that easily, he's just biding his time . . . then he's going to come and find me and finish what he started.'

'Surely not,' soothed Col. 'It won't come to that.'

'But what if it does? What if he threatens you and Molly – or the little ones?'

'We'll deal with that when it 'appens,' Molly assured her, handing her a cup of weak tea. 'We're not afraid of his kind.'

'But if Ivan does come looking for me, I'll have to leave here, and what will I do then?' Jenny's eyes searched Mae's for an answer. 'Who'd be mad enough to take me in? Who'd be on my side? Who'd stand up to Ivan and all his friends, and Mam, and . . .' Jenny stopped dead, remembering what Mae had promised. 'Did you see them – Tom and Nancy?'

Mae nodded.

'I talked to Nancy. She was in Bickerstaffe Street.'

'You gave her the letter?'

'Yes.'

'And what did she say?' Jenny refused to believe the look on Mae's face.

'She tore it up. I'm sorry, Jenny, I did try but she wouldn't listen to a word I said. She just kept telling me to go away and take you with me.'

Jenny felt her whole body sag.

'What about Tom?'

'I haven't seen him yet. I'll try and talk to him, but . . .'

'It's hopeless, isn't it? *Isn't it?*'

Mae paused.

'It doesn't have to be.'

'What do you mean?'

'I mean, perhaps no one around here *has* to stand up for you. You don't have to stay in St Helens at all.'

'Me? Leave St Helens – how? What could I do, how would I get a job? I'd have nowhere to live.'

Mae cleared her throat.

'Have you heard of Costigern's?'

'The holiday camps?'

'That's right. This one's the one in North Wales. Anyhow . . . Sid's been asked to put together a variety show for their summer season – singers, dancers, speciality acts, the lot.'

'What's this got to do with me?'

'He's been advertising for people, of course, only it takes time to find the right ones.'

'So?'

'So I thought . . . I just wondered . . . Look, Jen, I think I could persuade him to arrange an audition for you before we leave St Helens.'

Jenny stared at Mae in stunned silence. The words wouldn't come out right.

'An *audition*?'

'You always were a much better singer than me, Jenny. You've got the loveliest voice I've ever heard. Of course, you might have to dance a bit too . . .'

'I haven't sung anything since we did that revue in the church hall, and that was five years ago! And you *know* I can't dance . . .'

'Then I'll teach you.'

'By next week?'

'By tomorrow, if I have to. Think about it, Jen, we'd be working together. You'd be coming with me when we leave St Helens, we'd have a whole summer season in North Wales . . .'

'Stop!' Jenny put her hands over her ears. It was all too sudden and too much to take in. 'I can't.'

'You *can*.'

'No, you don't understand. I can't.' Jenny was looking at Molly and Col, willing Mae to understand. She'd always known she wouldn't be living in Canal Terrace for ever, but the money she brought in more than paid for her keep. If she left, how would they manage? 'I couldn't just . . . go.'

'Molly an' me'll be mad as hell if you don't try,' said Col. Molly nodded.

'Take your chances, Jenny. They'll only come once, you mark my words.'

Mae got to her feet and pulled on her gloves.

'I'd better go now, I promised Sid I'd be back by twelve. Think about it, Jenny,' she urged. 'You always said all you wanted was that one big chance. Now Sid's giving it to you.'

'I know I did, but that was before . . .'

'Before what? Before Ivan tried to rape you and your

91

mam threw you out? Jenny Fisher, if ever you needed a big chance, you need it now!'

The next few days passed in a kind of haze for Jenny. To begin with, she didn't really believe that Sid Dukes would ever agree to audition her for a real professional show, though a tiny part of her kept on hoping that he might. With all the will in the world, Mae Corlett's dancing lessons weren't going to turn her into Ginger Rogers.

One afternoon at the Alhambra, as she was sweeping biscuit crumbs from the foyer carpet, Mae bounced in through the front doors.

'Two o'clock on Wednesday,' she announced triumphantly. Snatching Jenny's brush and pan away from her, she dumped a huge bundle into her arms.

'What's this?' Jenny stared in bewilderment at the bundle. One gold-painted sandal was dangling out of it from its ankle-strap.

'Stage-clothes, Jen. For your audition – Wednesday at two, like I said.'

Jenny sat down, very heavily, on the floor. Her stomach turned a somersault.

'He's really going to audition me?'

'Yes, I told you he would, didn't I?' Mae was gabbling nineteen to the dozen. 'Actually it won't be Sid, it'll be Geoff, but it'll be all right, just you wait and see. Now, stand up and let's see if this outfit needs shortening. You've got to look the part, haven't you?'

'Not here!' exclaimed Jenny, hastily folding up the dress and pushing it out of sight behind the cigarette kiosk as Mr Gregson emerged through the swing-doors from the stalls.

'Everything all right, Jenny?' He had spotted Jenny's shocked expression and his voice registered genuine concern. He didn't often warm to the female sex, but he had become rather fond of Jenny Fisher.

'Yes, Mr Gregson. I was just . . .'

'It's entirely my fault,' cut in Mae with a winning smile. 'I've been distracting her. I just popped in to give her a message.' As she turned and walked back towards the door, she winked at Jenny. 'Two o'clock Wednesday, Jen. Don't forget!'

Forget! thought Jenny as she watched the doors swing shut behind Mae. How could I possibly forget?

Wednesday afternoon came far too quickly. Even as they were walking up the road to the theatre, Jenny was protesting.

'I won't do it.'

Mae swung round.

'Oh, yes, you will!'

'I can't . . . I'm terrified.'

'Good. If you're nervous you sing better, everybody knows that.'

'But my legs have forgotten how to move!'

'Rubbish. Now, let's see if you've got those steps right. It's one, two, three, *turn*, two, three . . .'

The two girls pirouetted along the pavement in the lightly falling sleet, Jenny with her tongue between her teeth, doing her best to concentrate on the steps. Mae seemed to glide over the flagstones, but Jenny's feet seemed to want to go off in two different directions.

'Ow!' she winced, turning her ankle. 'I'm not used to high heels.'

'Ah, well, we all have to suffer to be beautiful.'

'But it's pointless, Mae. I'm never going to be a proper dancer, I've got two left feet.'

'You're enough of a dancer to get by.'

Jenny was out of breath trying to keep up.

'If Mr Gregson finds out I'm doing this . . .'

'He won't.'

'But if he does – I had to tell him I was ill, you know. What if I lose my job?'

'You won't. Besides, you won't need it, will you?'

Jenny wasn't so sure.

'I wish I had your confidence.'

'Anyhow, Jen, we're almost there – sure you've got everything? Let's have a look at that make-up . . .'

Jenny paused under a shop awning, to endure Mae's primping and preening. She was wearing Mae's dress under her coat, Mae's gold sandals and silk stockings, and her freshly washed hair had been coaxed into fashionable curls, now dampened and a touch limp on account of the drizzle. Well, Jenny Fisher, she told herself, you've got everything except talent, confidence and good luck. She looked up at the façade of the theatre and realised that the moment of truth was only ten stone steps away.

'I feel sick.'

'Well, try not to throw up until *afterwards*, eh?' Mae seized Jenny by the arm and gave her a hug. 'Come on, count to ten and go straight in, it's the best way.'

It was a small theatre, but to Jenny it seemed immense and full of noise. People were running about all over the place, most of the girls half-naked, most of the men carrying musical instruments in large black cases. Up on the stage, five girls in satin shorts were going through a song-and-dance routine. Sitting on the steps at the side of the stage, a man in red braces was polishing the decapitated head of a ventriloquist's dummy.

There was an upright piano halfway up the middle aisle, and a young, curly-haired man in shirt-sleeves was bellowing commands as he hammered out a tune.

'Four-and-five-and . . . no, no, *no*! How many more times, Phoebe?'

'Sorry, Geoff,' squeaked a brunette, pulling her cardigan tightly about her shivering shoulders. 'It's so cold in here.'

'If you worked a bit harder, Phoebe, you wouldn't feel the cold.'

Mae nudged Jenny.

'That's Geoff – Mr Tait. He's Sid's deputy, takes care of things when Sid's busy. Writes quite a lot of songs, too.'

Jenny watched with mounting terror. Geoff Tait's approach to training a chorus-line seemed to be to shout at them louder and louder until they finally did what he wanted them to. It hadn't occurred to her that it would be like this: jumping about half-naked in a freezing cold theatre on a dismal, chilly day. This wasn't exactly glamorous, and to make matters worse Jenny's knees were knocking together. She tried to sneak back into the shadows but Mae was already powering ahead.

'Geoff, Geoff . . .'

Silence fell with terrible suddenness. Geoff Tait stopped in mid-tune, his hands poised over the echoing keys and his foot still on the sustain pedal.

'Mae Corlett, why aren't you up on that stage?'

'Sorry, Geoff. Mr Dukes said I could come a bit later and bring Jenny.'

'Oh, he did, did he?' Geoff Tait looked sourly at Jenny. She shrank from his gaze. Glancing around the theatre she realised that she had suddenly become the centre of attention. The five girls on the stage were giggling and pointing at her too-long skirt, the ventriloquist staring at her, Geoff Tait looking at her in a way that suggested he wasn't very impressed by what he saw. 'So you're the famous Jenny then, are you?'

There was no mistaking the note of sarcasm in his voice. Jenny had to bite her lip and force herself to be polite.

'Yes . . . sir.'

A stifled titter ran round the girls on the stage. Jenny coloured up, angry and embarrassed. Why had she let Mae persuade her to do this? All she was going to do was show herself up as the pathetic amateur she was. Geoff glanced up at the chorus-line and snapped his fingers.

'Five minutes.' As the girls came clattering down off the stage in their tap-shoes, he turned back to Jenny with arms folded. 'So – you can sing, can you?'

'Of course she can,' said Mae.

'I asked her, Mae, not you. I hope you've brought your music,' he added.

Jenny reached into her bag for the sheet music Mae had given her.

'*The Way You Look Tonight* – will it do?'

Geoff Tait glanced at it and set it on the piano.

'Well?'

'Well, what?'

Mae pushed Jenny forward.

'Get up on the stage, kid. Show him what you can do.'

The distance along the rows of seats and up the side-steps to the stage seemed impossibly far. Jenny's legs had turned to jelly, she could scarcely feel the floor; and sure enough, just as she took the very last step she stumbled, and had to put out her hands to save herself from falling flat on her face on the stage.

She got slowly to her feet. Muffled giggles from the wings made her ears burn with rage and humiliation. Mae was sitting about halfway down the auditorium, mouthing at her to do her best, but Mae wasn't standing up here now, was she? Jenny fiddled with the folds of the dress, conscious that the improvised hem had come down at the front and was flapping about her calves.

Three staccato piano chords brought her to· terrified attention.

'If you're *quite* ready?'

'Yes, sir . . . Mr Tait.'

Taking a deep breath, Jenny opened her mouth to sing. She knew the song, of course she did. Mae had rehearsed it with her a dozen times a day. It was a lovely song, and just right for her vocal range. She knew it backwards, she even hummed it when she was scrubbing floors at the Alhambra. If she half-closed her eyes she could see Fred and Ginger spinning gracefully across the silver screen . . .

And now she couldn't remember a single word of it.

She heard the introduction play a second time. How did it go? Mae was mouthing the words at her from the stalls, but she couldn't make them out and now blind panic was rising inside her. The harder she tried to remember the words, the more they refused to come. Tears were pricking at the corners of her eyes, blurring her vision. Everyone was laughing at her, and it was hopeless, hopeless, hopeless.

'Are you intending to *sing* this song, Miss Fisher?'

Geoff Tait's voice cut into her like an assassin's blade.

'I . . . I'm sorry. I . . .'

Jenny stopped in her tracks, realising that she was about to say 'I can't.' How often had she said those words over the last few weeks and months, and yet kept on going, kept on trying? Her father's words were whispering in her head: 'The worst sin of all is giving up.'

In her mind she was six years old again, and sitting on her mam's lap in the front parlour. She'd just had the chicken-pox, and Dad was singing to her as Mam brushed her hair. That old song, the one her mam loved so much, the one she loved too . . .

'Well?' Geoff slammed down the lid of the piano. 'I think you've wasted enough of my time, don't you?'

But Jenny didn't come down from the stage. She wasn't listening to Geoff Tait any more, or to the giggling girls or the mutterings from the orchestra pit. She wasn't singing for Geoff Tait either, or for Mae or even for herself. She was singing for Dad. It was almost as if he was right there beside her, reminding her of that beautiful song she loved so well.

Let Me Call You Sweetheart. Why hadn't she thought of it before?

Her voice began softly but firmly, the tone steady and pure despite the lack of any accompaniment.

Sitting in the stalls beneath the stage, Mae Corlett felt the silence deepen. She gazed up and was captured by the magic of the moment. When Jenny Fisher sang, she was transformed; she wasn't some gauche young girl in a borrowed dress, she was a star. Could the others feel it too? Could Geoff Tait feel the raw enchantment in that clear, pure, unaffected voice?

If Jenny had looked, she would have seen the scowl on Geoff Tait's face turning first to a look of incredulity, then to grudging admiration. But Jenny wasn't looking at Geoff or anyone else. She was lost in the music, living the pure joy and sadness of the old, unforgettable song.

She paused on the penultimate line, feeling the soaring exhilaration of the rising cadence as her voice filled the echoing vastness of the theatre; then ended as softly as she had begun.

The silence lasted beyond the echoes of Jenny's final note. A kind of shock had gripped the listeners in the theatre, Mae could feel their disbelief. That little, elfin-faced girl . . . that

97

enormous, extraordinary voice.

When Jenny looked down at Geoff Tait, she saw that he was staring back at her intently. Everyone else was staring too. Nobody was saying anything at all. Apprehension twisted Jenny's guts. Had she done the wrong thing? Had she thrown away her one big chance?

'Mr . . . Tait?'

Her voice seemed to drag him back to the present. Clapping his hands loudly, Geoff barked out instructions: 'Chorus – positions . . . Mae Corlett, that means you too.'

Mae threw off her jacket and walked towards the stage. Geoff looked at Jenny.

'Right, Miss Fisher. Let's see if you can dance as well.'

It was Bernie O'Brien who was first to spot Jenny coming up Canal Terrace. He ran back to number sixteen with Dora, Alice and Kenny at his heels.

'Mam, Mam, Mam!'

Molly O'Brien appeared at the door of the wash-house, her sleeves rolled up and somebody else's washing in her arms.

'What's up, Bernie? You've not hurt yourself again?'

'Mam, Mam, it's Jenny an' Mac . . .'

'. . . we saw 'em get off the trolley . . .'

'. . . they're comin' up the street.'

At this, Mrs O'Brien became uncharacteristically flustered. She dropped the pile of clean washing on to the wash-house floor and started fiddling with her hair.

'What did they look like? Was Jenny smilin', did she look upset?'

'Dunno, Mam, they weren't sayin' nothin' . . .'

'Annie, Aileen, put the kettle on, sweep the floor . . . Bernie, wash your hands under that tap . . . Kenny, here's sixpence, run an' get some milk . . . an' mind you don't drop it on the way back . . .'

By the time Jenny and Mae reached the back gate, two minutes later, most of the O'Brien kids were clustered around the doorstep.

'Jenny, Jenny, Jenny . . .'

'What 'appened?'

'Are you goin' to be a film star?'

Molly O'Brien emerged from the wash-house tying a clean apron over her torn dress. She looked from Jenny to Mae and back again, taking in their glum expressions.

'Oh, Jenny love, did it not go well? Never mind, there's a nice cup o' tea on to boil . . .'

Jenny and Mae looked at each other and exploded into gales of laughter.

'She did it, Mrs O'Brien, Jenny did it! She's going to be a singer in the summer show.'

'Just a backing singer and an understudy,' Jenny reminded her, but the grin on her face was growing wider and wider.

Molly's jaw fell open. Col, standing behind her, dropped his mug of tea with a clatter of dented enamel.

'Jenny Fisher! Well, I'll be . . .'

'Oh, Jenny love, Jenny love!' Molly threw her arms round Jenny and they hugged like mother and daughter. Suddenly Jenny and Mae were hugging everyone, Molly was laughing and crying all at once, and the kids were running about whooping and shrieking with delight like miniature Red Indians.

'Jenny's goin' to be famous, Jenny's goin' to be famous!'

When everything had quietened down a little, Jenny and Molly stepped back and looked at each other.

'Well done, love, I knew you could do it.'

'So did I,' cut in Mae.

'Well, I didn't!' confessed Jenny. 'I still can't believe it's really happening. Oh, Molly, I'm going to be able to get away, Ivan won't be able to touch me, he won't even know where I am, I'm going to be free!'

Molly smiled back at her, wiping the trace of a tear from her cheek.

'We're proud of you, Jenny. Right proud.'

'Oh, Molly.' The realisation had been slow in coming, but when it did it hit hard. 'It's not just Ivan I'm leaving, is it?' Jenny thought of Daisy and Billy who wouldn't understand, of Mam and Tom and Nancy who'd refused even to listen. And of the O'Briens who'd taken her in as if she was their own, and never once questioned that she'd told the truth. It was so very hard to walk away from such love and kindness. 'Oh, Molly, I don't think I want to go . . .'

'Of course you do, Jenny.' Col O'Brien put one arm round her and the other round Mae. 'Besides, you're not goin' for ever, is she, Mae?'

Mae smiled.

'Just for the summer,' she said. 'Just for one summer, Jenny.'

'You'll soon be back, girl, an' us lot aren't goin' anywhere, are we, Molly?'

'Just you take good care of her, Mae,' said Molly. 'Or Col an' me will know the reason why.'

Chapter 9

Everything happened very quickly, so quickly that Jenny scarcely had time to take stock.

One minute she was grateful to be cleaning the cinema; the next, Geoff Tait had offered her the chance of a whole new life. Well, a new life for one whole summer season, at any rate. Who could tell if her brand new singing career would last any longer than that?

The very next day she had to attend her first rehearsal with Mae. About ten o'clock that morning, Jenny went round to Mae's digs. She found her friend in her room, brushing lint off Sid's collar. He greeted Jenny cordially.

'Morning, Jenny, hope you're ready for anything.' He nodded towards Mae. 'You'll need to be, mind, with this one around.'

'Cheek!' She finished off with a peck on his cheek. 'Come on, Jenny, time to throw you to the lions.'

The "lions" were already gathering downstairs, in the sitting room. Jenny recognised some of them from her audition – especially the dancers who'd sniggered at her, although to be fair they looked pretty shamefaced now. One or two made an effort to be friendly. Mae performed a few quick introductions.

'This is Phoebe – she's the messy one – that's Moira, the redhead. Over there is Cathy . . . oh, and this is Dolly, she's one of the other singers, I expect you'll be working with her.'

Dolly seemed nice enough. She had porcelain-doll looks and a broad Cockney accent.

'Pleased to meet yer, I'm sure. Here, Bella, Pauline, come over 'ere a mo'.'

Bella came over. She was very willowy, with pillar-box red lipstick and matching nails.

'What is it?'

'This here is Jenny. You know, the new singer.'

'Really?' Bella stuck out a nicely manicured hand. 'Oh, yes, I remember hearing you at your audition. You were good. Met Joss, have you?'

'Joss?'

Mae eased Jenny away to meet some of the other members of Sid's new company. It wasn't until later that Jenny had a chance to question her properly.

'Mae . . .'

'Hmm?'

'Who's Joss?'

Mae gave a little, uncomfortable wriggle.

'Joss Flynn. She's the star singer – Geoff Tait's blue-eyed girl.'

Jenny sensed that her friend was avoiding her gaze.

'Is there something you're not telling me?'

'No, not really. Well, she's a bit . . . er . . . difficult. But I wouldn't worry about Joss. Just keep on the right side of her and you'll be fine.'

When she walked into the rehearsal with Mae, Jenny was rather alarmed to see Geoff Tait and Sid Dukes arguing by the side of the stage. Geoff Tait was scowling and jabbing Sid in the chest with his index finger. Sid had his hands up, fending him off.

Mae let out a sigh of exasperation.

'I ask you! You wouldn't think he was the boss, would you?'

'Who?'

'Exactly. Sid's too soft for his own good, Jenny, he lets Geoff walk all over him. It wasn't so bad when it was just the dance-band and a few singers, but what with the big summer show coming up, he's having to rely more and more on Geoff.'

'Can't he get somebody else – if they don't get on?'

'Trouble is, Geoff's good. He knows talent when he sees

it – after all, he picked you, didn't he?'

Jenny laughed.

'I see what you mean!'

'He's not a bad crooner either. Writes songs and does the odd romantic duet with Joss.' Mae pursed her lips. 'If you ask me, that's not all he does with her, but who am I to talk?'

Jenny's eyes were drawn to a third figure, standing almost – but not quite – alongside Geoff Tait. It was impossible not to notice her; she was a real glamour-puss with glossy nut-brown curls framing a high-cheekboned face, and thin, arching eyebrows which gave her eyes a permanent expression of disdain. She was leaning against the staging, a cigarette holder between her perfectly painted lips.

'Who's that?'

'Guess.'

'Joss Flynn?'

'Right first time.'

'She's very . . . glamorous.'

Mae chuckled.

'Common as a fly on muck, but you'd never know it, the airs and graces she gives herself. Of course she's the big star so Sid'll let her do whatever takes her fancy.' Mae sniffed. 'More fool him.'

'You don't like her much, do you?'

'I think it's more the other way round.'

The argument by the stage seemed to have calmed down, and Sid and Geoff were nodding and smiling over a sheaf of papers. At that moment Sid turned away from the stage and caught sight of Jenny and Mae.

'Ah, there she is. Come over here, Jenny love.'

She joined the group by the stage.

'Hello, Mr Dukes.'

'Now, Jenny, you've met Geoff of course . . . and this is Joss Flynn. Joss dear, this is Jenny Fisher.'

The woman transferred her cigarette holder to her left hand and flicked her hair off her high forehead.

'So you're our little shop-girl.' She spoke the words with such obvious relish that it was impossible to give her the benefit of the doubt. 'I've heard *so* much about you.'

Sid seemed not to have noticed Joss's venomous smile. He was chatting on happily.

'Jenny will be doing some chorus work in the summer show,' he continued.

'How lovely for her,' Joss smiled.

'But mainly she'll be in the close-harmony numbers, and of course,' he smiled at Jenny, 'you'll be Joss's understudy in case anything happens to our little star.'

Sid gave Joss's nut-brown curls an affectionate pat, as though she were a favourite spaniel. Jenny thought Joss would explode with annoyance, but all she did was glare.

'I . . . I'm sure it won't,' Jenny said nervously, just as a way of filling the awkward silence.

'Quite,' snapped Joss, and turning her back on Jenny, made it crystal clear that the royal audience was at an end.

The company was due to leave St Helens in three days' time. Jenny's bags had been packed and labelled and taken round to Mae's digs, ready to send ahead to Costigern's Camp at Llandew – not that she *had* much to pack. Everything she possessed in the world could be crammed into one small suitcase and an old string bag.

Jenny sat on the end of Mae's bed, deep in thought. She knew that if she didn't do something now, it would be too late; but on the other hand, perhaps it was better to do nothing. She was racked with indecision. Wouldn't it be best for everybody if she just left quietly, without a fuss? Mam and Nancy had made it clear they no longer cared tuppence about her, and Mae hadn't dared approach Tom at the pit, for fear of running into Ivan.

In any case, she had no reason to think that her elder brother would be any better disposed to her than Mam or Nancy. The close bond they'd had as little kids had been weakened when Dad died and both of them had to grow up overnight. In the months before Mam had thrown Jenny out, they'd scarcely exchanged more than hellos and goodbyes.

It was Billy and Daisy who most troubled Jenny's

thoughts. What had Mam told them? Was Nancy looking after them properly? Did she make sure Billy did his arithmetic and washed his hands before meals? Did she brush the tangles out of Daisy's hair and put a ribbon in it?

'If you don't try, you'll never know.'

Jenny turned round. Mae was leaning against the door, arms folded.

'Well, you won't, will you?'

'I suppose not.' Jenny swung her legs idly, her heels tapping softly against the leg of the bed.

'Then go round and see them.'

'What's the point? You saw Nancy, you know what she said.'

'People can change their minds,' pointed out Mae, coming in and sitting on the bed next to her. 'Look, if you go round now, Ivan and Tom will be at the pit.'

'Do you think I should?'

'Jenny, I'm not going to tell you what to do – you've got to make up your own mind.'

'But if it was you?'

'If it was me . . . I'd want to know, that's all. You know, set things in order. At least my dad's talking to me these days. If I hadn't gone round and had things out with him, we'd probably still not be on speaking terms.'

'So you think . . .'

Mae laughed.

'Don't ask me, kid. It's what *you* think. But if you're going to do anything, you'd better get a move on. We're leaving on Thursday morning.'

That was what made Jenny's mind up; the sight of the train ticket, printed with the date in straggly blue letters. In three days' time she'd be gone.

She dressed quickly but carefully, in the clothes Mae had lent her for "best". They weren't the sort of clothes she was used to; the wine-coloured suit was smartly tailored, with a pencil skirt and black velvet trimming, the shoes and stockings were fashionable and almost new, and the tiny, dotty veil on the hat was positively rakish.

She felt like a completely new person as she stepped out

on to the street. The sun was shining and there was real warmth in the spring air. It was impossible not to feel optimistic.

The feeling dimmed a little as she approached the corner of Jubilee Street. To get to Gas Street she would have to walk right past Mr Corlett's shop; she could see him moving about inside. What's more, people around this part of town knew her very well indeed and she knew they'd all be watching her. She could imagine what the gossips were saying, too: Well I never, it's that Fisher girl, the cheek of it! Everyone knows she's no better than she ought to be . . .

Of course, she could simply turn her head and walk straight past, but a reckless impulse drew her towards the shop. As she stepped up to the door her nerve gave out and she was about to turn and flee; but at that moment John Corlett looked up and their eyes met. It was too late, she'd have to go through with it now.

'Jenny Fisher. Well, I'll be . . .'

'Mr Corlett.'

She stood in the doorway, not sure whether she dared go in. John Corlett's face registered shock, or was that anger? Eddie the shop boy looked simply nonplussed.

The silence could only have lasted a few seconds, but to Jenny the distance between each thunderous heartbeat felt like a lifetime. Then, to her immense relief, Mr Corlett's stony expression melted into a smile.

'Jenny, come in, come in. Eddie, go out the back and sort those sacks of potatoes.'

'But Mr Corlett . . .' he whined.

'Do I have to tell you twice?'

'All right, all right, I'm going.'

Eddie sloped off with malevolent reluctance, no doubt desperate to know what was going on in the shop. But Mr Corlett waited until the stock-room door had clicked shut before he spoke again.

'Mae tells me you're leaving St Helens?'

Jenny nodded.

'Just for the summer. At least, I think so.'

Another silence followed, then both of them began talking at once.

'I meant to say . . .'

'I just wanted to . . .'

Mr Corlett smiled.

'You first.'

'I came to say I was sorry.' Jenny paused. 'What I did was wrong.'

'You did it because you thought it was right.'

'Yes. But that didn't make it right, it was still stealing.'

Mr Corlett thrust his hands into his pockets, the way he always did when he felt uncomfortable.

'I'm sorry too, Jenny.'

'I'd have paid the money back, I swear I would, only Ivan took away my wages . . .'

John Corlett nodded.

'I know that now. And I would have offered you your old job back, but I couldn't, the business was doing so badly.' He coughed to cover his embarrassment. 'I was sorry to hear what happened, you didn't deserve to be thrown out on the street like that. And if I was the cause in any way . . .'

Jenny shook her head.

'You weren't. I brought it on myself.'

'Well, I wish you better luck, gel.' He clasped her hand. 'Take care of yourself and . . .'

'Mr Corlett?'

'Take care of my gel Mae, will you? For me? She thinks she knows everything, that daughter of mine, but . . . well . . . I worry about her. That's the long and the short of it.'

'I will,' promised Jenny. 'We'll look after each other.'

All along Gas Street the net curtains were twitching. Jenny felt as though she was in a dream, one of those where you feel as if you're walking through quick-drying cement, your legs leaden and every step a greater effort than the last.

Number thirty-two, thirty-six, thirty-eight. She was walking more and more slowly. Number forty. She stopped dead in her tracks before a brown-painted front door.

Number forty-two.

Her palms were sticky with sweat underneath Mae's smart black gloves. She raised her right hand. Could she? Would she dare? She knocked. Waited. Nothing happened. Perhaps there was nobody in. A great surge of relief washed over her. If she turned and walked away right now, she'd have done her duty but nobody need ever know that she had been here.

Then she heard footsteps inside, coming towards the front door. Her blood turned to ice as the latch clicked and the door opened three or four inches, no more.

'I thought we'd seen the last of you.'

'Mam . . .' Jenny took a step forward but the door didn't open any further. Dot's eyes were cold as black ice. 'Mam, can I come in? I just want to talk.'

'How dare you show your face round here?' Dot's tone was one of barely controlled anger. 'Dressed like a painted trollop!'

The words stung like vitriol, but Jenny persevered; she had to, so much was at stake.

'Please, Mam. I'm leaving St Helens, I just want to come in for a few minutes and see the kids and . . .' She saw Nancy's face in the background, wary and pale. 'Nancy, please make Mam listen.'

'She doesn't want to see you, an' neither do I.'

'Please. Let me explain, about Ivan . . .'

'I've 'ad enough of your lies, Jenny Fisher. We all 'ave. Ivan's an honest man, he works all the hours God sends to keep a roof over our heads – and what do you do? You tell filthy lies about 'im.'

Dot was shaking with righteous indignation. Jenny put out her hand to touch her, to plead with her to listen, but Dot stopped her in her tracks with a look of pure hatred.

'Get out and stay out, Jenny.'

'Don't you understand, Mam? I'm leaving in a few days, I just want to make things right . . .'

'Right!' Dot greeted this with sarcastic laughter. 'You wouldn't know what was right if it jumped up and bit you.

You're a thief and a liar and a trollop, and you're no daughter of mine.

'Leave, and good riddance to you. There's nowt 'ere for you, Jenny Fisher. Not among decent folk.'

And with that, she slammed the door in Jenny's face.

So that's that, thought Jenny as she walked slowly up the road towards the railway station. She'd said her goodbyes in Canal Terrace, there'd be no one to see her off at the station, no one to wish her well in her new adventure. From now on she was well and truly on her own, Mam had made that only too clear.

As she stepped into the booking hall, she spotted a chattering gaggle of familiar figures. There was Mae and Moira, Sid and Joss, Bella and Dolly . . .

'Jenny – at last!' Mae waved her across. 'I was beginning to think you'd changed your mind!'

'Sorry I'm late, Molly . . .'

'Never mind that now, get a move on – the train's leaving in ten minutes. Now, you've got everything?'

'It's a bit late now if I haven't.'

'Got your ticket?'

Jenny patted the pocket of her jacket. It was there, one single to Llandew. She nodded.

'Then that's all you need. Come *on*!'

The company picked up its assortment of bags and boxes and streamed in a raggle-taggle crowd through the ticket barrier towards the platform. The train was already waiting, clouds of grey-white steam billowing about the engine; the guard hovering on the platform, glancing now and then at his watch. Sid wandered around rather ineffectually while Geoff ordered people about.

'You – in there, that's right. Joss, don't sit by the window, you know what the steam does to your upper register. Desmond, take Joss's bag for her. Mae, get a move on, we don't have all day . . .'

Jenny hung back to the very end. She was almost the last to get on to the train; most probably she'd have to stand in the corridor all the way to Wales, but right now she didn't

109

really care about that. Something was holding her back – not the love of St Helens, she didn't regret leaving her home town, it was something else: the feeling that she couldn't go because she was leaving unfinished business behind her.

'Jenny. *Jenny*, are you listening?' Mae was leaning out of the carriage window. 'I've saved you a seat, but if you don't shift yourself, Desmond'll nab it.'

'Just coming.'

Jenny picked up her one small bag and placed a foot on the step. Mae was right, it was time to get a move on and leave all this firmly behind her. With one last backward glance at the smoke-blackened station buildings, she stepped on to the train.

'Jenny – Jenny, stop a minute, will you, lass?'

The thunder of heavy boots on the platform. That voice. *Tom's* voice . . . She must be imagining it, it was nothing but wishful thinking. He didn't even know she was leaving today, let alone where she was going. Nobody did, she'd made very sure of that. But, no. Jenny caught her breath. It really was him, running towards her along the platform. She could see his face reflected in the glass of the train door.

Very slowly, still not quite believing, Jenny turned to face her elder brother. Beneath his thatch of shiny black hair, he was red-faced from exertion.

'By God, Jenny, I thought I'd missed you.'

'Tom? Tom, what are you doing here?'

He stopped a couple of yards short of where she was standing; he looked as if he was wondering the same thing himself. His lower lip jutted like a sulky child's.

'You could've told me you was leavin'.'

'Why?' countered Jenny. 'All these weeks and you've never once come near me.'

He looked awkward, ashamed even. He avoided looking directly into his sister's face.

'I didn't know where you was,' he said lamely.

'You could've found out.'

'It's . . . difficult,' he mumbled.

110

Jenny wanted to shake him for his bone-headed stupidity, but she wanted to hug him too, just for caring enough to turn up. The question was, now that he was here, what were they going to say to each other? There was so little time, the guard was unfurling his green flag and shuffling his feet.

'Difficult? It's *difficult* being thrown out on to the street for doing nothing but telling the truth, that's what *difficult* is, Tom!'

This time he did meet her gaze.

'Jenny, all this trouble you've caused at home . . .'

'Not me, Tom. Ivan. It's Ivan who's caused all this, and deep down you know I'm telling the truth, don't you?'

She searched his face, knowing that deep down he hated Ivan Price too, had loathed the man from the first time he'd set eyes on him, though for Mam's sake he'd always tried to hide that loathing.

'Mam's upset, Jenny. If you hadn't said them things . . .'

'So you'd rather Ivan had had his way, would you? Beaten me black and blue and . . .?'

'Jenny, don't. Don't keep on lying . . .'

'It's the *truth*. When are you going to believe me, Tom? When is anyone ever going to believe me?'

Somewhere at the back of her mind Jenny was vaguely aware of the guard, lifting his right arm. A hand on her shoulder made her jump. It was Geoff Tait.

'If you're not on this train in ten seconds flat, I'm leaving you behind.'

'Sorry, Geoff. I'll be right there.'

'You'll be there *now*.'

'Tom, I have to go.' She stepped on to the train, closed the door and leant out of the window.

'Running away's not the answer, Jenny.'

'I'm *not* running away. It's just that there's nothing left to stay for.'

'At least tell me where you're goin'.'

For a moment Jenny was tempted. Then she remembered Ivan and his threats, and the ways he had of getting what he wanted.

111

'It's best you don't know.'

A whistle blew somewhere nearby, and the train lurched, then began to slide slowly out of the station.

'Take care of Billy and Daisy, Tom. And Nancy, she needs someone to look out for her . . .'

He hesitated, then called back: 'I will.'

'And . . . and Mam.'

But she knew Tom couldn't hear. By now he was too far away, just a distant speck at the far end of a forgotten platform in the town she was leaving behind.

'Sit down, Jenny,' urged Mae. 'Don't upset yourself.'

'I'm not upset.' She pushed away the proffered hanky. 'Actually I'm happy.'

'Happy?'

'At least someone cared enough to come and see me off. At least Tom listened. I don't know if he believed me, but he *listened*.' Jenny glanced out of the window at the tall chimneys, belching smoke into the clouded sky. 'The only thing is . . .'

'What?'

'How did he find out I was leaving today? The only people I told were the O'Briens, and they'd never breathe a word.'

'Actually I've got a confession to make,' admitted Mae. 'It was me. Didn't I promise I'd contact Tom for you somehow? Dad and I thought he ought to know.'

'Thanks.' Jenny darted her a brief smile. 'But you don't think . . . Tom wouldn't tell Ivan he'd seen me, would he?'

Mae shook her head.

'Tom's no fonder of Ivan than you are, he just won't admit it. Besides, he's no idea where you're going. Don't worry, girl, think about the future – we're going to have an adventure!'

An adventure. It was true, it was true. Excitement tingled in the pit of Jenny's stomach. For once in her life she was going to do something just for herself.

Voices buzzed around her, deep in animated conversation.

'. . . they say it's just like Butlin's . . .'

'. . . even better than Butlin's! Fifteen hundred campers every week, that's what I heard . . .'

'. . . and right next to the sea. It'll be just like a holiday . . .'

'. . . don't you believe it, Bella love, Geoff'll work us till we drop and then some more!'

'. . . well, I've heard Jolly Jimmy Costigern's got a handsome son . . .'

'. . . why not go the whole hog and marry Jolly Jimmy?'

'. . . you're kidding!'

'. . . he's a widower, ain't he?'

'. . . yeah, and seventy if he's a day . . .'

Jenny turned her head away and looked through the window as the train slid away from St Helens. In a few hours' time they'd be in North Wales. She'd never been to Wales before, had only been on day trips to Southport and New Brighton, and you couldn't call them the proper seaside. She'd traced the route a dozen times on Mae's railway map. Jenny counted off the stations in her head: Prestatyn, Rhyl, Colwyn Bay, Llandew. What would it be like? An adventure, that's what it would be like! An adventure and the chance of a lifetime, and she was going to make the most of it, no matter what.

It would be a long, golden summer and whatever happened in the rest of her life, no matter how horrible or how ordinary it might turn out to be, she would never ever forget it.

Sunlight brightened Jenny's face, and sparkled on a solitary tear, trickling slowly down her cheek.

Chapter 10

The train slowed to a crawl as it climbed up the hill, nearing its destination, with heads poking out of doors and windows.

'That must be it . . .'

'. . . down below us, can you see all those chalets . . .?'

'. . . and the sea, and the swimming pool – and that building over there must be the theatre!'

Jenny joined the others at the windows. All her sadness about St Helens was forgotten in the gathering excitement, the mounting anticipation of this entirely new experience. Mae was at her elbow.

'That's it, down there, Costigern's Holiday Camp.'

Mae pointed to row upon row of brightly painted chalets, clustered in giant rectangles along avenues and boulevards that hugged the contours of the coastal site and sloped down towards a long, shingly beach. Around and among the chalets were dotted other, larger buildings and boating lakes, fountains, bowling greens, lawns and ornamental gardens that each looked as big as Taylor Park.

'It's enormous!'

'So big, it's practically a little town – in fact it's even got its own railway station,' commented Desmond the saxophonist, squeezing into the corridor to take a look out of the window. 'Let's have a squint at it then.' He jabbed a pudgy finger at the middle distance. 'See that?'

'Right at the back, near the big belltower thing?'

'That's right. That's the model farm, that is. Very fond of animals is Mr Costigern, 'specially pigs. Comes of starting out in the circus, I s'pose.'

'The circus!'

'Yeah, that's right. He had this troupe of performing piglets . . .'

'But in the paper it said he used to run a health spa or something.'

Mae laughed.

'He's had a few jobs in his time, has Jolly Jimmy. When he was in the circus he used to dose the sick animals with herbal remedies he'd made up himself. After a while, he started dosing people too.'

'That's how he got into the health business,' explained Desmond. 'Folk couldn't get enough of Costigern's Herb Cordial. Once he'd made his pile, he started running outdoor summer camps for young chaps – you know the sort of thing, all tents and cold showers. A couple of years ago, he heard a rumour that Billy Butlin was setting up a big family camp at Skegness, and decided to do the same with Llandew.'

'*We* won't have to sleep in tents, will we?' asked Jenny, aghast at the prospect. Bella overheard and burst out laughing.

'If we do, I'm on the next train back home!'

'Don't take any notice,' said Mae. 'We'll have nice chalets, just like Sid and the band did last year.'

'Nice leaky draughty chalets,' grunted Duncan the trombonist. 'So small you have to sleep with your head in the wardrobe.'

'I can forgive anyone who gives me four free meals a day,' said Desmond with relish.

'That's all you think about, your stomach,' commented Mae.

'And there's plenty of it to think about,' sniffed Bella.

'*Four?*' Jenny was sure she'd misheard. 'Four meals a day?'

'Four,' said Mae firmly. 'Breakfast, lunch, high tea and supper.'

'Healthy body, healthy mind, that's what Jolly Jimmy says,' explained Desmond smugly.

'Fat isn't the same as healthy,' retorted Bella. She

grinned at Jenny. 'If I were you, I'd give high tea a miss if you want to fit into your clothes come September!'

The train braked and slid into the flower-filled station. A signpost on the platform read: LLANDEW: ALIGHT HERE FOR COSTIGERN'S CAMP. Jenny's heart turned a somersault. She was here, she was really, really here!

The station buildings were plastered with brightly coloured posters of the camp, showing happy smiling holidaymakers, and young men and girls dressed in smart blue and yellow striped blazers. Posters announced: HAVE A WONDERFUL DAY, THE COSTIGERN WAY, HAPPY TO SEE YOU and EVERYTHING'S JOLLY WITH JIMMY.

'Bloody hell,' whistled one of the newer band members, getting off the train with his beloved ukelele case under his arm. 'This Jolly Jimmy thinks a lot of himself, doesn't he?'

'So long as we get paid, I don't care if he thinks he's Napoleon,' commented Dolly.

Jenny followed Mae off the train, her small bag clutched protectively against her body. She felt excited but rather lost too, like a child on its first day at school.

'Where do we go?' she whispered.

'Don't worry, everything'll be all right – look, they've sent someone to meet us.'

A girl in a blue and yellow striped blazer, yellow pleated skirt and white lace-up shoes was waiting for them on the platform. Her reddish-brown hair was pushed back from her cheery-looking face with a white Alice band.

'Welcome to Costigern's, everyone.' Her accent was softly, liltingly Welsh. 'Gwen Roberts, I'm a Stripey.'

'A *what*?' demanded Phoebe.

'A Stripey – that's what everyone calls us camp hosts and hostesses, on account of the striped blazers.'

'Bloody daft idea,' muttered Duncan, but Jenny noticed him looking appreciatively at Gwen's bare, nut-brown legs.

'Did you have a good journey?' she enquired.

'Hardly,' sniffed Joss Flynn, flicking imaginary specks of dirt from her coat. Who but Joss, thought Jenny, would travel on a smoky train in a brand new pastel pink outfit?

117

'Anybody seen our luggage?' enquired Sid, easing his way to the front of the crowd.

'Your baggage arrived yesterday, the trunks are waiting for you at the camp. If you'd just like to follow me, we can pick up your suitcases from the booking hall . . .'

They followed Gwen along the platform, past the ladies' waiting room, and turned right through double doors into the booking hall. It was fairly sizeable, but piled from floor to ceiling with suitcases. There was a mad scramble to match everyone with their luggage.

'Is this yours?'

''Course not, mine's blue.'

'Let go, that one's mine!'

'Here's yours, it's got your initials on it.'

Jenny hauled her solitary suitcase out from the very bottom of the pile. It was even more battered and squashed-looking than it had been three days ago, and hardly worthy of being in the same room as Joss Flynn's gorgeous set of matching monogrammed luggage.

Joss, of course, managed to foist her cases on to Geoff, Binky and Duncan. The rest of the dancers and singers had to manage theirs as best they could.

Gwen walked at the head of the straggling procession, telling them about the camp as they crossed the road and made their way towards the front gate. A huge arched sign formed the gateway, resting on tall white pillars. Blue neon tubes spelled out: COSTIGERN'S HOLIDAY CAMP. So this really was it.

'. . . that over there is the main reception building, where the campers register on arrival. Administration's down that avenue to the right, you go there if you have any problems with your chalets, that sort of thing . . . oh, and that's where Jolly Jimmy has his office . . .'

Jenny looked from left to right and back again, utterly dazzled by everything, scarcely able to take it all in. The camp was huge, extending in all directions along long, tree-planted avenues lined with row upon row of chalets, theatres, swimming pools, shops, kiddies' play areas. There were signposts everywhere: TO PETS' CORNER, TO THE

CINEMA, TO THE FUNFAIR. Jenny reckoned she was going to need them all . . .

Mae nudged her.

'We'll never find our way round here, it's vast!'

Jenny giggled.

'I expect we'll manage. Mind you – remember that time you went to Liverpool to meet your Auntie Fenella off the Isle of Man boat?'

'And I got lost and almost ended up in Bootle!'

The two of them were laughing so much that they fell behind, and had to hurry to catch up with the rest of the crowd. Skirting the boating lake, they passed four bowling greens and a double line of pink and yellow chalets which led up a steep incline to the crest of a hill. The sea lay below them, lapping at the edge of a sheltered, sandy beach.

'You're free to use the beach in your time off,' Gwen explained. She winked. 'But not too much "socialising" with the campers, it's one of Jolly Jimmy's rules.'

'He doesn't sound very jolly to me,' commented Dolly from somewhere to Jenny's left.

'Rules are made to be broken,' Bella reminded her.

'Is my chalet much further?' demanded Joss irritably. 'My feet ache.'

'Not much further,' promised Gwen.

As they followed her down Seagull Avenue to their secluded group of chalets, Jenny's attention was distracted by the solitary figure of a young man, standing with his hands in his pockets, watching them go by.

'Who's that?' asked Jenny.

'Beats me,' replied Mae. 'Nice-looking though. Bit like Errol Flynn.'

'Is he one of the campers?'

'Shouldn't think so, that's an expensive suit. Besides, the campers don't start arriving till next week.'

Jenny was so intrigued by the stranger that her mind wasn't on what she was doing. Catching the heel of her shoe in a drain-cover, she stumbled and dropped her suitcase, which burst open, strewing her bits and pieces all over the place.

119

'Oh, damn!'

On hands and knees, she started stuffing everything back in, crimson with embarrassment. Mae and Dolly helped a bit, Joss sniggered from a distance.

'Excuse me, would this be yours?'

Jenny looked up. The young man was standing over her, smiling and holding out a single, far from pristine shoe.

'Oh. Er . . . thank you.' She took the shoe from him and hastily thrust it back into the suitcase. Mae was right, he *was* rather nice, but wasn't she making an idiot of herself! And what must he think of her, with her terrible cheap underwear spread out all over Costigern's Camp?

'My pleasure.' Soft brown eyes crinkled at the corners when he smiled.

He looked as if he might be about to say something else, but at that moment Gwen produced a list of names and Sid started trying to organise everybody into their various chalets. By the time Jenny and Mae had finished squashing the last pair of knickers into the suitcase and forced it shut, the young man had disappeared.

'Joss, you're in number four with Moira.'

'Heavens no, Sid,' declared Joss. 'I can't possibly share, I wouldn't be able to sleep . . . and you know how lack of sleep affects my voice.'

He sighed and scratched his head.

'You're absolutely sure you couldn't . . .?'

'Absolutely not.'

'Bitch,' muttered Mae between clenched teeth. 'Why doesn't he stand up to her?'

'All right then, Joss, you take four and Moira can go in eight with Kate, Phoebe and Pauline. Mae, you and Jenny are sharing with Dolly and Gwen Roberts in number six.'

Gwen tossed them each a set of keys.

'Here you are, girls, keep 'em safe. It's a shilling if you lose 'em.'

Gwen unlocked the door of chalet number six. It looked exactly like a Wendy house, thought Jenny, or maybe a yellow garden shed. It wasn't much bigger either, she noted as she stepped inside, though whoever had designed it had made ingenious use of the space.

Two sets of bunk beds half-filled the single-roomed chalet. Apart from a fold-down table and a couple of chairs, there wasn't much else in the way of furniture.

'The sink's behind that partition,' explained Gwen. 'Only cold water, I'm afraid, but there's a shower and toilet block at the end of the chalet line. Oh, and you can hang your clothes in here.' She pushed aside a flowery curtain, revealing an alcove with a rail and a few coat-hangers.

'What – all four of us?' exclaimed Dolly.

''Fraid so. Your stage clothes will have to go in your dressing room at the theatre.'

'Just as well I haven't got much then,' remarked Jenny cheerfully. She bounced tentatively on the bottom bunk and almost broke her tailbone. It was rock hard beneath the thin mattress. 'Who's having which bed?'

Gwen shrugged.

'Doesn't bother me. When you've worked here a while, you could sleep standing up!'

'I think I could sleep right now,' murmured Mae, climbing up on to the bunk above Jenny's and flopping down.

Gwen filled the kettle and lit the tiny gas ring.

'Anyone for tea?'

'Ten cups,' declared Dolly. 'I'm parched.'

'One'll have to do,' said Mae. 'Sid's called a rehearsal for four o'clock, and then it'll be time to eat.'

As they drank their tea, they chatted about themselves and the camp. Gwen was from Colwyn Bay, and had worked as a hostess ever since the camp opened, in the spring of 1936. She knew just about everything there was to know about Costigern's, it was her second home and she loved it to bits.

'You'll like it here,' she promised. 'It's good fun, you'll soon settle in. In fact,' she grinned, 'some of us have already made a start.'

'How's that?' asked Mae.

Gwen looked at Jenny.

'You're a fast worker, I'll give you that!' she remarked.

121

Jenny swallowed a mouthful of digestive biscuit.

'What!'

'Remember that chap who helped you with your suitcase?'

'Of course I do. What about him?'

'That's Henry,' said Gwen, leaning forward over the little flip-down table for greater effect. 'Henry *Costigern.*'

'You're telling me . . .?'

'That's right,' said Gwen triumphantly. 'He's Jolly Jimmy's grandson!'

There was an ugly silence in the back alley behind The Feathers. Two dozen men, maybe more, had already gathered there, and now they were waiting for blood.

Ivan Price smiled to himself. The bare-knuckle fights he arranged were always well attended and if the police knew about them they hadn't caused any trouble. What's more, the money he earned from betting on the outcome more than offset his gambling debts.

He skirted the crowd and slipped through a gate into the back yard of one of the nearby houses. Jack Inglis was sitting on an upturned barrel, stripped to the waist and chatting to one of his seconds.

'Ready, Jack?'

Jack rose to his feet. The muscles under his skin flexed like knotted cables. He nodded.

'Ready as I'll ever be.' He spat into the palms of his hands and rubbed them together. 'Reckon I'll have him down in three.'

Ivan drew him to one side of the yard.

'You could beat him easy, boy, no doubt about it.' He nodded towards the unseen crowd outside. 'An' that's what they all think, an' all. You're twice the man Del Caley is. The thing is, Jack . . .'

Jack eyed Ivan suspiciously.

'What?'

'The thing is, I don't want you to win, not tonight.'

'Hang on, Ivan. You want me to . . .'

'No one's bettin' on Caley, see, the odds are sky-high. Stands to reason certain people have a lot to gain if he wins.'

'Is that so?'

Ivan carried on talking, the soul of reasonableness.

'I knew you'd see it my way, Jack. There's a bit extra in it for you, an' to be honest, you'll be doin' me a favour an' all.'

The muscles in Jack's jaw tensed with anger. He squared up to Ivan, eyes blazing.

'What do you think I am, Ivan Price? I won't do it.'

'Easy, boy. See reason.'

'Don't you "boy" me. I've never thrown a fight in my life an' I'm not startin' now. I won't do it for you, an' I won't do it for nobody.'

It was Ivan's turn to be angry now, an anger born partly from fear. He had betted heavily on Del Caley and stood to lose more than just his pride if Jack Inglis won. What's more, certain people had made it clear that they expected Del Caley to win against the odds. Certain people who expected Ivan Price to make sure it happened that way.

'Don't give me that, Jack. You don't mind breakin' the law for a few quid, do you? What's so different about this?'

Ivan was a powerful man, but Jack Inglis was a giant; Ivan flinched at the feel of Jack's fingers on his throat.

'I'll win this fight fair an' square, Ivan,' hissed Jack. 'An' if your friends don't like it, they can 'ave it out with you. Now get out of my way, before I break both your arms!'

There was no time to be bored at Costigern's Camp. With the first show only days away, rehearsals lasted practically from dawn to dusk. Jenny quickly discovered that the world she had entered was not as glamorous or carefree as she had once imagined.

Showbusiness meant aching legs and doing the same routine thirty times, until at last Geoff Tait was grudgingly satisfied. It meant learning every one of Joss Flynn's numbers off by heart, even though you knew you'd never be given a chance to sing them. It meant squeezing into tiny costumes in a freezing barn of a theatre, and learning how to smile, smile, smile, even when all you really wanted to do was burst into tears and run back home.

She adored it already.

One afternoon, in the break between rehearsal and high tea, Jenny and Mae were alone in the chalet.

'That roof leaks,' commented Mae, lying on her bunk and looking up at the spreading brown stain on the ceiling. 'If it keeps on raining I'll end up like a drowned rat.'

'I don't mind a bit of damp,' said Jenny. 'We can swap bunks if you like – your drip for my draught? It's giving me a stiff neck.'

They lay in silence for a few moments.

'Hardly home from home, is it?' observed Mae at last. 'You know these things are made of chicken wire and cement, don't you? That's why they're so perishing cold.'

'Oh, it's not that bad. It's not as if we get much time to ourselves anyway.' Jenny rolled on to her side and propped her head on her hand. 'Don't you wish you could be with Sid? I mean, the rules are a bit unfair, you're not even supposed to go to his chalet . . .'

'Oh, I wouldn't worry about that,' said Mae slyly. 'There are ways and means – you'd be surprised what goes on in this place after lights-out. The stories I've heard . . .' She swung her legs over the edge of the bunk and jumped down. 'I do miss being with Sid though. How about you, are you feeling homesick yet?'

Jenny thought hard. It wasn't that easy to say.

'I'm not sure. A little bit. This place . . . it's so completely *different*, not like a real place at all. It takes some getting used to.'

'New things always do.'

Mae rummaged in her bag, took out her compact and powdered her nose.

'Remember when me and Dad came to live in St Helens? I'd just turned nine. I thought Dad must really hate me to bring me to such a horrible place!'

'Well, it's no oil painting,' admitted Jenny with a smile. 'And I don't suppose it's much like the Isle of Man.'

'I'd never been off the island in my life till then. In fact, I'd hardly ever been out of Ballakeeill. I'd no idea places like St Helens even existed! And do you know what?'

'Hmm?'

'I suppose St Helens is my home now. Isn't that funny? I wasn't born there, I don't even live there any more, but it feels like home. Perhaps it's because Dad's still there . . .'

'I suppose home is wherever there's people who care about you,' hazarded Jenny.

They exchanged smiles.

'Then this place will be home in no time.' Mae threw Jenny a lipstick and she caught it one-handed. 'Here, kid, smarten yourself up. Sid says Jolly Jimmy might come to the rehearsal tonight.'

Chapter 11

'Jolly' Jimmy Costigern wasn't living up to his name this afternoon. His cherubic, rosy-cheeked face looked stern as he walked through the camp with Sid Dukes. For once, he was showing all of his seventy-two years.

'How long have I known you, Sid? Forty-eight years, forty-nine?'

'Ever since I was a nipper at Barnardo's.'

'Exactly.'

'You know I'm grateful for all you did for me,' cut in Sid hastily. Jimmy waved the words away.

'Never mind all that, Sid, I'm not fishing for compliments. What I'm saying is, after all this time I think I've a right to speak my mind.' He stuck his thumbs into the pockets of his waistcoat, exactly as he did on all the advertising posters. 'And I'm telling you, Sid, it won't do. It won't do at all.'

'No, Mr Costigern.'

'I've told you before, Sid, call me Jimmy. Everyone else does.'

'Yes . . . Jimmy. Sorry.'

Jimmy let out a small gasp of exasperation.

'Look, Sid, I'm not saying this is entirely your fault, but you've got to show that band of yours more discipline. They're young men, they need to be told who's boss or things are bound to get out of hand.'

'They were only . . .'

'As you know, Sid, I'm a lifelong abstainer myself, but I don't object to others having a drink or two – in moderation. But when half your brass section comes rolling back from Rhyl at midnight, blind drunk and singing bawdy songs . . . I won't have it, Sid, it's not good enough.'

'No, Jimmy. It won't happen again. I'll have a stern word with them.'

'Mind you do. And keep them out of those pretty girls' chalets too.' He appeared not to notice Sid blanch slightly at this, or perhaps he had simply chosen not to notice. 'You know it's a strict rule of mine, no shenanigans between the single folk. This is supposed to be a family camp – I've got a reputation to keep up.'

Lecture over, they walked on a bit further, passing a group of workmen who were supervising the filling of the paddling pool.

'What do you reckon to that then?' Jimmy cocked his head in the direction of the pool.

'Very . . . nice.'

At this, Jimmy looked a little jollier.

'You'll never believe how it came about. When we'd dug out all the soil to landscape the pitch-and-putt, we were left with this ruddy great hole – pardon my language. Well, James junior was all for filling it in, but straight off I thought, If you've got a hole, make the most of it. You can't be a successful businessman if you don't have an eye for the main chance, Sid.'

'I suppose not. But I'm a musician, not a businessman.'

Jolly Jimmy gave him a sharp look.

'That was always your trouble, Sid. Too many brains and not enough common sense.' His expression clouded. 'Bit like my son.'

Sid looked at him quizzically.

'Nothing wrong with James, is there?'

'No, no, just family trouble, you know how it is. I'll not burden you with it. Now, this variety show of yours . . . going to be a winner, is it?'

'I hope so.'

'Hope so's not good enough, Sid. Butlin may think he has the holiday camp trade all sewn up, but I've been around for twenty years and I'll not have him beat me at my own game. If he builds his campers a swimming pool, I'll build a bigger one. If he gives them free entertainment, I'm going to give 'em all-star variety shows they'll never forget. Got that?'

'There are some great song-and-dance numbers. And Joss Flynn of course . . .'

'Any speciality acts?'

'A troupe of jugglers. And a ventriloquist – oh, and Marvo's Mysteries of the Mind. That's a hypnotism and mind-reading act.'

'Good, good. I might as well tell you, I'm trying to persuade Gracie Fields to come and top the bill one Saturday night, but don't go blabbing about it, it might not come off.'

They were nearing the camp theatre; a huge white concrete box with a barrel-shaped roof and red masks of comedy and tragedy to either side of the front doors. Sid fidgeted with his bow tie.

'I'd better go in, I've a band run-through in five minutes.'

'Fine, fine. Just remember what I said: I won't have immorality in this camp, and I won't tolerate rowdy behaviour. Got that? Good.' Jolly Jimmy was already striding off towards the administration block. He called back over his shoulder, 'I'll be at the dress rehearsal tonight. Make sure it's a good one.'

Ron the ventriloquist leaned over and wiggled the head of his dummy in Mae Corlett's face.

'Gread and gutter!'

Its painted face leered horribly at her, showing its yellow teeth, and she pushed it away.

'Give over, Ron, I'm trying to listen to Sid.'

'What's got into Sid anyway?' asked Jenny, edging a little further away from Ron. He gave her the creeps.

'It's those idiots over there.' Mae nodded disdainfully at the sniggering brass section. 'Going out boozing and coming back half-cut. I've never seen him so angry.'

Jenny, Mae, Ron and Bella were all huddled together on the steps of the stage, listening to Sid address the company.

It wasn't so much a dress rehearsal as a dressing-down, thought Jenny.

Sid paced up and down in front of the jumble of musicians and instruments, pausing occasionally to glare at one or two of the worst offenders.

'Jimmy Costigern's nose is out of joint and I can't say I'm surprised. The way some of you behaved last night was a bloody disgrace. Do you want to get us all kicked out of Llandew before the show even makes it to the opening night?' He paused. 'Well?'

A few grudging murmurs of 'no' and 's'pose not' ran round the band. They looked embarrassed. Like naughty schoolboys who'd been caught having a smoke behind the bike sheds.

'I'm glad to hear it, because "Holiday Follies of 1938" opens next week and it's not even half ready.' Sid paused for emphasis. 'Right. Listen. The first lot of campers will be here on Saturday and you will behave like ruddy choirboys, or I'll know the reason why.'

At this, Geoff Tait let out a burst of laughter.

'Come on, Sid, don't you think you're being a bit hard on the lads? They're young, it's just high spirits. Relax. The show'll be all right on the night.'

Sid locked eyes with Geoff. It was obvious that for once the deputy bandleader had miscalculated.

'Not good enough,' snapped Sid. Geoff opened and closed his mouth like a stranded goldfish, clearly stunned. A ripple of surprise ran round the band. 'From now on this show is going to be all right *every* night, not just when you feel like it; in fact, it's going to be a lot better than all right or I'm scrapping it and sending the lot of you home!'

Sid snatched up a copy of *Moonlight Becomes You*, opened it, and plonked it on his music stand. Then he blew into his cornet a couple of times to warm it up.

'Page seven, from the top. Desmond, take the tenor sax solo; Joss, fill in the vocal line . . . oh, yes, there's one more thing I forgot to tell you.' He polished the cornet on his trouser-leg. 'Jolly Jimmy and I had a little chat this after-noon. He thinks if you insist on behaving like animals, you really ought to spend more time with them.'

Puzzled murmurs ran along the rows of chairs.

'Sid's cracked up,' hissed Ron's schoolboy dummy, its head shooting up and down on its wooden neck. 'Sid's cracked up.' Jenny took hold of the head and twisted it back to front.

'Ow!'

'Shut up and listen.'

'You're all going to be at the model farm tomorrow morning, eight o'clock sharp,' announced Sid with obvious pleasure and more than a hint of amusement. 'And that means *all* of you. Jolly Jimmy's kindly offered to let you clean out his pigs!'

Costigern's Holiday Camp had been bringing holidaymakers to North Wales since just after the First World War. In the early years, the whole camp had been under canvas; a regular mecca for healthy outdoor types with its bicycles, cold showers, gymnastics, nightly camp-fire sing-songs . . . and, of course, its model farm.

Although Costigern's had now evolved into a very different sort of holiday camp, Jimmy could never bring himself to get rid of the farm – partly because of nostalgia for the good old days, and partly through a sound grasp of economics. It made good financial sense to grow your own pork and chickens. Besides, the kiddies liked playing with the piglets, and with the piggery being right on the other side of the funfair, the smell was hardly noticeable unless there was a really strong onshore wind.

Or unless, of course, you happened to be standing right in the middle of the piggery.

Jimmy employed a miniature army of strapping Welsh labourers to take care of the dirty jobs around the farm, but today that special privilege had fallen to the Sid Dukes Band. Not surprisingly there was mutinous talk about the pigsties.

'The stink! God, Binky, I think I'm going to throw up.'

'You'll not catch me going in there.'

'My God, Dunc, look at those porkers, they've got teeth like razors!'

'That one's looking at you funny, Desmond. I reckon she fancies you.'

Everyone from the show had been roped in to do their bit, even Geoff Tait – well, everyone except Joss Flynn, who 'positively couldn't' come anywhere near the farm because she was 'horribly allergic' to animals of any sort (except mink, thought Jenny) and the smell would give her 'one of her thumping heads'.

'Allergic?' scoffed Marvo the Memory Man. 'Allergic to hard work more like.'

Jenny took another handful of corn from the bucket and threw it for the hens. She liked Marvo, they saw eye to eye on most things and especially about Joss Flynn.

'Don't let Joss hear you say that!'

'Doesn't bother me if she does. Stuck-up cow wants taking down a peg or two.'

'Anyhow.' Jenny straightened up and stretched her back. 'You can't talk. How come Sid lets you feed the chickens instead of shovelling pig-muck with that lot?'

Marvo grinned, displaying a double row of perfect white teeth; they contrasted sharply with the dark swarthiness of his tanned skin, making him look foreign in spite of his northern accent.

'Some of us,' he said importantly, 'have respect for our constitutions.'

'Eh?'

'I'm the Memory Man, aren't I? My mind's my livelihood – I'm not going to mess up my psychic powers by going out and getting plastered. Even if I do feel like it sometimes,' he added.

Jenny laughed.

'All this memory stuff is just a clever act though, isn't it? I mean, you can't *really* hypnotise people and read their minds?'

'Says who?' Marvo folded his brawny arms and leant against the hen-house, observing her through hooded eyes.

Jenny looked at him, intrigued.

'But I thought . . .'

'See this?' Marvo rolled up his shirt-sleeve to reveal an

impressive, brightly coloured tattoo. 'Got it when I was a merchant seaman travelling around the Indian Ocean. The natives there can do things with the mind that you just wouldn't believe. Saw one of 'em stick a six-inch nail through his nose, and not a drop of blood.'

'And they taught you – to read minds and predict the future?'

Marvo's deadly serious expression disintegrated.

'Nah. I bought the act off a bloke in Bradford, for fifty quid.'

Jenny wasn't sure whether to laugh at Marvo or kick him. One minute he seemed enigmatic and rather exciting, the next he was just a practical joker. She felt faintly disappointed.

'That's a pity. So you can't tell me my fortune then?'

Marvo laughed.

'Let's just say I wouldn't hold your breath. I'm a mind-reader, sweetheart, not Gypsy flaming Petulengro!'

The days were still lengthening, and when Tom's night-shift ended he stepped out of the cage into broad daylight. It made a pleasant change to feel the sun on his back, after twelve hours spent hacking away at the coal seam in sweltering darkness.

Mind you, it was good to be in work; normally at this time of the year the mine owners started putting the colliers on short time. Good, too, to be on a different shift from Ivan Price. At least with Ivan on days and Tom on nights, they were seldom forced to exchange more than the briefest of greetings.

The sun went behind a cloud as Tom was leaving the pit, killing the illusion of an early summer. It was a long walk home. By the time he reached the end of Gas Street, a fine, cold drizzle was coming down out of a muddy grey sky, plastering his hair to his scalp in oily black strands.

'Mam?' He pushed open the back gate of number forty-two and stepped into the yard. A couple of wet tea-towels were flapping dejectedly on the washing line. 'Mam, I'm back.'

The back door opened, but it wasn't Dot who walked out on to the step. It was Ivan, freshly shaven and dressed for the pit. Tom acknowledged him with a curt nod.

'Ivan.'

Ivan's eyes appraised him but he said nothing, just folded his arms and stood there, blocking the doorway with his broad bulk. Drizzle was trickling in a dozen separate rivulets down the back of Tom's neck, making his shirt stick to his back. He was impatient to get inside.

'Ivan, can I get by?'

'What's that, boy? Bit wet out there, is it?' Ivan's tone mocked him, daring him to rise to the bait. 'Don't suppose you'd want to come in, by any chance?'

'Stand aside and let me get past, will you?'

'Don't know if I can manage that, boy.'

Tom struggled to maintain his composure. He wasn't a hot-headed man, but Ivan had the power to turn his thoughts to violence. Still, an outburst of temper might make him do senseless things and he wasn't about to let Ivan use that against him. On the contrary, why not stay calm and play him at his own game?

He shrugged.

'Plannin' on standin' there all day, are you, Ivan? I'll just stay out here then, I can wait.'

The look which passed between them was one of mutual animosity and distrust; the guarded hostility of the cobra and the mongoose, each weighing up its chances. Then Ivan took his snap-tin from the kitchen table and went off whistling down the yard, leaving the gate swinging crookedly on its one remaining hinge.

Tom was grateful for the wall of warmth which hit him as he stepped into the back kitchen. There was always a fire in the coal-fired range, even in summer, and today it filled the house with the warm, yeasty fug of baking bread. Nancy was on her knees in front of it, sweeping cinders off the hearth.

'Oh.' She seemed to start at the sound of his pit-clogs on the floor. 'Oh, it's you.'

'Breakfast ready, is it?'

Nancy got to her feet, wiping her hands on her apron.

'There's bread and marge on the table. Ivan ate the last of the eggs.'

'Damn him,' Tom muttered under his breath.

'It's all there is, you'll have to make do.'

Anger quickened in Tom, but what was the point of directing his resentment against Nancy? She'd done nothing wrong. And in any case, she looked like a frightened rabbit and that worried him. She'd not been herself for weeks, not since the day Mam threw Jenny out and Ivan had knocked the kids about 'to teach them a bit of respect'. Surely she ought to be over that by now . . .

While Nancy put the kettle on, Tom had his wash then sat down at the table to read the morning paper.

'Billy and Daisy gone to school, have they?'

'Yes.'

'Where's Mam?'

'Still in bed, she's tired.'

Tom took a good long look at his sister.

'You look tired yourself.'

Something of the old spoilt, selfish Nancy resurfaced for a moment.

'You'd be tired an' all, if you had to scrub and cook and clean and . . . and all the rest.'

'It'll be easier once Mam has the baby.'

Nancy grunted.

'Oh, yes, much easier. She'll give it to me to look after and then she and Ivan'll go an' have another one!'

She turned away to fill the teapot with boiling water, and as she replaced the lid Tom heard it tinkle against the side. Nancy was shaking all over, he wondered how come he hadn't noticed it before. Perhaps there were other things he hadn't noticed.

'There.' She banged the pot down on the table. 'That'll have to do you, I've got the stairs to clean.'

Tom caught his sister's wrist.

'Nancy . . .'

'Let go of me.'

'Not until you tell me what's wrong.'

She wrenched free from his grasp.

'Nothing's wrong, I've told you. I'm just sick of playin' mother to you lot. So why don't you eat your breakfast and leave me be?'

Chapter 12

Llandew Station positively gleamed in the late-spring sunshine. Doorknobs had been buffed, paintwork washed until it gleamed, steps whitewashed and borders planted with row upon row of scarlet geraniums, surrounding the station's name picked out in painted stones. Blue, white and yellow bunting flapped above Jenny's head, beneath a banner which proclaimed: WELCOME TO COSTIGERN'S CAMP!

Jenny glanced up at the station clock. It read six minutes to two. Any minute now, a train would round the bend, laden to bursting with holidaymakers. So many people were already crowded on to the platform that she wondered if there would be any room for the campers.

The Stripeys – Jolly Jimmy's hosts and hostesses – stood in two neat lines along the edge of the platform, very smartly turned out in their yellow and blue striped blazers, yellow skirts and shorts, and white pumps. Behind them were the Sid Dukes Band and Singers, a chorus-line of Dukes' Dukettes, and finally, lined up along a length of red carpet which led through into the booking hall, three generations of the Costigern family.

Jenny recognised the young man who'd helped her with her suitcase, though he didn't seem to have noticed her. She nudged Mae.

'Isn't that Henry Costigern?'

Mae nodded.

'That's his dad next to him, James junior.'

'The one on the end? He looks fed up.'

'I expect he is,' cut in Dolly. 'Him and his dad never stop

rowing – don't agree on nuffink, at least that's what I 'eard.'

'What's he doing here then?'

'Jolly Jimmy's a stickler for doing things right. He reckons every camper's a VIP, that's why we have to go through all this rigmarole.'

The Costigern menfolk were a strange-looking trio, thought Jenny. You could see the family resemblance – the sandy hair, the roundish face and deep-set blue eyes – but apart from that the three men didn't look as if they had much in common. James was staring morosely at his feet, Henry whistling tunelessly with his hands in his pockets, and Jimmy was doing his damnedest to make certain that everyone, absolutely *everyone* in the whole world, was Jolly.

Unable to stand still for more than a few minutes at a time, Jolly Jimmy broke ranks and started wandering about on the platform, giving everyone last-minute instructions.

'You – yes, you – do up that top button on your blazer . . . and stand up straight. This is Costigern's Holiday World, not some second-rate holiday camp.'

'Yes, Mr Costigern.' Gwen Roberts hastily fastened the offending button and stood to attention. 'Sorry, Mr Costigern.'

'And you – the girl in the yellow dress.' Jenny almost sank through the platform.

'M-Me?'

'Yes, you. If you stand behind that bass player the campers won't be able to see you.' Jolly Jimmy beckoned Sid over. 'Can't you stand the girl on a box or something?'

'It's all right, she can swap with me,' said Mae, changing places in the line so that Jenny was thrust into the front row. 'There, that's better, isn't it?' Damn! thought Jenny. She'd been counting on anonymity for her very first public performance.

'Remember,' boomed Jolly Jimmy, 'bring 'em in snappy, send 'em home happy . . . that's the Costigern philosophy.'

He went on and on about giving folk a jolly day the Costigern way, but Jenny was only half listening. She was trying to remember the words of the camp song – it would look awful if she forgot them, like when she'd dried up at her audition. How exactly did that second verse go?

Sid indulged in a little last-minute reorganisation.

'Desmond, put your hat on. It's supposed to be on your head, not stuffed in your pocket.'

'Brushes or sticks for the side-drum, Mr Dukes?'

'Brushes, Binky, and pipe down in the middle eight – you'll drown out the singers. Now Dukettes, remember: sing up, give it all you've got, and whatever else happens, smile!'

A distant whistle sent a shiver through Jenny. The train! It was coming. Too late now for last-minute nerves.

'It's coming,' called one of the camp hostesses from her vantage point at the far end of the platform. Running back, she took her place in the immaculate blue, yellow and white row of Stripeys.

Steam plumed on the horizon, and the next minute the engine was rounding the bend, the brakes squealing as it slid towards the platform.

'A-one-two-three-four . . .'

The band struck up a hectic ragtime tune as the train drew nearer and nearer. There were people hanging out of every window, children laughing and shouting, parents too, while trying to restrain their excited offspring.

Once the train had come to a halt, there was no stopping them. The doors burst open, and the crowds and crowds of people in summer clothes spilled out on to the platform – more people than Jenny would have believed you could ever fit into one average-sized excursion train.

They looked like ordinary happy people, just like the ones she'd known in St Helens – why, some of them could even be her neighbours. People just like herself. Little boys and girls like Billy and Daisy, mums and dads, lads and lasses from the Lancashire cotton mills and factories and coal mines, determined that this was going to be the best week of their lives . . .

'There's the sea, Dad, the sea, the sea!'

'Where's lav? Want to go t'lav.'

'All right, all right, love, wait till we get to the camp.'

It would have been complete chaos if it hadn't been for

Jolly Jimmy's military-style organisation. At Costigern's, nobody was ever allowed to wander about aimlessly; there was always someone on hand to push them gently in the right direction – and if not the right direction, *any* direction. Stripeys swarmed about the campers like well-drilled ants, guiding them and their luggage towards the red carpet and the outstretched hands of Henry, James and Jolly Jimmy Costigern.

'Happy to see you, have a jolly holiday . . .'

The band paused briefly, then launched into the opening strains of *Happy to See You*, the camp's very own song. Now that Jenny was actually standing here, singing, it was absurdly easy; she couldn't have forgotten the words if she'd tried:

> *Happy to see you,*
> *Summer's on its way,*
> *Happy to see you*
> *This jolly, jolly day . . .*

It was exciting, and she loved every minute of it; but tonight was bound to be very different. Tonight the band would be playing at a huge camp dance. And she, little Jenny Fisher, the shop-girl from St Helens, would be standing in front of all these people, singing for her supper.

That same Saturday night, Costigern's Camp hosted its first 'Happy to See You' dance of the season. The idea of these weekly events was to 'loosen the campers up', as Jolly Jimmy liked to put it. When they arrived at the camp they might be fifteen hundred complete strangers; but by the time they left the following Saturday morning, they'd have become bosom pals. In fact, if previous years were anything to go by, over half of them would book for next year before they went home.

Down in the dressing rooms below and behind the stage, Dukes' Dukettes and the Sid Dukes Singers were milling about, putting the final touches to their make-up.

'Do me up, Dolly, there's a love.'

'Breathe in then. Gawd, Bella, you've a backside on you . . .'

'. . . and *you've* got a hole in your stocking, or hadn't you noticed?'

'What? Oh, bloody 'ell, lend us one of yours . . .'

Jenny was trying not to listen to the noise and chatter around her. Other people's last-minute panics only added to her own. Tonight was going to be all right, she kept telling herself. She wouldn't have to do much, just a little bit of dancing and a couple of close-harmony numbers with the other singers. Nothing that would make her stand out. The campers were here for the dancing, and to hear Joss and Geoff and Sid, not to gawp at her.

All the same, her hand shook as she tried to apply the thin blue line underneath her eye. No matter how hard she tried to get it straight, it wiggled about. Snatching up another ball of cotton wool, she dipped it into the pot of cold cream and started again.

'Damn, damn, oh, damnation!'

'Here, let me.' Mae held out her hand to take the thin stick of make-up.

Jenny shook her head stubbornly.

'I've got to learn to do it myself.'

'Yes, but you can practise some other time – we've only got a few minutes before we're on! Now, look up and hold still or it'll go in your eye.'

Jenny submitted to Mae. It wasn't easy to stand still and not blink.

'Are you sure I look all right?' she demanded, staring fixedly up at the ceiling so that Mae could run a thinner line of white along the line of her lower lashes.

'Absolutely hunky-dory. Will you stop worrying?'

'This dress. It's awfully . . . yellow.' She wriggled inside the thin evening gown of canary-coloured silky stuff and caught a glimpse of herself in the mirror. Nobody could have described the shade as subtle. 'I look just like a great big banana.'

'At least you can carry that shade, you being so dark. Pauline looks terrible with her red hair. Still, under the

141

lights the colour'll bleach out, you'll be surprised.'

The walls and ceiling of the dressing room were thin. From time to time gales of laughter floated down from the theatre. Somebody, at least, seemed to be having fun.

The door opened a few inches, and Gwen Roberts stuck her head inside.

'Five minutes, ladies.'

As the door snapped shut, another raucous peal of laughter sounded from above.

'Sounds like Harry's getting 'em warmed up for us anyway,' commented Moira, very leggy and athletic in her white satin shorts and sequinned top hat. She executed a few nifty tap steps on the bare boards, twirled her hat on the end of her finger, then threw it in the air and caught it on her head. 'What do you think?'

Mae laughed.

'Broadway beckons. Ready, Jen?'

Jenny nodded.

'Ready.'

Not ready at all, she thought, but that wasn't the sort of thing you could admit when you were supposed to be a professional. Everyone else covered up their nervousness with laughter, noisy banter and bawdy jokes, but Jenny felt half-throttled with terror, her throat tight and dry as dust. Sing? She could scarcely speak, and butterflies were dancing the Charleston in her stomach. She took a last sip of water.

'Oh, no, I think I need the toilet . . .'

Mae took her by the arm.

'There's no time for that now. Besides it's just nerves. Come *on*.'

'Get in line,' somebody called from the back, and the jumble of legs and arms resolved itself into two groups – Dukettes and singers. Jenny found herself standing in the corridor between Dolly and Bella on one side, and Pauline on the other. She wished she could be standing next to Mae, but she was with the other dancers. Dolly nudged Jenny.

'All right?'

Jenny pulled a face.

'No.'

''Course you are. Just follow Pauline if you get stuck, she never forgets the words.'

'And smile,' cut in Bella. 'They don't give a damn what you do so long as you keep on smiling.'

They shuffled along the corridor in their long frocks, and up a narrow flight of stairs to the wings. The sound from the stage got louder. Camp Host Harry Kaye certainly knew his job.

'Hello, campers!'

'Hello, Harry,' came straight back, but he wasn't satisfied.

'Harry can't hear you! I said, "Hello, campers!" '

'HELLO, HARRY!'

'That's more like it. Now, campers, it's getting to know you time. I want you all to turn to the person on your right, shake hands and say: "Happy to see you". Think you can do that?'

'Yes, Harry.'

'Harry can't hear you!'

'YES, HARRY!'

'Go on then, what you waitin' for? D'you want jam on it?'

Titters and squeals of laughter announced that the campers were getting acquainted.

'Any minute now,' hissed Dolly.

Jenny peered over her shoulder through the wings. On the dancefloor, crowds and crowds of campers in their new best frocks and jackets were giggling and grinning as they exchanged self-conscious handshakes. Harry Kaye, his spherical body tightly upholstered in a black and white check suit, was sending them into fits of laughter with daft jokes about Gracie Fields and Mussolini. Each punchline was signalled by a crashing piano chord and a bash of Binky's hi-hat cymbals.

'Now, lads and lasses, the moment you've all been waitin' for,' announced Harry to the accompaniment of a roll of drums. 'Yes, it's the only – the one and only – Sid Dukes Band and Singers . . .'

A loud cheer came from the audience.

'. . . with Dukes' Dukettes and your own, your very own . . . the lovely . . . JOSS FLYNN!'

Bright lights blazed in Jenny's eyes as she followed Bella and Dolly towards the battery of microphones, and she could hardly make out the audience at all for the spotlights trained on the stage. Smile, smile, SMILE, said a voice in her head. She smiled so hard that her jaw ached.

Joss Flynn was simpering at the audience from her special gilded chair by the side of Geoff's grand piano, but Jenny was much too scared and excited to be bothered by Joss. The only thing that mattered right now was doing her job, and doing it well.

Sid stepped up to the microphone. He looked quite debonair in his black evening suit, bow tie and silk cummerbund. His trademark golden cornet glinted in the stage-lights.

'Good evening, campers!'

'Good evening, Sid!'

'Take your partners please, ladies and gentlemen, for the first dance.'

He raised the cornet to his lips. For a few seconds there was complete silence in the hall, then the first high, sweet solo note filled the emptiness and Sid launched into the intro.

Eight bars of solo cornet, Jenny told herself, counting the beats on the fingers of her right hand. *Five*, two-three-four, *six*, two-three-four, *seven* . . .

The band kicked in with such gusto that it almost took her breath away. Remember the moves, girl, sway to the left then the right, make a half turn and . . . SING!

Down on the dance floor, the campers paired up and started moving in time to the music. It was incredible, utterly incredible! The first professional performance of her life, and Jenny had never dreamt it would feel like this. The fear completely evaporated the moment she opened her mouth and began to harmonise; and all of a sudden it transformed itself into heart-stopping exhilaration. She wanted this to go on for ever.

★ ★ ★

Where was Mae? Jenny stood on tiptoe and scanned the crowds in the Caribbean Bar but it was hard to spot any one person amongst the mad mêlée. Oh, there she was, talking and laughing with a group of young lasses by the bar.

Jenny felt faintly jealous, which she knew was unfair. Everyone in the band had been told that they must "mingle" after the dance, talk to the campers and make them feel at home; but after all, this was her very first performance, she'd got through it without disgracing herself, and a tiny part of her wanted to be . . . well, congratulated.

In the middle distance, a large group of campers had gathered round Joss Flynn and Geoff Tait, asking them for their autographs, jostling to gain their attention. Joss was smiling graciously and basking in glory, obviously loving every minute of it; it struck Jenny, not for the first time, that there was an awfully big difference between being the new girl and being the star of the show.

It was all something of an anticlimax after the triumph of the show. Oh, Jenny's part in it had been very small, she was under no illusions about that, but the 'Happy to See You' dance had been a brilliant success, everyone said so. After all the bad things that had happened to Jenny in the past, she wanted desperately to celebrate with someone who could really understand.

'Buck up, Jenny.'

She swung round. Sid Dukes was observing her from underneath the bottle-green leaves of a papier-mâché palm tree.

'Oh, Mr Dukes, I didn't see you there.'

'You look like you've lost a shilling and found sixpence. Something wrong?'

'No, nothing. I was just . . . you know, looking for Mae.'

'And you're at a loose end?'

Jenny nodded.

'It's silly, I suppose. But I don't really know any of the other girls, and I don't want to push in where I'm not wanted.'

145

'Mae's not forgotten you, Jenny, she's just doing her job, making sure folk have a good time.' Sid fiddled with his bow tie. 'It's your first time away from home, isn't it?'

'Does it show?'

He smiled.

'Look, Jenny lass. Mae's told me a lot about . . . the bad things you've been through. You've had it rough. What with this as well, it's a lot to get used to.'

Jenny looked up at Sid. He had a nice, honest face, you could tell just by looking at him that you could trust him. She was beginning to understand how Mae could think such a lot of a man who was old enough to be her father.

'It's just . . . what if I'm not good enough? What if I don't fit in?'

'Of course you'll fit in.' Sid folded his arms. 'Now, I wouldn't normally say this to a new singer, it's not good policy, but I don't think you're the swollen-headed type. I was watching you tonight, Jenny, and I could tell you were having the time of your life. You're a natural for this business.'

She felt a thrill of delight.

'Mr Dukes!'

'It's true, Jenny. Oh, you've a long way to go yet, but you'll get there. Now, go and get yourself a drink from the bar – tell them to put it on my slate.'

'But . . .'

'And then, for heaven's sake, go and *talk* to people, understand? They're friendly folk and so are you. Go on, what are you waiting for!'

Sid stood and watched her go, dodging through the crowd and exchanging words and smiles with campers as she went. He might not be the world's greatest businessman, but he knew raw talent when he saw it. And just like he'd told her to her face, Jenny Fisher was a natural.

Chapter 13

Jolly Jimmy Costigern had decreed that everyone would eat breakfast together – campers, Stripeys, entertainers, even the men who cleaned the dead leaves out of the fountains. This was supposed to encourage folk to get to know each other, and while they ate, the Stripeys went round handing out programmes and telling the campers all about the day's fun and frolics.

It was a nice idea – in theory. In fact, Jenny was the only one from chalet 6N to make it to breakfast at all on Sunday morning. Gwen Roberts was up and smiling at the crack of dawn, organising heats for the Diving Belle competition, Bella had a sore head from too many free port and lemons, and as for Mae, no one had seen her since the previous night. Jenny had a shrewd suspicion that wherever Sid Dukes was, Mae would not be far behind.

Jenny collected her plate of home-reared eggs and bacon and looked for a seat in the vast communal dining room. It had just been refurbished according to Jolly Jimmy's own designs, and he had decided to call it the Roman Room. Jenny supposed this was because of the high ceiling, with its dozens of white fluted columns, and the real grape vines which twined around and between them, dangling tantalisingly low over the tables. In reality it was so noisy and chaotic that it was more like the monkey house at Chester Zoo.

'Happy to see you,' trilled Jenny with her best Costigern's smile. 'Room for a little 'un?'

'Happy to see you, 'course there is. Budge up, Sadie.'

A gaggle of factory girls squeezed up to make room for

Jenny, and she plonked herself down at the end of their table.

'Having a nice time?'

'Oh, it's grand, really grand. I've never been to a place like this before.'

'Never even had a proper holiday,' volunteered her friend, gulping down a forkful of fried egg.

'So where are you from?'

'Bolton. It's a bit different from here, i'n't it, Trish!'

'Sadie come last year with her mam,' said the first girl. 'We got sick of her tellin' us how wonderful it was, so when we heard we was gettin' a week's paid holiday, we decided we'd all come here.'

'I still can't get over them great big baths!' enthused Sadie. 'You could 'ave ten baths a day if you wanted, all lovely an' hot.'

'Mind you, them chalets is a bit draughty,' commented Trish. 'Still, who wants to stay indoors?' She looked Jenny up and down. 'You're one of them singers, aren't you?'

'That's right.' She was surprised they recognised her, she looked so different without half an inch of pan-stik plastered all over her face.

'Know Joss Flynn, do you?'

'Er . . . yes.'

'Well, next time you see her, tell her she's wonderful – you tell her that from me. She's better than our Gracie, is Joss Flynn.'

'An' that Geoff Tait, he's lovely an' all – do you know him too?'

'Sort of,' said Jenny.

'Lucky you! Maureen love, pass us that programme and we'll tick off what we're going to do today. How d'you fancy your chances in the Knobbly Knees?'

Jenny ate slowly, fending off so many questions about the camp that by the time the campers had finished eating, she was still only halfway through her toast. They bounced up from their seats, ready to face the day.

'See you round the camp, then?'

'I'm sure you will.'

148

'Is there another show on Monday?'

'Yes . . . see you there.'

Jenny watched them go, a happy crowd in bright new frocks and identical hand-knitted cardigans. This week probably meant just as much to them as it did to her. They'd been looking forward to it all year, their one escape from the drudgery of boring lives and boring jobs.

She thought about St Helens. About the little house on Gas Street, about Mam sitting by the fire knitting clothes for the baby and Nancy getting all dressed up to go to the flicks. About Canal Terrace too, with its rats and bugs and all-pervading smell, and the warm smiles of the people who had welcomed her in when she had nowhere else to go. As soon as she got her first week's pay, she'd send something to the O'Briens, with a letter telling them all about what she was doing.

She tried to focus on Molly and the O'Briens, but her thoughts drifted back to Gas Street. Did Mam and Nancy ever think about her? Did Mam ever regret one harsh word of what she'd said? What would Tom and Billy and Daisy think if they could see her now, eating more food in one meal than she was used to in a day?

'Er . . . mind if I join you?'

The polite, nicely spoken voice gave her such a start that she jumped and hit her knee against the leg of the table.

'Ow! Oh.' She rubbed her throbbing knee. 'Hello.'

Henry Costigern pulled out a chair and sat down opposite her.

'Sorry, did I startle you?'

Jenny peeped under the table at her knee. There would be a lovely bruise there later.

'I was miles away, that's all.' She took her first proper look at Jolly Jimmy's grandson. Henry was no more than three or four years older than she was, with attractive, twinkling brown eyes, unmanageable sandy hair and a mouth made for smiling. 'I . . . didn't thank you properly, did I?'

'Thank me – for what?' He looked nonplussed.

It occurred to Jenny in a rush of embarrassment that he

probably didn't even recall their one brief meeting. He must meet dozens and dozens of girls, all of them prettier than she was.

'The other day. I dropped my suitcase by the chalets and you helped me pick up my things. You probably don't remember.'

Henry grinned.

'Of course I remember. Your shoe rolled halfway across the road.'

'It was very kind of you to help like that.'

'Poppycock! My pleasure.' He stuck out his hand. 'Henry Costigern.'

She accepted his handshake with a slightly more confident smile.

'I thought you must be. Jenny Fisher, pleased to meet you.' She took a sip of frighteningly strong tea. 'Do you always eat with the campers? I've not noticed you in here before.' And I'm sure I *would* have noticed you, she thought to herself.

Henry toyed with a piece of black pudding.

'Only when Grandpa insists – doesn't that sound terrible? The thing is, I've never felt comfortable in great big crowds of people, I'm not a showman like him. Apart from "happy to see you", I'm never sure what to say.'

'Oh, surely . . .'

'No kidding. I just don't have the knack, nor does Dad really.' He dabbed at his mouth with a napkin and pushed away his empty plate. 'You were jolly good last night.'

'The band, you mean? Yes, I thought the dance went well. And of course Joss . . .'

'Not the band, you.'

Their eyes met.

'*Me!* All I did was stand at the back.'

'That's not true, I could hear you singing in those close-harmony numbers. You have a lovely voice, you know.'

'Th-Thank you.' Jenny wasn't quite sure whether to be flattered, embarrassed, mystified, or all three.

'It's funny, you know – can I pour you another cup of

150

tea? – this place reminds me a bit of school.'

'Where was that?'

Henry dabbed milk into the thick white cups and poured two cups of tea, as delicately as if he were pouring Darjeeling at the Ritz.

'I boarded at Winchester. Grandpa never got much schooling, you see, so he made up his mind I was going to get a proper education, no matter what. I'd rather have stayed at home, but Ma and Pa were hardly ever there and Pa was always tied up with the business . . .'

'So what does your dad do?'

Henry stirred his tea.

'To be honest, I'm not quite sure. Helps Grandpa in the business – when Grandpa can bear to let him. What about yours?'

'He was a collier,' said Jenny.

As the mundane truth left her mouth, she wished for an instant that her past life could have been more glamorous, that she could have something to say that would interest Henry Costigern. And in the same instant she felt thoroughly ashamed; after all, no one could have been a better father than Dan Fisher.

'Was?'

'He was killed down the pit. The lift cage fell on him . . .'

She stopped as abruptly as she had begun, suddenly feeling the pain of loss all over again. It was all such a long time ago, dead and buried like Dad. What on earth had possessed her to blurt it all out to a complete stranger?

Henry looked mortally embarrassed.

'Oh, gosh, I had no idea. I'm awfully sorry.'

'Don't be, it was years ago.' Jenny curled her fingers around her tea-cup. 'Do you like it here?'

'Sometimes. And you?'

'I love it! This is my big chance to do something with my life. I've always wanted to be a singer.'

'I bet your mother's proud of you?'

'Well, no, not . . . exactly. We fell out. It's a long story.' Jenny glanced at the big clock above the entrance. It was almost half-past nine and the kitchen staff had started

151

clearing up. 'Look at the time! I said I'd be back long ago . . .'

'Do you have to?'

'I'd better.'

'Still, I expect I'll see you around.'

'I expect so.'

It took more effort than it should have done to get up from the table and walk away. She felt an unaccountable urge to sit there all day and tell Henry Costigern her entire life story. Not that he'd want to listen. As she kept on reminding herself as she walked back to the chalet, her life contained nothing that could be of interest to a man like Henry Costigern.

Henry Costigern in Gas Street? The thought was ludicrous. Henry taking afternoon tea in Canal Terrace, making polite conversation about Winchester with Molly and Col O'Brien while the cockroaches nibbled at his jam butty? At a pinch, Jenny could just about imagine Jolly Jimmy walking through the streets of St Helens, but not his grandson. She and Henry Costigern were characters from two separate films, people so different that they had never been meant to meet.

All the same, Jenny couldn't help wishing that someone would write the delectable Henry into her life story . . .

'Holiday Follies of 1938' opened to an enthusiastic reception. Even Jolly Jimmy seemed satisfied, and the campers were still humming the songs as they made their way to bed along the darkened chalet lines.

As each night's performance passed without any major disasters, Jenny found that she was beginning to relax. The singing was easy – all she had to do was remember her part, and harmonising came naturally to her. The dancing was a bit more tricky, but Geoff had wisely sidelined her from most of the complicated dance routines, so no one noticed her few trips and stumbles. Her one really big fear – that Joss Flynn would fall ill and not be able to perform – had receded far into the background. Joss Flynn was as strong as an ox, she didn't *need* an understudy.

What's more, Jenny had other things to think about. She had acquired a new friend . . .

It was Mae who first noticed that wherever Jenny went, Henry Costigern always seemed to be there too. Judging the Bonny Babies at the boating lake, playing tag with the kids at the Fun House, partnering the campers at the afternoon tea dances . . . Henry always turned up sooner or later and found an excuse to talk to Jenny.

'He's here again,' Mae grinned, nudging Jenny one afternoon at the outdoor roller-skating rink.

Jenny looked over her shoulder. Henry was at the other side of the rink, helping a little boy to buckle on a pair of skates. She almost caught his eye as he looked up, and hastily looked away again.

'It's a coincidence,' she said firmly, hauling herself up by the handrail and trying to stand up straight.

'Rubbish! That boy's been mooning over you ever since you got here.' Mae lowered her voice. 'I'd make the most of it if I were you, his grandpa's filthy rich.'

'Mae!' protested Jenny. 'I'm not Joss Flynn, you know.'

'I know, I know, I was only teasing. But he's not bad-looking, is he? And it's obvious he's got a thing about you. Where's the harm in a bit of fun?' She raised her arm and waved cheerily at Henry. 'Coo-ee!'

'Mae, don't!'

She kept on waving.

'Henry! Over here . . .'

'Don't you *dare*!'

'Why not? Just letting him know we've seen him.' Mae pirouetted cheekily on her skates. 'Come on, let's take a turn round the rink. We might *bump into* somebody interesting . . .'

'I . . . oh! . . . I can't!'

'Let go of the rail, Jenny, it's easy!'

'I can't, honest, I can't.'

With immense difficulty, Jenny managed to detach one hand from the rail, waving it about to stop herself overbalancing. By now she had attracted a gaggle of small children, all of them fascinated and offering their own brand of advice.

''Seasy, yer just let go.'

'Kick yer 'eels, it skids a bit but yer can balance wiv yer arms.'

'Strap a cushion to 'er backside, then lass won't 'urt herself when she falls over.'

'Don't know why she's botherin'. Girls can't roller-skate for toffee.'

'Can!'

'Can't!'

'Flippin' can!'

'Flippin' can't!'

'Can, Terry Porteous, can, can, can!'

'Well, this one can't,' said Jenny cheerfully. 'If I let go, I'll fall on my bum.'

'Told yer,' said young Terry with obvious satisfaction, sticking out his tongue at his small sister.

'But it's so *easy*,' pleaded Mae. 'Isn't it, Mr Costigern?' she added with a charming smile as a long-limbed figure skated across the rink towards them.

'Mae!' hissed Jenny, furious and embarrassed. But Mae beckoned Henry across.

'Isn't that right, Mr Costigern? Roller-skating's easy.'

Henry slid smoothly to a halt with a slick half turn, catching hold of the rail with his right hand. He looked cool, handsome and athletic with his rolled-up shirt-sleeves and light grey flannels.

'Having a spot of bother?'

'Jenny says she can't do it, but I know she can,' said Mae. 'I bet Mr Costigern could show you how,' she added with a look that contained a dozen shades of meaning.

'Bet I could too,' nodded Henry. 'Tell you what, Jenny, why don't you let go of that thing and take my hand?'

'N-No, it's very kind of you, but I don't think I'm cut out for roller-skating.'

''Course you are, you just need to get the hang of it. Go on, let go with your right hand and take mine. I won't let you fall – promise.'

'Go on, Jenny,' urged Mae. 'I can see you're in capable hands.'

154

Jenny threw Mae a murderous look, but she just kept on smiling, with that wicked twinkle in her eye. I'll get my own back on you for this, Mae Corlett, vowed Jenny, but she did as Henry asked and held out her right hand. He caught it and held it fast.

'Right-ho, now the other one.'

'I'd rather not.'

'How am I going to teach you to skate if you won't let go of the rail?' With the gentlest insistence, Henry prised her remaining fingers from the rail and captured her hand. He was facing her, holding her with both hands, the only thing stopping her from falling. 'Good. Now try sliding your right foot forward . . . just a few inches . . .'

She tried. It slid forward with such suddenness that she almost did the splits, and let out a squeak of alarm.

'Oh! Oh, I . . .'

'That's it, you're doing fine. Look down at my feet. When I slide my left foot back, you slide your right foot forward, does that make sense?'

Jenny nodded, and they began skating, painfully slowly, towards the centre of the immense rink. She was convinced that everybody was staring at her ungainly efforts, but she was concentrating so hard on Henry's feet that she had no opportunity to look left or right.

'Now the left foot, that's it . . . and the right . . . that's wonderful! You're really getting into the swing of it now.'

'Don't let me go . . .'

'I won't.'

They paused, and Jenny stole an upward glance at Henry. His sandy hair was dishevelled about his flushed face, and he looked more boyish than ever; but the look in his velvety brown eyes held something deeper, something much more complex . . .

'Perhaps we ought to go back now – I can try again tomorrow.'

'Nonsense! More practice, that's what you need. Come on, let's try you out on the Boulevard, it's nice and straight there . . .'

There was no point in protesting. Henry was already

155

towing her off the skating rink like a stranded vessel, towards the broad, straight road which led from the camp administration offices to the main gate and out beyond towards Llandew railway station. All she could do was giggle breathlessly, and try to stop her feet skidding from under her.

'Mr Costigern . . .'

'Henry.'

'Henry, if you don't slow down I'm going to fall over!'

'You won't. I won't let you.'

'I *will*.'

'Then I'll pick you up again.'

The Boulevard stretched out before them like a wide white ribbon, laid flat on the gently sloping ground between the two rows of saplings which would eventually grow into tall lime trees.

'I'm moving . . . I can't stop!'

'Just let yourself roll forward, that's it. Now I'm going to let go with just one hand, I've still got hold of you . . .'

'Henry . . .'

'There, see, you can do it.'

'Henry, will you listen to me . . . there's a car coming!'

And there was. A red, open-topped Bugatti with frog-eye headlamps and highly polished chrome that glinted in the afternoon sunlight. The horn sounded once, twice, three times; the irritable sound of someone in a hurry.

Henry swung Jenny to the side of the road as the car slowed to a stop. The woman in the driving seat was dressed like a Paris fashion-plate, with white driving gloves and a gauzy scarf draped over her tight golden curls.

'Henry!'

All the colour seemed to drain out of his face.

'*Mother!* What on earth . . .?'

The woman leant out of the car and offered her cheek.

'Don't you have a kiss for your dear mother, Henry? And don't stand there with your mouth open, have you forgotten all your manners?' She took in her surroundings with a series of sharp, critical glances. 'I always told your father this place was a bad influence on you.'

Jenny looked at Henry. He was obviously very, very uncomfortable.

'I'll . . . perhaps I'd better go,' she suggested.

Henry shook his head.

'No, stay, it's all right.'

He was still holding her hand, refusing to let go of it. When he spoke again, Jenny noticed an edge of anger in his voice.

'Mother, why didn't you let somebody know you were coming?'

'Really, Henry, I might have expected a warmer welcome from my own son.'

'We haven't heard from you in months, Mother! You didn't even write.'

'Well, I'm home now, dear. I'm sure we can make up for lost time.'

Jenny felt the woman's gaze fall upon her, the eyes weighing her up and finding her wanting.

'Aren't you going to introduce me to your . . . little friend, Henry?'

He smiled at Jenny and pushed her forward.

'This is Jenny, Mother. Jenny Fisher. She's one of the singers in the variety show.'

'Yes. Yes, I can see that.' The words were cutting in their tacit dismissal; Jenny had to rein in a sudden impulse to slap the woman across her smoothly powdered face. 'Well, I can't stay here chatting all day, I must go and see your grandfather.'

The Bugatti leapt forward and charged on up the Boulevard, leaving dusty tracks where its tyres had bitten into the roadway.

'That was Miranda Costigern.' It wasn't so much a statement as an apology, thought Jenny. Whatever was going on, she wasn't at all sure she wanted to be part of it. 'My . . . er . . . mother.'

'I think I'd better go now,' she said gently, detaching her hand from Henry's.

'Really, there's no need.'

'Oh, I think there is,' she replied, and unbuckling her roller-skates, walked back towards the skating rink.

157

Nancy had thought she would never get to bed. With Mam away at Auntie Jane's and the kids to look after and Ivan and Tom to wash and cook and clean for, she hadn't had a moment to herself all day. Sometimes she thought it was better that way. The busier she was, the less time she had to think.

She lay in the bed that had been Jenny's, staring up into the darkness. Her body was exhausted and aching, longing for sleep, but her mind refused to let her escape. Perhaps that was her punishment.

Oh, Jenny, she whispered silently. Jenny, I'm sorry now for all those terrible things I said to you. I wish I hadn't said them and made you go away for ever . . . but I was angry, and now I can't stop being angry. You were always the favourite, weren't you? Dad's little favourite. I was so jealous that I really hated you sometimes, did you realise that? And I'm hating you now. Did you know how *glad* I was when Dad died, just because you wouldn't have his love any more?

Nancy rolled on to her side. The tears on her cheek soaked into the pillowslip and she sniffed them away. Why did it hurt, why did everything have to hurt so much?

Cinderella, she told herself. That's what you are, Jenny Fisher; Cinderella. Why did it have to be you who got away? Everything always goes right for you in the end. Why couldn't it be me instead?

Why couldn't *I* be the princess, just for once in my life?

Chapter 14

Ivan Price was an important man and he knew it.

As pit overman, he was responsible for over ninety colliers in one of the mine's "districts"; and any man who wanted to get on in his job knew that he would also have to get on with Ivan Price.

The colliery under-manager rarely ventured underground, and that was how Ivan liked it. Men with soft hands and suits had no place down the pit.

'You wanted to see me, Mr Forbes?' The whites of Ivan's eyes gleamed in his coal-caked face.

The under-manager scanned the underground roadway in the beam from his Davey lamp. Bare-chested labourers were hard at work in the sweaty darkness, some completely naked, their bodies streaming with rivulets of perspiration as they hauled timbers to shore up the roof.

'Any problems in your district?'

'No, Mr Forbes.'

'Those timbers – regulation distance apart, are they?'

'You know me, sir, never cut corners where my men's safety's concerned.' The corners of Ivan's mouth twitched in an ironic smile, then it was gone.

'Glad to hear it. How's the seam holding up?'

'Plenty of coal. We're havin' to work harder to get it out, mind. Still, my men understand 'ard work.'

'No agitators, then?'

'They wouldn't dare! They know if they don't toe the line, I'll have 'em out, see.'

Mr Forbes nodded slowly, approving Ivan's words with a thin-lipped smile.

'You're a hard man, Ivan Price. I can see we'll have no troublemakers in this district.'

When the under-manager had gone, Ivan made his way down the line of coal-tubs and sought out Phil the roadman.

'Remember that little favour we talked about the other night?'

'Yes, Mr Price.'

Ivan reached into his pocket and handed over a numbered tally.

'Do it now, and we'll see if we can't forget about that three pounds you owe me.'

Tom whistled softly to himself. Piecework suited him. He prided himself on working hard, and today had been a better day than most. For every tub he'd filled, he and his drawer would receive a bonus, and this week's bonus would be a good one – even Ivan Price couldn't put a dampener on his optimism.

'Tom. TOM!'

He caught sight of one of the daywagemen, signalling to him, and turned off the coal-cutting machine.

'What is it?'

'You've been called up out o' mine.'

'Why?'

'Summat to do wi' weigh-house.'

Puzzled, Tom made his way back along the underground roadway to the pit-bottom, passed Ivan's office and took the long, slow journey back up to the surface in the cage. He felt irritated, knowing that he was losing valuable coal-cutting time; whatever was going on, it was obviously some mistake.

He blinked in the daylight for a few moments before crossing the yard, past the fan-house and the stables, to the weigh-house.

'Tom Fisher?'

'What about it?'

'You're tally number fifty-three?' The weighman picked the numbered tally out of the tub. He was examining it suspiciously.

'Aye, that's mine.' Tom stepped forward. 'Summat wrong, is there?'

'This tub's weighing over-heavy. We'll have to tip it out.'

Tom stared as the coal-tub was upended on the ground. At least half of what came out wasn't coal at all, but dust and wet, heavy dirt.

'It's full o' scuftings,' said the weighman, kicking the pile of dirt with the toe of his boot. 'Over half dirt, by look of it.'

'That's not mine!' protested Tom. 'I put nowt but coal in my tubs.'

'It's got your tally in it, lad, so it must be your tub – I wouldn't have thought it of you, mind. Never 'ad you down as a shirker.'

'Now look here . . .'

The checkweighman confirmed what the weighman had said.

'Sorry, Tom lad, you'll be off home wi' no pay today.'

'Somebody must've . . .'

'Go home, lad. Don't make trouble for yourself. You'll make up some o' money tomorrow.'

Still disbelieving the evidence of his own eyes, Tom walked very slowly back to the lamp-house and handed in his safety lamp. Make trouble for himself? It looked very much as if somebody round here was already doing that for him.

He thought of Ivan Price's smug expression as he'd stepped into the lift cage, and had a shrewd idea who that somebody might be.

'Happy to see you!' chorused from the bowling green and the swimming pool as Jolly Jimmy Costigern and his family paraded around the camp on their regular Sunday afternoon stroll. Jolly Jimmy beamed, oozing munificence as he shook hands with all and sundry; he was always at his happiest when he was passing the time of day with the people who'd helped to make him rich.

'Happy to see you, Mrs . . .?'

'Call me Irene.'

'And these are your children?'

'That's right, Terry and Gwen. Say hello, Gwennie. Terry, stop picking your nose.'

Jolly Jimmy ruffled two shocks of tousled brown hair, much to the small boy's indignation. Jimmy affected not to notice the pink tongue sticking out at him.

'Enjoying yourself, young fellow?'

Mrs Porteous glared at her son and raised her hand as if to slap him. Terry knew better than to annoy his mother.

'Yes, fanks, Mr Jimmy.'

'Good lad. Here's sixpence, buy your sister an ice-cream.'

The procession carried on through the camp: Jolly Jimmy striking out in front, with James and Henry following rather more reluctantly in his wake. Gwen Roberts, who was helping with children's team games outside the Fun House, noticed that there was a fourth member of the group today: Henry's mother, Miranda.

As she handed out the prizes of sticky lollipops and balloons, Gwen took the opportunity to get a proper look at Miranda Costigern. She must have been in her early forties, but was the most glamorous creature Gwen had ever seen – the sort of woman who dressed to be noticed. In any case, news spread like wildfire round Costigern's Camp, you couldn't keep anything quiet for long; and what with Jenny Fisher practically getting run over by her, the news of Miranda's arrival had reached everyone within the hour.

Despite working at Costigern's for three seasons running, Gwen had only ever seen Miranda once before; *that* was how often James Costigern junior's wife showed her face in the camp. There was a lot of gossip about her and Mr James, what with them hardly ever being in the same place for more than five minutes. And to judge from the expressions on their faces, they weren't much enjoying each other's company today. She blew her whistle for the egg and spoon race, but kept half an ear open to catch any juicy snippets of conversation.

'You'd think he was Queen Victoria, to look at him,'

commented Miranda loudly to Henry. He looked embarrassed and tried to shush his mother, but James swung round and glared at his wife.

'If you insist on coming round the camp with us, you might at least enter into the spirit of things,' he hissed.

His expression changed to a charming smile as a young married couple greeted him with a cheery: 'Happy to see you!'

'Happy to see you too.' He smiled. 'Hope you're having a jolly time with Jimmy . . .'

'*I* didn't insist on anything,' sniffed Miranda, ignoring the young couple and turning her back on their gurgling baby. 'It's your father who expects everyone to behave like grinning imbeciles.'

If Jolly Jimmy heard this exchange, he gave no sign of it. He just strolled on, dispensing smiles and sixpences as the mood took him. Henry followed some way behind; he seemed torn between wanting to please his grandfather and trying to stop his parents scratching each other's eyes out.

'If you can't make the effort to be civil,' snapped James, 'I don't know why you bother coming home at all. Your society friends sick of you sponging off them, are they? Or are you just bored with living it up in the Mediterranean?'

Miranda's eyes flashed a danger sign.

'We both know why I've come back,' she said. 'Though how you can call this place home . . .'

'The answer is no, Miranda. It was no yesterday, and it will be no tomorrow. Now keep your voice down, the campers are staring at us.'

Miranda laughed, but there was only anger in the sound.

'So they are,' she observed, and looked down her nose at the mother of two toddlers who were tugging at the hem of her skirt. 'You know, dear, you really shouldn't let them chew with their mouths open – they look just like cattle.'

'What!'

James junior stepped in, mollifying the young woman with smiles and blandishments. When she had gone, he swung round to face Miranda.

'One more word from you and I'll . . .'

'You'll what?' Her smile was glacial and victorious. 'Give me a divorce?'

Jolly Jimmy and Henry had stopped to banter with the parents of the winning children's team. Gwen and her fellow Stripeys stood to attention respectfully, like troops being reviewed by the King, but it was James and Miranda Costigern who kept drawing everyone's attention.

'Happy to see you, er . . .?'

'Sonia. Happy to see you, Mr Costigern.'

James bestowed his suavest smile on a teenage girl in a pink print frock.

'Charmed to meet you, Sonia. That's a very pretty dress.'

'Thank you.' The girl blushed to the roots of her strawberry-blonde hair.

'And where are you from?'

'Birkenhead, Mr Costigern.'

'Having a jolly time?'

'Oh, wonderful, really lovely. We've nothink like this at home, It's just like . . . like . . . oh, it's . . .'

'Glad to hear you're enjoying yourself. Perhaps I'll see you again before you leave.'

If he had deliberately attempted to infuriate Miranda, he couldn't have done it more successfully, thought Gwen Roberts. You could see from the look on her face that she wanted to smack her husband's face – and that of the pretty girl in the pink dress. She strained her ears to listen, wondering what Jolly Jimmy was making of it all.

'Still up to your sleazy little games, James? I'd have thought you'd have better taste.'

'I don't know what you're talking about.'

'Oh, really? Don't bother denying it, James, you always were a hopeless liar. And a letch. I know what you've been up to with these cheap little factory-girls . . .'

'What!' He rounded on her so furiously that every eye within fifty yards turned to the warring couple. Even Jolly Jimmy couldn't pretend he hadn't noticed. Not that either James or Miranda seemed to care. '*You* dare accuse *me* of . . . of . . .'

'Infidelity, James. Or do you prefer "adultery"? I believe

164

that's what the lawyers call it.'

'How dare you! Everyone knows what you did when we lived in Hampstead, and with whom . . .'

'Ah, but James, whatever I did in the past, I did discreetly.' She was sneering at him now. 'Not like you, with your taste for common little sluts.'

'You foul-mouthed hag!'

Gwen caught her breath. James was actually raising his hand, curling the fingers into a fist; surely he wasn't going to strike his own wife, right in front of several dozen campers? Somewhere behind her, someone giggled nervously.

''E's goin' ter slap 'er one! 'E is, tha knows!'

It was Jolly Jimmy who intervened, voice booming through the sudden silence. Henry trailed behind him, eyes downcast and face flushed with suppressed rage or embarrassment, it was difficult to tell which.

'Get over to the tennis courts, James – you're umpiring the mixed doubles in ten minutes,' commanded Jolly Jimmy, taking James by the arm and stepping between him and Miranda. The look he gave his daughter-in-law was more expressive than a thousand expletives, but Miranda just kept on staring back at him, bright-eyed and defiant.

'I'll see you later then,' she said brightly. And turning on her expensively shod heel, sauntered off in the direction of the chalet lines, leaving Henry and Gwen standing amid a crowd of wide-eyed, open-mouthed campers.

'Come on, Ray, come on, Ellie, on you get.'

'Lift us up, lift us up!'

'Oh, all right. Hold tight then.'

Jenny picked up the sturdy four year-old and lifted her into one of the seats in the tiny railway carriage. Jolly Jimmy's miniature steam railway ran all round the perimeter of the camp and right along the seashore, and was a tremendous hit with the kids.

'Me next!'

'Come on then, chop-chop and lickety-spit.'

'Wanna sit a' front . . . next t'engine . . .'

Small children swarmed about Jenny's legs, pulling at her yellow skirt and striped blazer with the monogrammed blue "CC" on the pocket. They were unruly, badly behaved, happy as Larry and screeching their tiny heads off – and no doubt their parents were delighted to be free of them for the afternoon. But Jenny was happy enough to play "mum" for an afternoon; she liked little kids . . . they reminded her of visits to Stanley Park with Billy and Daisy when they'd been the same age.

The engine driver blew the whistle with a shrill blast of steam. Sitting astride the first carriage – it was too small for an adult to sit in – Jenny held little Ellie on her lap.

'All aboard.'

'Toot-toot!'

'Choo-choo!'

'Hold on tight now!'

Just as the train was about to move off, a long-legged figure vaulted over the white picket fence and came bounding up to the engine.

'Just a mo', driver . . .'

'Henry!'

'Room for one more?'

The engine driver winked.

'Go on then, Mr Costigern, seein' as it's you.'

Henry scrambled aboard the train. Grabbing hold of the nearest available child, he sat behind Jenny and plonked it on his knee. Seconds later, the train began chugging slowly out of 'Jolly Jimmy's Junction'.

'Thought I'd missed you,' said Henry as the train snaked between the bowling greens and headed off towards the shoreline and the sea. Llandew Point stretched out in the distance, its rocky outline reduced to a hazy green line in the sunshine. Jenny looked back over her shoulder at Henry, one hand holding on to Ellie and the other trying to keep the hair from blowing across her face. She looked at him curiously. He seemed not quite himself, a bit agitated.

'Is something the matter? You're as red as a beetroot.'

'Am I? I've just escaped from Grandpa's Sunday afternoon walk, that's all. Aren't you pleased to see me?'

'Of course.'

She looked away, not sure that she should let him know just *how* pleased she was to see him. After all, they'd only met a few times and Henry's mother had made it very clear that she didn't think much of her only son associating with a common show-girl.

'Look, look, I can see the sea!' Ellie waved her short, fat arms at the horizon. As the train chugged over the hill and down the slope, the shore and the sea came into panoramic view, an expanse of blue-grey water sparkling in the afternoon sunshine.

'Yes, the sea, Ellie, isn't it lovely?' Jenny screwed her head round to look at Henry. 'You know, I've been here almost a fortnight and I still haven't even had a paddle! I've been so busy . . .'

'You're free on a Wednesday afternoon, aren't you?'

'Yes, but . . .'

'Let's go for a swim then. I could bring a picnic, if you like? We could eat on the sands.'

'Well.' Jenny thought of Miranda Costigern's disdainful expression. 'I'm not sure.'

'Oh, go on. Say you will?'

It was a lovely afternoon, thought Jenny. Perfect. The sun was beating down on her neck and shoulders, making her feel relaxed and lazy and excited, all at once. What's more, the children's unbridled enjoyment was infectious.

'All right then.' She smiled as the tiny steam-engine took the bend and began chugging along past the bathing huts. 'All right then, why not?'

'Hmm,' said Sid Dukes, unscrewing the mouthpiece of his cornet and tapping out the spittle. 'That wasn't bad . . . but it wasn't good either.'

The band shuffled restlessly in their seats, muttering to each other about "ruddy perfectionists" and "blood out of a stone". Jenny exchanged sighs with Bella and Pauline. They were sitting on the edge of the stage, waiting for their next number to be rehearsed. Mae attracted Jenny's attention and pulled a face – the one that signalled 'Watch it, Sid's in one of his moods'.

'It was note-perfect,' protested Geoff Tait from the piano stool.

'The horns were flat, the tempo dragged, and you can do a lot better. Right. Saturday's programme.' Sid reached into his music case and pulled out a sheet of paper. 'I'm making a few changes.'

This was greeted with groans and sotto voce comments from the back, and Jenny couldn't help noticing the look of annoyance on Geoff Tait's face. Did he and Sid ever see eye to eye about anything?

'*More* changes?'

'What's wrong with the numbers we've rehearsed?'

'I've only just got the hang of the last lot . . .'

'Now,' said Sid, glancing down the new running order, 'as I see it, the programme's too samey. We're giving 'em two hours of the same stuff. What's needed is a bit more variation.'

'What they want,' countered Geoff, 'are good, up-tempo numbers they can dance to. And plenty of new tunes.'

'They want some new stuff, sure they do. But that's not *all* they want. They want something they can sit and listen to as well, especially the older campers. That's why I've decided to reinstate a few of our more established numbers.'

'*Established?*' There was no mistaking the sneer in Geoff Tait's voice.

'That's right – a couple of the popular classics we tried out in the lunchtime concerts, one or two of the old music hall numbers for the campers to sing along to . . .'

'Dead music for dead people! I might have guessed.'

Geoff Tait's reply was muttered so softly that it was scarcely audible beyond the front row of the band, but Sid wasn't going to let him get away with it. Jenny had never seen him look so angry or so hurt.

'Was there something you wanted to say, Geoff?' Sid's voice shook with angry sarcasm. 'I mean, if an expert like you's got something really *important* to say, I think you should share your pearls of wisdom with the whole band.'

'You're making a mistake, Sid.' There was ambiguity in Geoff's words, a spark of contempt in his eyes. 'A big mistake.'

A fat, worm-like vein was pulsing at Sid's temple. Jenny looked at him and felt quite frightened. His face had turned an unhealthy red and was running with sweat; his lips were wet with spittle. Glancing across at Mae, Jenny saw that her jaw was set, her facial muscles tense and clenched.

'So you think it's a mistake, do you?' Sid slammed down the lid of the baby grand, narrowly missing Geoff's fingers. 'Well, you know what you can do if you don't like the way I run things. You can get out and stay out – and let me tell you, Geoff, you won't be missed!'

Jenny saw that Sid was breathing heavily as he turned and marched away from the band.

'Take five.'

Sid disappeared through a side door into the corridor which led down to the dressing rooms.

'Oh, God. Not again, please . . .' murmured Mae.

'Mae?' Jenny turned to question her friend, but Mae was already on her feet and half walking, half running after Sid. 'Dolly, what's happening?'

She shrugged.

'Don't ask me, kid.'

Alarm bells sounded in Jenny's head. Against her better judgement, she sprang up and went after Mae. As she went through the door she could hear her friend's voice in the distance.

'Sid? Sid, are you all right? Sid, please . . .'

The door of his dressing room stood wide open. Jenny stopped with a gasp at the sight of Sid Dukes slumped over a chair, his face purplish-red and streaked with sweat, his shoulders heaving with the sheer effort of breathing. His hand was clasped across his chest, over the place where his heart must be, and Mae was bending over him, unfastening the collar of his shirt.

'Mae . . . Sid . . .'

Mae turned abruptly towards the door. She looked pale

and drawn, her eyes bright with the effort of not crying. Seeing Jenny standing there, she made an effort to smile.

'Don't worry, everything's all right, Jenny. You get back to the practice.'

'But, Mae! Sid's ill . . . I'll get the doctor . . .'

'No,' he gasped, sitting up abruptly. 'No, everything's fine. This . . . it's not . . .'

'This just happens sometimes,' said Mae. 'When he and Geoff . . . you know. It just gets Sid a bit worked up, that's all. He'll be fine in a minute.'

He didn't look fine, thought Jenny; and one look at the expression on Mae's face made her doubt that she believed it either.

Chapter 15

After the late-afternoon sing-along show, Jenny took herself off to the shower block for a nice, hot soak.

As the water thundered into the bath, she hummed happily to herself. She still couldn't get over the sheer luxury of being able to have a bath whenever she wanted it; and not just a lukewarm wash in front of the fire, in water that three other people had already bathed in. This was real, fresh, hot water out of gleaming taps that never seemed to run cold.

Mae had been right about Sid's funny turn, after all, and that was a big relief. By curtain-up, he'd seemed as right as rain and Geoff Tait hadn't said another word, so everything was sweetness and light . . . for the moment at least.

Jenny tested the temperature with her toe, slid under the water and luxuriated in its warmth. As she began washing herself, she found the same tune slipping into her mind again and again. A happy, carefree little tune – the song Geoff Tait had written especially for Joss Flynn.

' "*Let me be your butterfly . . .*" ' she sang to herself. No, wait, that wasn't quite right – it was a C sharp, not a C natural. ' "*Let me be your butterFLY.*" ' That was better, though she always had trouble with the little twiddle at the end. ' "*Your flutter, butter, butterFLY, and you can be my BEE.*" '

It was such a simple, almost childish song to listen to, but it was deceptively difficult to sing. Joss made a good job of it, thought Jenny; it was just as well she was only the understudy and would never have to stand up and sing it in public.

' "*Be my BEE, my honey BEE* . . ." ' She arched her back to reach the difficult bits with her sponge, practising the same phrase again and again. ' "*My honey BEE* . . ." '

The sound of laughter outside the cubicle made her stop in mid-note, suddenly embarrassed. She must have been singing at the top of her voice, whatever would the campers think?

But it wasn't a camper's voice which sang back at Jenny through the thin plywood door. It was a voice she knew only too well, and it made her heart sink to the bottom of the big enamel bath.

' "*My honey BEE*," ' came an imitation of her own voice, cruelly exaggerating her intonation and emphasising the mistakes she'd made.

'Joss?' Jenny sat bolt upright in the bath. 'Joss, is that you?'

'Right first time, honey BEE.' Joss kicked open the cubicle door and leant against the doorframe. She looked leggy and coolly beautiful in a sleeveless top and soft, wide-legged trousers. ' "*Honey BEE*," ' she sang with cruel precision. ' "*Honey BEEEEE*." '

'Joss, don't!'

'Don't what, Jenny dear? Don't show you what a pathetic little amateur you really are? Face it, darling, I'm doing you a favour. You ought to thank me.'

All of a sudden, Jenny felt cold and shivery. She wrapped her arms about herself, but was all too painfully aware of her nakedness and vulnerability.

'Did you want something?' she demanded, determined not to let Joss Flynn get the better of her.

'Only a little word in your ear, darling,' Joss smiled with the sweetest hint of venom. 'Just to remind you.'

'Remind me – about what?'

Joss looked down on her, smile hard and fixed.

'You were singing *my* song, Jenny.'

'I was only practising . . .'

Joss silenced her with a look.

'My song, my band, my show. Got that?'

'Yes, but . . .'

'Good. Now make sure you don't forget it.'

That night, Jenny sat down at the tiny table in the chalet. The sheet of writing paper looked very white and very blank under the feeble glow of the table lamp.

'Are you *ever* coming to bed?' grumbled Mae sleepily from her bunk.

'In a minute. I'm having another go at that letter.'

'Well, get a move on and switch off that bloody light,' muttered Bella. 'Some of us want our beauty sleep.'

'Some of us,' commented Dolly drily, 'need it more than others.'

'Flamin' cheek!' Bella lobbed a cushion at Dolly, but it bounced off the wall and fell on Gwen's upturned face, provoking fits of giggles.

'Shush, I'm trying to *think*,' said Jenny, biting the end of her pen.

'Oh, Lor',' groaned Dolly. 'We'll be here all night.'

Ignoring the jests and jibes, Jenny got up from the table and reached under her bunk. Her best shoes were safe and sound in the box where she'd left them . . . but what about the money? A shiver of relief ran through her as she felt the thin roll of paper and the few coins pushed down into the toe of the right shoe. It wasn't much, but it was all she had, every penny she'd managed to save since she arrived at Costigern's Camp.

How should it be shared out? There'd be ten shillings for Molly O'Brien – no, fifteen, it was the least Jenny could do for the O'Briens after all they'd done for her. Molly must have the money, but would she take it? Jenny would have to find some way of making sure that she did.

And then there was Daisy and Billy . . . and Nancy; sullen-faced, unhappy Nancy who hated her so much and blamed her for every bad thing in the world. There must be something she could do for them, too. Even if Ivan Price had curbed his temper since Jenny had left, he didn't amount to much as a stepfather.

The thought of Ivan made Jenny shiver. His threats still burned in her memory and she certainly couldn't risk writing direct to Nancy or Mam or even Tom. Ivan would be sure to get hold of the letter, and that could only bring more trouble for everyone.

She sat down again and picked up her pen. Like Tom, she'd never been much of a writer. She could have asked Mae to write the letter for her, but was determined to do it herself.

'Dear Mr Corlett . . .' she began. She glanced at the small mound of money at her elbow. It seemed a huge responsibility. Such a small amount, yet it could make such a difference if she used it wisely.

Dear Mr Corlett,
I hope you are keeping well. I am well and so is Mae. She is showing me the ropes and we are settling in. The camp is so different from home, it takes a lot of getting used to.

Home? Where *is* home? Jenny wondered. Is it Gas Street, or Canal Terrace, or this tiny chickenwire chalet on the edge of nowhere?

'Mae says she's missing you and sends her love.' That much was true, at any rate. Whatever disagreements they'd had, Mae had always worshipped her father. All the same, Jenny thought she'd better not mention Sid Dukes to Mr Corlett, he probably wouldn't approve. 'The campers seem to like the show and it hasn't rained much.'

She paused. This wasn't why she was writing to John Corlett. Her pen moved steadily across the paper again as she got into her stride:

I've saved a bit of money and am sending it to you with this letter. I couldn't think of anyone else who would help me. Please could you make sure Molly O'Brien gets fifteen shillings? I know she will refuse the money, but please try to find a way – she has been very kind to me. If she won't take the money, perhaps she will take food instead.

The half-crown and the sixpence are to buy things for Billy and Daisy. You know how Billy loves his

174

toffees, and Daisy always used to buy sherbert lemons when she had tuppence off Mam or me. And liquorice torpedoes. I don't suppose they get pocket money off Ivan. Please could you keep the money behind the counter and make sure they get treats now and then? Perhaps it's best if you don't say it's from me, I don't want Ivan finding out.

Please, please look out for them and tell me if there's anything else they need. Those kids mean the world to me.

There was still a ten-shilling note left, thought Jenny. She visualised herself folding it and popping it into her purse, crisp and brown and capable of buying all sorts of nice things. Face powder or stockings . . . lipstick . . . sticky buns. Yes, if she had any sense, she'd keep it for herself.

The rest of the money is for Nancy. Ten bob's not much, I know, but it might buy her something she wants. She won't take the money off me, she blames me for everything, but perhaps from you?

Thank you, Mr Corlett. You're a good, kind man and I'm sorry for what happened, really I am. Please look out for Tom and the little ones, and Mam. And Nancy.

There's no one else to look out for them, thought Jenny to herself. And rolling the coins inside the two ten-bob notes, she slipped them quickly into the packet before she had a chance to change her mind.

Miranda Costigern was standing in her bedroom, admiring herself in the mirror. Her father-in-law had such vulgar taste in furniture, but what could you expect from such a common little man? Still, even Jolly Jimmy's walnut-veneered wardrobe couldn't dim the brilliance of her reflection.

The past seven months in Greece had put highlights in her hair, and given her normally pale skin a fashionable golden glow which looked absolutely sensational against

175

the crisp white of her halter-neck evening gown. It was backless, cut low at the neck and skimmed her hips, giving her a long, lean, yet desirably feminine silhouette. Tonight, she thought with savage humour, even her husband might find her attractive.

Ah, yes. Miranda might be on the wrong side of forty, but you'd never know it to look at her. She'd worked damn' hard to take care of her body and it showed. Men everywhere fell at her feet, worshipped her, found her utterly adorable.

But would they still find her so irresistible in a few months' time? That was the question. Anger flared inside her as she ran her hand down over her flat, smooth belly. In a matter of months everything would be spoiled, the child would make its presence obvious, and her looks would be ruined for ever.

Little bastard, she thought. Little *bastard*.

Why should this happen to her? Why should she be made to pay for one small mistake? She must and would have her divorce and her financial settlement, whether James wanted it or not. But there was no way that he could be tricked into thinking the child was his. So it must be soon, if she was going to come out of this with her honour and – most of all – her financial independence assured. If he found out about the baby – the concrete proof of her infidelity – he'd divorce her for adultery and she'd be left without a penny.

She paced back and forth across the room. *Her* room. At least Jimmy hadn't insisted on her sharing with James – not that he would have been any happier with that arrangement than she. How was it possible for two people to loathe each other so heartily, and yet still stay married? It hadn't really mattered much until now, she'd been content to go along as they were and live on the generous allowance James paid her; but now, suddenly, everything had changed.

The clock on the wall above the bed read five past eight. Miranda checked her watch; it agreed. In ten minutes' time, fifteen at the outside, she would have to go down to dinner with Jimmy and James and the rest of the Costigern menagerie. Where was that man? Where *was* he? If he dared to let her down . . .

A knock at the door interrupted her train of thought. Miranda let out her breath in a gasp of mingled irritation and relief.

'Who is it?'

'Burkiss.'

'Come.' The door opened to reveal a young man with dark, wavy hair and a Costigern's striped blazer. 'Where have you been?'

'Couldn't get here earlier, Mrs C, the Ugly Face competition was running late and . . .'

'Shut up. And listen.' Miranda scrutinised the young man from head to toe. 'You know why I chose you?'

''Cause I'm . . . discreet?'

'Precisely. And because I know certain things about your petty criminal record which Jolly Jimmy might also be very interested to know. But, of course, he doesn't have to find out, does he, Burkiss? Not if you do as you're told.'

'Right, Mrs C.'

Sammy Burkiss had the effrontery to go on smiling like some kind of scouse gigolo. There was no denying the fact that he was very, very good-looking in a low-class sort of way, even charming if you liked your diamonds rough. Small wonder he'd talked his way into a job at Costigern's on the strength of a couple of forged references.

'If you do your job well, you'll be paid well. If you fail . . .'

'I won't let you down.'

'I'm glad to hear it.' Miranda felt close to smiling for the first time in quite a while. 'I want information about my husband's *activities*. You know the sort of activities I mean?'

'Bedtime activities, Mrs C.'

'Do whatever you have to, but find out what he's been up to and with whom. Names, places, dates, times, photographs. I want the evidence quickly, do you understand, Burkiss? And watertight.'

'Oh, I understand, Mrs C. Clear as crystal.'

'Good. And Burkiss—'

'Mrs C?'

'Make sure it's *dirty*.'

Chapter 16

It was just before the Tuesday afternoon rehearsal that Sid Dukes broke the news.

'Marvo's assistant's got mumps.'

'Nasty,' commented Bella, buckling up her tap shoes.

'Even nastier for her boyfriend,' giggled Mae.

'So one of you will have to stand in for her tonight,' said Sid. 'Any volunteers?'

The girls exchanged looks that said 'Not a chance'.

'Come on, girls,' said Marvo, his head appearing over Sid's left shoulder. 'It'll be a nice change from all that hoofing about.'

'I am *not* wearing that cat costume,' said Bella. 'And that's flat.'

'It can't be me,' said Mae promptly. 'Lindsey's about four inches shorter, the costume wouldn't fit.'

Jenny caught Marvo's gaze at just the precise moment that inspiration struck him. She knew that look only too well.

'Oh, no . . . not me!'

'You'll do, Jenny,' declared Marvo. 'You're just the right size. All right if I borrow her, Sid?'

He shrugged.

'I suppose it'll have to be. But, Dolly, you and Pauline'll have to double up on the melody lines tonight or the band'll drown you out. Oh, and Marvo—'

'Hmm?'

'You owe me one. A big one.'

In which case Marvo owes *me* at least a dozen, thought Jenny that night as she squeezed herself into Lindsey's cat

179

costume. Remember, she told herself, tonight you're not Jenny Fisher from Gas Street – you're Diana, Mysterious Cat-Woman of the East. Or, in other words, a girl in a black body-stocking with a tail sewn on to the backside, an alice-band with furry ears, and whiskers painted on to her face with grey make-up.

'I look . . .' Jenny struggled to find exactly the right word.

'Gorgeous?' suggested Mae.

'Enigmatic?' volunteered Bella.

'Stupid. I look absolutely stupid. And I'm going to trip over this tail, it's miles too long.'

'Never mind that, they'll think it's part of the act. Just try and remember what Marvo told you – the code. Have you got it straight in your head?'

'I *think* so.'

'You'd better be sure. The act depends on it.'

'That's Marvo's problem, not mine! I never wanted to do this in the first place.'

Jenny rehearsed the act in her head as she slouched along the corridor to Marvo's dressing room. It was an awful lot to get the hang of in one afternoon – she'd had no idea there was so much lowdown trickery involved in being Marvo the Memory Man. The verbal codes, the see-through blindfold, the hand signals, even the different tones of voice. So much for the Mysteries of the Mind! And there was such a lot to remember . . .

Marvo came out of his dressing room, resplendent in wide-legged trousers and a multi-coloured turban.

'Ready?'

'You're a rat, Marvo. A rotten sewer-rat.'

He eyed up the tight-fitting cat costume. It clung in all the nicest places.

'Does that mean you're going to pounce on me?' he enquired hopefully.

'Don't push it, Marvo. I might ask Lindsey to give you mumps.'

Jenny spent the first half standing in the wings with Marvo, half watching the other acts whilst mentally running through the divination routine. Pick the right kind of objects, hold them up, give Marvo the right code . . .

'It's a full house,' she commented, her mouth dry with apprehension. If anything she felt even more nervous than she had before her singing debut: at least when she was singing she knew what she was doing – whatever Joss Flynn might think about that.

'It's *always* a full house on a Tuesday, there's free beer and sandwiches in the Caribbean Bar afterwards. That's why there's so many young lads in tonight.'

They were on straight after the interval, and the audience – a rowdy lot – took some settling down; especially when the young men caught sight of Marvo's shapely new assistant. Wolf-whistles erupted from all corners of the theatre, and the front row started stamping their feet. Jenny could tell she was in for an eventful evening.

Harry Kaye bounded off-stage and Geoff Tait stood up to do the introductions, hamming it up for all he was worth while Desmond played *The Sheikh of Araby* on the soprano saxophone.

'LadEEZ and gentleMEN . . . Costigern's Camp is proud to present . . . Marvo's Mysteries of the Mind!'

Marvo was certainly a showman, Jenny had to admit that. Within the first minute of his act he had the audience on the edge of their seats, ooh-ing and aah-ing at the sight of him *apparently* hammering a six-inch nail right through his own hand. It was a good trick; so good that Jenny had almost fainted the first time she saw it.

This bit of the act was easy. All Jenny had to do was strike a few poses and hand Marvo his props. He levitated, he did the Indian rope trick, he fooled about with a bed of nails. But after Secrets of the Fakirs came Mysteries of the Mind. This was where her job began in earnest.

'And now, ladies and gentlemen,' announced Marvo, 'my beautiful assistant, the mysterious Diana, will apply the blindfold.'

Jenny knew what to do, Marvo had rehearsed this bit with her over and over again. The blindfold had to be put on in a special way, so that Marvo could see through a narrow, thinner band of gauze sewn into the thick black fabric. If he couldn't see through the blindfold, he wouldn't be able to make out the hand signals she gave him and the act would fall flat.

Marvo sat down cross-legged on a gold-tasselled cushion, raising his arms to receive "astral inspiration".

'The lovely Diana will now pass among you to gather items of personal and sentimental value.'

'Watch out, she'll 'ave yer wallet, mate!' called out one of the youths, but he was shushed into silence.

Jenny felt uncomfortably conspicuous as she walked down the centre aisle in her cat outfit. People were waving watches, handkerchiefs, brooches, a cigarette case, desperate to be chosen even though they knew it was all an elaborate con. As she reached over to take a woman's handkerchief, she felt a sharp tug on her backside, and a gale of raucous laughter erupted around her. Swinging round, she confronted the offender with a stony glare, but he just smiled back innocently.

'Summat up, love?'

Just managing to keep her temper in check, Jenny moved on and held up the handkerchief in the way Marvo had told her. Now, she must get those code words exactly right.

'Take your time, Marvo. Take your *time*. Tune in to my thought-waves.'

'Ah, yes. It is coming to me now.' Marvo raised his hands higher, palm upwards, as though receiving vibrations from the air around him. 'I see . . . I see a handkerchief . . .'

'And what can you *tell* me about it? Can you feel the vibrations, Marvo?'

'A woman's handkerchief. It belongs to a beautiful woman.'

The woman who owned the handkerchief could hardly have been described as beautiful, but she blushed and simpered and was plainly delighted when Jenny gave her back her hanky. People applauded warmly. All in all, everything was going quite nicely. It was as Jenny was holding up a man's wristwatch that she felt another tug on her tail.

'Will you *stop* that?' she hissed. This time the offender

was a red-haired youth in a blue shirt. He grinned back at her, displaying a gap where his front teeth ought to be.

'You can feel my vibrations any time you like, darlin'.'

Mocking laughter ran along the row of young men with their identical open-necked shirts and brilliantined hair. Friends, no doubt, from the same town – probably the very same factory or office. They were obviously egging each other on; Jenny wondered how Lindsey put up with this kind of nonsense night after night.

Snatching her tail from his grasp, Jenny took a deep breath and counted to ten. There was no way of getting to the owner of the cigarette case except by squeezing her way along the entire length of the row, past jiggling knees and wandering hands.

'Excuse me. *Excuse me.*' A young man was obstructing her way with his leg. She stepped slowly and deliberately on his foot, and he moved it with a muttered 'strewth' of pain. 'Excuse me, *sir*, if I could just get by, thank *you*.'

Standing beside the owner of the cigarette case, she held it up.

'Now, Marvo, what can you see? Are my thought-waves travelling to you across the dark sea of the mind?'

'Ah, yes, Diana, I see it clearly . . . a cigarette case . . . it's silver-plated . . .'

'Think *harder*, Marvo.'

'. . . no, not silver, it's chrome . . . and I can read the initials on it. They're . . . they're . . .'

Jenny really didn't mean to drop the cigarette case on that poor man's head, but at that precise moment a hand delivered a hearty slap to her bottom and she almost fell headlong into Row K.

This time they'd gone too far. Jenny saw red. Turning round, she confronted a whole row of grinning, sniggering faces.

'Summat wrong, darling?' enquired a fat-faced lout with a boil on the end of his nose.

'Only your manners,' she snapped back, whisking the end of her tail from between his pudgy fingers and flicking it across his smirking face.

'You what?'

She looked daggers at him.

'Is this the way you behave at home? Would you like someone to do that to your sister? Well, *would* you?'

For a split second, Jenny's blood froze as she realised that she had done The Unthinkable. She had actually lost her temper and shouted at a camper! Her mind reeled. The one rule that was constantly drummed into them was: no matter what the campers do, no matter how obnoxious they are, you must never, never, NEVER retaliate. She stared at the spotty youth in horror. He deserved it, right enough, but that was hardly the point. She'd really done it now . . .

'Bloody 'ell,' he yelped. 'She can't speak to me like that.'

He looked around for moral support, but suddenly the whole theatre was rocking with laughter and clapping wildly.

'Serves yer right!' shouted a woman from the back.

'That'll teach yer,' called out a middle-aged man in front of the youth. 'Nasty-minded little lout.'

'Tell 'im straight, lass, it's no more'n 'e deserves!'

Jenny darted an anxious glance at Marvo. He was quivering with laughter behind the blindfold. Sid Dukes was shaking his head reprovingly, but couldn't wipe the smile from his face. Relief washed over Jenny and with an impish curtsey to the audience, she crossed the aisle, held up a pair of cufflinks and carried on with the act.

Nancy Fisher cowered away from the kitchen table, her hands crossed defensively in front of her face.

'Please . . . please, Ivan, I'm sorry.'

'Sorry, girl? This is muck. Muck, d'you hear?'

He stood up, hurling the tin plate across the room. It crashed against the wall and bounced off, rattling to the floor in a slimy mess of tepid stew. Tom glared a silent warning to Billy and Daisy, who had been watching hungrily from the doorway, and they backed off into the passageway. They knew better than to stay around when Ivan Price was angry.

'I'm sorry, really I am.' A spark of the old Nancy

surfaced for one brief instant. 'It's the best I can buy with the money you give me.'

Ivan was unbuckling his belt.

'Back-chat me, would you, you little slut? I'll teach you a lesson you won't forget . . .'

'Ivan.' Tom was on his feet now. He couldn't just sit there and watch Ivan knock seven bells out of his sister. 'Leave her alone, she's done nowt.'

Ivan rounded on him, piggy eyes narrowed to slits of evil.

'What's that you said, boy?'

'I said, leave Nancy alone.'

'Keep out of this – or d'you want a taste of the strap an' all?' He wrapped the belt round his knuckles, savouring the look of terror on Nancy's face.

'Get out of the way, Nancy,' said Tom. But she just stood there, rooted to the spot, afraid to move a muscle. 'Nancy, are you listening?'

Ivan laughed, a rough growl of malice.

'Nobody's listenin' to you. You're nothin', Tom Fisher. You can't even fill a coal tub without toppin' it up with dirt . . .'

'You bastard,' hissed Tom. And anger enveloped him in a blood-red mist. He sprang forward, fist swinging up at Ivan Price's grinning face.

'Tom, don't!' squealed Nancy, and for a crucial moment he hesitated – long enough for Ivan to catch his fist and twist his arm behind his back in a single, brutal movement. Tom swore and struggled to free himself, but despite his youth and strength, Ivan's cunning had him beaten.

'I always said you were nothin' but a runt, Tom Fisher. A whining, useless whelp.' With a snort of contempt, Ivan let him go. ''Sides, boy, your sister 'ere knows I'm a fair man. It's your Nancy that's at fault, ain't that right, girl?'

Tom was angrier at himself than he was at Ivan. He should have kept his temper, should have known he'd come off worse in a brawl.

'Nancy, don't – you've done nowt wrong.'

For a moment, Nancy's eyes met his. They were full of a dull and silent desperation. He willed her to defy Ivan.

Together they could get the better of him, maybe even talk some sense into Mam when she came back from Auntie Jane's . . . but Nancy looked away and mumbled something.

'What's that, girl?' snapped Ivan.

Nancy raised her face and whispered the words a little louder.

'Yes, Dad.'

Ivan Price's face crinkled into a broad triumphant grin.

'See, boy?' He clapped Tom on the shoulder as though they were father and son. 'See? One big 'appy family, that's what we are.'

'Jenny . . . Jenny, come back here this minute!'

Laughing so hard she could scarcely breathe, Jenny dived off the end of the jetty and began swimming for the shore. Henry Costigern jumped in after her, but she knew he'd never be able to catch up with her; she'd been the strongest swimmer in her class at school, boys included.

It was a fine, hot day and the beach was crowded as she waded out of the water. There were more pebbles than sand, but nobody seemed to mind. It took more than pebbles to daunt the spirits of Costigern campers.

She turned towards the sea, pushing the wet hair out of her eyes.

'Slowcoach!' she laughed.

Henry was panting as he staggered out of the sea.

'Jenny, you *witch*. Wherever did you learn to swim like that?'

'In the Sankey Canal, of course!'

Henry wrinkled his nose.

'In a *canal*?'

'Where else? Tom threw me in as soon as I could walk, I soon got the hang of it.'

'Tom?'

'My big brother.'

'Oh.' Henry picked up his towel and shook the water out of his ears. 'Weren't you frightened?'

'No, all us kids learned that way; besides, he wouldn't have let me drown.'

186

'I should hope not!'

Wrapping a towel around her shoulders, Jenny flopped down on the sand.

'Where did you learn, then?'

'At school. We had this awful brute of an instructor who'd swum the Channel in December or something – he used to make us break the ice on the lake . . .'

Jenny shivered.

'I think I prefer the canal.' She waved and smiled back at some of the campers she recognised from the audience at the previous night's show. 'Happy to see you, Mrs G . . . you too, Rodney, glad you enjoyed the show, hello, Davey . . .'

'Jenny.'

'Hmm?'

'I'm not very fascinating, am I?'

She turned back.

'Oh, sorry, Henry, am I neglecting you?'

'Don't mind me, I'm just wildly jealous of those handsome young chaps.'

'Them? The campers?' Jenny put her hand over her mouth to stifle a giggle. 'Oh, Henry, that's silly. That one over there – the blond one, see?'

'What about him?'

'You can see Llandudno through those bandy legs. And that spotty lad tried to pinch my bottom in the show last night.'

Henry rolled on to his belly on the sand.

'What about me? What are *my* bad points?'

Jenny laughed.

'Yours? You haven't got any. You're a *gentleman*.'

'According to my father, that's the worst thing about me. He thinks being nice to people is a waste of effort.' Henry grimaced. 'You've probably noticed.'

'Well . . .' Jenny wasn't sure what to say. She thought of what Gwen Roberts had told her, and the rumours that were spreading like wildfire around the camp. 'I did hear something about him and Mrs Costigern last Sunday, by the Fun House . . .'

'I should think everyone in the camp's heard about it by now,' said Henry grimly.

'Sorry, I didn't mean to poke my nose in.'

'Don't worry about it, Mum and Dad don't. They fight like cat and dog and don't give a damn who hears.' He shook his head disbelievingly. 'I don't know why Mum came back. She's been gadding about the Continent for as long as I can remember. Besides, she and Dad can't stand the sight of each other.'

'Perhaps they're going to try and get along . . .'

'Fat chance.' Henry picked up a handful of pebbles and threw them into the sea with a sigh. 'Parents.'

'At least you've *got* parents.'

Henry looked up sharply.

'You and your mother – you don't get along?'

For a moment Jenny was tempted to tell Henry exactly why; to tell him all about Ivan's brutality and Mam's drinking, and spill out all her angers and anxieties and regrets. She was sure she could trust him . . . but not so sure that he would understand.

'It's a long story,' she said.

'Try me.'

'Some other time, maybe.' She leapt to her feet, determined not to let dark shadows fall across this sunny, happy day. 'Fancy another swim?'

'Why not?'

'Race you to the point.'

'You'll beat me hands down!' She felt Henry's hands on her arms, gently turning her round to face him. 'Jenny . . .'

She smiled back at him.

'Yes?'

'Jenny, listen. I like you . . . I *really* like you.'

'I like you too.'

'Can I . . . kiss you?'

For a dark and horrible instant, Ivan Price's leering face loomed into Jenny's mind and she heard the threatening hiss of his voice: 'If you can't earn me money, you'll make yourself useful in other ways.'

'Henry . . .'

188

'Please, let me kiss you.'

The dark shadow crept away as she looked into his innocent and guileless eyes. Henry Costigern was not Ivan Price. She wanted very much to kiss him, yet still something held her back. She dropped a tiny peck of a kiss on the end of his nose.

'You'll have to catch me first!' she laughed. And sticking out her tongue at him, she turned and scampered back towards the sea.

Chapter 17

It was Sunday morning and Joss Flynn was determined to look her best. She bent half-double in front of the tiny square of mirror, trying to get a better look at herself.

'Drat these horrible little chalets! Why can't they have proper mirrors? I'm the star of the show Geoff, I *ought* to have a proper mirror.'

Geoff Tait stood by the door of the chalet, arms folded.

'Calm down, Joss, you look wonderful. As usual.'

She darted him a small smile of acknowledgement.

'Are you sure the blue suits me . . . would I look better in the mauve with the matching toque?'

Geoff shrugged in an embarrassed, masculine kind of way.

'Don't ask me. I'm not even supposed to be in here. You look fine, really you do.'

Joss straightened up and turned first to the left, then the right, admiring her reflection as she smoothed the blue crêpe de chine over her sleek hips.

'It'll have to do, I suppose.' She looked Geoff up and down. 'You could at least put on a suit and tie.'

'Why? I'm not going anywhere.'

Joss's brittle smile faded.

'You said you'd come to the Sunday service.'

'No, I didn't,' he corrected her, firmly but gently. '*You* said it would be a good idea, *I* said not in a million years. I've not been near a church since Sunday school.'

'But Jolly Jimmy *always* goes to the open-air service on a Sunday morning, it'd be the ideal opportunity for you to talk to him.'

'No, Joss. Sucking up to Jimmy Costigern isn't the way to get things done. He's not stupid, he'd see straight through it.'

Joss pursed her lips, their natural rosebud shape accentuated by a hint of uncharacteristically chaste pink lipstick.

'You have to talk to him, Geoff. You know what about.'

'All in good time.' He shifted uncomfortably, but Joss wasn't letting the subject drop that easily.

'Sid's past it and we both know it. It's time for a younger man to take over.' She was right in front of him, practically jabbing her varnished fingernail in his chest. 'The opportunity's there and if you don't grab it now, somebody else will . . .'

'I said, no.'

'Are you telling me you're happy with the way Sid's running the band?'

Geoff said nothing. He couldn't deny the truth of what Joss was saying, but that didn't mean he liked the way she was going about it.

'And the show, Geoff – the songs he puts in – they're ten years out of date. He takes shop-girls off the streets and thinks he can turn them into professionals. He hasn't a bloody clue!'

'Just leave it, will you?' There was a warning note in Geoff's voice, but Joss ignored it.

'He's an old has-been. He's going nowhere and so is the band. But with you in charge and me as the star . . .'

'Sid Dukes gave me my first big break in the business. I owe him.'

Joss reacted with a burst of sarcastic laughter.

'Oh, so it's *gratitude* that's holding you back, is it? Come off it, Geoff! You owe Sid nothing. You've carried that band for four years, it's time you got something back.'

'Now listen, Joss . . .'

'Or are you as spineless as he is? Is that it?' Her blue eyes held the steely glint of naked ambition. 'Yes, that's it. When it comes down to it, you just don't have the guts to go out and take what you want.'

'Shut up, Joss.' Geoff's temper was always on a short

fuse, and she had lit the blue touch paper. His voice rose to a bark of rage, his fist driving into the flimsy wall of the chalet. 'Shut up!'

Joss squared up to him, her pink lips wet with spittle, taunting him the way she taunted every lover who didn't match up to her expectations.

'Or you'll make me? Don't make me laugh, Geoff. You're a loser, just like Sid Dukes.'

He caught her by the shoulders.

'Listen to me, Joss. I'm not afraid of anyone: not Sid, not Jimmy Costigern, and certainly not you.'

Joss said nothing. She just stared back at him, her blue eyes narrowing with satisfaction. He might not realise it, but she had Geoff just how she wanted him: fired up and angry enough to make things happen.

'When the time's right, I *will* put a band together. But I'll do this *my* way, understand? Not yours.'

He slammed the door behind him as he left Joss's chalet, walking slap-bang into two Stripeys.

'Happy to see you, Mr Tait, sir. Lovely morning, isn't it?'

One of the young men was looking at him in a way which made him wonder. Just how much had they heard? Those chalet walls were damnably thin . . .

'Get lost.'

He turned and walked, very quickly, in the direction of his own chalet.

Billy and Daisy Fisher were careful not to step on the cracks in the pavement as they chased each other down the street. Monsters lurked down between the flagstones, and Billy and Daisy knew more than most about monsters.

It was a lovely morning, and the sun was hazy in a patchy pale sky. Ivan Price would be at the pit all day with Tom, Mam was at Auntie Jane's waiting for the baby to come, and Nancy was busy doing the washing – so she had given Billy and Daisy housekeeping money to go to Mr Corlett's shop. It wasn't much money, but it dangled importantly in Daisy's pocket.

'Two slices corned beef, two pound of 'taters, carrot, loaf

of bread,' she chanted as she bounced along. 'Two pound of 'taters, loaf of bread, carrot, two slices corned beef . . .'

''Snot much,' commented Billy. ''Snot fair.'

'There's bread an' jam in pantry.'

'But Ivan'll get a whole slice of corned beef, an' Nancy always gives Tom hers an' says she's 'ad summat already. When I'm grown up,' he announced, 'we'll all live in a big house an' we'll 'ave meat an' 'tater pie *every* day.'

'All of us? Mam an' Nancy an' Tom an' you an' me?'

'All of us. But not Ivan.'

'No.' Daisy stared at the scuffed toes of her shoes. 'I don't like Ivan. But Mam does. Mam might want 'im to live in the big house too.'

It was with this thought that they reached the door of Corlett's Family Grocer's. The seductive aroma of freshly baked meat pies drifted halfway up the street; it was enough to set even the fullest of stomachs grumbling.

'Look at them pies!'

'An' them sticky buns . . .'

'An' the big jar of gobstoppers, an' the liquorice twist, an' the bags of toffees . . .'

'I want to go in first!'

'No, me!'

'Me!'

Scuffling like kittens in a basket, the two of them fell through the door, setting the shop-bell jangling and almost knocking over Old Mrs Pargeter, Father O'Leary's house-keeper from Lowe House Church.

'Saints preserve us!'

'Sorry, missus,' they chorused, helping her to collect her apples and onions and putting them back into her shopping basket.

'Ah, well, no harm done, I suppose.'

John Corlett watched them from behind the counter, waiting for Mrs Pargeter to leave and the shop door to jingle shut behind her.

'Well now, if it isn't Daisy and Billy. And what can I do for you?'

'Two pound of 'taters, two slices of corned beef,'

chanted Daisy. 'An' . . . an' . . .'

'. . . a carrot an' a loaf of bread,' cut in Billy helpfully.

'I know!'

'You forgot.'

'Didn't!'

'Did!'

Mr Corlett smiled to himself as he weighed out the potatoes and bagged them, sliding them into the string bag which Billy had brought with him. The carrot was popped neatly on top.

'There's your veg and your bread. Now, two slices of corned beef, was it?'

'Two, that's right.'

'How much have you got?'

Daisy uncurled her sticky palm to reveal the meagre collection of copper and silver. There was enough – but only just enough – to cover what the kids had bought. It was a tragedy, that's what it was; two men in that house earning good money, and Ivan Price drank or gambled away every penny of his wages, leaving Tom and Nancy with the burden of feeding the lot of them. Surreptitiously, he slipped an extra slice of corned beef into the greaseproof paper packet. With luck, Nancy would think he'd made a mistake.

Slipping the last of the packets into the string bag, Mr Corlett leant over the counter, beckoning the children closer.

'I bet you like sweets?' he asked.

Daisy and Billy nodded vigorously.

'Yes!'

''Course!'

'What sort do you like best?'

'Treacle toffees! An' mint balls . . .'

'Sherbert lemons!'

'Well, well.' John Corlett shook his head as if in wonderment. 'Isn't that funny? Because, do you know what?'

'What?'

'What, Mr Corlett?'

'Those are the very sweets that Jenny has sent you as a present.'

195

Two pairs of eyes became very round and bright.

'Jenny? Jenny! Is she coming back?'

'No. Not yet.'

'Jenny's gone away . . .'

'But she hasn't forgotten about you.' John Corlett reached under the counter for the two white paper bags of sweets. 'See? She sent these 'specially for you.'

Sticky fingers reached out, eyes widened with fascination.

'Where's Jenny gone, Mr Corlett?'

'I can't tell you – it's a secret. And you mustn't tell anyone about the sweets, that's a secret too.'

'Not even Tom?'

'Not even Nancy?'

'No, not even Tom or Nancy. It's a very big secret, understand?'

Two heads nodded solemnly.

'Promise?'

'Promise.'

Mr Corlett was speaking to them quietly and seriously now.

'Especially Ivan. You won't tell him you've had presents from Jenny, now will you? It's very important.'

Daisy shook her head. Billy drew himself up to his full height.

'Ivan give us strap,' he said. 'An' he 'it our Nancy. We wouldn't tell 'im owt.'

It was a rainy Tuesday evening, and Jenny was sitting in the Caribbean Bar.

On those evenings when there was no variety show, the band played for dancing. On these 'Happy to See You' nights, singers, dancers and Stripeys were all expected to dress up and do their darnedest to give the campers a holiday to remember.

Jenny was almost falling asleep as she sat at the bar, gazing into the depths of a glass of cherry brandy without having the energy to drink it. It had been pouring with rain for the past three days and everyone was having to work twice as hard to keep the campers happy. What with indoor sing-a-long sessions instead of bike hikes, and tea dances instead of pony rides, the Dukettes had their work cut out from the moment *Happy to See You* blared out of the tannoy system at seven o'clock sharp every morning.

Mae clapped a hand over her mouth.

'You know what, Jen? I'm bushed.'

'Me too. Think they'd notice if we slipped off back to the chalet for forty winks?'

'Jolly Jimmy notices *everything*,' said Mae darkly. 'Do you know, he's even been going through the kitchen rubbish bins to find out what meals the campers don't like! *And* he goes round with a torch after lights out, to see if he can catch any campers misbehaving behind the chalets.'

'You and Sid had better watch out then,' pointed out Jenny with humour.

Mae winked.

'Don't you worry – I'm an old hand at climbing in and out of windows in the dark. Remember at school . . . that time we got into the needlework room and put those worms in Miss Grainger's sewing box . . .'

'Yes, and Dodie Perks got locked in the stock-room and we thought we'd have to break down the door . . .'

'You know, I always hated needlework, but I'm glad I learnt it now. These Costigern uniforms fit where they touch.'

'Ah, well, they're not supposed to look good, are they?'

'How d'you mean?'

'Jolly Jimmy doesn't want us inflaming all those young men's passions, now does he?'

They were still giggling together when Mae noticed an elderly lady, sitting alone and sad beside the edge of the dancefloor.

'Duty calls. Looks like she's short of a dancing partner.'

'Shall I?'

'Not you, she doesn't want her bunions stepped on. You stay and finish your drink, eh?'

Jenny was grateful for a chance to sit and relax. Surreptitiously she eased off her shoes and wriggled her battered toes. Lost in a world of her own, she let her mind drift away from the music. She wondered how Mam was; the baby must be due in a few weeks' time. Her little brother or sister . . . well, half-brother or sister. The other half . . . the Ivan half . . . she didn't really want to think about. But it wasn't the kid's fault it had Ivan Price for a dad, was it? Any more than it was Jenny's fault that Mam had thrown her out for telling the truth.

'Penny for 'em.'

She jumped. One of the Stripeys was sliding on to the stool next to hers; a tall young man with an oil-slick of black hair – quite handsome in a way, though shifty-looking with it.

'Oh. Hello. Burkiss, isn't it?'

'That's right. Sam Burkiss. And you're Jenny, aren't you? I've seen you in the show. Buy you a drink, can I?'

She looked down at her half-empty glass.

'I've not quite finished . . .'

But he was already clicking his fingers and pushing a note across the bar.

'Same again, Tony. And a pint of best for me.' He settled himself on his stool, swivelling it round to get a better look at Jenny. 'Enjoying it here, are you?'

'Very much. I've made a lot of friends.'

He took a swig of beer.

'So I've heard. Friends in high places, eh?'

'What?'

'Come on, girl, everyone knows young Henry Costi-gern's sweet on you. Courting strong, are you?'

'I don't think that's any of your business!'

'No offence meant.' He sounded sincere enough. 'I was just wondering . . . you being close to young Henry and that . . . talks much about the family, does he?'

Jenny stared at him, puzzled and instinctively suspicious.

'Why do you want to know?'

'Oh. Just curiosity. I mean, the whole camp's talking about James and Miranda, aren't they? I just wondered if you might have heard anything?'

Jenny fiddled with her glass.

'I'm sure if there *was* anything, Henry wouldn't tell *me*,' she said. Sam Burkiss was beginning to make her flesh creep.

'Good-looking man, James Costigern,' commented Burkiss airily. 'Prime of life, well-off, knows how to treat a lady.'

'What're you getting at?'

He shrugged.

'Only that I can't see why any woman . . . any *attractive* woman like you . . . would choose the son over the father. If you ask me . . .'

'I didn't!'

'If you ask me, James is a far better bet for a young woman who wants to get on. Henry's just a young pup, he's still wet behind the ears . . . is that one . . .'

'What's that?'

Henry Costigern's voice cut Sam Burkiss's short. He looked up to find Henry practically standing over him, spare and handsome in his dark blazer and flannels.

'What was that?' repeated Henry. 'I didn't quite catch what you were saying.'

'I . . . er . . . nothing.'

Henry's eyes twinkled in the flashes of light from the sparkly glass ball which turned slowly on the ceiling.

'Care to dance, Jenny?'

She felt warmth wash over her; not just the sneaky, alcoholic burn of the cherry brandy she wasn't quite used to, but the delicious warmth of being with a man she really, really liked. She felt childishly excited as she took his hand and slid off the bar-stool.

'If you'll excuse me,' she said sweetly to Burkiss. He buried his face in his pint.

'What was all that about?' enquired Henry as they danced cheek to cheek, their bodies so close that they were almost one. There were dozens of couples on the floor, but the Caribbean Bar could have been empty for all the notice Jenny took of them.

'Oh, nothing really.'

'That Burkiss fellow . . . I thought I heard him mention my name.'

'Really?' She nestled her face into the crook of Henry's neck, breathing in the faint, lingering scent of expensive cologne. The scent of a gentleman, so different from a collier's sweat and carbolic. 'Let's not talk about him.'

'No, you're right.' Henry drew Jenny a little more tightly to him, and she felt the beating of his heart, almost as fast and frantic as her own. 'There are far more important things to do.'

He kissed her tentatively on the cheek, and she smiled up at him.

'That was nice,' she said.

'In that case, I'll do it again.'

Early on Wednesday afternoon, Dot arrived back in St Helens. She got off the tram just outside the town and started walking slowly up the hill.

It was a hot day for early summer, still and sluggish like her heavily pregnant body. A slight breeze rattled the leaves of the occasional tree, but there was no cool air to lick away the sweat which was running down her neck and back, pooling at the base of her spine and making her clothes stick to her.

At thirty-eight, Dot hadn't expected to be pregnant again, but she'd been lucky to find a man like Ivan Price to take on her ready-made family, and of course he had wanted what any husband had a right to want. Besides, he hadn't troubled her much since she'd fallen pregnant.

She rubbed her back with the heel of her hand. Not quite eight months gone, and almost another two to go before the baby was born. She felt as heavy as a whale. Still, these last two weeks at her sister's had done her the world of good: so much so that she'd decided to come back home a day early.

Up the street she trudged, towards number forty-two.

'Afternoon, Dot,' called Mrs Carter from the other side of Gas Street. 'How you doin', luv?'

'I'll be right as rain, soon's I've had a nice cup o' tea.'

'Well, just you let me know if you need owt doin'. Your Nancy looks proper worn out.'

Dot nodded her thanks and walked down the alleyway to the back of the house. She pushed open the back gate and clicked it shut behind her, then walked down the yard and up the steps to the back kitchen.

It was empty, save for a pile of dirty pots. That Nancy! She wasn't fit to leave on her own for five minutes, not like Jen . . . She stopped that train of thought in its tracks. At least Nancy wasn't a lying little trollop!

What she needed was a bit of a lie-down. Her ankles were swollen up like balloons and her head was muzzy; she didn't feel quite right really. Well, Ivan'd be on shift till six, he'd never know she'd had a little doze on the bed.

It seemed a long way to the top of the stairs, and she had to use the rail to pull herself up. Halfway up, she thought she heard voices, then sudden silence. If she caught Billy and Daisy wagging school, she'd tan their hides.

At the top of the stairs, she turned right and pushed open the bedroom door. For a split second, nothing made sense.

There were two figures on the bed; one half-naked and sprawled across the covers, the other on top, bare-backed with his trousers pushed down low on his thighs. She saw the girl freeze, her eyes opening wide, staring, full of fear and pain.

'No. No . . . please, don't . . .'

Dot's breath escaped in a low, juddering gasp. They were in her bed, doing it in *her* bed. This couldn't be true, it couldn't. It must be some sickening nightmare.

Ivan rolled sideways, pulling up his trousers.

'What you doin' back here, woman?'

She stared at him, speechless, shaking. He tucked in his shirt-tails.

'Pull yourself together. This isn't what it looks like.'

At last Dot's anger found voice.

'You think I was born yesterday, Ivan Price? Or d'you think I'm so grateful for you marryin' me that I won't mind you takin' my own daughter to bed?'

Nancy crawled slowly off the bed, clutching the rumpled bedspread to her nakedness, trying to cover her bare breasts and thighs. She was white-faced, save for the darkening circle of bruising that would be a black eye in the morning.

'Mam, I'm sorry . . .'

'Shut it!' Dot's eyes flashed with an ice-cold fire.

'Mam, he made me, I swear . . .'

'Oh, he *made* you, did he, you two-faced little slut?' But at the back of Dot's mind, a treacherous voice was whispering: You know it's true; he made Jenny, didn't he? Only when she told you, you didn't believe her. 'Don't give me that . . . oh!'

A sharp pain stabbed through her belly and she clutched at it, doubling up as a second, cramping spasm took hold of her. Her hand reached out for the doorframe, but she was too weak to hold herself up, and her fingers, wet with perspiration, slid down it as she sank to her knees.

'Mam, what is it? What's wrong, Mam?'

'No,' gasped Dot. 'No, it's not time. Not yet. The baby can't come yet.'

Chapter 18

Jolly Jimmy Costigern's office was situated on the first floor of the administration block, with huge rectangular windows which offered a panoramic view of the camp. People said Jolly Jimmy knew what you'd done before you'd thought of doing it; perhaps they were right, thought Henry as he stepped into the office.

'You wanted to see me, Grandpa?'

Jolly Jimmy looked up from his desk. It was strewn with papers, an advertisement for Costigern's Herb Cordial (BY 'ECK, IT DOES YOU GOOD), and a half-eaten wholemeal sandwich.

'Come in and sit down.'

Henry closed the door and sat down on the other side of Jimmy's large mahogany desk. Every chair in the room was deliberately lower than Jimmy's, to make sure that all visitors immediately felt at a disadvantage. In Henry's case there was no need for the chair; he had always been in awe of his dynamic grandfather.

Jolly Jimmy spent the next five minutes signing a pile of letters. Henry was used to this. It was another of Jimmy's ploys for making people feel uncomfortable. Henry spent the time gazing out through the window, watching the campers splashing about in the swimming-pool as Joey the Jolly Jester clowned about on the high diving board.

At last Jimmy threw down his pen.

'You're a bloody fool, Henry.'

'I beg your pardon?'

'Like father like son. Your father's a bloody fool with women, and so are you.'

'I'm sorry. I don't know what you're talking about.'

'Don't give me that, Henry. I pay for a first-class education for you, no expense spared, turn you into a proper gentleman, and what do you do? You start carrying on with the first chorus-girl who throws herself at you.'

'If this is about Jenny Fisher . . .'

Jimmy raised a bushy eyebrow.

'How many other chorus-girls have you got on the go?'

'Jenny and I are good friends.'

'From what I've seen, you're more than that, lad.'

Henry felt anger tightening his throat. He stood up.

'Have you been spying on us?'

'Spying!' Jimmy was on his feet now. 'I've a right to look out for my own flesh and blood.'

'You've nothing of the sort! I'm twenty-two years old, I'm my own man.'

'Look, lad, I know what you've been getting up to with this girl. It's all over the camp, you're making a fool of yourself – and you're making a fool of me too, and I won't stand for that.'

'Jenny Fisher is a lovely girl – bright, talented, natural . . .'

'Oh, she's pretty enough, lad, but she's not your kind.'

'Not my *what*!'

'She's out for what she can get, lad, they all are. So you'll stop seeing her right now, before it goes any further.'

Beneath his calm, almost meek exterior, Henry was coldly furious.

'Grandpa . . .'

'I won't hear another word on the subject, Henry. If this Fisher girl gives you any trouble, send her to me – I know how to deal with her sort.'

'Grandfather!' Henry thumped the desk, and for a split second at least, Jimmy Costigern was taken aback. 'I will *not* have you prying into my private life and trying to run it for me. I will *not* have you telling me who I can and can't be friendly with!'

'How dare you? How dare you speak to your grandfather like that!'

204

'How dare *you* insult a lovely young woman who has never had anything but good to say about you!'

Jimmy was on the defensive now; he could see that he had used the wrong tactics and was trying to turn the situation to his own advantage.

'You know very well that I have your best interests at heart. I want you to be a success in the world . . . find a suitable girl and make a good marriage . . .'

'Well, I don't need your good intentions, Grandpa. And I'd be grateful if you'd stop poking your nose in where it isn't welcome.'

Jimmy Costigern stared aghast at his grandson, normally so mild-mannered and diffident.

'She's put you up to this, hasn't she?'

'No, Grandpa, nobody's put me up to anything. I'm quite capable of thinking for myself. And, frankly, I can do perfectly well without your marriage guidance as well.'

'Henry!'

'In fact, I'm willing to bet my father would have been a lot happier if you hadn't tried to run *his* life for him.'

Henry got up and walked across to the door. He was beginning to shake with the shock of his own outburst, but was determined not to lose his cool until he'd closed the door on Jolly Jimmy. He turned and looked back at his grandfather, red-faced and perspiring behind his monolithic desk. Henry wondered how long it was since anyone had dared to tell Jolly Jimmy Costigern that he was wrong.

'It *was* you who insisted on Mum and Dad getting married, wasn't it?'

'And what if it was?'

'Think about it, Grandpa. Some things are better if you just leave them well alone.'

Tom Fisher knew something was wrong the minute he rounded the corner into Gas Street.

He could feel the eyes boring into him, watching him from behind twitching net curtains – and more than that, there was a cluster of people standing outside number forty-two. He could make out the tall, stooping figure of

205

old Mr Pateman from next door, Mrs Pateman too, and fat Nellie from the wash-house. And wasn't that Nancy, standing a little apart from the rest, holding her apron to her face with clenched hands?

What the hell was going on? Apprehension quickened his step, and he called out before he reached the house.

'Nancy?'

Startled out of some speechless trance, she looked up. Her eyes were two red circles in a pastry-white face.

'Nancy, for God's sake, what's up? It's not the kids, is it?'

She shook her head soundlessly. She seemed to move in slow motion, and the people around her just kept on staring and muttering to each other under their breath. Impatience got the better of Tom.

'Won't somebody tell me what's goin' on?'

'It's yer mam, lad,' said Mr Pateman, putting his arm around Tom's shoulders.

'Mam? What's wrong with her? 'As she been took ill?'

'She's . . . it's babby, lad.'

Before Tom had time to respond, the front door of number forty-two opened with a click and a woman in a navy blue dress and round-brimmed hat stepped out, closing it quietly behind her. The crowd parted respectfully, questions spilling out now.

''Ow is she, nurse?'

''As she 'ad it?'

'Is it a girl or a boy?'

The midwife looked up and shook her head sadly; turned away and fastened her black bag to the back of her bicycle. Words weren't necessary. A ripple of condolence passed through the crowd.

'Poor Dot.'

'Babby weren't ready to come yet.'

'It were the shock, see . . .'

'If I get my hands on that Ivan Price . . .'

'Shock?' Tom pushed his neighbours aside. 'What shock, nurse? What's Ivan Price got to do with this?'

The nurse straightened up.

'Never you mind about that, lad. Your mother's had a bad time, she's tired and she'll need her family round her. Why don't you go up and see her? Don't tire her out, mind.'

'I'll go to 'er now.'

Tom turned to Nancy. She was shrinking away, slowly distancing herself from everything and everyone, arms hugging herself as though they offered the only comfort she could hope for.

'You comin', Nancy?' She shook her head. There was something she wasn't telling him, that much was obvious. '*Nancy?*'

But she just kept backing away.

'Leave her be,' said a voice from the back of the crowd. 'I'll take care of her. You go to yer mam.'

Tom pushed open the front door. The door that was only ever used for bad things, like when they'd brought Dad back from the pit, spreadeagled like cold cod on a slab; or when Mam and Ivan Price had come back from the chapel, to eat boiled ham salad in the front parlour.

He stepped into the house. It was horribly quiet and cold, almost completely silent except for the soft sound of the kitchen tap, dripping into the shallow brown sink. He didn't want to go upstairs to his mam, he was afraid of what he would find – and more afraid still of the anger it would provoke in him.

Each step lasted an eternity, his boots echoing on the bare wooden treads. Now he was near the top of the stairs he could hear another sound, the sound of somebody quietly sobbing.

'Mam? Oh, Mam . . .'

Dot Price was sitting propped up in bed, her dark, grey-streaked hair untied and wet with sweat. Her face was red, her eyes swollen.

'It's dead, Tom. The baby's dead.'

He didn't know what to say. He took another leaden step towards the bed and sat down on the edge.

'You'll dirty the bedspread wi' those mucky clothes.'

'Then I'll wash it meself.' He took her hand in his. It was

like a child's, cold and sticky after a bad dream. 'Mam, what happened?'

A sob escaped her. He'd never seen her like this before, a crumpled, deflated shell of a woman.

'It were Ivan. I caught 'im . . . wi' our Nancy . . . That's what set it off, see, the shock of it.'

'What you sayin', Mam?' But Tom was already two steps ahead, he understood only too well what Dot was saying. He'd closed his eyes for far too long to what was happening; they all had.

'Do I 'ave to spell it out, lad? Him and her – in this bed.' Dot's fingers clutched at the candlewick bedspread, twisting it almost to the point of tearing.

'I'll kill 'im.' He pictured Nancy in the street below, white-faced, red-eyed, shrinking away from him and from her own guilt. 'No, I'll kill them both. The little whore . . .'

'No, Tom.' There was steel in Dot's weary voice. 'No. I'll not 'ave Nancy driven away like Jenny was. It weren't her fault, lad, Ivan forced her – all this time he's been doin' this to my own daughter and I was blind to it.'

Tom sprang to his feet.

'Where is he, Mam?'

'Gone. Scarpered an' took his things.'

'I'll make him pay, I swear I will. I knew he were no good, Mam, I tried to tell you but he made you 'appy . . .'

Tears streamed in silent rivers down Dot's cheeks.

'Jenny tried to tell me an' all, but would I listen? I called her a liar, Tom, I threw her out and now she's gone.'

'I'll find 'er, Mam. I'll bring 'er back.'

'You don't even know where she is.'

'If I say I'll find 'er, I will.'

Dot turned her face away.

'You're a good lad, Tom. But she'll want nowt to do with us now, not after what we did to 'er.'

Chapter 19

It was Friday night, the biggest night of the week. With ten minutes to go till curtain up, there was still no sign of Joss Flynn.

'That girl,' sniffed Bella, 'thinks she's Lady Muck.'

'We all know there's one law for Joss and one for the rest of us,' agreed Mae, bending forward to adjust her suspenders. 'Of course she'll swan in at the last minute, as per usual.'

Jenny breathed in and zipped up her yellow dress. It was starting to look rather tired after several weeks of wear, and there was a thin line of make-up around the neckline.

'This looks awful,' she commented.

'It won't show up under the lights,' Mae assured her. 'Besides, Sid was talking about us getting new costumes for the revue – apparently Jolly Jimmy wants everything in Costigern's colours.'

'He doesn't look happy,' commented Dolly, nudging Jenny's elbow. She looked across the dressing room. Sid Dukes was standing by the door, deep in conversation with Geoff Tait. She couldn't hear what they were saying, but Sid was flushed and kept looking at his wristwatch.

'Neither does Geoff,' observed Jenny.

'Hardly surprising. Joss has been giving him the runaround ever since we got here.'

'I don't know why he puts up with it,' said Jenny.

'Must be love,' grimaced Mae. 'God help him.'

Desmond the saxophonist struggled past with his arms full of music stands, managing by some marvel of dexterity to pinch Jenny's bottom as he squeezed by. She jumped up with a startled squeak.

'Desmond!'

He beamed back like a naughty fifth-former.

'Whatever it is, the answer's yes.'

'Do that once more, and I'll have your guts for garters.'

'Five minutes, everybody,' called a voice from the doorway.

'Oh, no, I'm not ready!' wailed Mae, fiddling with the buckle on her tap shoe. 'Somebody help . . . Jenny, can you do this up for me? The end's stuck.'

It was while she was crouching down, trying to free the buckle, that Sid called across, raising his voice to make himself heard above the general hubbub.

'Jenny!'

She raised her head, looking around for the source of the voice.

'Jenny, leave that and come over here.'

'Sorry, Mae, you'll have to manage it yourself.' Wondering what she could possibly have done wrong, Jenny crossed the dressing room. 'Yes, Mr Dukes?'

Sid looked furious, Geoff Tait on edge.

'Sid,' Geoff said, 'are you sure this is a good idea?'

Sid turned a cold eye on him.

'Have you got a better one?'

'We could wait . . .'

'We're on in less than five minutes, and I'm not delaying the start of the show for anyone. Besides, it's not just that, Geoff, she's done this to us once too often. Now then,' he turned his attention to Jenny.

She held her breath, guessing yet not wanting to know what he was going to say. The words she'd been waiting to hear for weeks, the words she'd never believed she *would* hear. And suddenly she wasn't sure that she wanted to hear them at all.

Sid cleared his throat to project his straining voice over the noise around them.

'Joss has let us down, Jenny, you'll have to stand in for her tonight.'

She heard gasps of surprise all around. Everyone had heard; momentarily everything stopped. Conversations were halted then began again just as suddenly, weaving a maze of words about her head.

'Did I hear that right? Did Sid just . . .?'

'He did!'

'Jenny Fisher! No, never . . .'

'Good on you, girl.'

'Scheming little bitch . . .'

'Joss'll be mad as hell about this.'

Jenny put her hand to her mouth. Her lips were dry, her throat suddenly so constricted that she could scarcely breathe.

'Oh, Mr Dukes!'

'Think you're up to it, Jenny?' asked Geoff, his eyes searching her face. Jenny had the feeling that he was willing her to say no.

'Of course she is,' snapped Sid. 'You know the songs, don't you, lass?'

Jenny felt hot and cold, all at once more alive than she had ever been before and yet curiously distanced. She had never been so afraid in her life.

'Yes,' she said, not at all sure that it was true. But of course she knew the songs, hadn't she been practising them for week after week after week? 'Yes, Mr Dukes.'

'Good girl.'

'But, Mr Dukes . . .' In her mind, Jenny was picturing Joss's face, remembering her taunts and her threats. Perhaps she had been right. Perhaps Jenny really wasn't up to it and was just going to make an idiot of herself. She clutched at straws. 'Joss'll be here in a minute, she's just a bit late, that's all . . .'

Sid shook his head. Jenny saw that he had made up his mind and wasn't going to change it now.

'Take Joss's numbers in the first half and we'll see how it goes. Now go and get changed, curtain's up in two minutes.'

'Come on, kid,' said Mae, bundling Jenny off towards Joss's beautiful white silk gown. 'We've only got two minutes to make you look like a star.'

★ ★ ★

'Can't you go faster than this?'

'We're already doing sixty.'

'Go on, put your foot down! I love going fast . . .'

Joss Flynn laughed and threw back her head, enjoying the sensation of the wind in her hair as the Speedster hugged the curves of the country lane. She'd had a wonderful day out, and tonight she would give the performance of her life.

Peregrine Lacey had money, good looks and a fast car – everything Joss needed to enjoy herself. More than that, he knew how to have fun – and if Geoff Tait refused to give her the attention she deserved, she'd show him that there were plenty of other men who would.

'Have some more champagne, sweetie.'

Peregrine held out the half-empty bottle to her. She took a long swig and found herself overcome by giggles. She was a bit tipsy. Ah, well, she'd always found that a couple of drinks helped loosen up her voice.

The car accelerated out of the bend and on to the long road which led along the Welsh coastline to Costigern's Camp.

'Hurry, Perry darling,' she laughed. 'I'm frightfully late. They'll all be waiting for me, so they can start their silly little show.'

The lights blazed. They had never seemed so dazzling, and the white spotlight almost blinded Jenny as she stepped up to the microphone. She heard Sid's voice in the background, very faintly as though in a dream.

'And now, ladies and gentlemen, it's time for our first solo spot. Unfortunately Joss Flynn is indisposed . . .'

She could feel the disappointment in the audience, hear the murmurs of discontent running along the rows.

'. . . but Costigern's Camp is proud to present its very own St Helens sweetheart . . . Jenny Fisher!'

She couldn't see anything. Why couldn't she see anything? All the faces in the audience had turned into anonymous dark shapes, barely distinguishable beyond the footlights. Would they love her or hate her? Would this one moment pass in the blink of an eye and be forgotten for ever?

The intro to her opening number was playing behind her, Desmond's tenor sax floating the melody above a jaunty four-four beat. On the upbeat of the second bar she began singing, not so much inspirationally as automatically. She had sung the song so many times before that the words and melody had become a part of her.

It was a good song, a brand-new hit from Hollywood; it ought to have gone down a storm, but Jenny could feel the distance growing between her and the audience. It wasn't working, it wasn't working! The more she worried about it, the more tense she became; and the more tense she became, the harder it was really to feel the song.

It wasn't until the final chorus of *You Must Have Been A Beautiful Baby* that Jenny felt the audience beginning to warm to her. It was hard for them, she knew that. They'd been expecting the ebullient, super-confident Joss Flynn, and instead of her they'd got Jenny Fisher, pinned into a gown that didn't fit her and scared half out of her wits.

There was mildly enthusiastic applause for the first number. The second was *You Are My Sunshine*, which was a great favourite with the old campers; and by the last verse she even had a few of them clapping and singing along. This was the last night of their week's holiday, they wanted a night to remember; Jenny had to make sure they got exactly that. So why did she feel as if she was just going through the motions? This is your big chance, girl, she kept telling herself. The biggest chance of your entire life. Don't throw it away now.

Her eyes were becoming accustomed to the lights, and she could make out a few of the faces in the audience. They didn't look too hostile. She tried smiling at them. One or two of them seemed to smile back. Looking across to the right, she saw Mae and Dolly in the wings. They were smiling too, and making silly faces that almost made her burst out laughing. 'Go on,' mouthed Mae. 'You can do it. Go *on*!'

'Thank you,' said Jenny, forcing the tremor out of her

voice as she acknowledged the applause. 'And now for a very special number, written by our own Mr Music – Geoff Tait.'

As Geoff stood up at the piano and took a bow, Jenny remembered only too well that he had written *Honeybee* not for her, but for Joss Flynn. Not to mention the cruel taunts that Joss had thrown at her, that afternoon when she'd heard her singing it in the bath . . .

The band struck up the intro; two, two-three-four; three, two-three-four; four, two-three *and* . . .

' "*Honeybee, my darling honeybee* . . ." '

Suddenly the old electricity came rushing back; the crackle and buzz of being up alone on the stage, of not just singing a song but living her whole life through it. For these three minutes and twenty seconds at least, *Honeybee* was Jenny Fisher's song, and hers alone.

> *Why won't you let me be*
> *Your butter-flutter-butter-fly,*
> *And you can be my bee . . .*

She was carrying the audience with her; she could feel it in every note she sang, her voice soaring with the sheer elation of knowing that this was something she could do, and do supremely well.

They were clapping along, singing the chorus with her, some of the audience even getting up and dancing in the aisle during the middle eight. The cheeky, bouncy beat was so infectious that even the band were swaying in time as they played along. It was all going a hundred times better than Jenny could ever have hoped.

Out of the corner of her left eye, Jenny caught sight of something going on in the wings. But she was lost in the song, and if she'd turned to get a better look she'd have lost her concentration.

> *Honeybee, you're sugar-sweet,*
> *So sweet and neat,*
> *My Honeybee . . .*

As Jenny powered into the chorus, Marvo the Memory Man was standing in the wings, having a last-minute word with his assistant.

'This time, don't forget the marked cards . . .'

'All right, all right.'

'And keep an eye on your tail, you know what happened with Jenny Fisher.'

'Yes, yes, I know.' Lindsey adjusted her cat-costume and took a peek out on to the stage. 'She's not bad, is she?'

'Not bad at all.' Marvo watched the small figure in the white dress; such a huge voice soaring out of that tiny frame. 'Mind you, she's wasted on that lot.'

'Her and me both.'

The screech of anger which erupted behind them was so loud that it almost drowned out the band. On stage, Jenny hesitated mid-note and glanced sideways, her eyes widening momentarily; then she turned back and went on belting out the song like a true trouper.

Startled, Marvo swung round.

'What the . . .?'

'Get that bitch off the stage! Get her off!'

Joss Flynn was running up the steps from the dressing rooms to the wings, face distorted with jealous rage.

'The bitch . . . she's singing my song! *My* song . . .'

Marvo caught her just as she reached the top of the steps. The smell of drink hit him full in the face.

'Steady on, Joss.'

'Let go of me!'

'Calm down, you've had one too many.'

Joss lunged forward, but Marvo had her by the shoulders and wasn't planning on letting go.

'That common little cow – she's stolen my song! Let me get at her, I'll scratch her eyes out.'

'Shut up, Joss.' Lindsey spoke with such vehemence that Joss did just that. 'Shut up and give the kid a chance.'

The applause was warm and sincere, and it seemed like ages before Jenny could take her final bow and leave the stage. As she turned to walk off, Jenny saw Joss Flynn standing in the wings. The look on her face was not so much hostile as murderous.

'Bitch,' she hissed as Jenny stepped into the wings.

'Take no notice,' said Marvo. 'She's half-cut.'

'I am *not*. That bitch . . . that common little bitch stole my song!' Joss lunged at Jenny, fingers clawing.

'Now wait a minute, Joss, I only went on for you because you didn't bother turning up for the show!'

'Don't give me that, Jenny Fisher. You've been after my spot ever since you persuaded that senile old idiot to take you on.'

That was one insult she couldn't let pass.

'Oh, really? Well, why don't you tell that to Mr Dukes? I'm sure he'd be very interested to hear what you think of him!'

'You'd like that, wouldn't you? Get me the sack and take my spot for yourself, that's what you've wanted all along.'

Behind them, the band was playing the final notes of *Bei Mir Bist Du Sheyn*. In a few moments, most of them would come off the stage, leaving just a four-piece to provide the incidental music for the ventriloquist act.

'For God's sake, Joss,' said Marvo. 'Do you want Sid to see you like this? Go back to your chalet and sleep it off. I'll tell him you're . . . ill.'

'I'm not bloody ill, I'm just bloody angry!'

It was too late anyway. The band was coming down off the stage in a flurry of blue and yellow. Sid was talking to Desmond about a mistake he'd made in the second number, but he soon cut the conversation short when he saw Jenny and Joss.

'You did well, Jenny. I'm very pleased with you.' He treated Joss Flynn to a glare which would have turned most people to stone. 'So, Joss, I see you bothered to turn up at last.'

She greeted Sid with an ingratiating smile, wrenching herself free from Marvo's grasp and swaying slightly on unsteady legs.

'Sid *darling*, I didn't see you there.'

'Where have you been?'

216

'I was . . . unavoidably delayed.'

'You're drunk.'

A small giggle escaped from Joss's lips before she could stifle it.

'I may have had a glass of champagne . . . or two . . . anyway I'm here now, so I can go on in the second half, can't I?'

'You most certainly will not!'

The smile wavered, then disappeared from her face and became the beginnings of a scowl.

'But . . .'

'I am sick and tired of your behaviour, Joss. I will *not* tolerate it any longer. You will go back to your chalet and Jenny will sing your numbers for the rest of tonight's show.'

'That bitch! You can't let her have my songs . . . she's trying to get rid of me, the common scheming little slut. She's even sleeping with Jolly Jimmy's grandson so she can get her hands on his money . . .'

Jenny sprang forward.

'How dare you! That's a filthy lie and you know it. Take it back.'

'Make me,' sneered Joss.

Sid intervened, stepping between the two women.

'Desmond – take Joss back to her chalet. And make sure she stays there. Jenny.'

'Yes, Mr Dukes?'

'Get Mae to pin up that dress properly, it's coming down at the shoulder. You want to look your best for the second half, don't you?'

A knock on the dressing room door made Jenny look up.

'Can I come in?'

'Yes, of course.'

She was alone in the dressing room. Everyone else had gone, it was late, even the campers had gone back to their chalets; but Jenny couldn't think about sleeping. Sid Dukes yawned as he walked in, his bow-tie dangling round his collar and the top stud out of his dress shirt. Mae followed him at a distance, his black dinner jacket over her arm.

'Are you all right, love?'

'Yes. Yes, thank you, Mr Dukes.'

Sid pulled up a stool and sat down.

'It's late, you ought to be in bed.'

Jenny shrugged.

'I feel too fidgety. D'you know what I mean? I'd never be able to get to sleep.'

'You did well tonight, I was proud of you.'

She looked up, searching his face for any trace of a lie.

'Really?'

'You know me, I say what I mean. And you enjoyed yourself on that stage, didn't you, once you got going?'

Jenny nodded. Even now the memory of the excitement was still inside her, tingling and addictively strong.

'It was wonderful,' she admitted. 'Until . . .'

'Until Joss Flynn came along and spoiled it all?'

'Well . . . I suppose she had every right to be angry. I mean, Geoff did write that song for her, and she's the star, not me.'

Sid sighed. He exchanged a look with Mae and she smiled, the way a mother smiles when a child says something naive and endearing.

'Listen, Jenny,' said Sid, 'you're not to worry about Joss Flynn. It's all sour grapes with her. You see, she knows talent when she sees it – and she doesn't like what she sees.

'Joss has gone as far as she's ever going to go in this business,' he added, getting to his feet. 'But you, Jenny . . . well, between you and me, the sky's the limit.'

218

Chapter 20

'Mam.'

Nancy hesitated on the threshold, the cup rattling on the saucer as she tried to hold it still.

'Mam . . . I brought you a cup of tea.'

Dot sat propped up in Dan Fisher's old armchair, pillows and cushions behind her head and a quilt over her legs. For a moment she said nothing, then attempted a smile.

'That's nice.'

Nancy took this as encouragement and stepped into the front parlour. She held out the cup in both hands.

'Will you drink it now, Mam?'

'Not now. Put it there, I'll have it in a minute.' Dot stared into space for a little while, then glanced at her daughter. 'Better get a cold compress on that eye.'

'I'll be all right. It'll mend.'

The silences between the words were far more painful, and more telling, then the words themselves. Desperate for some comfort, some sign of understanding, Nancy sat down on the floor at her mother's feet, taking her hand.

'Mam . . . I'm sorry.'

Dot patted Nancy's hand dismissively, her eyes focused on the middle distance as if fixed on something that only she could see.

'We won't talk about it now.'

Then when? thought Nancy. When will we ever talk about this big black thing that's gnawing away at our insides? Are we just going to go on pretending it never happened?

'But, Mam, I need to know . . . can you forgive me? Please say you forgive me.'

Dot made a very real effort to look into her daughter's face.

'It's in the past. I won't 'ave that man's name spoken in this house again.' She pulled her fingers from Nancy's grasp. 'Where's Billy an' Daisy?'

'Out back somewhere.'

'I want them 'ere. Where *he* can't get at them.'

'He won't, Mam, he's gone.'

'I want them kids 'ere where I can see them. Go an' fetch them before it gets dark.'

Nancy got up and went outside. Billy and Daisy were down the bottom of the yard, skulking in the alley.

'Come in, you two, Mam wants yer.'

Billy shook his head violently.

'Can't.'

'What's up with you two?'

'Mam's ill an' it's our fault.'

'Not comin' in,' said Daisy, backing away.

Nancy grabbed her by the elbow.

'You'll do what you're told, you little madam.'

'Gerroff.' Daisy shook herself like a wet dog, but Nancy hung on, her fingers digging into the soft flesh of her little sister's arm. There was not one ounce of gentleness left in her, not any more. 'Gerroff, I won't, you're hurtin'!'

Nancy took Billy by the scruff of the neck and dragged the two kids back up the yard.

'Now wash yer 'ands before you go in.'

They obeyed sullenly, holding their hands briefly under the tap then wiping them on their clothes and holding them out to be inspected.

'That's not clean. Still, it'll have to do. Get in there and be nice to Mam, she's not well.'

Nancy walked several feet behind them, cold and shivery on this warm summer's night. She didn't want to go back into the parlour any more than the kids did.

Dot brightened at the sight of Billy and Daisy.

'Come to yer mam . . . look at the state of yer! 'Ave you combed that 'air today?'

She held out her arms to the children but they hung back.

'Go on,' said Nancy, prodding Daisy forward. But she took one faltering step then stopped.

'Can't.'

'What's up wi' you?' Dot's eyes darted from one child to the other, full of concern.

Billy and Daisy remained ominously and resolutely silent, looking daggers at each other as though each was daring the other to break the silence.

'Answer your mam when she's talking to you,' said Nancy, her impatience turning to resentment.

Dot waved her away.

'There's no need to get angry, Nancy. Come 'ere, you two, an' tell yer mam what's up,' she said gently. 'It don't matter what you've done, I won't be angry.'

'Promise?' asked Billy doubtfully.

'Promise. Now, what's all this about?'

'Ivan 'urt you, Mam,' blurted out Daisy, running to her mother. 'Didn't he?'

'He hurt us all,' said Dot quietly.

'Ivan 'urt you an' that's why babby died an' you've been took poorly, i'n't it? He 'urt you an' it's me an' Billy's fault.'

'*Your* fault? How?'

'Ivan hurt you 'cause we made 'im angry,' said Billy. 'So it must be our fault.'

Dot shook her head sadly.

'Nay, it's not your fault. It's nowt to do wi' you two kids.'

'But, Mam,' protested Daisy, 'it were the presents . . .'

'. . . what our Jenny sent . . .'

'. . . Ivan must've found out about 'em, see, and that's what made 'im angry, an' then . . .'

'What's that you said?' Dot leant forward, her tired features drawn with concentration.

'The presents, Mam. It were only sweets an' stuff, honest.'

'From Jenny? Jenny's been sendin' you presents?'

Billy and Daisy looked at each other, shuffled from one foot to the other, then Billy spoke up.

'Mr Corlett said it were a secret.'

Dot's mouth fell open.

'John Corlett knows where our Jenny is?'

'He made us promise not to tell nobody . . .'

'. . . 'specially Ivan, 'cause he'd be angry an' go lookin' for 'er . . .'

'Oh, Daisy . . . Billy!' Dot welcomed them into the biggest of hugs. 'This isn't your fault – none of it's anybody's fault but mine.' Her eyes lighted briefly on Nancy, then she looked away. 'An' Ivan's gone away now. He's a bad man but he won't bother us no more.'

'Is our Jenny comin' home now then, Mam?'

'I don't know, Billy. I don't know, we'll have to see. Poor kids, did you really think it was your fault?'

As Nancy watched her mother hugging her little brother and sister, she felt the pain of alienation more sharply than ever. How easy it was to soothe away the trivial hurts of childhood with a simple hug and a kiss of reassurance. Poor Daisy. Poor Billy. There, there.

She wanted to scream at the top of her voice: What about poor Nancy, who had to let Ivan do that to her again and again, in fear and pain and silence? She closed her eyes for a moment, trying to escape the memory of his grunts and groans, the foul, stinking weight of his body on hers; and each hateful thrust of him inside her, that had meant one less bruise for Daisy and Billy.

Yes, what about poor Nancy? A voice inside her head whispered that maybe it wasn't just Ivan Price's fault, maybe it was true what he'd said and it was *her* fault too, Nancy's fault, the little slut, who'd led him on.

Anyway, what was the use? They all hated her now. And no one could hate Nancy Fisher more than she hated herself.

Saturdays were always busy at Costigern's Camp. With fifteen hundred campers packing up ready to leave, and another fifteen hundred due to arrive by two o'clock, there was hardly time to think.

Chalet maids bustled about with mops and buckets,

dodging between the long columns of campers with their bulging suitcases and sticks of souvenir rock. Farewells sounded across the camp as the convoy of motor-coaches rolled up the Boulevard, ready to take everyone to Llandew Station.

'Same time next year then?'

'Wouldn't miss it for anything!'

''Bye, Glad. 'Bye, Tommy. 'Bye, Cilla . . .'

Sid stood and watched it all from the door of the camp theatre. They all looked so happy, though doubtless every one of them was going back to a mess of assorted problems. That was what Costigern's was for: to give people a chance to forget their problems for one precious week every year. It was a pity Sid couldn't forget his problems quite so easily and completely.

Joss Flynn came up to the theatre door with Geoff Tait in tow.

'You wanted to see me?' she demanded airily. She looked a bit pale, no doubt the result of all that champagne. 'I hope it's not going to take long, only Geoff has a new song he wants me to run through . . .'

'You'd better come inside,' said Sid tersely. 'It's more private.'

Without lights, campers and performers, the theatre was just a cold barn, devoid of glamour. People made a theatre, not bricks and mortar. Sid walked in through the stage door and Joss followed, her high heels tip-tapping on the concrete floor. Geoff hung back.

'You might as well hear this too,' said Sid. He took a deep breath. 'Last night's performance was a disgrace, Joss.'

She sniffed.

'I told you that common shop-girl wasn't up to the job. If you'd just let me go on in the second half . . .'

'I'm not talking about Jenny Fisher. I'm talking about you. You turn up late and blind drunk . . .'

'I was just a bit tipsy, that's all . . .'

'. . . blind drunk, Joss. If Marvo hadn't been holding you up you'd have fallen flat on your face. Then you try to throw a punch at Jenny and almost ruin the show . . .'

'Ruin it! For God's sake, Sid, I'm the only good thing in it!' She turned to Geoff. 'Tell him. Tell him he's talking rubbish.'

Geoff stared at his boots, cleared his throat then looked up.

'I think you should apologise, Joss,' he said quietly.

Her elegant features contorted in fury.

'Apologise! It's *he* who should be apologising! If he wants proper professionals in his show, he has to learn to handle them like professionals.'

'If you were a professional,' pointed out Sid with barely controlled anger, 'you'd stop behaving like a spoilt child.'

'Geoff! Geoff, you can't let him talk to me like this.'

'I'm sorry, Joss, this time I agree with Sid.' Geoff's eyes reflected twin images of Joss's self-righteous rage, and perhaps just a glimmer of his own resentment. 'Just say you're sorry, and we can forget the whole thing.'

Joss spat her bile in his face.

'The only thing I'm sorry about is that I ever set eyes on you. *All* of you!'

'If you don't care for the company,' said Geoff, 'you know what you can do.'

'And let that cow Jenny Fisher take my spot? Oh, you'd all love that, wouldn't you? Well, I'm not giving you the bloody satisfaction.'

She ran out into the noonday sunshine, slamming the door behind her. People were rushing about all over the place, shouting to each other, waving goodbyes, being Jolly just like Jimmy Costigern wanted them to be. His odious, fat, red face seemed to beam down at her from every corner of this wretched camp complex.

Her head throbbed. What she needed was a hair of the dog. Spotting the Caribbean Bar across the way, she made straight for it. It would have opened ten minutes ago; she could just about bring herself to go in there in exchange for a double gin and tonic.

Tony was behind the bar as usual, drying glasses.

'Don't often see you in here, Miss Flynn. Not in the daytime anyhow.'

'Only a social outcast would be seen in a place like this before dark.' She sat down on one of the high stools. 'Double gin. No, make that a treble.'

'Celebrating something, are we?'

Joss gave a sarcastic laugh.

'What are you, my father-confessor? Look, just give me the drink.'

She paid for the gin and took it to one of the tables in a quiet corner. There was hardly anyone in the bar at this time of day, what with one lot of campers leaving and the other lot not yet arrived. A couple of Stripeys were feeding bits of banana to the macaws, and a maid was polishing the beer stains off the tables, but apart from that she was alone; for that, at least, she was grateful.

Peace didn't last long. A tall, dark-haired figure in a striped blazer appeared from behind the plaster galleon, and came across to Joss's table.

'Mind if I join you?'

'As a matter of fact, I do.'

He ignored her reply and sat down next to her, setting down his pint glass.

'Sam Burkiss.' He extended his right hand but Joss didn't bother taking it.

'Am I supposed to be impressed?'

He chuckled.

'Is that any way to talk to a man who's got a business proposition for you?'

Joss took a gulp of gin, only very slightly diluted with tonic.

'You don't honestly think I'd be interested in anything you've got to say?'

'That depends, don't it?' Sam sat back and folded his arms. 'I mean, everyone's got their price.' He grinned. 'Even you.'

Joss's lip curled.

'Has anyone ever told you you're a disgusting little oik? Now just go away, and leave me alone.'

Sam kept on talking, unperturbed.

'You know that Miranda Costigern?'

'Of course I do, I could hardly miss her.'

'Between you an' me, she an' James junior don't get on.'

'Tell me something I don't know! They had a stand-up row in front of the Fun House.'

'Ah, but I'll tell you somethin' else that *is* a secret. She wants to divorce 'im, only he won't play ball.'

Joss displayed only the mildest of interest in this juicy tidbit.

'So?'

'*So*, if he won't give her grounds for a divorce, she'll get them herself, know what I mean? Miranda's paying me to . . . ease things along, see. All she needs is the right evidence . . . papers and photos to prove that some pretty girl's spent the night with him . . . and bob's your uncle.'

'I don't see what this has got to do with me.'

'You're a pretty girl, Joss. An' that James Costigern, well, he's not a bad-looking chap. Rich with it.'

Joss stared at him, not so hung-over that she couldn't see what he was getting at.

'You're suggesting that I let James Costigern . . .?'

'You could do worse. There's money in it if you get the evidence – plenty of money. More than you earn in this dump, that's for sure. That family stinks of money. An' so what if you get your picture in the papers? You want to be famous, don't you?'

Joss sprang to her feet.

'What do you think I am – a common trollop like Jenny Fisher?' She slapped him a stinging blow across the cheek. 'How dare you!'

Grabbing her handbag, she stalked out of the bar. She didn't turn to look, but Sam Burkiss was smiling as he rubbed his face and called out after her: 'Think about it, Joss. It makes sense. If people won't give you what you want, take it.'

Chapter 21

'Look, Sid, don't take this the wrong way. Let's just say I'm . . . concerned.'

Jolly Jimmy Costigern was standing with Sid Dukes, looking out of his huge office window at the scuttling campers beneath.

'Concerned about what?'

'I hear all the things that go on in this camp, Sid. It's my job to hear things – and I've heard that the Friday night show went less than smoothly.'

Sid went on looking out of the window.

'It was nothing, I've sorted it out.'

'That's not what I heard. Star of the show too drunk to perform, that's what I heard – you put some kid on in her place and then there was trouble.'

This time Sid turned to look at Jimmy.

'Nothing serious happened, you have my word – the campers didn't even notice. And what did happen certainly wasn't anything to do with Jenny Fisher. She did a wonderful job, she's got real talent.'

'Ah, yes. Jenny Fisher.' Jimmy's eyes followed a young couple in swimsuits, chasing each other around the fountain. 'You do know about the company that girl's been keeping?'

The penny dropped.

'I don't think it's any of my business who my singers see in their spare time.'

'Oh, really? Well, I think it's *my* business when they spend their time with my grandson.'

Sid sighed.

'Mr Costigern – Jimmy – don't be hard on Jenny. She's a good girl, talented too . . .'

He waved aside Sid's protestations.

'You're a good man, Sid, your loyalty does you credit. But you've always been a soft touch and I know a gold digger when I see one.'

'It's not like that! Like I said, Jenny Fisher's a good girl, straight as a die, and as for Henry . . . he seems happy enough to me. These last couple of weeks he's really come out of his shell.'

'Henry – happy?' Jimmy laughed scornfully. 'Sid, that boy hasn't a clue what's good for him. If he had, he'd be putting his back into the family business, not mooning around after chorus-girls. I want you to have a word with that girl, Sid.'

'I don't follow?'

'She trusts you. If she's a good girl like you say she is, you'll make her see sense. If not, well . . . money talks to girls like that. I'm sure we can persuade her to keep away from Henry.'

'We!' Sid stared at Jimmy Costigern with a mixture of anger and amazement. 'You can leave me out of this, Jimmy.'

'Look at it this way, Sid,' he went on, his tone calm and even, 'you'll be doing the girl a favour. After all, if Miss Fisher wants to stay in showbusiness . . .'

Sid blanched. Now Jimmy was playing his trump card.

'I'll give it to you straight, Sid. No point in beating about the bush. I know an awful lot of people in the entertainment business – in fact, think about it, who *don't* I know in the North-west?'

'This sounds a lot like blackmail, Jimmy.'

'Call it what you like, Sid. But the fact remains that I got you your start in this business when you were a raggy-arsed urchin . . .'

'. . . and you could finish me just as easily?' Sid gave a dry laugh. Temper whirled like a cyclone inside him; he could feel his blood pressure rising and the dull ache as his chest tightened. 'Well, go on then, do it.'

'Sid . . .'

'Do it, Jimmy, if that's what you want. Jenny Fisher is the best thing in my show, and if you ruin her life you'll be ruining me too.' His breath came in short, difficult gasps as anger overwhelmed him.

'Sid, pull yourself together and listen!'

'No, Jimmy. I'm tired of listening, and I won't do your dirty work for you either. If you want Jenny Fisher out of your precious grandson's life, you can "Jolly" well tell her so yourself.'

It was a very dark night, the pure black of the sky softened only by the distant glow of the chalet lights.

Jenny lay beside Henry Costigern on the scrubby headland, his jacket draped over her shoulders, listening to the gentle swishing and sighing of the unseen sea.

'I should be back in the chalet by now,' she whispered as he curled his arm about her waist. 'It'll be lights out in ten minutes.'

'Nobody will find us up here. And you said yourself Mae would cover for you.'

'I know, but . . .'

'Please don't go.' He wound a curl of her hair round his fingers and kissed it, very softly. 'Stay here with me and count the stars.' He paused, and she listened to the rhythm of his breathing. 'You know something, Jenny?'

'What?'

'You're the best thing that's ever happened to me.'

A thrill of fear and excitement shivered through her body.

'Don't. You don't mean that.'

'You know I do.' This time Henry rolled on to his side and drew Jenny's face down to his, kissing her on her brow, her closed eyelids, her chin, and finally her lips. 'You mean the world to me.'

They kissed again, and this time Jenny rolled back on to the dry, stony grass, submitting to the gentle insistence of Henry's urgent caresses. They both sensed that tonight their lovemaking would go far beyond kisses.

229

'Jenny – oh, Jenny, I've wanted you so much.'

'I've wanted you too.'

Henry's fingers moved ever so slowly down from her bare throat, over her shoulder and then to the small, hard swell of her breast. She could scarcely breathe for excitement. Her whole body tingled with delicious anticipation; she wanted so much for him to touch her there, she had waited so long for this moment, dreamed and fantasised about what it would be like, and yet . . . and yet . . .

'Henry.'

'Mmm?'

'Henry, please.'

Jenny felt suddenly afraid, unable to go on. A few moments more, and there would be no going back. Coldness gripped her. She was in mortal fear of the closeness, this intimacy, which was drawing its velvety cloak about them. Yet it took a real wrench to break free from his kiss.

'Please . . . stop.'

He drew back a little way, his hand moving up to rest lightly on her shoulder.

'I'm sorry, I thought . . . don't you like me touching you?' The disappointment in his voice was palpable.

'O-Of course I do.'

'I won't if you don't want me to.'

'I . . . you know I like you. I like you very much.'

'Then what's wrong? Tell me, Jenny, what have I done? Is it because . . . because it's your first time? I'd never do anything that would hurt you . . .'

'I know. You've done nothing wrong, I swear.'

She wanted to tell him what was wrong, truly she did. But how could she begin to explain to Henry Costigern about the invisible scar which Ivan Price had burned into her soul? About the violence and brutal lechery of his caresses, the hissing menace of his threats, the beery stench of his breath as he had forced her down on to her own mother's bed?

'I'm sorry, I didn't mean it to be like this. I wanted it to be special.'

'It *is* special. Just being with you is special.' Henry's

fingers traced the curve of her cheek, felt the fine trail of wetness. 'You're crying – oh, Jenny, don't cry.'

She didn't answer him, but sighed a little 'oh' of gentle pleasure as he kissed away the tear that had escaped from the corner of her eye.

'I meant what I said, Jenny. You're the best thing in my life and all I want to do is make you happy. I can wait as long as it takes. For ever if need be.'

There was such warmth in his voice that it melted right through the walls of her fear. He cradled her in his arms, and she returned his kisses with a new and honest need.

'I want to make you happy, too,' she whispered; and meant it. Taking Henry's hand, she guided it to her breast. This time, she felt only pleasure.

'Are you sure?'

She smiled up at him in the darkness. This wasn't Ivan Price, this was Henry; sweet, gentle, honourable Henry who filled her with happiness and wanting.

'I couldn't be surer.'

The following morning, Mae and Sid were too late to catch breakfast at the Roman Room, so they made do with a fry-up in Jim's Cafe, just across the way from the boating lake. It was cheap and cheerful, if a bit tacky; and best of all, at this time of the morning, completely free from campers.

Mae chattered happily between mouthfuls of bacon and eggs.

'She was out all night, you know.'

Sid prodded the overcooked fried egg on his plate.

'Hmm?'

'Jenny . . . she was out all last night. Sid, are you eating that egg or waiting for it to hatch?'

'To be honest, I'm not very hungry.'

Mae swallowed a lump of fried bread.

'Not hungry? You? That's a new one on me.'

He pushed away his plate.

'I think I'll have another cup of tea.'

Mae watched him ladle three spoonfuls of sugar into his

cup. He didn't drink it, just kept on stirring it round and round with a Costigern's monogrammed teaspoon.

'There's something on your mind, isn't there?'

'What makes you say that?' he asked evasively.

'Well, for a start off you've not been listening to a word I said. And you've lost your appetite. And you've had a face as long as a wet Wednesday ever since yesterday morning. Come on, Sid. Why don't you tell me what's up?'

'If you really want to know,' he said in a low voice, glancing around to make certain that the waitress wasn't listening, 'it's Jimmy Costigern.'

'He's not been going on about the stage costumes again, has he?' Mae patted Sid's hand. 'Take no notice of him, he's just got a thing about yellow and blue stripes.'

Sid didn't return her smile. His eyes were sad, and the wrinkles at the corners seemed deeper than usual. In the unforgiving light of morning, Sid Dukes looked old and tired.

'Sid, you can tell *me*, surely?'

'I didn't know he had it in him, Mae, really I didn't.' Sid ran his fingers through his thinning hair. 'That man was like a father to me, he practically brought me up when I was in the kids' home – paid for me to have music lessons, even took me camping once . . .'

'I know, Sid. Jimmy's been good to you.'

'He was always so generous, so kind. He gave me my start in life, I really looked up to him. And now he does this. He *threatens* me.'

'Threatens you? With what?'

Sid lowered his voice to an angry, barely controlled whisper.

'Seems he doesn't approve of Henry getting friendly with Jenny, thinks she's out to get his money . . .'

'Jenny!' exclaimed Mae, her mouth agape. 'Jenny's not like that. She'd never . . .'

'I know, I know, that's what I told him. I reasoned with him, I told him she's a good girl, but he wouldn't listen. He wanted me to warn her off Henry, make her "see reason". Even told me to offer her money to buy her off!'

Mae stared at Sid. His whole body was tense with rage.

'And you told him where to get off?'

'What do *you* think? I'm not Jimmy Costigern's lapdog. Whatever I owe him, I'll not sink that low. But I've never seen him like that, Mae, he was ruthless.'

'I expect . . . maybe it was just a fit of temper, maybe somebody'd said something to upset him – you know what he's like. He'll have forgotten about it by now.'

Sid shook his head.

'Oh, no, he meant it all right. You know, Mae, it's really shaken me up. I thought I knew him . . .'

'I know.' She tried to soothe him, laying her hand on his, but Sid's knuckles were white with anger. 'But best forget about it, eh? No sense in upsetting yourself.'

'Forget about it? How can I? It makes me so angry. Jenny's had a rotten life, Henry's been like a lost soul till now – they're good kids, they *deserve* something good to happen.'

'Yes, Sid, you're right – but calm down. You know the doctor said you mustn't upset yourself like this.'

Sid ignored her. His face was white and filmed with sweat, jaw set and clenched.

'Then along comes the great god Jimmy bloody Costigern, who thinks he's got a right to run other people's lives for them when even his own son hates him . . .'

'Sid.'

'And we all have to jump to attention and . . . and . . .'

All of a sudden his eyes closed and he clapped his hand to his chest. His voice became very small and far away, his breathing a slow rasp of pain. Mae leaned across the table, seized him by the shoulders.

'Sid, listen to me, what's wrong?'

'Mae . . . Mae, get me back to the chalet. Before someone sees . . .'

He got to his feet, hardly able to stand upright.

'Let me get the doctor.'

'No! No doctor, I know what's wrong with me, it'll pass. For God's sake, Mae, get me home. I can't let anyone see me like this.'

Back in Sid's chalet, Mae helped him on to the bed and drew the floral curtain across the window.

'Sid . . . Sid, are you all right?' She knelt on the bed astride him, fingers fumbling to pull off his tie and unfasten his shirt collar. 'Sid, don't *do* this to me!'

'Gawd, Mae,' he joked through the pain, 'you could've picked a better time to rip my clothes off.'

'Look, let me fetch the camp doctor, he won't tell anyone.'

'No.' Sid caught her wrist and drew her hand to his lips, kissing it. 'No, Mae. I know you're thinking of me but I'll be better when I've rested for a minute or two.'

'But what if . . .?'

'I'll be fine, I promise.' A little colour was returning to Sid's cheeks, and his breathing began to ease as the iron band slackened around his chest. 'And you've got to promise me something, Mae. You've got to promise not to tell anyone about this. Not even Jenny. And especially not Geoff Tait.'

She nodded silently, determined not to show the tears that were pricking beneath her eyelids.

'I promise. But, Sid . . .'

'But nothing.' He eased himself slowly upright and Mae propped a couple of pillows behind his back. 'You don't think anyone saw?'

'No one saw.' She forced a smile. 'And if they did, they'd have taken you for a drunk.'

She kissed the end of his nose and lay down on the narrow bed beside him, her arm curled lightly over his belly.

'Will you really be all right?'

'Right as rain.' Sid hugged her to him. 'Just you wait and see. *Everything*'s going to be all right.'

'Steady on, Mr Potter, I can hardly keep up!'

'That's the trouble with you young 'uns, no stamina!'

Jenny did her best to keep up with the *Lambeth Walk*, though she had a stitch in her side from too much laughing.

Joby Potter was seventy-five if he was a day, a champion clog dancer and as nimble on his feet as most men thirty years younger. He was also the winner of this week's Gorgeous Grandad competition, and had been trying out his chat-up lines on her all afternoon.

'. . . All together now . . .'

'OI!'

One hand hanging on to his cardboard laurel wreath, Mr Potter jabbed his thumb in the air and bellowed out the tune.

'Sing up, lass, you've a grand little voice!'

These old folks certainly knew how to have fun, thought Jenny. They'd spent the morning playing bowls, eaten a three-course lunch in the Roman Room, cheered on the kids in the Donkey Derby, and now they were all enjoying a knees-up before high tea. The pace was enough to wear anybody out, but Jenny was so happy that she could have danced and sung for days on end, and never stopped.

She thought of Henry again. In fact she found herself thinking about him almost all the time. She felt excited, strangely grown-up and very, very alive. What use was sleep, unless it was to dream about Henry Costigern?

After a Paul Jones and a couple of foxtrots, everyone formed a giant conga line which threaded its way round and round the Viennese Ballroom, out through the French doors, once round the fountains and back inside. Then, at last, the music stopped and everyone took a breather.

'Come on, Mr Potter, time for tea and biscuits on the sun terrace.'

It wasn't until Jenny went across to the trestle table to get Mr Potter a second cup of tea that she noticed Jolly Jimmy Costigern. He was standing by the French doors, arms folded, looking straight at her. She gave a little start as their eyes met. How long had he been standing there? Had he been watching the entertainment or – horrors of horrors – had he been watching *her*?

Her heart skipped a beat at the thought. Surely even the all-seeing Jimmy Costigern couldn't have found out about her and Henry, and what they'd done last night? A fire-and-brimstone church man like Jolly Jimmy would never approve. She looked away and started chatting to the campers, certain that the truth must be written all over her face.

'Miss Fisher . . .'

Jolly Jimmy didn't need to raise his voice, it had a natural booming quality which made it carry effortlessly across the ballroom. Old Mr Porter poked Jenny in the ribs.

'Ow! Mr Porter, behave!'

'Best be off, lass, t'owd bugger wants you.'

Jenny crossed the ballroom to where Jimmy was standing.

'Mr Costigern?'

'Ah. Yes. Miss Fisher . . . Jenny, isn't it?'

'That's right. I was just . . . helping.'

'So I see.' He paused, seeming unnaturally hesitant, as though he had something on his mind but couldn't quite decide how to put it. 'Do you like it here, Jenny?'

'Oh, yes, thank you, Mr Costigern. It's what I've always wanted to do, and the campers are lovely.'

'Get homesick, do you?'

She paused.

'Sometimes.'

'Where are you from?'

'St Helens.'

'And your father . . . what does he do for a living?'

'He's dead. He was killed down the pit when I was eleven.'

'Ah.' Jimmy cleared his throat to cover his embarrassment. 'So . . . you'll be going back to your family when the season's over?'

'I . . . don't know.' Jenny realised that she hadn't thought about it; ever since she'd come here she'd put off thinking about the future. 'I suppose it depends on how the singing goes . . . whether Mr Dukes wants me to stay on with the band.'

Jenny wondered if Jolly Jimmy had heard a word of what she had said. His eyes were on her, but he seemed to be looking straight through her, his mind elsewhere. On impulse, she added: 'Mr Costigern?'

'Yes?'

'Am I doing something wrong? I'm trying hard, but I don't really know, you see. It's all so new.'

Jimmy Costigern looked hard at her for a few seconds, as though searching her face for an answer. He opened his mouth to say something then closed it again.

'I've done something wrong, haven't I?'

He laid a large red hand on her shoulder.

'Don't worry,' he said at last. 'You're fine. You're just fine.'

Chapter 22

Sam Burkiss wasn't hard to find – his sort seldom were, thought Joss Flynn as she pushed her way past a group of young campers and into the Caribbean Bar.

It was two o'clock, and most of the Stripeys were out organising team games or mashed-potato-eating competitions. Burkiss was propping up the bar in a haze of cigarette smoke, a copy of the *Sporting Life* in front of him whilst he carried on a conversation with three of Jolly Jimmy's pigmen.

'Well, if it ain't Miss High and Mighty,' he commented, stubbing out his cigarette in a dish of monkey-nuts. He gave his companions a meaningful stare. 'Scram, will yer? I'll catch up with yer later.'

Burkiss bought himself another beer; he didn't bother to offer to buy Joss anything. She lit up an Abdullah and slid on to the stool beside him.

'That business proposition of yours . . . still on, is it?'

A thin smile twitched the corners of Burkiss's mouth.

'I knew you'd see sense.'

Joss felt like hitting him again, but held herself back.

'This place is a hole,' she snapped. 'Sid Dukes is a cretin and Geoff Tait has completely lost his nerve. If I'm ever going to get my name in lights . . .'

'If you want something doing, do it yourself, that's what I always say.' Burkiss lit up again, inhaled deeply, and blew out the smoke in a bluish coil which drifted into Joss's face, making her cough.

'So?'

'So what?' he asked innocently.

Joss watched Tony go off to the other end of the bar, to serve a couple of men in flat caps.

'So what do you want me to do?' she hissed.

Burkiss's smile broadened.

'That's more like it.' He grinned. 'Now, why don't I buy you a drink?'

As Joss Flynn was making plans for the future, Jenny and Henry were out walking in the woods, a couple of miles from the camp.

'There – that's a nuthatch,' said Henry, pointing to a distant flutter of departing wings.

'Missed it,' sighed Jenny. 'I'm no good at birds – all we get in our backyard are sparrows, and they're black with soot!'

'Then I'll teach you. See up there, near the top of that oak tree?'

Jenny shaded her eyes and peered up.

'What am I looking for?'

'A bird. Can't you see it?'

'What – that little brown thing?'

'That's the one. It's some kind of warbler, I think.'

'How on earth can you tell? It's just a brown blob with a beak!'

Henry laughed and hugged Jenny to him, kissing her tenderly on the brow and the lips.

'I used to think that,' he said. 'Until Dad insisted I join the school Scout troop. I tell you, Jenny, I hated everything about scouting, all that knot-tying and dib-dib-dobbing and those awful hats. And then we went on summer camp, and I started learning about flowers and birds and things.'

Jenny smiled up at him.

'You're full of surprises.'

'As a matter of fact, I thought about reading Botany at university, but of course Grandpa had set his heart on Law.'

'He wouldn't let you choose for yourself?'

'You know how it is. He hauled me into that office of his and lectured me for hours: "What's the use of knowing all about flowers when you can know all about how to make money?" ' Henry ground the toe of his shoe into the soft leaf-mould. 'That's Grandpa for you.'

'Funnily enough . . . Jolly Jimmy spoke to me yesterday.'

Henry looked up.

'Grandpa did?'

'While I was helping with the old folks' dancing in the ballroom. I noticed him watching me and he called me over.'

'What did he want?' Henry's voice seemed to hold a note of suspicion. Then he smiled it away and took Jenny's hand, and they strolled on together, under the sun-dappled trees.

'That's just it, I still don't really know what he was on about. I kept thinking he was going to say something important or to tell me off or something, but all he did was ask questions.'

'Questions – about what?'

'Silly things really. Where I came from, and what my dad did for a living. What do you think it was all about?'

For a moment, she thought Henry actually knew. Like Jolly Jimmy, he seemed on the point of saying something momentous. Then he shrugged and laughed it off.

'I haven't the faintest idea. But that's Grandpa for you – he likes to keep people guessing.'

At the top of the hill the ancient woodland thinned out, giving a clear view across fields to Llandew Point, and round the sweep of the bay towards Costigern's Camp, with its ever-turning ferris wheel and its patchwork of many-coloured chalets trailing down the hillside to the sea.

'You know, Henry . . .'

'What?'

'Sometimes I think . . . all this is too good for me, I don't deserve it.'

'Don't talk nonsense!'

'No, I mean it. It's too good to be true, isn't it? It can't last.' She thought back to the happy days of her childhood, and the big yellow sun that had always shone, no matter how thick the smog might be. 'Good things never do.'

'This one will,' he promised, slipping his arm round her waist and pulling her closer. She rested her head on his shoulder, feeling the warmth of him beneath his shirt.

'How can you say that?' she murmured.

'I'll *make* it last. For ever and ever. This is the best thing in the world, and I'm not going to let anyone spoil it.'

It had taken many days to do it, but Tom Fisher had finally come to a decision. He would have to go and see John Corlett.

It was early in the morning when he reached the corner of Jubilee Street. The shop wasn't due to open for another hour, but he could see Mr Corlett moving about inside, arranging tins of peaches on a shelf behind the counter. There was no sign of Eddie, so that was one thing to be thankful for. Tom rapped on the glass.

'Open up, will yer, John?'

Mr Corlett looked up at the second knock and called across: 'We're closed.'

'Let us in, John. It's important.'

Impatience gnawed away at Tom as the key grated in the lock and the door swung inward. Now he had come here he wanted to get it over with as quickly as possible.

'What's up? Dot run out of something, has she?'

'I want a word.' He followed John into the shop, hands thrust deep into the pockets of his work trousers. 'About our Jenny.'

John Corlett's expression registered cautious surprise.

'What about her?'

'Billy and Daisy told us you know where she is.'

'And if I do?'

John Corlett went on setting out the tins, three deep, building them up into meticulously symmetrical rows. He was a methodical man, thought Tom, methodical but no man's fool.

'Look . . . man to man, John. Do you know where our lass is? It's really important.'

'Well . . . perhaps I do.'

'Have you told her owt about what's been going on?'

242

The Manxman hauled another box of tins on to the counter, and wiped his hands on his brown shopcoat.

'Now, boy, do you really think I'd bother your sister with gossip and hearsay? She's more to think about than a lot of vicious rumours. Credit me with some sense.'

Tom let out his breath in a rush.

'Thank God for that! Listen, John, what folk have been sayin' . . . it's not the half of it. I want you to know the truth.'

'I don't want to pry . . .'

'It's not prying, I want to tell you. You were a good friend of my mam's once, John, you did your best to warn her off Ivan, the least you deserve is the truth.

'Fact is, John, Mam caught Ivan in bed with our Nancy . . .'

'She what!' The shock loosened John Corlett's grip on a can of pineapple chunks and it crashed to the floor, rolling away to rest against a sack of potatoes.

'Oh, 'twern't Nancy's fault, he beat her till she gave in. He'd been forcing her for weeks. He'd tried it on with Jenny too, only she told Mam and Mam thought she was lying. That's why she threw Jenny out.'

'For the love of God, Tom . . .'

He looked John Corlett squarely in the face. It wasn't easy. Shame made him want to hang his head and stare at his boots.

'She weren't lying, John. It were all true. If we'd listened to Jenny, Nancy'd not be sobbing in corners and our mam'd have her baby. I'll have him, John, I'll have Ivan Price for what he's done!'

John Corlett stood stock-still, his steady gaze on Tom.

'There was a lot taken in by that man. Dot was on her own for a long time, she wanted someone who'd take care of her.'

Anger flared in Tom, anger against himself.

'She wasn't on her own. I'd have looked after her, John! D'you not think I'd take care of my own mam?'

'Of course you would, but you were only a boy. There's no reason to be so hard on yourself.'

Tom wasn't listening. He didn't want kind words. He reached into his pocket for the envelope and held it out.

'I want to put it right, John, if it's not too late.'

'What's this, boy?'

'It's a letter to our Jenny, what I wrote. I'm not a writer, but it's best I could do. Will you give it to her?'

John Corlett took the envelope, turning it over, reading the way 'Miss J. Fisher' had been printed so carefully, too carefully, across the front.

'I could give you the address, you could send it yourself?'

'No. You send it. After all this . . . mebbe she won't want to know us. I couldn't blame her if she didn't. I don't want to know where she is if she wants nowt to do with us.'

'I'll send it,' promised John, slipping the letter into his pocket.

Tom walked back to the door, then turned at the last minute.

'Be honest with us, John. Do you think she'll ever forgive us?'

He reached into the box for another tin of pineapple chunks.

''Course she will, boy. 'Course she will.'

Well, that's done and there's no more to be said about it, thought Tom as he walked through the colliery gates and across the yard to the lamp-house. No use brooding on it; either she'll read the letter and understand, or she won't.

There was work at the pit today, and he was profoundly grateful; not just for the money, but for the liberation of sheer hard, physical effort. You couldn't dwell on things when you were hacking coal out of a narrow, rocky seam. But you could swing your pick at the coal-face and imagine that every lunging blow was stabbing into the treacherous body of Ivan Price.

Men were lining up to collect their lamps and tallies.

'Morning, Len.'

'Morning, Tom.'

'Work again today, thank God. Our Kenny's been laid off from PBs. There'd be nowt t'eat if it weren't for my wages.'

244

Tom clapped Len on the shoulder.

'Come down The Black Horse tonight, I'll buy you a pint.'

He stepped out into the sunshine, aware of the weight that had been lifted from his shoulders. He'd told his sister everything, and for the moment at least, he could do no more.

As he crossed to the winding-house, deep in thought, he heard a voice behind him.

'They not sacked you yet then, boy?'

Tom whirled round, sick to his stomach.

Ivan!

He didn't know why it came as such a surprise. After all, Ivan still worked here, they were bound to meet up sooner or later. But that voice, that sneering, vicious hiss of a voice! It made his blood boil in his veins. If Ivan Price was feeling the slightest twinge of remorse, there was no sign of it.

Tom chose not to acknowledge him. That was best, just keep on walking. His fists clenched and unclenched in his pockets. Just keep on walking. Ivan would get the message and go away. But the footsteps were still there, right on his tail.

'Hey now, boy, is that any way for a son to behave with his *da*?'

That word touched the one raw nerve Tom could not ignore. He spun round, fury in his eyes.

'Go to Hell, Ivan!'

He smirked.

'How's your ma, boy? I'll be home soon to see 'er.' The menace in his voice was chilling. 'Don't look so surprised now, boy. It's my house an' I'll do what I like in it.' He grinned. 'With whom I like. Got that?'

The impulse to swing his fist at Ivan, to knock him down and stamp on his grinning face, was almost too strong to overcome. But that wasn't the answer, Tom kept telling himself; all it would do was give Ivan the upper hand, hand him the perfect excuse to get Tom the sack – and then where would the Fishers be?

He turned on his heel and kept on walking away. Ivan quickened his pace and marched in step with him.

'She'll have me back, boy, like a shot.'

Tom darted him a look of venomous hatred.

'Only to put a knife in your guts.'

The sneer in Ivan's voice was as unbearable as the scratch of wet chalk on a blackboard.

'Why's that, boy? You not man enough to do it yourself? You as big a *nancy* as your sister?' He laughed. 'That's what you are, boy. A coward an' a filthy little queer.'

Tom's fist itched to slam into Ivan's face. But instead he simply stopped in his tracks, turned and spat on Ivan Price's boots.

'I wouldn't dirty my hands on you,' he said; and kept on walking towards the winding-house.

Wednesday lunchtimes usually found Geoff Tait in the Caribbean Bar, drinking with the boys from the band.

'Your round, Desmond.'

'What, again? It can't be!'

'Get your hand in your pocket, Des. Mine's a pint of mild.'

With obvious reluctance, Desmond pulled out the contents of his trouser pocket: a greyish handkerchief, chalet key, one furred-over boiled sweet and a packet of ten Capstan. A couple of half-crowns followed still more grudgingly, tinkling on to the bar-top.

'You know what they say, Desmond,' said Duncan the trombonist. 'It's better to give than to receive.'

'Oh, and you'd know all about that,' commented Geoff, draining his beer glass.

'What's that supposed to mean?'

'It's all right, I won't tell Jolly Jimmy about that little fiddle you and Binky are running on the Holiday Princess competition.'

'That girl won fair and square!'

Desmond spluttered into his half of shandy.

'Square? She *was* square. She was built like a flippin' brick shithouse. Besides, me and Geoff saw her dad slipping you a backhander behind the dodgems.'

'Two quid's not much when you have to split it with four judges,' replied Duncan serenely. 'Pass us that ashtray, will you, Geoff? Anyhow, the best bit is consoling the runners-up afterwards.'

'You're a dirty dog, Duncan,' observed Geoff. 'Is there any woman in this camp you *haven't* had?'

'None worth having,' he admitted. 'Except that Miranda Costigern. I wouldn't mind giving her one.'

'Jolly Jimmy'd have your knackers for breakfast,' retorted Desmond, blowing out a noseful of shandy.

'Jolly Jimmy wouldn't know, would he?' Duncan surveyed the bar like a white hunter scanning the African veldt. 'Bit of savvy, that's all it takes to get the women running after you, 'specially in a place like this.'

A gaggle of pretty lasses were sitting at a table across the bar, being terribly sophisticated and daring. It was probably their first time in a pub, their first time without their mums and dads to keep them in check. They kept nudging each other, looking across at the boys, then giggling and looking away again.

'Take that lot over there,' said Duncan. 'I could have all three of 'em by teatime if I wanted.'

'So why don't you?' asked Geoff.

'Can't be fucking bothered.' Duncan stubbed out his cigarette as though it had insulted his grandmother. 'Chasing skirt is all very well, but that's all there is to do in this place. It's like living in a sodding knocking-shop.'

Geoff set down his glass, took out his silver cigarette case and offered it round.

'Here – have one of mine.'

'Ta.' Duncan looked at him quizzically. 'You're not usually so generous.'

'So – you don't reckon much to Costigern's then?'

''S all right,' shrugged Desmond, lighting up.

'But it's not what we started out to do, is it?' pointed out Duncan. 'Look, four, five years ago this was a great band, we knew where we were going – straight to the top. We were first with all the new material, that's why I joined. I

247

wanted to play hot dance nights at the Café Royal, not bash out old music hall songs and accompany some second-rate juggler who's always dropping his balls . . .'

'It's regular money, though,' said Desmond.

'Yeah – till the end of the season. Then what? Tea dances in Wigan? Besides, Sid's in Jimmy Costigern's pocket. One word from him and we'll be back here for Christmas fortnight an' all. I tell you, I'm sick of it.'

'You know,' said Geoff quietly, 'I worry about Sid. He's not getting any younger.'

'Neither is his material,' said Duncan. 'Old music, old pals, old hat.'

'Yeah . . . well, maybe you're right. Sid's getting past it. The band's been going downhill for too long.'

'So what are you going to do about it? Have another stand-up row with him and get yourself the sack?'

'Look, Duncan. We could do it again. You, me, Desmond, six or seven of the other lads. We could start up the band from scratch again, really go places.'

Across the bar, a cheer went up. A group of campers were raising their glasses to a middle-aged bloke who was dancing on the table, his trouser legs rolled up to the knees.

'Happy birthday, you old sod.'

'Happy fiftieth, Reggie luv, hope you like the slippers.'

Duncan looked Geoff in the eye.

'Are you serious?'

'We could do it, Dunc.'

Duncan looked at Desmond. He nodded. Behind him, the man on the table had started singing *Any Old Iron* and conducting his friends with a beer glass.

'All right, Geoff, you're on. If we stay here much longer, we'll all end up like him.'

The pit was a hot, claustrophobic hell of dust and blackness. Noise from the coal-cutting machinery and the winding gear covered any attempt at civilised conversation. The colliers worked in silence, paying no attention to anything but the work. Nobody took any notice of Ivan Price as he moved along the roadway towards the coal-trucks. After all, he was the overman for this district; he was just doing his job too.

Tom was at work on the seam, lying on his belly to steady the bar machine cutter. It was a bad seam, very low and hard to get at, and there was water everywhere, a hot rain falling on him continuously, leaving him to work in several inches of wetness. He might get another shilling for working in water, he might not. You didn't complain, particularly when Ivan Price was doling out the work. Make a fuss, and maybe tomorrow there'd be no work at all.

The machine reached the end of its rope, and he signalled to his drawer to turn off the compressor. He got up from his knees and he and Len finished loading coal into the tub.

'Ready?'

'Ready.'

They began pushing the tub from the coal face to the roadway, where it would be hauled up to the surface. The tub held ten hundredweight and it was a steep incline to push it up, but Tom was used to the work. They walked slowly up the slope, one on either side, hands clamped to the edge of the tub.

Tom didn't see Ivan ahead of him, standing astride the rails; didn't see him smile as he unhitched the clips that coupled a "journey" of coal tubs to the moving steel rope which lay between the tracks. Nor did he see him slip the jack catches that prevented the tubs from running backwards down the slope.

The first he knew was the bell sounding, and then the shout: 'A runner – get out way, it's a runner!'

There was no time to do anything. All he knew was the rush of air and the rumble of the ground beneath his feet as the tubs came charging down the incline towards him. Then Len's fists hitting him in the stomach, punching him away to one side so that when the runaway tubs crashed into him, only his right arm was caught between them.

The blow was so sudden and so savage that at first Tom felt no pain, only the numbness of shock. Through eyes blurred by sweat, he saw Len go down without a sound, the first tub knocking him flat and pinning him against the second.

'Len! Len, oh dear God, Len . . .'

He wrenched his hand free. Other miners were coming, running, calling to each other, their lamps making criss-cross patterns in the darkness. One of them tried to pull him back.

'Tom lad, you've hurt your 'and . . .'

Tom shook him off.

'I'm all right. Len!' With his one good hand he started trying to push and drag the tub off his friend's prostrate body. 'Help me! Help me get this off him.'

Strong hands pushed and pulled, the steel rope going into reverse to drag the train of coal tubs back up the slope. Len lay very still across the rails, his right leg twisted at an unnatural angle.

'Tom, what's wrong with me, why can't I move?'

Somebody behind him called out: 'Where's stretcher? Get bloody stretchers! Two men hurt down here.'

'What happened?' asked someone else.

'It were an accident – aye, a terrible accident.'

An accident? Tom knelt protectively over Len. They'd worked together for six years, looked out for each other; his hand was starting to throb, but he wasn't leaving Len now. An accident? Everyone knew the coal tubs were dangerous, many men had been injured by them, but something inside him knew that this was no accident.

He looked up, straight into the face of Ivan Price. Ivan looked away, and in that instant Tom knew why.

That coal tub had been meant for him.

Chapter 23

'You spoke to Duncan then?' Joss Flynn stood at the mirror, attacking the slight sheen on the end of her nose with dabs of face powder.

'Uh-huh.' Geoff sat at the table in Joss's chalet, doodling on the back of a cigarette packet. 'He was interested.'

She gave a wide smile, put her arms round Geoff's neck and kissed him lightly on the cheek.

'Oh, darling, you see? I said you could do it.'

'It's a start,' he conceded. 'So far I've had four yeses and three maybes. That's not bad going.'

Joss lounged on the edge of the bed and eased her feet into a pair of elegant court shoes.

'So who've you got so far?'

'Binky and Con Parry . . . and Desmond.'

Joss pulled a face.

'*Must* you?'

'He's a good saxophonist. Mel and Andy said they'd think about it too . . .'

'Which means yes.'

'Don't jump the gun. Oh, and I think I could persuade Johnny Peroni.'

'Then do it! Johnny's the best vibes player on the northern circuit.'

'I don't want to push it, he might spill the beans to Sid.'

Joss snorted.

'Sid? You're still thinking about that old has-been? I keep telling you, Geoff, you'll never be anything until you start looking after number one. Now, who else are you going to ask?'

He twiddled his pencil. He hadn't been looking forward to this.

'A couple more brass players . . . a clarinettist . . . oh, and Jenny Fisher.'

Joss's jaw dropped.

'The Fisher girl? Is this some kind of sick joke?'

'She's a good singer. Very good.'

'Oh, it's like *that*, is it?'

'It's nothing of the sort, Joss. But if the band's going to get the prestige venues, we'll need a second singer, it's as simple as that.'

'Then get somebody else.'

'Jenny Fisher's right for the job. And she's new to the business, so she won't want too much money.'

'Let that little cow come and steal all my other songs? No, Geoff, I won't stand for it!'

'Sometimes you're like a spoilt kid, d'you know that?' He seized her by the wrists. 'What the hell *do* you want – Joss Flynn and her Nobodies? 'Cause at this rate, nobody's going to want to work with you. Me included.'

Joss opened her mouth to let fly with a torrent of abuse, then another thought seemed to cross her mind. She pouted.

'I like it when you come over all masterful with me, d'you know that?'

'What?'

'It gets me all excited.' She smiled as she drew him down on to the bed beside her. 'I'm all excited now, can't you tell?'

'Joss, this isn't the place . . .'

'You don't need anyone but me, honeybee,' she breathed. 'Why don't you let me prove it to you?'

She kissed him, and it was a skilful, provocative kiss. He could easily have given himself to it, body and soul. When she drew back, she flicked the tip of her tongue seductively across her lips.

Geoff pulled away and got to his feet.

'No, Joss. Every time you want something, you do this to me. This time I'm not playing along.'

'Geoff. Geoff, come back!'

He turned and walked out, breathing a sigh of relief once he was outside the chalet. Sod you, Joss Flynn, he thought. You're more trouble than you're worth.

Jenny Fisher, you don't know it yet, but I'm going to make you a star.

'You tell me that, in your opinion, Ivan Price deliberately sabotaged the coal tubs with intent to cause you injury?'

Tom stood before Mr Costain the pit manager, cap in his good hand, the other arm still in bandages. His mouth was dry. He wished he had Ivan Price's skill with words.

'Yes, sir.'

There were three men in the room: Tom, the manager and the pit owner, who had a copy of the mines inspector's report on the desk in front of him. They looked at each other and wrote notes on typed sheets. Panic gripped Tom. It was obvious they thought he was lying. Leaning across the desk, he looked the mine owner right in the face.

'Sir, I swear it's the truth.'

The man in the dark suit and stiff collar waved him away.

'You've given your evidence, Mr Fisher, you may go now.'

That's it, Tom thought to himself as he opened the door and stepped out of the manager's office. They don't believe a word I've said, and who can blame them? Poor Len's delirious in Providence Hospital, in no fit state to say one thing or another, and nobody actually saw Ivan do anything. It's my word against his; collier against overman. What chance do I stand?

The last person he wanted to see right now was Ivan, but he was sitting there in the outer office, self-righteous and smart in his Chapel suit.

'Had your say, 'ave you, boy? Told your little lies?'

Tom clenched his teeth.

'I told 'em the truth, which is more'n you'll do.'

Ivan laughed.

'You think they'll believe your fairytales, boy? It just so 'appens Peter Costain is a friend o' mine – goes to the same Chapel, see. He's a God-fearing man like me.'

Tom turned aside, sick to his stomach. So it had all been a waste of time. No wonder Costain and the mine owner had seemed so cold towards him. There seemed little point in hanging around to watch this charade reach its conclusion. Bitterly, he jammed his cap on his head and pushed his way out into the hazy summer afternoon.

About five minutes after Tom had left, the door opened and the manager beckoned Ivan into his office.

'You may come in now, Mr Price.'

'Much obliged Peter . . . Mr Costain . . . I'm sure.'

He stood confidently before the men, staring straight in front, the only sign of tension a single muscle twitching spasmodically in his jaw.

'You were present when the injuries occurred to Mr Fisher and Mr Dawson?'

'Yes, sir. I've been on day turn these last three weeks.'

'Give us your account of the incident, Mr Price.'

''Twas an accident, sir, plain an' simple. The couplings were faulty, the tubs came loose and ran down the incline. Naturally I sounded the alarm . . .'

'You are responsible for safety in your district, Price?'

'Yes, sir. But when I looked at the clips they'd sheared right through. Must've been wear an' tear, see.'

'So you are confident that the injuries were caused as a result of a regrettable accident, nothing more?'

''Course, sir. What other reason would there be?'

The pit owner folded his hands and leant forward over the desk. Ivan Price's respectful smile did not flicker.

'Tom Fisher gives a rather different account of the affair. He says you tried deliberately to injure him, that you bear a grudge against him and his family . . .'

Ivan laughed, but there was an edge to his laughter.

'The boy's imagining it, sir.'

'He tells me you and Mrs Price have had . . . difficulties.'

'Nothing that can't be mended, sir.'

'Indeed.' The mine owner patted the pile of papers in front of him. There was a look of distaste on his face. 'Personally, Price, I don't much care what you may get up to in the privacy of your own home, but what Tom Fisher told me did set me thinking. The fact is, nobody round here knows a thing about you. You're a man with no past, and that intrigued me.'

Ivan looked uneasy now.

'What's there to know, sir? I come 'ere from the Rhondda three year ago, lookin' for work . . .'

'Yes. From the same village Mr Costain was born in, wasn't it?' The mine owner shot a glance at the manager. 'I can't think why he didn't ask a few questions about you when he hired you. If he had, perhaps he'd have found out about the Parry boys.'

'What's that you say, sir?'

'The mines inspector who's been looking into this incident is a Mr Pugh-Jones – I think you may remember him? He certainly remembers you, Ivan. And he remembers what happened to the Parry boys – that was another unfortunate mining accident, wasn't it? Two dead and another so badly injured he's never worked since.'

'They never . . .' Ivan's face blanched beneath his weather-worn skin.

'Never proved that you were involved? True. But you left Wales after that, didn't you? And now you're leaving this pit too.'

'Sir! You can't . . . that bastard Tom Fisher . . . you can't listen to his lies!'

'Lies, Ivan? I think the only liar here is you.' The mine owner held out a sheet of paper. 'I'm giving you your cards. Collect whatever money's owing to you and don't bother coming back.'

Dot didn't make a sound, but Tom knew his mam was crying. As he looked in through the kitchen door he could see her shoulders heaving, her face buried in her hands.

'Mam.'

She looked up, hastily wiping her face on the corner of her apron and sniffing away the last of the tears.

'I thought you were down The Black Horse.'

Tom shook his head.

'Not tonight.' He crouched beside his mam and put his

bandaged left arm about her shoulders. 'Look, Mam, he's gone now, he's been sacked, he's not comin' back.'

'I know, son. It's not that . . .'

'What then?'

'I don't want the kids to hear.'

'Don't worry about them, Mam, they're in bed.' He pulled up a chair. 'What is it, Mam? Tell me.'

'We're not managin', love.'

''Course we are. We don't need him.'

'No, you don't understand. It's the money.' Dot upended her purse on to the table and a few copper coins spilled out. 'That's all we've got to last us till Friday. It's not enough, son.'

Tom felt in his pocket and brought out a sixpence. He laid it on the table next to the pile of change.

'Have this. I've nowt else.'

'You're a good boy, Tom, you do your best. But it's not enough, we can't manage.' Dot swallowed hard. 'We'll have to go on the Assistance.'

'Mam!' Tom looked at her, aghast. 'It's got that bad?'

Dot nodded.

'What with short-time workin' at the pit and you with your hand all bandaged up, there's not enough to keep us all. I pawned your dad's watch to pay the rent.'

'Mam, no, not Dad's watch!'

'I had to lad, I'll get it back somehow. But where's next week's rent comin' from, tell me that?'

'I'll find the money. Give me a few days.'

She pressed her hands gently to his cheeks, framing his face as she had done when he was a small boy and she wanted to tell him something really important, something he had to try and understand.

'Tom, you can't keep on livin' here. They'll means-test us, they'll find out you're bringing home a wage, an' they'll give us nowt.'

'Leave here? Leave you an' the kids?'

'You have to. Else we'll all starve, don't you see?' She kissed him on the forehead and smoothed his hair back.

'There's got to be summat else.'

'No, lad. If we go on like this, things'll be so bad they'll take the kids off me.'

'No, never. I'd never let them do that.' He hesitated, then blurted out, 'Look, Mam, I gave John Corlett a letter for Jenny. He promised he'd get it to her. She'll come back an' we'll all be together again, like we used to be.'

'You're a good lad, Tom.' Dot shook her head slowly and sadly. 'But there's no way round it, there's nothing else we can do. You've got to go.'

'But where? Where would I go?'

'You can stay at your Auntie Jane's. 'Course, you'll need to lie low an' we'll have to tell the Assistance man we don't know where you are . . .'

'Come on, Mam.' Tom took her small, work-roughened hands in his. 'Smile for us. We'll get through this, just you see.'

She watched him go, so tall and strong and yet so vulnerable, his bandaged arm a reminder of that vulnerability. Jenny had been vulnerable too, and Nancy; and she'd let them all down and now she was going to let them down again.

Alone in the kitchen, she sat for a while just listening to the ticking of the clock; the clock she would have to sell before the Assistance would give them a penny. Her dead husband's watch, the clock her parents had given them for a wedding present, and now her son . . . what else were they going to take from her?

In the cupboard, behind the pots and pans, Dot had a secret. She'd kept the gin bottle there for two and a half years; that was how long it had been since she'd had a drink. It was just over two and a half years since she'd met Ivan Price at the Miners' Welfare.

She sat herself down at the table and wiped the dust and cobwebs from the bottle. It was solid, reassuring, seductively comforting. A few glasses and the pain would quickly go away.

Standing in the passage, just outside the kitchen door, Nancy watched in sullen, resentful silence as Dot drank from an earthenware mug. Jenny had run away, now Mam was running away too. Damn them both to Hell.

Chapter 24

Jenny swam another length of the outdoor pool, then rested on the rail at the shallow end. Even by eleven o'clock the weather was swelteringly hot, and the water felt deliciously cool. This was the life; a whole day and night off, to do exactly as she pleased. If Henry had been free to spend it with her, it would have been just like being on holiday.

The campers were obviously having a whale of a time in the sunshine, chasing each other about and pushing Stripeys in and out of the pool. Jenny could see Gwen Roberts and Phoebe Haynes in fits of laughter, dripping wet and wringing the water out of their hair.

Harry Kaye, the camp host, was a real virtuoso. He had worked the campers up into a frenzy of silliness with his That's My Elbow competition, and Joey the Jolly Jester was leading a giggling conga-line of girls in bathing costumes all the way round the edge of the pool, up to the top of the diving board and back down the other side.

All this activity was being watched by Jolly Jimmy Costigern, who was standing by the deep end next to two men with a film camera, waving his arms about and shouting directions.

Jenny yawned and lay back against the rail, kicking out her legs lazily. She couldn't be bothered with all that running about. Another few minutes of wonderful laziness, then she'd go back to the chalet and find Mae. Maybe they could walk into Llandew and blow a few bob on a cream tea.

She glanced around the pool. Gwen and Phoebe were noisily chasing one of the campers now, a young boy dressed as a Red Indian. Who was that over there, reclining on a deck-chair beside the lifeguard's post? Jenny shaded her eyes. She might have guessed – it was Joss Flynn, queening it over everybody with her white silk swimming costume and her nose in the air.

It was while she was watching Joss that she felt a tap on her shoulder.

'Thought I might find you here.'

'Geoff!' Jenny looked up at him, puzzled. 'Joss is over there.'

'I know.' He stood and surveyed Joss just long enough to be absolutely sure that she had seen him with Jenny Fisher, then sat down on the edge of the pool, dangling his legs in the water. 'It's you I wanted to talk to.'

'Oh.' Jenny wasn't sure whether to be flattered or alarmed. Geoff Tait scarcely bothered talking to her except to moan about something she'd done wrong, or some last-minute change to the act.

He slid down into the water beside her, gasping at the coldness.

'Hasn't Costigern heard of heated swimming pools?'

Jenny grinned.

'Cold water strengthens the constitution and purges improper thoughts, remember?' Jolly Jimmy's personal commandments were listed on the back of every chalet door, the wall of every toilet block and even the bingo hall. By now, she knew most of them off by heart.

'Oh, yes? It doesn't seem to have worked very well on some people I could mention.' Geoff looked across at Joss. His eyes lingered for a few seconds, then he fixed them on Jenny. 'On your own today then?'

'Mae's having a sleep in the chalet.'

'I wasn't thinking of Mae. Henry Costigern deserted you, has he?'

Jenny felt a hot blush creeping up her cheeks. She supposed she should have known it would be like this – if she was with Henry everyone started talking wedding bells; if she wasn't, they all assumed he'd seen sense and given her the push.

'Geoff . . .' Her grey eyes flashed him a warning. He waved it away.

'It's all right, I'm not prying. Well, not as such. But I *am* interested in your . . . future.'

'Not *another* person trying to warn me off Henry Costigern!'

'No, no, not at all. A smart girl like you can make her own decisions.' Geoff rolled on to his back and floated, staring up at the fine puffs of cloud in the brassy blue sky. 'Like what you're going to do with the rest of your life.'

Jenny looked at him, puzzled.

'That depends,' she said.

'On?'

'On how you and Mr Dukes think I'm getting on . . . and whether there's a chance of any more work?'

'But you want to stay in the business? You still want to be a singer?'

'Of course! But . . .'

'Never mind the buts.' Geoff moved his hands and feet gently in the water, making tiny waves which lapped against Jenny's sides. 'The first time I saw you, I thought you were a nobody,' he said abruptly. 'A stupid little nobody with no talent and no future.'

His words stung Jenny.

'I . . . see.'

'I said that was what I *thought*.' Geoff turned over and got to his feet, smoothing back his wet hair. 'I was wrong. You've got talent and I want to help you make the most of it.'

Jenny looked at him in amazement. Was this really Geoff Tait – the same Geoff Tait who'd been infatuated with Joss Flynn and sure that Jenny Fisher wasn't up to the job?

'How?' she asked, hardly daring to be intrigued.

'I've got a proposition to put to you, Jenny – but until I say different you have to keep it to yourself. You're not to tell anyone, not even Mae.'

'But why . . .?'

'No one, it's important. Understood?'

Reluctantly, Jenny nodded her assent.

261

'I'm sick of Costigern's,' said Geoff. 'I'm sick of playing second-rate tunes to second-rate people. I'm setting up my own band when the season's over.'

'Geoff!' The implications struck Jenny in a rush. 'What about Mr Dukes, does he know?'

'I told you, Jenny, for now you keep this to yourself.' He paused. 'There'll be me and seven or eight of the lads, we'll be doing new material and playing good venues. We've got several London bookings already. I'll need a singer . . .'

Jenny's heart thumped crazily in her chest.

'But . . . Joss?'

'I'll need a singer,' he repeated. 'Think about it. Good venues, new material, and more money – if things go well, I should be able to double what Sid's paying you. Interested?'

Jenny's head reeled.

'It . . . it's all a bit sudden.'

'Take a few days to think about it. But not too long, eh?'

And with these parting words, Geoff Tait swam off towards the deep end.

'Mam! Mam, I'm 'ungry.'

Dot ruffled Daisy's hair.

'You can 'ave some bread an' scrape when we get in.'

'Mam, I want chips.'

'We can't afford chips. Friday maybe, we'll see.'

She pushed open the back gate and walked up the yard, the two kids trailing behind with the bag of coal they'd picked from the spoil-heap. Ten bob's worth of food vouchers, that was all the Assistance had given her this week; it might help feed the kids, but where was the rent money coming from? And the money for another half-bottle of gin.

There were four large loaves in the bags she carried; they'd keep them till they were stale, that way they went further. Climbing the steps, she half-turned towards the kids.

'Put the coal in coal hole, then come in an' wash yer hands.' She stepped into the back kitchen and the bags of bread fell to the floor. 'Oh, my God, no . . .'

Ivan Price was sitting at the table like Banquo's ghost, cleaning his fingernails with the blade of a pocket knife. His smile was like the leer of a stalking hyena.

'Well, if it ain't my own dear wife.'

'Dear God, Ivan! You've not come back?'

He threw back his head and roared with cruel laughter.

'Come back? To you? To this place? Don't make me laugh, woman. Leavin' 'ere was the best thing I ever done.'

'Then why, Ivan? Why 'ave you come back?'

He got to his feet, slowly and deliberately, slipping the knife into his pocket.

'Come 'ere, woman.'

'No.' Dot backed away towards the half-open door.

'I said, come 'ere. You're still my wife, Dot Price, an' don't you forget it. I can make you remember it any time I want.' He took her by the waist and pulled her forcibly towards him, crushing her against the hardness of his body.

'Ivan! Ivan, please . . .'

He forced a kiss on her lips then pushed her away, so hard that she fetched up against the draining board, wiping the taint from her face with the back of her hand.

'Go away, Ivan. Leave us alone.'

''Fraid I can't do that.'

'We've got nowt. Can't you see?' Out of the corner of her eye Dot saw Daisy and Billy coming back up the yard. 'Nowt. So why don't you just go? You're not wanted 'ere.'

'Ah, but there's summat *I* want. You always was a stupid woman, Dot. You borrowed money from Cecil Stokes, didn't you? Four quid, weren't it?'

Dot's face grew whiter than white.

'It were to pay off the debts . . .'

The door opened a fraction.

'Mam, can me an' Billy 'ave . . .?' Daisy's face froze in an expression of horror.

Ivan smiled.

'Why don't you come in an' give your *da* a nice big kiss, girl?'

'Daisy, go out – get out an' stay out!' cried Dot, swinging

round and slamming the door shut on both children. Their shocked faces stared at her through the back kitchen window. Ivan seized her and turned her round to face him.

'Four quid you 'ad off 'im on reasonable terms, only you've not been payin' 'im back, 'ave you?'

'I couldn't! Daisy got the scarlet fever, an' we 'ad to get doctor. Then we 'ad no food . . .'

'Mr Stokes don't like excuses, Dot. He wants 'is money, see, an' he wants the interest what's owin'.'

'I . . . I'll pay what I can, you know I will.'

'That's not good enough, Dot. Now, you can pay me, nice as pie, or you can pay Mr Stokes. You got a week to get the money.'

'I'll find it. Somehow.'

'Good. 'Cause in a week I'll be back to collect. An' if you don't pay up, well . . .' He smiled, a devil's smile. 'Well, I'll just 'ave to take whatever I can find.'

'I've told you, I've got nowt!'

'You got your precious kids,' replied Ivan. 'P'raps I'd better see what *they* can give me.'

Mae was still flat out on the bottom bunk when Jenny got back from the pool. She tried tiptoeing about, so as not to disturb her, but dropped one of her sandals on to the wooden floor with a tremendous clatter.

Mae opened her eyes and rolled over, squinting in the sunshine which was filtering through the curtain. She yawned.

'What time is it?'

'Almost one. If we don't get a move on there'll be no food left.'

Mae wrinkled her nose.

'Boiled mince and cabbage? Don't think I'll bother.'

'We could walk into Llandew, if you like? Get a bite to eat in a cafe.'

'Sounds good to me.' Mae slid off the bed and wriggled about to stretch her stiff muscles. 'I think I slept too long.' She winked. 'Must've been dreaming about Sid.'

The mention of Sid Dukes set the butterflies fluttering in

Jenny's stomach. She desperately wanted to tell Mae what Geoff Tait had told her: that he was planning to set up a rival band behind Sid's back. In all the years of their friendship, Jenny had never hidden anything from Mae Corlett. But Geoff had sworn her to secrecy, so how could she tell?

'Something on your mind?'

'No,' said Jenny a bit too sharply. 'Why, should there be?'

'No need to bite my head off.' Mae gave her a curious look. 'Where's love's young dream today then?'

'Henry? His dad's sent him off on a ten-mile hike with two hundred campers. I don't think he's very pleased about it.'

'I bet.' Mae ran a comb through her blonde locks. Her eyes met Jenny's in the mirror above the sink. 'You and Henry are as thick as thieves these days, I hardly ever see you.'

'You see me all the time!' protested Jenny, guiltily covering the fact that it was true; she'd been spending an awful lot of her spare time with Henry Costigern.

'On stage, yes, but that's hardly *seeing* you, is it?' Mae picked up her handbag. 'You and Henry are getting pretty close, aren't you?'

'I . . . well . . . sort of.'

'Oh, come on.' Mae dug her friend in the ribs. 'I know what you two have been getting up to. It isn't a crime you know, whatever my dad might think.' She opened the chalet door. 'Come on, let's see if there's any post for us. I've had nothing in ages.'

They walked together across the camp towards the administration block.

'Talking of scandalous behaviour,' said Mae, 'did you see Joss last night?'

'In the Caribbean Bar?'

'Where else! In *that* dress you could hardly miss her.'

Jenny giggled.

'Dress? It was more like a couple of pocket handkerchiefs held together with ribbon.'

Mae squealed with delight.

'Jenny, you bitch!'

'I must be getting it off Joss, she's such a good teacher!'

Jenny and Mae laughed together like gossipy schoolgirls as they walked down the avenue past the bowling green where a tournament was in progress. The competitors' silent concentration contrasted oddly with the hysterical laughter from the kiddies' paddling pool, where a dozen men with rolled-up trousers and tall Welsh hats were wading about, trying to spear cardboard fish.

'Did you see the way she was making up to James Costigern?' asked Jenny.

'She hardly left him alone all night.'

'And him a married man.'

'Not that he seemed to mind.'

Jenny shook her head.

'Dunno what Geoff'll make of it. All these men she's been seeing – she's making a proper fool of him.' She thought of what Geoff had said, and how he hadn't answered her when she'd asked if Joss would be singing with the new band.

'Well, if I was him, I'd give her the push,' declared Mae. 'Of course . . .' she grinned '. . . the way things are going, she might end up as your mother-in-law!'

'Don't!'

'No, really. If James ditches Miranda for Joss . . .'

'Mae!'

'. . . and Henry pops the question . . .'

'He wouldn't!'

'Ah, but what if he did?'

'Don't talk daft.'

'I'm serious. He's like a lovesick puppy – you want to snap him up before Joss does. That woman's a nympho-wotsit. At least that's what I overheard Geoff calling her the other night . . .'

'Mae, you've not been eavesdropping again?'

'You know those chalet walls, they're awful thin!'

Still laughing, they arrived at the administration block, where Bella and Gwen were sorting the staff post into pigeonholes.

'No rest for the wicked,' said Gwen cheerfully, rummaging in the pile before her and handing over a couple of envelopes. 'Here, these are yours.'

'Ta very much.' Mae took the envelopes and scanned them. 'A letter from Dad – *two* letters from Dad! I'm usually lucky if I get one a fortnight. Wait a minute, though, this one's for you.'

She held out the envelope and Jenny took it. It was rather thick for a letter. Curious, she tore it open. Another envelope was inside, together with a short note from John Corlett.

'What does it say?' Mae craned over Jenny's shoulder. She unfolded it and read aloud: ' "Dear Jenny, I hope you are well. Your brother asked me to make sure you got this letter. He said it was important. Regards, John Corlett." '

Jenny stared at the envelope, and at the name written so carefully across the middle of it: 'Miss J. Fisher'. There was no mistaking it, she knew that painstaking hand, that of a man unaccustomed to doing much writing. Her mouth fell open; her heart skipped a beat.

'Oh, God,' she whispered.

Mae laid a hand on her arm.

'What is it?'

Jenny looked up.

'It's from Tom!'

Chapter 25

'Jenny? Jenny, sit down, you look terrible.'

Mae's hands guided her to a seat beside the fountains. Children were shrieking with pleasure as they rode past on the back of an Indian elephant, but Jenny didn't even notice. All she saw was the sheet of paper in front of her, the letters blurring out of focus, remembered phrases echoing in the silence of her mind.

. . . caught Ivan with Nancy . . . threw him out . . . baby died . . . hardly any money coming in . . . come back, Jenny, come home for Mam's sake, we should have believed you . . .

Mae took the letter gently from between her fingers and scanned it quickly.

'Ivan's gone then?'

Jenny nodded.

'And they know you were telling the truth?'

Jenny clenched and unclenched her fingers.

'Oh, Nancy. Poor Nancy. It's all my fault.'

'No, how could it be?'

'She's only a kid. If I'd stayed, it would have been me instead of her.'

'If you'd stayed, it would have been both of you. He's an animal, Jenny, he likes hurting people. Do you really think it would've stopped with you?'

Jenny wanted to cry or shout, but nothing came out but a dry, colourless whisper.

'I *should've* stayed. Coming here . . . it's just selfish vanity. It's not for me.'

'No, don't you dare talk like that!' Mae took Jenny by the

shoulders and held her firmly, one second away from shaking the sense into her body. 'You've got talent, Jenny, more talent in your little finger than the rest of us have in the whole of our bodies.'

'Mae, I know you want to make me feel better, but . . .'

'It's nothing to do with making you feel better, you stupid girl! Look, you've spent your whole life caring for that family, when your drunken mother couldn't even be bothered to get out of bed. It's your life and it's your turn. You deserve to have something good for once!'

'What am I going to do?' Rationally Jenny knew Mae was right, that staying wouldn't have done any good, but guilt weighed heavy in her heart. 'Tom wants me to go back.'

'What good would that do?'

'He says Mam's drinking again and Nancy's a nervous wreck . . . who's looking after Billy and Daisy? And I've got a bit of money I've saved, I could help them . . .'

'Look, Jen.' Mae stared down at the shiny toes of her shoes. 'Go and see them, give them a bit of money if you've got it. Then turn right round and *come back*.

'If you return to live in St Helens, all it'll do is drag you down. What'll you do – clean the Alhambra till you find another Ivan Price to knock you about and mess with *your* daughter? If you don't take your chances, Jen, they'll not come again. You'll end up like your mam and spend the rest of your life hating everybody.'

Mae's words carried more meaning even than she understood. Tom's words mingled with Geoff's in Jenny's mind: 'Come back and look after Mam and the kids'; 'Come with me and I'll make you a star'.

'I've got to do *something*,' she said.

Mae's fierce expression softened.

'Of course you have. Did I say you shouldn't? We'll talk to Sid about it. He'll let you have a few days to go back and see them. Let's go and find him now.'

Sid. Good, kind, honest Sid who'd given her her one big chance. Jenny could hardly bear the deceit of keeping Geoff Tait's secret from her best friend. She wished with all her heart that he had never spoken to her about the new band, but he *had* spoken and there was no forgetting it. Or the money he had talked about – a vast amount by her standards, twice what Sid was paying, enough to buy a decent life for Nancy and Billy and Daisy.

'I suppose . . .' hazarded Jenny.

'Come on.' Mae pulled her to her feet. 'Strike while the iron's hot. But just you promise me one thing?'

'What's that?'

'Make sure you come straight back. Billy and Daisy aren't the only ones who need you, you know. You're part of the company now – we need you here, too.'

Later, at the afternoon rehearsal, Mae looked mysteriously pleased with herself. Jenny wondered why. The letter from St Helens was hardly any cause for celebration.

'Mae . . .'

'What?'

'Why are you smiling?'

'I can smile if I like, can't I?'

'Yes, but why?'

'Shush, Jenny, I'm trying to listen to Sid.'

He leafed back through the pages of sheet music on his stand until he reached the beginning of *Play, Orchestra, Play* and tapped with his pencil on the music stand.

'All right, everybody, one more time.'

'Oh, Sid,' came a chorus of groans.

'Once more, then we'll break for ten minutes. And this time, Geoff, remember it's a happy song – not a funeral dirge.' He threw a look at Geoff, who avoided eye contact and fiddled with the signet ring on his finger. 'Right, one-two-three, two-two-three . . .'

Jenny sat in the second row of the stalls and watched Sid's Dukettes going through their song and dance routine. She wished she could dance like Mae, who managed to look graceful even in silly satin shorts and rabbit ears. And she wished she knew why her friend looked so suddenly – and smugly – happy.

Jenny hummed along with the tune. Even though it wasn't one of her numbers she knew it by heart. She knew every word and every note of every show the company had staged since they arrived at Costigern's. She even knew the comic's patter off by heart.

The Dukettes moved into *I'll See You Again*, then Jenny and the other singers joined them on stage for *Thanks For The Memory*, which ended the Friday night show.

'Gawd,' panted Bella as she jumped down off the stage, 'is that man a slave-driver or what?'

'At least Geoff didn't stick in his three penn'orth,' observed Dolly. 'He's hardly said a word since we started.'

Jenny sneaked a look at him. He was standing near the back of the band, talking quietly to Desmond and Duncan. She could imagine what about.

'Sid looks happy enough anyway,' said Phoebe, pinning up a broken shoulder-strap. 'Makes a change.'

Sid did look happier than usual, thought Jenny with a pang of guilt. Less careworn, younger even, as if he'd shaken off some of the worries which weighed heavy on his shoulders. And as for Mae, her smile was a mile wide and she had Sid by the hand, towing him across the theatre.

'Jen! Jen, come here. Sid's got something to tell you.'

Puzzled, she went across. Mae looked like a little kid, bursting with some wonderful secret she could hardly contain. An overgrown kid at that, what with her being a full head taller than Sid. They made a funny pair.

'Mr Dukes?'

'Go on, Sid. Go on, aren't you going to tell her?'

Sid aimed a not-too-convincing glare at Mae.

'Honestly, Jenny, it's impossible to keep anything to yourself with this one around.' He folded his arms. 'Mae's had a word with me and she tells me you need a bit of time off?'

'Well, I don't want to cause problems . . .'

'You won't. We can manage without you for a couple of days. In the circumstances, you'll want to go back home and . . . deal with things. Why don't you go tomorrow and come back on Friday morning?'

'Thank you! Oh, Mr Dukes, that's ever so kind of you.'

Sid put up his hand to halt the torrent of gratitude.

'There's something else. I've decided to give you a regular solo spot in the show.'

Sid's words were a white-hot bolt of lightning, straight through the heart. For a moment Jenny couldn't take it in, couldn't believe what she was hearing. Then she thought of Geoff Tait, and the offer she hadn't accepted but hadn't exactly turned down either. She should have been elated, but instead felt almost petrified with shock.

'Nothing spectacular,' continued Sid. 'Just a couple of songs after the interval.'

'I . . .'

'Something wrong, Jenny?' asked Mae.

'What? No, it's just a bit of a shock, that's all.'

'You'll be wonderful,' beamed Mae, the dimples in her cheeks deepening as her mouth curved into a broad and generous smile. She gave Jenny a bone-crunching hug, just like the countless hugs they'd shared when they were kids together. 'I'm ever so pleased for you, you really deserve it.'

'Now, Jenny,' Sid went on, 'I don't want you getting the idea I'm some kind of charity, but there'll be a bit of extra money in it for you, that's only right. Not a fortune, mind, just a few bob extra.'

Jenny's heart contracted. Geoff Tait's words were echoing at the back of her mind: 'I'll be able to pay you twice what Sid gives you . . .'

'Th-Thank you.'

'No need to thank me, I'm just doing the sensible thing. Fact is, Joss Flynn's getting unreliable and I need a second soloist in case she lets me down again. Besides, you're good. The campers love you. I'd be a fool not to use you more.'

'You'd best get back to the chalet and pack,' said Mae.

'Oh. Yes, I suppose I had.'

'I've checked the trains. There's one to Liverpool first thing in the morning – you'll need to change there for St Helens.'

'Thanks.'

Jenny could hardly bear Mae's searching looks, but at least Sid seemed not to have noticed that anything was amiss. On the contrary, he looked happier and more relaxed than he had done in days.

'Off you go then, Jenny – oh, just one more thing.'

'Yes, Mr Dukes?'

'Geoff. You'll need to see him before you go, to work out which songs you're going to sing in the show.'

'Where are you going to stay?' asked Henry, jumping up and perching on the edge of the top bunk.

Jenny kept on thrusting bits and pieces into the overnight bag she'd borrowed from Mae.

'At Mr Corlett's. You know you're not supposed to be in here, don't you?'

'I'll go if you want.'

'No, stay. I like having you here.'

'Don't worry, no one saw me. And I can always jump out of the window if anybody comes in. Corlett . . . that's the man with the grocer's shop?'

Jenny nodded.

'Mae's dad. It's lucky he's got a telephone. She rang him for me and he said I could sleep in Mae's old room if . . . you know . . . if things don't work out with Mam.'

But they must, she thought to herself. Somehow I've got to make them.

'This trouble with your folks . . .'

'Please, Henry, I don't like talking about it.'

'. . . you've never really told what it's all about.'

No, thought Jenny. I haven't. And how can I? She turned and smiled up at him, saying it as gently as she could.

'You wouldn't understand.'

Henry sighed and swung his legs disconsolately.

'How do you know if you don't try me?'

'I can't. It was . . . to do with my stepfather and something he did, that's all I can say.'

'He hurt you?' Henry was willing the full, unexpurgated truth from her. She resisted him with all her might.

'Henry . . .'

'He hurt you, didn't he?' He jumped down off the bunk bed. 'Let me go with you.'

Jenny shot bolt upright.

'I could go with you. Dad and Grandpa hardly notice I'm here most of the time anyway.'

For a split second, the thought was seductive enough to be almost possible. She imagined walking down Gas Street, arm in arm with Henry Costigern; thought of the looks they'd get as they passed by in their Sunday best.

And then reality kicked in like a body blow. Take Henry to St Helens? To Gas Street? To Canal Terrace?

'No, Henry.'

'Why not? You'd be safer with me to look after you.'

'I don't need anyone to look after me,' she snapped, then relented, stroking the side of his face. 'I know you mean well, but it's best you keep out of this.'

'I want to go with you. I want to be with you. Don't you understand? If I could, I'd be with you every moment of every day.'

Jenny backed away almost imperceptibly, not so much comforted as threatened by the strength of Henry's feelings. She tried to make a joke out of it.

'What on earth would you want to come to St Helens for? It's just a hole, a big black hole.'

Henry took her hand and spoke to her quietly.

'You could introduce me to your family.'

No! screamed a voice inside Jenny's head. No, never. She was startled by the force of her own reaction. But how could she tell Henry how she felt? That this relationship, this thing between them, was more than friendship but less than love . . . that it could only exist here, in the summer sunshine? Take it to the dour, grime-darkened streets of her home town, where the smoke from the chimneys sometimes turned the sun to a feeble haze, and how could it hope to survive?

She picked up her toothbrush and carried it across to the open suitcase on the bed.

'Jenny?'

'I'm sorry, I can't.'

'Why not?' In desperation, Henry stepped in front of her. 'Are you ashamed of me, is that it?'

'No!'

'You are, aren't you?'

'Don't talk rubbish, Henry. It's you who should be ashamed of me, not the other way round.'

Or am I ashamed of him? she asked herself. Am I afraid of what my ordinary family would think of this nicely brought-up young man, with his soft hands and his manners and his university education?

'Then tell me why.'

'I told you, you wouldn't understand. It's not . . . it's not a nice place, not like you're used to. It's dirty and it's poor – I'm not ashamed of it, and I'm not ashamed of you, but . . .'

'But you won't let me come with you?'

'No.'

Her lips trembling, she looked into Henry's face, waiting for the look of love to turn to anger, half expecting the vicious slap that would prove to her that he was no better than Ivan Price.

'All right,' said Henry.

'What?'

'All right, I can see you've made up your mind.' He kissed her lightly on the forehead and stepped back, forcing a smile. 'I'll just have to stay here and wait for you, won't I?'

I've changed, thought Jenny as the train rattled along the track and into Shaw Street Station. This place is supposed to be my home, but I feel like a stranger now.

'Live 'ere, do you, love?' asked the woman next to her.

I don't know, thought Jenny. Do I?

'I . . . my family do.'

'Can't think why anybody'd want to come back,' sniffed the woman, getting up from her seat and hauling a suitcase off the luggage rack. 'Come far, have you?'

'From Wales . . . Llandew. I'm working at the holiday camp.'

'Well, I'd get back there sharp if I were you, looks like it's comin' on to rain.'

It did too. Jenny squinted up at the watery sun, disappearing behind thundery grey skies. There were no trees to be seen here, just roofs and chimneys and acres of smutty grey sky. It was all so very different to Costigern's Camp, with its lines of rainbow-coloured chalets and the endless sea, sparkling along the faraway horizon.

The train slowed and came to a juddering stop at platform one. Doors opened, people shouted to each other through clouds of steam.

'Here, Johnny! Over here.'

'You've grown!'

'Just look at the smuts all over your new coat.'

There was no one there to meet her, but then she hadn't expected there to be. Only John Corlett knew that she was coming, and she'd asked him to keep it to himself. It could all go so horribly wrong.

She stepped down on to the platform and walked slowly towards the ticket barrier. Tom's letter was in her pocket; all her hope resided in that letter. Could it really be true?

Please God, let it be true, she prayed silently. Let me belong to my family again.

Chapter 26

Ivan Price was sitting with his racing paper in the back room of The Feathers when Denny Finch came in. Ivan glanced up from his paper and went on reading. He was glad he'd "persuaded" Denny to give him free bed and board. Proper cosy it was.

'You got that baccy for me then, boy?'

Denny slapped it down on the table.

'That's one and six.'

'I'll owe it yer.' Ivan spat into the spittoon by his chair. 'What's 'appened, seen a ghost, 'ave yer?'

Denny put on his cellerman's apron.

'Nowt important. I'm off to put that new barrel on.'

Ivan grabbed him by the upper arm and pulled him back.

'Don't gi' me that, boy. What's on yer mind?'

Denny turned frightened eyes to Ivan.

'She's back.'

Ivan's eyes narrowed to malevolent slits. His body tensed in expectation.

'Who?'

'T'lass. Jenny Fisher.'

Aggie Finch appeared in the doorway to the bar.

'Bitter's still off.' She caught sight of Ivan and shrank back. 'When tha's ready.'

'Get out, woman,' snarled Ivan. 'Get out, an' keep your nose out of other people's business.'

The door closed. Ivan took Denny by the lapels and pulled his face down closer to his own.

'You're sure?'

'I . . . I think so.'

'I said, are you *sure*?'

'Yes. It were Jenny all right. She were comin' out o' Shaw Street Station wi' a suitcase.'

Ivan let go of Denny and pushed him away like a toy that had lost its allure.

'So, she's come crawlin' back 'ome, has she?' he growled. 'Back to 'er hag mother an' her whingeing sister. That family's poison, you know that? They reckon I'm out the way for good, so they're all bandin' together, plottin' against me.'

'Nay, Ivan,' said Denny, as conciliatory as he dared. 'They'd not do a thing like that.' Ivan ignored his attempts at peacemaking.

'She's the worse of 'em all, she started it,' he hissed.

'Jenny? But . . .'

'She's the cause of it all, the little bitch! If it weren't for 'er . . .' He thumped the table. 'They think they've got it all worked out between 'em, but they're nothin'. I've got that family where I want 'em – Dot, Tom, Nancy, the brats. I could finish 'em in five minutes if I wanted. But Jenny . . .'

Denny Finch tried to distance himself from Ivan but the room was too small for him to put more than a few feet between them.

'Steady now, Ivan.'

'I'll 'ave her, Denny. I'll 'ave that bitch for what she's done to me.' He got to his feet and put on his jacket. 'This time I'll break 'er good an' proper.'

'Nay, Ivan, tha's not goin' after her?'

He laughed into Denny's white face.

'You always were a milksop,' he sneered. 'No more marrow in yer than Tom Fisher. No, boy, now Jenny Fisher's back 'ome she can wait till I'm good an' ready for 'er. Right now I've got a bit of business needs doin' for Mr Stokes.'

The last time I stood in front of this door, thought Jenny, my mam only opened it to tell me to go away. What will she say when she sees me here again? Maybe Mae was wrong, maybe I should have asked Mr Corlett to tell her I was coming. Maybe I shouldn't have come here at all.

The street was deserted, save for the old woman sweeping her front step at number thirty-three. But Jenny knew that all eyes were secretly on her. The minute she'd rounded the corner she'd caught the telltale twitch of bleached nets. Not that anyone would speak to her to her face, mind. They were all waiting to see what kind of reception she'd get at number forty-two.

She set down her bag on the pavement. The oranges rolled about and the bottles of lemonade made a chinking sound as they fell against each other. With a deep breath, she raised her hand and knocked.

The latch clicked back. To her complete amazement, it was not Mam who opened the door.

'Well, I'll be . . .'

Molly O'Brien stood and gawped in delighted astonishment, before flinging her arms about Jenny's waist and practically dancing a polka down the street.

'Jenny! Jenny . . . oh, Jenny love, is it you? It *is* you, 'ow could it be anyone else? Come in, come in.' Her eyes twinkled as she turned and called out: 'Dot, there's someone here wantin' to see you.'

A faint, lacklustre voice replied from somewhere at the back of the house: 'Tell 'em I'm busy.'

Molly beamed at Jenny.

'Take no notice, love, it'll be fine.'

'No . . . perhaps I'd better not go in.'

'Don't talk nonsense. Come on in.'

More afraid than she cared to admit, Jenny clutched at Molly's arm.

'Why . . . I mean, how . . .?'

She took Jenny's hand and squeezed it affectionately.

'Your mam's 'ad a rough time these past weeks, and your sister too. Round 'ere you help each other out a bit when times are bad.'

Jenny marvelled at Molly O'Brien's serene smile. The woman was like a bottled ray of sunshine. And who'd have believed it of the Fishers and the O'Briens – the proddy dogs and the papists? Time was when Dot and Tom

281

wouldn't have had a Catholic across the threshold. It seemed that Jenny wasn't the only one who had changed around here.

She found her voice at last.

'Nancy, Mam – they're all right?'

'Don't fret, Jenny love, just come in an' see your mam.'

'What about Billy and Daisy?'

'Right as rain, Tom's took 'em out for the day.'

Jenny's heart sank. She'd been counting on seeing Tom, had been so sure he'd be at home today to offer moral support.

'I need to see him, Molly, he wrote to me . . .'

She nodded.

'He told you he doesn't live here now?'

Jenny's jaw dropped.

'No. Why?'

'Had to move out, see, 'cause of the Assistance men pokin' their noses in, askin' questions. He's been at your Auntie Jane's these last three weeks, layin' low.'

Jenny took a deep breath to steady her racing pulse. Assistance men, Tom having to move out . . .

'I didn't realise . . . I didn't know things had got so bad.'

'Where are you stayin'?'

'Corlett's. Over the shop. But only tonight and tomorrow. I have to be back in Wales on Friday, because of the show . . .'

'I'll make sure you see him, don't you worry. An' the kids. Now are you comin' in off the street or what? Stand out there any longer, an' you'll take root in the pavement.'

The familiar smell of Jenny's old home surrounded and engulfed her as she took the first, all-important step back into number forty-two Gas Street. It was a mixture of so many workaday things: wet washing and boiling mutton bones, floor polish and damp coal. The walls of the house were thick and the smell never seemed to escape, even when the doors and windows were wide open; Jenny supposed that by now it must have soaked right into the bricks.

'You're sure . . . I mean . . . will Mam want to see me?'

Molly led her down the passage, like a timorous puppy on an invisible leash.

'She's in the kitchen. You'll find her a bit . . . you know . . . tired.'

A pang of the old bitterness twisted like a knife in Jenny's guts. What Tom had said was true, though she had prayed with all her heart it wouldn't be.

'You mean Mam's drunk?'

'Look . . . she's been worryin' herself sick about everythin' – Ivan an' your sister an' the money. She'll be fine now you're back. There.' Molly stopped at the door. 'In you go.'

'Come in with me. I don't know what to say.'

'I'll not go in, I'd just be intrudin'.'

'But, Molly . . .'

Molly's eyes were sparrow-bright in her sallow face; Jenny knew she understood a lot more than she was saying.

'You're a kind lass, Jenny, you're like a daughter to me an' Col. But your mam's your mam an' nothin' can change that. Try to forgive 'er.'

Turning that doorhandle was one of the most difficult things Jenny had ever had to do. At the quarter turn the latch clicked and the door moved inwards a little.

'Who . . . who's that?' It was Dot's voice; a little slurred and indistinct, but it was Dot's voice all the same.

'Mam? Mam, can I come in?'

There was no reply and for a moment, Jenny was a child again. A child not daring to enter the room for fear that its mother would be drunk and incoherent for the umpteenth time. But she wasn't a child, not any more. She was a grown woman and the past was dead and gone. She pushed open the door.

Dot was sitting at the table, her head resting on her folded arms and a half-empty square green bottle in front of her. At the sound of the door opening, she lifted her head and cast a bleary, red-rimmed gaze in Jenny's direction.

'Wh-What . . .?'

'Mam, it's me.'

Dot sat up, instantly sobered by the shock of seeing her daughter.

'Jenny? My God, Jenny.' It was almost soundless, the words not so much whispered as mouthed.

It wasn't until Jenny stepped into the kitchen that she realised her sister had been in there all this time. Nancy was standing very still and white by the larder, one hand on the door, frozen and silent as an ice sculpture.

'What do you want?' she said colourlessly. 'We don't want you here.'

Jenny looked from Mam to Nancy. Mam's face expressed shock, amazement, the beginnings of happiness. Nancy's was a mask of suspicion and resentment.

'I've come . . . to see you.'

'Why?'

'Because . . . because Tom wrote me a letter. He told me what happened. With . . . with Ivan.' She dropped the bag with the oranges and the lemonade on to the kitchen floor with a dull clinking sound. They seemed irrelevant right now, irrelevant and downright insulting. 'Oh, Nancy, I don't know what to say, I'm so sorry . . .'

Nancy's grey eyes, which were so nearly a mirror of Jenny's own, glittered with ice-cold anger.

'Oh, yes, you're always *sorry*, aren't you?' she spat. 'Always sorry when it's too late.'

'Nancy, listen . . .'

'All you ever cared about was yourself,' she snarled. 'Saving your own precious skin. Getting out so somebody else could take what was meant for you. Make trouble for others, that's what you do, then run away.'

'No, it wasn't like that, Nancy, you know it wasn't! I only left because I thought it would be better for you . . .'

She laughed sarcastically.

'Oh, really? I thought you left because Mae Corlett said you were going to be a big Hollywood star.'

'Nancy, please, don't say that.' Tears pricked Jenny's eyes, trembled there and spilled down her cheeks. Don't say it, echoed a voice in Jenny's head. Don't say it, because it just might be true and I don't ever want to believe that.

'Stop this!' Dot's voice rang out with sudden, unexpected fury. 'Hasn't Ivan Price brought enough trouble on this family? Haven't we had enough hate?'

Silence reigned for a long and oppressive moment, then Nancy turned on her heel.

'Nancy, don't go,' pleaded Jenny.

Nancy threw Jenny a look of alienation and disgust.

'I'm not staying in the same room as *her*.' Then she ran down the steps out into the yard, banging the door behind her.

Jenny's heart was thumping. She felt sick.

'I'll go after her.'

Dot got unsteadily to her feet and put out her hands to prevent her leaving.

'No. Don't. There's no point.'

'But, Mam . . .'

'She'll get over it. It's been hard enough on her, but it's been hard on us all.' There was an edge of callousness in Dot's voice, overlaid with bitterness. 'She'll just 'ave to get by, like the rest of us.'

She sank back on to her chair, supporting her head with her right hand. It was only too obvious from the half-empty bottle how she was managing to get by.

'I've been a fool, Jenny.' Her tired eyes searched her daughter's face. 'What I did to you . . .'

Conflicting emotions were fighting for supremacy inside Jenny. Part of her longed for the warmth of her mother's long-forgotten love, another wept for something which was lost and would never be found again. And a darker part of her could not shake off the angry resentment and the guilt which had dogged her for so long. Why should she forgive and forget, just because Mam wanted it? Why should she deny the angry pain which just wouldn't go away?

She laid her hand on her mother's shoulder.

'It's in the past, Mam.'

'But I can't forget. How can I forget?'

'I know.' And I can't forget either, thought Jenny, and perhaps none of us ever will. The best we can do is pretend. She sat down opposite her mother, gently pushing

285

the gin bottle to one side. 'But drink won't mend anything, will it?'

Dot didn't answer. She was gazing down at her own shaking hands as they gripped her empty glass, totally absorbed in the comfort of her own misery. Jenny let her gaze wander around the kitchen. Things had changed here, too, more than she had realised at first sight.

'Mam?'

'Hmm?'

'Where's the wireless gone? And Grandma's copper kettle?'

'We had to sell 'em.'

'Why?'

'The Assistance said we had too much money comin' in. That's why Tom had to go to your Auntie Jane's.' Dot's expression hovered between pain and resentment. 'They'd not give us a penny-piece till everythin' was gone, even your dad's watch.'

'Oh, Mam.' Jenny thought of the things she had brought with her, the little presents, the few luxuries. They seemed like a drop in the ocean in a house where just getting by was the best you could hope for. 'Mam, how are you getting on? *Really*. I want to know.'

Dot pushed back a trailing strand of lank hair.

'We manage. On the Assistance money. Molly O'Brien helps when she can. An' John Corlett's been good to us.'

'You've enough? To feed yourself and the kids?'

'Like I said,' repeated Dot sharply, 'we manage. When Nancy's . . . when she's feelin' better, p'raps they'll give her her job back at the bottle-works. P'raps not. Anyhow, we'll get by.' She looked up, stubborn pride engraved deep in the lines on her face. 'Don't you worry about us, you've got your own life now, what with your singin' an' your new friends.'

Jenny sensed there was more to all of this than met the eye. There was a weird restraint in Dot's tone, something that Jenny remembered only too well. It meant that there was something she wasn't telling her.

'Mam.'

Dot half rose from her seat.

'I'll put kettle on, shall I?'

'You'll sit there until you've told me what things are *really* like.' The years were rolling back. Jenny remembered the long torment of Dot's drinking bouts, how much she'd resented the fact that her mother used the drink as an escape, an excuse to push every responsibility on to Jenny. Just like you did with Nancy, whispered the treacherous voice inside her head. 'It's a struggle for you, isn't it, Mam?'

Dot gripped her wrists so hard it hurt.

'You're not to breathe a word to Tom. He'll only worry.'

'Just tell me what's going on, Mam. I'm not going till you've told me everything.'

'I borrowed a bit of money. Daisy was sick, she needed the doctor. Then there was the rent to find . . .'

And the price of the next drink, thought Jenny; but she banished that cruel thought from her mind. The worst that Dot had ever been was weak and lonely, and Jenny ought to know how that felt.

'How much, Mam?'

'A few quid.'

'How much? Exactly.'

'Four pound. Off that Mr Stokes.'

Jenny's blood ran cold.

'Stokes! Not that bloodsucking leech, Mam, how could you? He's a crook, he's . . . everybody knows!'

'What choice did I have?' Dot stared at a stain on the distempered wall. 'I tried to keep up the payments, but with hardly any money comin' in . . .'

'Has he been threatening you?'

'Not him.' She took a deep breath. 'Ivan.'

'Ivan!' All Jenny's worst nightmares closed in on her in a sea of dark panic.

'He got the sack from the pit and now he's working for Stokes. He says . . .' Dot's voice quavered. 'He says if I don't pay up by next week he'll find ways . . . ways of making me.'

'What ways? Mam, what's he going to do?'

Dot shook her head in utter misery, trying to ignore the truth; only it refused to go away.

'I don't care about myself, Jenny. It's the kids. He said . . . he said what I wouldn't give him, he'd take from the kids.'

Black horror made Jenny's fingers cold and unresponsive as she struggled to take her purse from her bag, opened it and tipped it out on to the table.

'Take it.'

'Jenny?'

'Take all of it, I want you to have it. Pay off your debts, look after the kids.' She thought of Geoff and Sid and Mae, of the offers and the hopes and the deceit. And especially of the hope that she might be able to earn enough through her singing to make everything all right. 'It's not much, I know, but they say they'll give me a pay rise soon . . . and if Geoff Tait sets up the new band . . .'

Dot pushed the money away.

'I can't.'

'Why not?'

'It's your money. Your savings.'

'I don't need it, you do. Take it, Mam, if not for yourself then for Billy and Daisy and Nancy.' She reached out and touched her mother's hand, squeezing it lightly. It was the first real contact between them in years. Dot looked into her face, uncomprehending.

'You mean it?'

''Course I do. I'll always do what I can for you and the kids.' It hurt to say the words, but they were true. 'Family comes first.'

It was after dark when John Corlett lifted the latch on the back door and let Tom Fisher into the shop.

'She's 'ere, me sister?'

John nodded.

'Upstairs, waiting for you. You all right, lad?'

Tom was far from all right, but he nodded.

'Don't think any of them Assistance men were snoopin' round . . . can't be too careful though.' He looked at John

288

squarely. 'She wants to see us then?'

'Did you think she wouldn't?'

'Aye. Reckon I did. I've missed 'er, Mr Corlett.'

'I know you have, Tom. Let's go up and see her now, eh?'

There was a kind of foggy dampness at the corners of Tom's eyes. He swabbed it away ruthlessly with the sleeve of his jacket. No good blubbing like some big wet lass. He put his foot on the bottom tread of the staircase and looked up at the door at the top. It seemed an awfully long way away.

Jenny got up as the door opened. John Corlett came in first, and for a second she thought perhaps Tom had turned tail and fled. But there he was, tall and awkward-looking as ever, his fingers twisting the cap in his big red hands.

'Jen.' He swallowed. 'Y'all right, lass?'

She didn't speak, simply flew into his arms, and he lifted her up and swung her round just like he'd done when they were kids together.

'Tom, put me down, I can't breathe!'

He set her down and they stood looking at each other.

'You got the letter then?'

'' Course I did, thanks to Mr Corlett.'

John Corlett smiled.

'Don't thank me, all I did was post it. It's Tom who had the sense to write it.'

'I had to tell you,' explained her brother. 'I'm no good with words, only I had to find a way. I'm sorry, sis. Mam's sorry too, I know she is, only she finds it hard to say.' He coughed. 'I brought somebody to see you.' He winked to John Corlett, who called down the stairs: 'You can come up now.'

The thunder of small feet on bare boards was enough to fill Jenny with an elation she hardly dared feel. Could it be? Would it be . . .

'Jenny, Jenny!'

'I told you she was 'ere!'

'Where's me present?'

'Is the sea big?'

Jenny didn't bother trying not to weep. The tears seemed natural, it would have been far stranger not to let them come.

'Billy! Daisy! Billy, I swear you're two inches taller . . . Daisy, just look at your lovely long hair . . .'

She put her arms round them and cuddled them tight, doing her best to answer their flurry of questions.

'Are you stayin'?'

'Just for a little while.'

'Are you comin' back home?'

'Not this time.'

'Why not?'

She stroked their hair. It was soft and fluffy. They were young for their age; Ivan Price had kept them that way with his taunts and his beatings. Baby birds that had not yet fledged. It wasn't easy to make them understand.

'Maybe next time. But I'll send you lots of letters.'

'I'd rather 'ave you,' said Billy ruefully.

'And I'd rather have you. But I've got to earn money to buy you nice things. Look, I've brought lots of presents for you. See? In the bag? There's oranges, and chocolate, and toffees . . .'

'And sherbert lemons?' pleaded Daisy.

'And sherbert lemons. Why don't you and Mr Corlett have a look for them while I talk to Tom?'

They sat down on John Corlett's sofa.

'They don't really understand,' said Jenny.

'I'd as soon they didn't,' replied Tom grimly. 'You've been home?'

Jenny nodded.

'Things are bad, Tom. Nancy hates me so much she won't even speak to me, and Mam . . . I'm worried about her too. Did you know she's been borrowing money she can't pay back?'

He let out a groan.

'I thought . . . I've been givin' her every spare penny out of my wages.'

'But the Assistance money doesn't go far, and she's on the drink again.' Jenny paused. 'Ivan Price is working for

Stokes. He's been round threatening to do something to Mam and the kids if she doesn't pay up.'

'Ivan! That scum's been to our house an' she never even told me?'

'I'm frightened, Tom. You know what he's capable of.'

Tom's jaw clenched, taut with knotted muscle. When he spoke, his voice was chillingly quiet.

'I'll kill him.'

'Tom . . .'

'I tell you, I'll cut his black heart right out of his stinking chest!'

'No, Tom!' Jenny's fear intensified at the sight of his wild anger. She saw that this time Ivan had pushed him too far. Never one to seek out violence, Tom had finally succumbed to the hatred which had simmered within him for three long years, and it was screaming to be let out. 'Tom, you'll be sensible.'

He stopped in his tracks and stared at his sister.

'*Sensible?*'

'Yes, Tom, sensible. What use will you be to Mam if you're in the nick?'

His breathing moderated a little, though his chest still heaved with emotion.

'I don't care what you say, Jenny. I'll not let him get away with this.'

'I know, I know, but there are other ways. You don't have to kill a man to teach him a lesson.'

'I s'pose.' He hesitated. You've not come home to stay then?'

'Not this time. I've to go back to the camp on Friday – I've no choice and I need the money for Mam. Please, Tom, for my sake, look after the kids and keep an eye open for any trouble.'

He gave a brief nod.

'I will. Don't you worry about that, not now I know what's going on.' He glanced at Mr Corlett's clock. 'I'd best be off, I've to be up for early-mornin' turn.'

Jenny felt a strong urge to hold him back, to talk to him into the small hours the way they used to do when they were small; but she smiled and accepted his big bear-hug.

'Will I see you again? Before I go?'

'I'll come here after I get off shift. You'll be here?'

'I'll be here.'

Tom went back down the stairs to the shop, John Corlett following close behind. As he unlocked the back door to let Tom out, John paused.

'Your mam got trouble with Ivan again, has she?'

Tom shook his head.

'No, Mr Corlett,' he said firmly. 'Leastways, nowt I can't handle.'

Chapter 27

Geoff arrived at the Caribbean Bar ten minutes early. He ordered a whisky and stood it on the table in front of him as though just looking at it would provide him with all the answers.

By the time Sid arrived, five minutes after they'd agreed to meet, Geoff was beginning to feel edgy. He'd convinced himself that it would be easy, but things weren't quite so clear-cut now that Sid was actually standing in front of him. To make matters worse, Mae was hanging on to Sid's arm; these days the two of them seemed to be stuck together with invisible glue.

'No Duncan?' enquired Sid.

'Not tonight. I wanted to have a quiet word.' Geoff and Mae eyed each other. 'Alone,' he added.

Sid smiled affably.

'Don't worry about Mae. Nothing we say'll go any further than these four walls. Will it, Mae?'

'No, Sid.' She pecked him on the cheek. 'You can rely on me.'

'Right then. I'll just get myself a pint. The usual for you, Mae?'

'That'd be lovely.'

Sid went off to the bar. For the umpteenth time, Geoff rehearsed what he was going to say. Mae sat down next to him.

'What's all this about then?'

'You'll know soon enough.'

'If you're going to upset Sid again . . .'

'Give over, Mae, Sid's a big boy now.'

There was no point in beating about the bush, thought Geoff. Not when Mae Corlett's suspicions about him were entirely justified.

'Sid . . .' he began as the bandleader slid into the seat next to him. 'It's about the band.'

'You've got some new songs you want to try out?'

'Not exactly. Look, Sid, you and I haven't been seeing eye to eye just lately – we've got different ideas on how things ought to be done.'

'True,' conceded Sid. 'But we're working things out, the show's going down a storm.'

'Yeah – with a load of old fogeys! The young kids want something different, something new.'

'We've had this conversation before, Geoff. A bit of new material's fine, but you can't just cater for the youngsters . . .'

'You've got to move with the times, Sid!'

'Geoff!' Mae glared at him with all the force of her protective love for Sid.

Geoff took a few deep breaths. In a way Mae was right, there was no point in letting this degenerate into a shouting match. Still, there were things that had to be said.

'It's nothing personal, Sid,' he said quietly and calmly. 'And it's not been easy. But I've made up my mind: I'm leaving at the end of the season.'

Sid's face registered shock, then sorrow; Mae's lit up with a mixture of relief and elation.

'Come on, Geoff lad, things can't be that bad,' said Sid.

'Sorry, my mind's made up.'

'Well, I can't say I won't be sorry to lose you. You're a first-rate musician.' Sid drained his glass. 'Can I get you another?'

He made as if to get up, but Geoff pulled him back down into his seat.

'There's something else, Sid . . .'

'What?'

'I won't be leaving on my own.'

Understanding dawned with painful certainty. Mae sat bolt upright, frozen to her seat. Sid, shocked to the core, spent several long seconds in silence, the sadness on his face turning slowly to cold anger.

'How many, Geoff? How many are you taking from me?'

'Desmond, Duncan, Binky . . . Ron and Charley . . . eight in all, maybe nine if Pete decides to go.'

'The best. Every one of my best musicians. You'll ruin me, is that what you want?'

'No, of course not.'

Sid drew in a deep, shuddering breath and expelled it harshly.

'I took you from that second-rate speakeasy trio . . .'

'I know, Sid. And I'm grateful.'

'I took you into the band, I made you my deputy – I trusted you, for God's sake!'

This hurt more than Geoff had expected. He didn't like seeing the bitter pain in Sid's eyes or the hatred in Mae's.

'You bastard,' she hissed. 'I should have known that was what you wanted all along. You've just been using Sid, haven't you?'

'It's not like that, Mae.'

'Oh, yes, it is! You've been using Sid to get where you want to be, never mind if you have to walk all over him to get it.'

Sid took Mae's hand and squeezed it. The anger had gone from him, to be replaced with resignation.

'What's the point, Mae? He's made up his mind.' He looked Geoff in the eyes. 'Of course it'll fail, you know that, don't you?'

Geoff shook his head.

'We've already got bookings up to Christmas. We'll stick to what we can play well, then introduce the new material slowly.'

'Oh, they're good players, Geoff, don't get me wrong.' Sid laughed humourlessly. 'Nobody knows them better than me – I discovered them. But they're playboys, the lot of 'em. They don't know the meaning of discipline, and all you do is let them get on with raising hell. And if you're thinking of relying on Joss Flynn . . .'

Geoff swallowed hard.

'Actually, no. Not Joss Flynn.'

Mae looked first at Sid, then at Geoff. Hatred turned to horrible suspicion.

'Who then?'

'Jenny Fisher. I asked her last week if she'd be my lead vocalist.'

Henry Costigern was waiting on the platform at Llandew Station, handsome and studiedly casual in white shirt and light grey flannels. As Jenny stepped down from the train, he greeted her with the broadest, most wholehearted grin she had ever seen.

'Jenny!'

She strove to match the brilliance of his smile, happy to see him but already feeling overwhelmed.

'Henry, it's lovely to see you.'

'Don't I get a kiss?'

He pulled her to him and pressed his mouth against hers. The warmth and strength of his body outdid the July sun overhead. She emerged from his embrace breathless and dishevelled.

'Say you've missed me,' begged Henry, as though he had detected some lack of enthusiasm in her response and wanted her to reassure him that things hadn't changed between them.

''Course I did.' She stood on tiptoe and put her arms round his neck, kissing the soft, smooth skin just in front of his ear. 'Did you miss me?'

'Can't you tell? Here, let me take your case, it must be heavy.'

'It's fine, really, I can manage . . .'

'No, please, let me.'

Their hands met on the handle of the suitcase. Henry's soft brown eyes were so insistent that Jenny gave in and let go, even though she could manage the case perfectly well on her own.

'You mean the world to me, Jenny,' he murmured. 'You do know that, don't you?'

She knew only too well what he was hoping she would

say – that he meant the world to her too, that she couldn't live without him – only somehow she couldn't quite frame the words. Being away from Costigern's for the last few days seemed to have brought so many things into sharper focus. Henry Costigern was a lovely boy, but maybe that was just it: however lovely and handsome and kind and gentle he was, he was still a half-grown boy for all his twenty-two years.

'Let's go back to the camp, I mustn't be late,' she said, avoiding the issue by kissing him lightly on the cheek.

'Will you have dinner with me tomorrow night?' The brown eyes were full of questions and longing. 'I know this really nice little place in Llandew.'

She smiled.

'I'd love to, if I can get the time off, only I'll have to ask . . .'

She was halted in mid-sentence by a hiss of cold rage.

'Jenny! Jenny, you bitch.'

'What?'

Jenny swung round and was confronted by Mae, her face twisted into a parody of a smile.

'What's wrong?'

Mae's open-handed slap caught her across her right cheek, and Jenny yelped in pain. The slap felt like a hornet sting and she clapped her hand to it, startled and confused. Henry dropped Jenny's suitcase and rushed to her side, putting a protective arm about her shoulders.

'Mae Corlett, what on earth did you do that for?'

'Ask her,' snapped Mae. 'She knows.'

Jenny stared back, shaking her head.

'I don't understand . . .'

'Don't you give me that, you backstabbing bitch! How could you . . . how could you do it, Jenny?'

'Do what?' cut in Henry, desperately trying to get to the bottom of this sudden, inexplicable confrontation. Mae rounded on him, shouting into his face.

'Keep out of this! This is between me and her.'

'You're making a scene,' said Henry lamely. 'People are staring.'

'Let them. Do you think I care? After what she's done?'

Jenny stood transfixed, not wanting to understand why Mae could be so angry with her.

'I know what you've been up to,' said Mae, moderating her voice to a furious, trembling whisper. 'Plotting with Geoff Tait behind Sid's back, after all he's done for you.'

All at once Jenny felt very cold. The guilty secret she had been keeping was a secret no more. The secret she had known all along it was wrong to keep.

'No, Mae, it's not like that. Geoff only asked me . . .'

'To be his lead singer, right? In his wonderful new band.'

'Well, yes, but . . .'

'But nothing! You knew all about him splitting up the band, didn't you? You knew and you kept it to yourself. You kept it from *me*, Jenny!'

'Geoff made me promise . . .' she said, knowing how lame it sounded.

'Made you? Like Ivan *made* you?' The knife-blade thrust into Jenny's guts and twisted viciously. 'I'm beginning to wonder if that wasn't all lies, too!'

'No!'

Henry tried to stand between her and Mae, but Jenny shook him off, close to tears but angry too.

'Leave me be, Henry.'

'What's all this about? You can't let her talk to you like that!'

'Look, Mae,' pleaded Jenny, 'he asked me, I admit that . . . but I haven't said yes.'

'But you *knew*. You knew and you didn't say one word.'

It was an inescapable fact. Jenny hung her head.

'No.'

Mae's eyes blazed.

'I thought we were friends.'

'We are!'

'Not any more,' replied Mae, and she walked quickly away, not once looking back over her shoulder.

Tom Fisher stood in the alleyway behind The Feathers, watching the darkening sky with relief. Soon it would be dark, and darkness would cover the mean, black thing that he must do.

'This the place then, Tom?'

'Just keep out of sight till I tell you. You know what to do?'

The lad nodded, and joined the others in the shadows. There were about a dozen in all. Tom hadn't realised he had so many friends, or that so many men in St Helens had a grudge against Ivan Price. Some of them owed Tom a favour, some were friends of Len Davey, so cruelly injured down the pit. All of them hated Ivan Price's guts.

Jack Inglis was one of the last to arrive, his massive bulk seeming to fill the narrow alleyway, blocking off the last of the daylight. He held out his hand and, after a moment's hesitation, Tom took it. It was the first civil gesture they'd exchanged since they left school.

'I'm obliged to you, Jack.'

Jack's impassive face registered no trace of emotion.

'There's no need. I've waited a long time for this.'

There was no sense of excitement or elation. Nobody liked being here, or the idea of what they were about to do. They just knew that it had to be done.

Darkness crept through the streets of the town with damnable slowness on these summer nights. Men shuffled their feet, coughed, shushed each other.

'Is that 'im?'

'Nay, lad, not yet.'

They waited. At last came a whisper in the darkness that chilled Tom's blood.

'I can see 'im – 'e's just turning corner of Jubilee Street.'

'You know what wants doin'?'

'Aye, lad, us'll not let thee down.'

Tom took a deep breath, then stepped out into the street, walking towards Ivan then falling in step beside him. Ivan greeted him with the usual sneering smirk.

'Well, if it ain't the young runt 'isself.'

All the fear had gone out of Tom; he wouldn't be cowed by Ivan, not any more.

'You're not wanted round 'ere, Ivan.'

'Is that so? Well, it just so 'appens I've got a bit of business to attend to round your 'ouse. Your mam's been a naughty girl, Tom, takin' money she can't pay back.' He leered. 'Still, there's other ways of payin', ain't there?'

Tom almost swung a fist into his face. But no, why give him the satisfaction of rising to his taunts?

'I'm tellin' you to go 'ome, Ivan, you're not wanted.'

'Oh, an' you're goin' to make me, are you?'

Tom stepped in front of him, halting his progress.

'Yes.'

Ivan threw back his head and laughed.

'You an' whose army? Out of the way, boy, I got important business needs attendin' to.'

A shape stepped out of the alleyway, then another. Ivan looked from one to the other, puzzled.

'Charley Baines, Fred Gurney . . . what's this, a welcomin' party?'

Another figure, another and another. They formed a circle around him, a circle that grew slowly but steadily tighter. Arms folded, they stood and stared and said nothing. Ivan moistened his lips with the tip of his tongue.

'Now 'ang on a minute, boys. We got no cause to quarrel, that's right, ain't it?'

Silence.

The beginning of panic showed on Ivan's face. He took a step forward. The circle of men did not move.

'Now, boys, this ain't a very funny joke . . .'

Tom smiled.

'Joke, Ivan? The joke's on you.'

Ivan swung round and made a break for it, pushing two of the men aside. They did not resist – they didn't need to. Jack Inglis was already waiting for him, sleeves rolled up in anticipation.

'Hold 'im still for me, Jack,' said Tom between clenched teeth. 'I want to make sure he feels every punch.'

'Cheer up, Jenny,' said Henry as they got up to leave the restaurant. 'Things aren't so bad, surely? Here, let me help you into your coat.'

'I'm sorry,' she sighed. 'This hasn't been much fun for you, has it?'

'I spent the evening with you, I can't think of anything I'd rather do.'

'That's a nice thing to say, but . . .'

'It's true.'

They hardly spoke as they walked back from Llandew to the gates of the holiday camp.

'Jenny, what's making you so sad? Is it what happened with Mae?'

'I . . . suppose so.'

Mae, Mam, Nancy, Henry – the question was, where to start? These last few days, something small but very significant had changed inside her as though a tiny, unseen switch had been thrown, turning her life upside down. She moved to walk on, but Henry held her back.

'Is it me?'

'Of course not.'

'You're sure?'

'I'll be fine, don't worry about it.'

'Shall I walk you back to your chalet?'

'No need. I'll see you tomorrow sometime.'

'Well, if you're sure?'

They kissed goodnight and went their separate ways. She could feel the regret in Henry's gaze as he stood and watched her walk away from him. Had he recognised the slightly distant quality in her kiss, the awkwardness that simply hadn't been there a couple of weeks ago?

She would have to do something about Henry, she told herself as she walked along the darkened chalet lines, her torch-beam picking out the numbers on the painted walls. But not yet. Perhaps if she waited things would go back to the way they'd been before: blissfully, unquestioningly happy.

A noise somewhere ahead startled her, then she smiled to herself. Whispering and giggling in the darkness – whatever Jolly Jimmy might have to say about it, you were always stumbling over red-faced campers, doing what came naturally in the shadowy lanes behind the chalets.

'Shhh,' came the exaggerated whisper. 'Shhh, someone'll hear.' A woman's voice, which ended in a strangled giggle.

'I don't care who hears.' A man's voice now, rather cultured for a camper's. Vaguely familiar, too. 'Come on, open the door.'

Another giggle.

'I can't find the key!'

'Come on, Joss. I can't wait, I want you . . .'

Joss! Jenny stopped in her tracks just as the beam of her torch picked out two figures against the wall of a chalet. *Joss Flynn's chalet*.

She almost dropped the torch in shock. A couple of seconds more, and she'd have switched off the torch and tiptoed away. But it was too late, they'd seen her. Two white faces caught in the torch-beam, two expressions that turned instantaneously from passion to horror.

'Joss!' gasped Jenny. 'Mr Costigern . . .'

James Costigern detached himself unsteadily from Joss's clinging embrace. She was even drunker than he was, thought Jenny, one hand clapped to her mouth to stifle hiccups and the other fumbling in her bag for the chalet key. Joss was dishevelled to say the least, her normally immaculate hair tousled and unpinned, and her blouse half unbuttoned at the front, revealing a glimpse of white lace underneath.

James shaded his hand.

'Who . . . who's that?'

Jenny stepped nervously forward, lowering the torch beam.

'Jenny Fisher.'

'Oh, God,' groaned James. Joss dropped her evening bag with a curse, bent to pick it up and nearly fell over. 'Oh, God, this is just what I was afraid of.'

He came forward, leaving Joss stumbling about drunkenly trying to pick up the things that had fallen out of her bag. She at least seemed too inebriated to realise what was going on. James gripped Jenny by the shoulders with a desperate urgency.

'You mustn't tell . . . oh, for God's sake, you won't tell, will you? I'll give you anything you want. How much do you want to keep your mouth shut?'

Jenny shook her head, shocked and dumbfounded. Perhaps a little disgusted too.

'I don't want your money.'

'Please, Jenny.' There was a pitiful, fearful expression in James Costigern's eyes. 'You mustn't tell Henry, he wouldn't understand.'

'Yes. Yes, all right.' All Jenny wanted was to get away. Turning off the torch, she half ran in the opposite direction, trying to shake the memory of James and Joss out of her mind.

It was only when she was walking up the line towards her own chalet that it struck her: something that James had said. 'He wouldn't understand.'

That's it, she thought. People never do understand. And she felt a sudden, unexpected sympathy for James Costigern and his bungled attempts to find consolation away from his horrible stuck-up wife. Nobody ever understands, she thought bitterly. Not even Mae, not this time. All you can do is what you have to do to get by, what you think is right. That's all anyone can do. And if people don't understand that, then bugger the lot of 'em.

She held her head high as she turned the key in the chalet lock. It had taken time and agonies of indecision, but her mind was made up. She'd take Geoff Tait's offer. What other choice did she have? Mam and the kids needed money and she had to earn it for them, the best and quickest way she could. Anyone who couldn't see that wasn't worth bothering about.

'There you are, Nancy.'

She looked up from her work on the production line. It wasn't much of a job, just a bit of part-time packing, but at least it stopped her thinking. The foreman shouted over the noise of the machinery.

'There's a bloke askin' after you. At gate.'

'A bloke? What bloke?'

'Big man. A collier, I'd say. Looks like 'e's bin in wars an' all.'

'Oh, no. Tom must've got hurt down the pit. Can I go to him?'

'Aye, but be quick about it.'

She left the main production building and hurried past the offices to the main gate. Poor Tom. Still, he couldn't be that badly hurt, or he'd not have come here to see her. As she drew closer to the gates she saw that there was nobody there. Had the foreman been playing some kind of joke on her?

'Nance.'

The voice nailed her to the ground. She couldn't move forward or back, only stand there shaking like a rabbit mesmerised by a stoat.

'Come 'ere, Nance.'

Nancy moved round, almost imperceptibly, a fraction of an inch at a time. Her worst nightmare stood there in front of her.

Ivan Price. Oh God, no!

'Like what you see, girl?' He fingered his bruised and swollen face, the bottom lip split, the nose crooked and pulpy from a crushing blow. 'Still fancy your da, do you?'

She stepped away from him. The bogey-man, the nightmare monster of her childhood dreams, his bloody claws outstretched as though to grab her.

'Don't! Please, don't.'

He stopped a few inches short of her.

'You did this, Nancy. You an' your bitch sister. After all I done for you . . .'

'No.' She was shaking all over, her hands clutching and twisting the skirt of her overall. 'No, no, no! I won't listen, I won't listen.'

'You'll listen all right. You'll listen to this. You an' Jenny done this, an' you and her is goin' to pay for it, right?' He took Nancy's chin between the fingers of one hand and jerked it upwards, forcing her to look into his face. 'I'm not restin' till I paid you back, understand? Paid you back twice over.'

He let go and she slipped to the cobbled roadway, a crumpled, defeated, sobbing heap, her head down and her hands held protectively above it, waiting to ward off the blows as best she could.

But they didn't come. When she opened her eyes, she was completely alone.

And that was more frightening than anything.

Chapter 28

The canal was the last place left to Nancy. The last happy place, never tainted by the presence of Ivan Price. This was the only place in the world where Nancy Fisher had never been sad.

She walked down the bank towards the towpath. Midges buzzed and milled about her head in the sultry, overheated air. She didn't bother waving them away, didn't care if they bit her all over. All she cared about was what was in her head.

The sickness in her stomach lurched and was still. She stood at the water's edge and looked down into the murky depths. You couldn't see the bottom, the water was a murky brown and comfortingly deep. She heard the echo of her mam's voice in her head, scolding her when she was little: 'Don't you go swimmin' in that canal, you'll catch your death.' Nancy wanted to laugh, but the sound stuck in her throat.

This was where she'd end it all, she'd made up her mind. This would be her escape. There'd be no more Ivan, and no more brats who'd grow up into little Ivans, nor sisters so dazzlingly, shinily bright that she could never hope to step out of their shadow.

Hazy evening sunlight cast weird, kaleidoscopic patterns on the filthy canal water. It looked coaxing, inviting. Nancy put the bottle to her lips and drank down the rest of her mam's vile-tasting gin. The bottle swam in and out of focus, but she found the strength to swing it hard against the underside of the bridge, shattering it into dazzling fragments.

The jagged neck of the bottle was still in her hand. She took a deep breath and drew it purposefully across the inside of her wrist. She was surprised at how little it hurt.

And then, with a single forward step, she plunged soundlessly into the canal.

Nancy was only vaguely aware of the rough hands clutching and dragging at her, and the man's voice calling for help.

Help? What help? She didn't need help. She wept. The water was her friend and they wanted to take her away from it. No, no help. Don't want your help. Why can't you just leave me here, where I'm happy?

Faces looked down at her – she couldn't be sure if they were real or part of a dream.

Mam, Jenny . . . don't make me. Don't make me come back. Don't let him, don't let him hurt me again.

The voices and the hands seemed fainter and further away. Everything was receding into the distance: light, shadow, pain, reality. She was slipping out of her body, towards a world where everything was bright and warm and silent.

Then, without warning, everything went completely black.

Sam Burkiss rounded the corner of the old barn between the riding stables and Jimmy Costigern's piggery. He whistled, hands in pockets, a small package tucked under his arm.

As he came into view, there was a muted sound of scuffling and whispering from inside the barn.

'Bloody 'ell, somebody's comin'!'

'Put it away, gerrit put out!'

Two transparently guilty, slightly green faces peeped out at him from the doorway of the barn. Burkiss stood and regarded the miscreants: two of the campers' kids, gangly Liverpool lads of twelve or thirteen with sleeves too short for their skinny arms. The smell of cigarettes hung heavy in the air.

'Well, well.'

'We weren't doin' nothink'.

'We was just lookin'.'

'Relax, lads.' Burkiss smiled. 'I'm not Jolly Jim. Mind you, he'll skin you alive if he catches you smokin'.'

'You'll not tell 'im, will yer?'

'Go on, sling yer 'ook. I ain't seen yer.'

'Thanks, Mister. Sorry, Mister.' One of the lads looked back over his shoulder as they retreated towards the distant chalet lines. 'Happy to see yer!'

He watched them go, laughing and cuffing each other as they ran back towards the camp. The sun was setting after a hot, hazy day, turning the sky shades of apricot, blue and orange. Leaning against the doorpost, he lit up and inhaled deeply.

Miranda Costigern arrived a couple of minutes later, flustered and angry-looking.

'You're late,' commented Burkiss laconically.

'Who are *they*?' She jabbed an elegant finger at the distant figures of the two boys.

'Just lads. I caught 'em catching a crafty fag in the barn.'

'You said no one would see us if we met here.'

Burkiss shrugged.

'Look, those two wouldn't know who you were if you handed 'em a bleedin' signed photograph.' He glanced at his wristwatch. 'Best go in, we've business to do.'

Once inside the barn, he took an oil lamp and lit it. He balanced it on top of an orange box and laid down his brown paper package on a stack of hay bales, opening it up carefully and laying out the contents. He stood back, arms folded.

'So, what d'you reckon? Pretty good stuff, eh?'

Miranda stepped into the circle of light and looked down. Photographs of James, photographs of Joss, photographs of James *with* Joss.

'Is that it?' she sniffed.

'You ain't paid me anythin' yet, remember?'

'And I won't be paying you if you don't come up with something better than this.'

Burkiss looked smug. He pointed to a photograph of Joss and James, walking out of the Caribbean Bar together, dangerously close.

'How about snaps of what they did next?'

'You have photographs of them?'

'Good ones. And statements from two witnesses, what saw the slap an' tickle. *And* . . .' He paused for effect and picked up a photograph of Joss. 'I got her statement that James wouldn't leave her alone, got her drunk an' had his wicked way with her.'

Miranda said nothing. She stared at the photographs, her mouth set tight, the scarlet lips pursed.

'He bought her posh undies, you know,' said Burkiss.

Miranda winced but still said nothing.

'French silk, Brussels lace, the good stuff. She give me some of 'em an' all.' Burkiss patted his jacket pocket. 'You can 'ave the lot if you meet my price.'

Miranda's gaze lifted.

'And if I don't?'

'I'll tell Jimmy-boy what you've bin up to. I mean, I'm a loyal Stripey an' that, aren't I? That crystal clear, is it?'

'Perfectly,' said Miranda, quietly and disdainfully.

Burkiss packed up his things, pushing a photograph of James and Joss across the hay bale to Miranda.

'Think about it. But don't take too long. This should jog yer memory.'

He left. Miranda did not watch him go. She was too busy brooding over the terrifying power she had suddenly acquired.

As the sun set over Costigern's Camp, the camp theatre resounded to the sound of the Sid Dukes Band. It was a packed house and the show was going well tonight, really well; the band sounded the best they had all season. The campers were in holiday mood too: even the novelty paper-tearing act was going down a storm.

In the interval, Sid found Mae on her own, standing in the passageway sipping from a glass of lemonade. She was staring into space and hadn't even noticed he was there.

She looked preoccupied, perhaps a little sad.

He touched her on the shoulder and she jumped.

'Oh! Oh, Sid, it's you, you gave me a fright.'

'Come into my dressing room, Mae, there's something I want to talk to you about.'

'If this is about me and Jenny . . .'

He shook his head.

'You know I wouldn't interfere. No, this is something different.'

'There's only ten minutes till the start of the second half.'

'This'll take five.'

They went into Sid's dressing room and he closed the door. He took a deep breath.

'I won't beat about the bush,' he said slowly. 'And I want you to be the first to know.'

'To know what?'

'Geoff's right. I *am* too old for this game. I've decided to jack it in and hand the band over to him.'

Mae sprang to her feet, horrified.

'Sid, you're mad, you can't let him bully you like this!'

'Nobody's bullying anybody, Mae. I've given this a lot of thought.'

'But why? Why, when things are going so well?'

Sid perched on the edge of the dressing table.

'Because the band's good. I've not spent five years building it up, to watch it tear itself apart.'

'This is Jenny's fault, isn't it? If she hadn't kept things to herself, gone behind your back . . .'

'No, Mae. It's not Jenny's fault. It's nobody's fault, it's my choice. Sooner or later this was bound to happen.'

'Sid. Oh, Sid.' Mae sank down on to the battered old sofa in the corner of the room. 'I can't believe it.' There was anger, confusion, relief and joy inside her, so many feelings, all mixed up together. 'I just can't.'

'There's another reason,' he said, sitting down on the sofa beside her.

'What reason?'

'I've got a weak heart, Mae, you know that. The doc's

been nagging at me to take it easy for years. And I'm giving up the band now because I don't want to leave you a widow.'

She stared at him, uncomprehending.

'What did you say? I thought you said . . .'

'A widow.' He took her hands in his, smiling nervously at her. 'Dammit, Mae, I'm proposing to you. Will you take an old man like me?'

'Marry you? Marry *you*?'

Sid's face fell.

'You're turning me down then?'

Mae flung her arms round Sid's neck, squashing all the breath out of his body.

'Turn you down – do you really think I'd turn you down? Of course I'll marry you, you daft ha'porth, what took you so long?'

There was no time to kiss, because at that moment all hell erupted around and beneath them.

'What the bally 'eck is *that*?' Sid got to his feet, went to the door of the dressing room and flung it open. People were running up and down, milling about, shouting at each other. There seemed no sense to any of it.

Mae appeared at Sid's shoulder. She called out to Desmond as he ran past.

'What's going on?'

'It's the hay store by the stables – it's caught fire and half the model farm's burning down!'

Jenny could hardly believe that the heat and noise from one burning barn could be so intense. Sweat coursed down her face as she swung another bucket of water up the line to fight the fire. Blazing timbers cracked and popped and groaned as the flames leapt higher, licking at the night sky above Llandew Point.

It was pandemonium at the model farm. The moment the alarm was raised, half the camp had turned out to fight the fire; campers and singers, musicians, chalet maids, even Marvo, his bare chest wet and glistening in the eerie, flickering light.

A double human chain extended all the way back from the stable block to the boating lake. Jenny craned her head to make out their shapes, some bent almost double under the weight of buckets, tin baths, kettles, anything that could and would hold water.

'Where the hell is the fire brigade?' she heard someone call out. But no one had an answer.

'More water, quickly!' That was the big, booming voice of Jimmy Costigern, not so jolly now, marching up and down the lines giving orders. James and Henry were at the head of the chain, doing what they could. Poor Henry looks like a lost soul, thought Jenny, scared and out of place.

People were rushing about, not panicking but doing their jobs as quickly as they could; leading terrified horses away from the stables, herding the pigs and chickens into safer enclosures, farther away from the flames.

Some cruel twist of fate had placed Jenny and Mae next to each other in the chain of firefighters. Jenny tried for the umpteenth time to make Mae talk to her, panting with the effort of swinging the heavy water-filled buckets along the line.

'Mae.'

'What?'

'Please don't do this.'

'Do what?'

'Freeze me out.'

'Just leave me alone, will you?'

'Mae, I'm *sorry*.'

'So am I.'

For a moment their eyes met, and Jenny thought that Mae was about to relent. Then the moment was gone.

'Sorry that I ever trusted you,' she said, and moved away to take a different place in the line.

Those words stung so much – did Mae mean them to hurt so cruelly? It hurt still more to know that this time she, Jenny Fisher, was in the wrong.

She had no time to brood. The work was hard and the fire seemed to be taking more of a hold by the minute.

'It's really catching now,' said someone at her elbow. 'If we don't stop it soon it'll spread to the piggery.'

'You don't think it'll reach the chalets?'

''Ardly,' said a thin man in a flat cap and pyjamas. 'There's bloody boating lake in way.'

A couple of people were pushing through the ring of gawping sightseers; Joss recognised them as Gwen Roberts and that shifty-looking Stripey, Sam Burkiss. Gwen was hailing Jimmy Costigern. He didn't look pleased, especially when Sam Burkiss stepped forward.

In fact, that was when all the Costigerns started shouting at each other.

Jimmy Costigern turned to his son.

'Where the hell is the fire brigade? You telephoned them, didn't you? Or are you incapable of that as well?'

'Of course I bloody telephoned them,' snarled James. 'And if you'd taken my advice and trained your own camp fire brigade, like Butlin did, we wouldn't be in this mess now!'

'Dad, Grandpa . . .' ventured Henry.

'For God's sake,' snapped James. 'Make yourself useful, or don't they teach you that at public school?'

'This is no time for arguments,' barked Jimmy. 'We have to stop the fire spreading. We'll have to demolish the barn so the fire's got nowhere to go.'

Gwen Roberts and Sam Burkiss pushed their way to the front of the crowd.

'Mr Costigern – Mr Costigern, please!'

Three pairs of eyes were turned on the two newcomers.

'Not now,' snarled Jimmy.

'Mr Costigern, it's *important.*'

Henry stepped forward.

'What is it?'

Gwen panted, trying to get her breath back.

'Is Mrs Costigern safe?'

Henry and James exchanged puzzled glances.

'Haven't seen her since yesterday,' said Jimmy. 'No inclination to, either.'

'What do you mean, is she safe?' demanded James. 'Why shouldn't she be?'

Gwen pushed Burkiss forward.

'Go on. Tell him what you told me.'

Burkiss coughed. He looked deeply uneasy.

'I saw her 'ere – in that barn.'

'When?'

'Not more'n an hour ago.'

James looked like he'd seen a ghost.

'Oh, God. No.'

'What is it, Dad?' demanded Henry.

'It's your mother. I went looking for her, we had a lot to talk about, but I couldn't find her. She wasn't anywhere – and her car's parked just inside the camp gates . . .'

He turned round to face the fire, contemplating the inferno for a few, desperate moments.

'Dad, no – you can't!'

But as hundreds of people stood and watched in silent horror, James Costigern walked straight into the blazing barn.

Chapter 29

Dr Runciman stood up and packed away his stethoscope. He cleared his throat.

'Keep her warm, plenty of fluids, and make sure you keep those dressings clean.'

He paused, and looking down at the patient in the bed, tried to force eye contact with her. She looked away, burying her face in the pillow.

'I'll be back tomorrow morning to see how she is.' He clicked shut his black bag and prepared to leave.

Dot put her hand on his arm.

'Please, Doctor . . . she'll be all right?'

'Physically, yes, she should be. Given her condition, she's been very lucky. There's no real damage done.'

'Her . . .?' Dot followed the doctor out of Nancy's bedroom and made sure the door was firmly shut behind her. 'Her what?'

'Give her these pills tonight if she can't sleep.' He placed two white tablets in Dot's hand.

'Doctor . . .'

'Yes, Mrs Price?'

'Why did she do it, Doctor? Why did my Nancy try to do away with herself like that?'

Dr Runciman sighed.

'I think you should ask Nancy that, not me. I'll bid you good day, Mrs Price. I'm sure Nancy will be much less distressed by tomorrow. Goodbye, I'll let myself out.'

Dot listened to the doctor's footsteps on the stairs, and the sound of the front door clicking shut. Looking down the stairs, she saw the white circles of faces, Daisy's, Billy's

317

and Tom's, anxiously waiting for news.

'Doctor says she'll be fine,' she called down to them, then she turned and went back into Nancy's room.

Nancy did not acknowledge her mother's presence. She just went on lying there, white and still, her hair still damp from the canal and her eyes vacant and cold.

Dot sat down on the edge of the bed, pushed back the cover and gently took her daughter's hand. It was small and pale, dwarfed by the cotton wadding and bandages around her wrist.

'Doctor says you'll be all right then, Nancy.'

She didn't reply.

'Why did you do it, love?'

Nancy glanced at her mother, then looked away again.

'You'll have to tell me sometime.'

A tear escaped from the corner of Nancy's eye and rolled down on to the pillowcase.

'Why do I 'ave to?'

'I'll just go on askin' you till you do.'

'I just wanted it all to go away.'

'What, love? What did you want to go away? You can tell your mam, Nancy love.'

Nancy was still stonily silent again. Dot tried another tack.

'Dr Runciman said you'd been lucky, considering your condition. What did he mean?'

'No . . .'

'What did he mean, Nancy? Did he . . . you're not . . .' She swallowed. The word didn't want to be uttered. 'Are you in the family way, Nancy?'

Nancy's frail body convulsed with sobs. Rolling on to her belly, she clutched the pillow to her face, losing herself in its white softness.

'No,' whispered Dot, the shock reverberating through her. It was a hot July night, but she felt freezing cold. 'You can't be . . .'

Nancy raised her head from the pillow. It was awash with tears – angry, bitter tears.

'That's right, Mam. It's Ivan's.' She dragged her hand

out of Dot's grasp. 'Now do you see why?'

She fought to grasp the truth, the sickening truth she didn't want to contemplate.

'The bastard! That vicious, evil bastard.' She softened, stroking Nancy's matted hair. 'Oh, Nancy love, why didn't you tell me?'

'So you'd hate me even more?'

'*Hate* you?'

'You already hate me, don't you? All of you. Not like your precious Jenny. Little Miss Perfect. I couldn't bear any more, I just couldn't . . .'

'Oh, Nancy. Nancy love, I never knew, I swear I never knew.'

Shamed beyond endurance, Dot took Nancy in her arms and hugged her, the way she had never hugged any of her children when they had really needed it.

'Mam, Mam, I'm sorry, he made me . . . he said he'd punish me for what Tom did . . . an' Jenny too . . .'

'I know, Nancy, I know. But I swear I'll never let him touch any of us, ever again.'

Geoff opened his chalet door to find Joss on his doorstep.

'Hello, honeybee,' she beamed. 'Can I come in?'

He stood aside to let her in.

'You're looking nice,' he commented. 'Going somewhere special?'

'I dressed up 'specially for you. I know how you like me in pink.'

'And what about James Costigern? Does he like you in pink, too?'

Joss coloured slightly, then recovered her composure. She pouted winningly.

'Oh, *Geoff*, don't be silly. I thought you'd be pleased to see me.' She lunged at him, as though to plant a kiss on his lips, but he backed off at the last moment. 'You're not *angry* with me, are you, honeybee?'

'Angry? No. Just surprised that you'd bother coming halfway across the camp to see me. I don't suppose . . .'

'What?'

'James Costigern wouldn't have dumped you, by any chance? I mean, after heroically rescuing Miranda from the flames and all that? I hear they're getting on together really well just now.'

Anger made Joss purse her lips but she held it back.

'Why should I care what James Costigern does?' she said with a defiant toss of her head. 'You're much more interesting.'

'Really? So why the change of heart? Last week you'd hardly give me the time of day. I wonder if it's anything to do with my getting to be boss of the band – *my* way.'

Joss was wearing her most winsome, little-girl smile. She toyed with the brown kiss-curl on Geoff's forehead.

'Geoffie darling . . . please don't be angry with your little honeybee. All she wants is to be best friends again. If you let me be in your new show, I'll prove I'm a *much* better singer than that stupid girl Jenny Fisher.'

Geoff sighed as he put his arm round Joss and kissed her lightly on the cheek.

'Relax, Joss. Just relax. I've got plans for you.'

'Really?' Her eyes lit up with childlike anticipation.

'Really. Now why don't you go and look stunning by the pool or something? I've got a whole new show to write.'

You never knew quite what was going to happen next at one of Uncle Ronnie's Punch and Judy shows. The string of sausages might eat the crocodile, or the baby chase the policeman down the stairs. That was the thing about Uncle Ronnie: he wasn't just a Punch and Judy man, he was an *artiste*.

It was a slightly grey afternoon, threatening drizzle, but the campers' kids were loving every minute of Uncle Ronnie's Funtime. Not just the kids either, thought Jenny, as she walked slowly towards the kiddies' playground. Apart from one or two parents, plus the obligatory Stripeys to keep everything in order, Jenny made out the back of Sid Dukes' head, its almost circular bald patch gleaming despite the lack of sunshine. He was sitting near the front, surrounded by kids, arms folded, evidently enjoying the show.

'Know what this is, boys and girls?' squeaked Uncle Ronnie in the guise of Mrs Punch.

Back came the enthusiastic reply.

'Yeees!'

'That's right, boys and girls, it's a nice big rolling pin.' Thump, thump, thump went the rolling pin on the front of the red and yellow booth. 'Listen, boys and girls, has Mr Punch seen Mrs Punch?'

'No!'

'You're sure?'

'Yeeees!'

'Shall Mrs Punch hit Mr Punch with the rolling pin?'

The children were at fever pitch now.

'Yes, yes! Go on, go on!'

The hook-nosed puppet waggled its rolling pin at the spellbound children.

'Shall she do it then?'

'YEEEES! 'IT 'IM, 'IT 'IM!'

The rolling pin struck Mr Punch with a thwack of wood on wood. Something about that sound made Jenny feel queasy. She'd never liked Punch and Judy shows. Perhaps she should go back to the chalet and write a letter to Billy and Daisy instead. No, she'd made up her mind to speak to Sid and that was what she'd do. If he didn't want to hear her out, well, that was a chance she'd have to take.

She squeezed her way through the huddle of children to the front.

'Ow!'

'Sorry. Did I step on your foot?'

'Shush, we're listenin'.'

''Appy to see you, miss.'

'Happy to see you too.' At last she found Sid, sitting on the grass among the children. He looked happy, less careworn, in spite of all the trouble with Geoff Tait.

'Mr Dukes . . . Sid . . .'

Still laughing from the sight of the crocodile swallowing a miniature Costigern's deck-chair, Sid swivelled round his head. His smile faltered momentarily but immediately returned, much to Jenny's relief.

321

'Jenny! Come and sit down.'

'You don't mind?'

'Of course not. Here, I'll make room – budge up, young 'uns, make room for the lady.'

After much shuffling of small bottoms on grass, the children made a big enough space for Jenny to sit down.

''Ere, that's singer what sings in show.'

''Snot!'

'Is.'

'Isn't. That one's prettier. An' she's got *legs*.'

'That's t'other 'un, stupid.'

''Ere, miss, my dad says you're a bit of all right.'

Jenny suppressed a smile. She slid her legs underneath her.

'I was wondering, Sid . . . could I have a word?'

'What about?'

Jenny's fingers fiddled with her yellow pleated skirt.

'I'm really sorry, Sid. I can't tell you how sorry I am.'

'About?'

'About what happened . . . with Geoff Tait. I know it was wrong of me to keep it from you and Mae like that, but he told me not to tell anyone. I just didn't know what to do. He said if I didn't keep it to myself he might change his mind about offering me the job . . . and it was so much money, I just couldn't make up my mind what to do.'

She willed him to understand, knowing that she couldn't blame him in the least if he didn't.

'You were in a tight spot,' said Sid. 'From what I've heard, you need the money more than most.'

'But all the same . . . I should have told you. I wish I had.' Anger flared briefly inside Jenny. 'And Geoff had no right, telling you I was going to be his singer before I'd even made up my mind. I really am sorry, Sid, I wish it hadn't happened the way it did. I'm so grateful for everything you've done for me.'

He gave her hand a fatherly pat.

'You know your trouble, Jenny?'

'What?'

'You worry too much.' She joined in the clapping and

cheering as the policeman knocked off Punch's head with his truncheon, and fed it to the crocodile. 'What happened with Geoff just forced me to make up my mind, that's all. I should have given up the band before now, I just didn't want to let go. Besides, you were only looking after your future – doing what anybody would've done.'

'Even you?'

His gaze was steady and honest.

'Yes, Jenny, even me. Nobody knows the value of hard-earned cash like I do. When Jimmy Costigern found me I was a Barnardo's kid with the arse hanging out of my pants. I didn't even own the clothes I stood up in. Believe me, I know what it feels like to have nothing.'

'Mae was right,' said Jenny softly, a dull ache of loss gathering inside her.

'About what?'

'The first time I met you, she told me you were a good man, honest and kind. She said if I really got to know you, I'd see that.'

'And you didn't?'

'I couldn't understand what she saw in you, you were so much older than her.'

Sid smiled.

'Well, that's true enough. *I* don't know what she sees in me either, to be honest with you.'

'But I do,' said Jenny, swallowing down her emotion. 'Now I understand. Her and me – well, I made a right mess of that, didn't I? I know she wants nothing to do with me now, but I still care about her.'

'I know you do. And Mae cares about you too.'

'You really think so?'

'It's just that she's too stubborn to admit it.'

'Sid . . .' she began hesitantly.

'Yes?'

'Can I ask you something else?'

'Fire away.'

'Do you trust Geoff Tait?'

Sid let out his breath in a surprised murmur.

'I . . . well, he's a good musician, one of the best.'

323

'But do you *trust* him?'

Jenny watched the brightly coloured puppets hurling themselves and each other across the miniature stage above her, and the young faces filled with delight and expectation.

'Well . . . you've put me in a bit of a spot there. I don't really know.'

'I don't know if I do, either. The thing is, he's been pestering me.'

Sid looked astounded.

'Pestering you? Making a pass, you mean? That doesn't sound like Geoff.'

'No, nothing like that. He says he wants to manage my career.'

'Oh.' Sid shrugged. 'He's ambitious, knows the business inside out, has all the contacts . . . and he obviously thinks he can make money out of you.'

'So you think it's a good idea then?'

'That's not for me to say, Jenny.'

'No. No, you're right, I'm sorry. But you see, I just can't trust Geoff, not completely . . . not after what he did, going behind my back like that.'

'You're going to turn him down?'

'I have to. Really, there's only one person I'd want to be my manager.'

'Really? Who's that then?'

Jenny's heart thumped. She prayed she wasn't about to make an idiot of herself again.

'You.'

Sid stared at Jenny, open-mouthed.

'Me? Be your manager?'

'I know it's a huge favour to ask, and I know the way I've behaved I've no right to expect anything from you, but . . .' She caught her breath, suddenly dizzy with her own audacity. 'But I knew I had to ask.'

Sid considered for a moment.

'All right, I'll do it.'

'What!'

'If you're serious, that is?'

It was Jenny's turn to be shocked half out of her skin.

'You really mean it?'

'I'll need something to do with my time when I hand over the band, won't I? And I can't think of anybody I'd rather manage. Of course, I'll want my ten per cent!'

'Oh, Sid. Thank you, thank you!'

In an explosion of happiness, she threw her arms round him and hugged him, almost crying with gratitude.

'Steady on, Jenny, you'll knock all the stuffing out of me.'

A third voice rose above the childish giggles and cheering.

'Jenny Fisher, what the . . .?'

Jenny sprang back, wheeling round to see Mae standing not two yards away, an ice cream cornet in either hand. Sid smiled and beckoned her over.

'Mae love, come and sit down. Jenny and I have just been having a chat.'

'So I see.' The flat, expressionless quality in Mae's voice distressed Jenny more than anything. It would have been far easier to bear if she had simply let fly at her with a torrent of abuse. Mae held a cornet out to Sid and he took it.

'Here. I got you a fourpenny one.'

'Ta very much. Sit down, eh?'

Mae shook her head slowly, her eyes fixed on Jenny.

'No, thanks. I don't much care for the company.'

Her words were like a well-directed slap across the face. It was almost more than Jenny could bear. Mae had even moved out of their chalet, swapping places with Phoebe so that she and Jenny wouldn't have to spend any more time together than they absolutely had to. They hardly spoke to each other. Jenny was caught between pain, guilt and resentment: if Sid could understand and forgive, then why not Mae, her oldest and – she had foolishly thought – her closest friend in the world?

'Mae, please . . .'

She turned on her heel, obviously intending to leave. With a despairing look at Sid, Jenny got to her feet, shaking the grass off her skirt.

'It's all right, Mae, you don't have to go. I can see I'm not welcome.'

Mae stood and watched Jenny walking away, until she had turned the corner of the Fun House and disappeared from sight. Drips of melted ice cream truckled unheeded over her fingers and on to the grass beneath.

Sid took her by the waist, laid out his jacket on the grass and persuaded her to sit down.

'What was all that about?' demanded Mae, her gaze not so much questioning as accusing.

'Jenny wanted to talk to me. She wanted to apologise for what happened . . .'

'Apologise!' snorted Mae. 'That's easy, isn't it, *after* the harm's done?'

'What harm? She didn't tell me about Geoff's offer because he made her promise not to. She feels bad about that, really she does. Now, personally, I don't think she should feel bad, and as a matter of fact I told her so.'

'You did what!'

'Look, Mae, you know better than I do what that kid's gone through at home. You know practically everything there is to know about Jenny Fisher, more than her own mother does. Your problem is, you don't *understand*.'

'Now just hold on . . .'

'No, Mae, you hold on. And listen. How *can* you understand? You've got a good father who dotes on you, you've never gone short of anything in your life, you've got money in your pocket, you've never been out of work . . .'

'So?' she demanded with uncharacteristic aggression.

'So how can you begin to imagine what life's been like for Jenny? She's worried sick about her family, especially the kids . . . she sleeps with half an eye open in case that thug of a stepdad comes after her . . . her own mother threw her out on the street without a penny to her name – do you really blame her for taking her big chance when it came along?'

Mae said nothing. She just went on staring at the Punch and Judy show.

'Well, do you?' Sid's voice quietened and he took Mae's hand in his. 'Listen. Remember when *you* got your big chance? Did you hesitate? Did you take any notice of your dad when he begged you not to take it?'

'That was different.'

'Yes,' said Sid softly. 'It was. It was different because you already had a nice life, a decent job – and Jenny had nothing. All you were doing was following your heart. Do you begrudge Jenny following hers?'

Mae didn't reply, but allowed Sid to stroke the back of her hand as he continued talking.

'My guess is, nine out of ten people would have done the same thing in Jenny's situation.' He laid his hand against Mae's cheek and gently turned her head so that she was looking at him. 'Jenny came to see me to ask if I'd consider managing her.'

'She *what*! That scheming . . .'

'I said yes, Mae. Jenny has a great singing talent, and I can make sure it doesn't go to waste. In your heart of hearts, I think that's what you want too.'

Chapter 30

'*Step* – dum-dee-dee-dum-dum – *turn* – dum-dee-dee – *back* – dum-dee-dee – *up* – two, three, four – *catch* . . .'

Mae sat with the other Dukettes in the second row of the stalls, watching Jenny rehearsing *Me and My Shadow* with one of the other dancers. Jenny's singing was terrific, her dancing so-so. Her new partner's dancing, on the other hand, was turning into a nightmare of clumsiness and nerves – feet all over the place, tripping over each other, getting all the steps mixed up.

'That Katie's not up to much, is she?' commented Phoebe, lighting up a cigarette and passing round the packet. 'All the grace of a baby elephant. Here, have one of mine.'

Bella took a cigarette from the packet.

'Ta very much. Ooh, Russian ones, very swish. 'Spect it's just nerves.'

'Can't think why Geoff picked her,' said Dolly. 'Unless he wants to turn it into a slapstick routine.'

'It was supposed to be you, wasn't it, Mae?' said Bella curiously.

'What's that?' Mae was miles away, staring dreamily at the two figures on the stage.

'You. It was supposed to be you, doing that routine with Jenny.'

Mae shrugged dismissively.

'What if it was?'

'You two still not speaking then?'

'Leave it, Bella,' warned Phoebe. 'Can't you see it's a sore point?'

'Dunno what all the fuss is about,' sighed Dolly. 'A girl's got to make a living, best way she can. Good on Jenny, that's what I say. Just wish it was me, that's all.'

Bella chuckled.

'Yeah, well, *you'd* sell your granny just to be the back end of a pantomime cow. Some of us've got standards, darling.'

'Which is why *some* of us are never going to be stars.'

Mae watched the routine on the stage. It was impossible to take her eyes off it – it had been her routine, hers and Jenny's. Before . . . when Mae had trusted Jenny and everything had been all right.

That girl Katie really was useless. Just look at the way she kept treading on Jenny's toes! 'It's one, two, step, tap, not one, two, tap, step, you silly girl,' muttered Mae under her breath, her feet silently going through the steps underneath the seat. 'Come on, girl, it's not difficult. All you have to do is let the music guide your feet.'

They just didn't look right together, Jenny and Katie. They lacked that essential something that made the perfect double-act, that secret understanding which made words unnecessary. You and I used to have it, thought Mae, her eyes following Jenny's attempts to look confident whilst dodging out of Katie's way. There were feelings inside her that she didn't want to acknowledge: uneasy misgivings about the way she'd treated Jenny, the uncomfortable beginnings of doubt.

I wonder, she thought. I wonder if we could ever find that understanding again.

Jenny was *not* having a good rehearsal. For a start off, Mae was sitting bang in the middle of the second row of the stalls, watching her with a kind of fixed, accusing stare which made her feel not only uncomfortable, but sad. As if that wasn't bad enough, poor little Katie Purvis was a complete bag of nerves and just couldn't get the hang of the dance routine.

They were preparing *Me and My Shadow* for the next Friday night show – Geoff hated it, but it was one of Jimmy Costigern's favourites, and a bit of fun for the campers.

The idea was that Jenny would begin the song, then Katie would come on in the chorus, all dressed in black, and dance just behind her, shadowing her. That was the *idea*. The reality was that Katie kept tripping over her feet, which of course threw Jenny completely. Dancing had never been her strong point – hadn't she and Mae laughed about her two left feet time and time again?

Geoff stopped the music and ran his fingers irritably through his curly brown hair.

'Stop. I said, STOP! Katie, what are you *doing*?'

Jenny felt for Katie. She intervened.

'It was my fault, I missed the half-turn and she just sort of . . .'

'Just sort of fell over her own feet?' queried Geoff sarcastically. He took a deep breath and sighed. 'Sorry, Katie, you did your best but this just isn't working.' Katie looked not so much disappointed as relieved. 'Take a break, and we'll try this again with just Jenny.'

As he raised his hands over the piano keys, a peal of laughter could be heard above the low hum of chatter. Heads turned. People stopped talking and looked towards one of the side doors. Joss Flynn was swaggering towards the orchestra pit, three-quarters of an hour late and snootily casual in wide-legged silk pants and a sleeveless blouse.

'What a good idea, Jenny,' she said smugly. 'And *then* we'll try it without you altogether. That'll be best of all.'

The sudden silence was laden with delicious expectation. Was there going to be a cat-fight, a shouting match? Was little Jenny Fisher going to get her comeuppance? There were some here who'd like nothing better than to see her face rubbed into the dirt. Jenny felt her face and neck burn with fury. She took two steps towards the edge of the stage.

'I've had just about enough of you, Joss Flynn.'

'Really?' Joss smiled sweetly. 'Funnily enough, we've all had enough of you too. So why don't you just go back to your smutty little corner shop and leave showbusiness to people who know what they're doing?'

'You hard-faced bitch!'

Jenny was about to jump down off the stage and slap Joss

331

Flynn's smug face for her, when Geoff Tait cut in.

'I'll deal with this, Jenny.' He looked Joss up and down. 'Well, well, Joss. So glad you could make it. I wouldn't want you to leave without saying goodbye.'

'Good . . . what do you mean, goodbye?'

'You're leaving us, Joss, didn't I tell you?'

Joss's face froze between malice and horror.

'If this is a joke, it's not funny.'

'You should know me by now, Joss, I never joke. Let me put it simply, so's even you can understand. You're lazy, you're arrogant . . .'

'Geoff! Geoff, you can't do this!'

'. . . you're slapdash . . .'

'She's turned you against me, hasn't she, that little whore?' Jenny felt Joss's eyes burn into her but she wasn't afraid of Joss Flynn any more, just angry. 'Been sleeping with you as well as Henry Costigern, has she?'

Geoff just carried on, as if he hadn't heard a word she'd said.

'. . . and you're talentless. I think that's about it.' He idly picked out the notes of *So Long, It's Been Good To Know You* on the piano keyboard. 'Oh, yes, I forgot. You're fired.'

'Tell me, woman, where is she?'

Ivan Price's hand came down across Dot's face again, with such force that she slumped back against the kitchen wall.

'I told you, I don't know.'

'An' I know you're lyin'.' Slap, slap, thump. Dot's body absorbed the blows almost silently, her arms crossed over her face. 'Where is she? Where's that bitch Jenny?'

'I. Don't. Know.'

Ivan paused, his fist raised about shoulder height. There was a white froth of spittle about his lips, his face still distorted and bruised from the beating he'd received.

'Don't give me that! You know where she is. She's bin 'ere, ain't she? Come to visit 'er lovin' da, did she? You should'a told me she was comin', woman, I'd 'ave give her a proper welcome . . .'

Dot ducked under his arm and ran to the far side of the kitchen.

'You're the devil, Ivan Price!'

'That right?' Ivan's lips tightened into a leering rictus of a smile. 'Don't matter what you do, I'll 'ave her, Dot. Set the police on me, she did . . .'

'No! No, she never . . .'

'Paid me a little visit this mornin', did Constable Harries. Seems someone's bin tellin' tales about me. Just as well it's all lies, eh?' He picked up the poker. 'Where is she, woman?'

Dot moaned softly, half from pain, half from fear. But her eyes were bright with inner strength.

'I'd not tell you, even if I knew.'

As the poker swished through the air, a child ran forward through the open kitchen door.

'Leave 'er alone! Leave me mam alone!'

Ivan kicked out at Billy but the boy was quick and light on his feet. He dodged round behind his stepfather and leapt on to his back, tearing and biting and clawing like a tiger cub. Dot slid down the wall, her whole body shaking, as Ivan whirled round, trying to dislodge the boy.

'Billy – no, Billy!'

Tears of rage streamed down Billy's face.

'Gerroff 'er! Gerroff me mam. I 'ate you, I 'ate you! I won't let you 'urt 'er no more.'

'Little bastard!'

Ivan flung Billy from his back in a single vicious movement. The child fell to the floor with a cry of pain, his wrist twisted beneath him. Ivan aimed a kick at his side and he scrambled away, out of reach.

'Billy – oh God, Billy, run . . .'

'Mam!'

'Want some more, do you, boy? Want to fight your da like a man? Come on then, whelp, what you waitin' for?'

'I said run, are you listenin', Billy? Run an' get 'elp . . .'

He might take to his heels, but there could be no escape for Dot. She was little more than a crumpled heap at Ivan's feet, too lost in fear to think about anything else.

'Where is she?'

'You'll not find out from me.'

Rage overtook Ivan and he seized Dot by the scruff of the neck.

'Will you tell me, woman?'

Her voice was weak, exhausted.

'No.'

'Bitch!' Taking her by the hair, Ivan ran forward, slamming her head into the kitchen window.

'Aaah . . .' Dot slumped limply over the edge of the stone sink.

The window had shattered with the force of the impact, shards of bloody glass flying into the sink, on to the draining board, all over the floor.

'Where is she?' roared Ivan. 'Where is she? Where the hell is she?'

But Dot's body lay motionless, not responding, not anything. There seemed no more life in it than in a bundle of old rags. He shoved it to the ground in disgust. Stupid cow, never was good for much. He looked around him. The answer must be here somewhere. There must be something that would tell him where to find Jenny, that bitch who was the cause of all his troubles.

There would be letters. Where would that devious cow have hidden them? Empty drawers broke into matchwood as he pulled them out and threw them down. The brown earthenware teapot smashed against the cooking range as he found nothing inside it but rolled-up bills and a few copper coins. Nothing. Just rubbish. But it had to be here somewhere. With a savage sweep of his arm, he dashed the pots off the stove, sending them clattering to the floor.

It was then that he caught sight of it; the picture postcard resting on the windowsill, partly obscured now by fragments of glass. He brushed them away and picked up the card.

There were only seven words on the back: 'This is where I work. Love, Jenny.'

He turned it over. The photograph showed one of those new holiday camps by the sea, with happy campers running

334

about in bathing costumes, playing stupid games. In the middle, Jolly Jimmy Costigern's fat face beamed above the message: HAVING A JOLLY TIME AT COSTIGERN'S, LLANDEW.

Ivan might have stood there gloating for a long time – if not for the sudden commotion in the street outside.

'What's goin' on?'

'Summat's up at Dot Fisher's 'ouse.'

'Terrible shoutin' an' screamin' an' that.'

Damn that boy – that was Billy Fisher's voice, shouting fit to bust: 'Quick, Mr Corlett, quick! It's me mam.'

He cursed under his breath. 'No one crosses Ivan Price. You not learned your lesson yet then, boy? I'll be back to teach it to you, soon as I've taught it to your bitch sister.'

By the time John Corlett reached the back kitchen of number forty-two Gas Street, Ivan Price was long gone.

'Mr Corlett, where's me mam? Is she all right?'

There was no time to stop Billy from following him into the kitchen. It was a sight John Corlett wouldn't have had the boy see for all the world. His poor mother was lying silent and still on the kitchen floor, her head all bloody and surrounded by a halo of broken glass.

'Mam! Mam, wake up!' Billy had to be dragged back by old Mrs Pateman.

'Nay, lad, stay back. Best let Mr Corlett see to her.'

John Corlett knelt beside her, putting his ear to her mouth.

'She's breathing. Just knocked out, I'd say. Billy, run for the doctor.'

'I want to stay with Mam.'

'Now, Billy. I'll stay with your mother and make sure she's all right. Mavis, you'd best send to the pit for Tom. Mr Pateman—'

'Aye, John?'

'Fetch Constable Harries. I think we all know who's responsible for this.'

Still kneeling beside Dot's unconscious form, he stroked his hand lightly over her face, pushing back the matted strands of hair. Lying there she seemed very young, almost childlike, and with the fear and pain gone from her face, she looked quite beautiful.

'Oh, Mrs Fisher,' whispered John Corlett. 'Oh, Dot.'

After rehearsal, Jenny met Henry for a glass of Vimto and an ice cream at Jolly Jim's Cafe. She really did enjoy being with Henry; he was gentle and clever and fun. If only there weren't so many other things to preoccupy her, so many other feelings that had to be sorted out and dealt with.

'How's your mother?' asked Jenny.

'Mum? Oh, she's right as rain – couple of superficial burns on one hand, but she's fine. And between you and me, she hasn't been so nice to Dad in years.'

'I'm not surprised,' said Jenny. 'Going into the fire like that, to rescue her. The whole camp's talking about how brave he was.'

'Not just brave,' Henry replied. 'What he did was completely out of character.'

'How do you mean?' asked Jenny, puzzled.

Henry drained his glass. His eyes rested on her, not demanding anything, just holding her attention.

'Let me tell you a story, Jenny – a love story.'

She laughed nervously. What was this all about? Surely Henry wasn't going to go and do something really silly like propose? Dolly and Bella had been teasing her that he might for weeks now . . .

'It's about Mother and Dad,' he continued. 'When they were young they were very much in love.'

'Your parents!'

'I know it's hard to believe, but they were so devoted to each other they were practically famous for it. In fact, they were *so* famous that Pinero actually put them into one of his plays!'

'Fancy,' said Jenny, wondering who Pinero was. 'So what went wrong?'

'Grandpa, that's what. He steamrollered them into getting married when they were still too young to know what they were doing. He made Dad work in the family business, and made sure he got Mother in the family way so there'd be an heir.'

'Surely . . . couldn't they just have said no?'

'Have you ever tried saying no to my grandfather? The thing is, there's so little love left between Mother and Dad now that Mother practically had to get herself killed to make Dad show it. And yet she still can't believe he cares enough about her to risk his life for her.'

'But . . . why did they stop loving each other? Where did all that love go?'

'Oh, Jenny, I wish I knew. The thing is . . .'

She saw the turmoil enter his eyes.

'What is it, Henry?'

'I'm afraid that the same thing might happen to us.'

Dumbstruck, she slowly lowered her glass.

'Us? But we're . . . different.'

'There are so many things I want to do, Jenny, lots of things I want to see. Do you know what one of them is?'

'Tell me.'

'Five years from now, I want to be sitting in the best box at the London Palladium, watching you singing for the King.'

'Henry!'

'And another thing. I want to go to the pictures and see you on the screen, dancing with Fred Astaire.'

'But . . .'

'I want the best for you, Jenny, the best of everything. And that won't happen if I ask you to marry me, will it?'

Jenny saw that the look in Henry's eyes was more than friendship, or kindness, or adolescent lust; it was real, unselfish love. How often had she known love in her life? Often enough to turn it away?

'No,' she said softly.

His hand slipped across the table and covered hers. Their fingers linked, sharing their warmth.

'We're too young,' he said. 'We'd end up like my parents – and I couldn't bear to do that to you.'

'We could never be like them,' Jenny assured him. 'I can't imagine not liking you.'

337

'And loving me? Do you think you could love me too? Not today . . . but sometime?'

Jenny smiled as she leant across the table and kissed him, provoking a chorus of whoops and cheers from the campers at the next table.

'Why don't you ask me in five years' time?' she said. 'When you come to see me at the London Palladium.'

Chapter 31

'Bitches and bastards! I hate you all. I hate the whole damn' lot of you . . .'

Joss Flynn was not at all happy. She was also very, very drunk. An entire bottle of Dubonnet in the Caribbean Bar had taken its toll, and it took her ages to get her key into the chalet lock. When she finally managed to get the door open she almost fell inside.

'Bastards! BASTARDS! I won't let you get away with this, I bloody won't.'

A passing Stripey, out on night patrol, swung his torch towards her and shushed her as she wrestled with the door handle.

'Please . . . Miss Flynn, isn't it? Do try to keep the noise down. It's after eleven-thirty, you know.'

'Fuck off,' snarled Joss. 'Just bloody fuck off and leave me alone!' She slammed the door shut behind her, switched on the light and stumbled towards the bed.

'It's here somewhere, I know it is . . . Where the hell is it?'

Scrabbling about in suitcases and hatboxes, she searched for the elusive slip of paper. It had to be here somewhere, she was sure she hadn't thrown it away – the telephone number of that newspaper reporter in Manchester who couldn't keep his eyes off her tits. He'd been nice to her, he'd listen – and she had plenty to say.

She'd fix 'em all good and proper, that's what she'd do. Joss took out the drawer from the dressing table and upended the contents on to her bed. She rummaged among the lipsticks, train tickets and powder compacts.

Once it got into the papers, Joss Flynn's story would put a bomb under this whole sorry pigsty of a holiday camp.

Got it. She kissed the scrap of paper and slipped it into her pocket.

Right, James and Miranda. Right, Geoff and smug little Jenny Fisher, you'd better watch out. And you'd better keep an eye on the morning papers – 'cause the headlines will be about *you*.

The Friday night show came round with frightening speed. Backstage at the camp theatre, things were really buzzing. Hairgrips clenched between her teeth, Bella was pinning up Phoebe's hair while Dolly was standing on a chair so that Jenny and Katie could make emergency repairs to her torn costume.

'Gawd,' commented Bella, glancing critically at Dolly's rear end. 'Best get that tear fixed, I can see your knickers.'

Phoebe chuckled.

'I dunno, Dolly. Anybody'd think you were Joss bleedin' Flynn!'

'Hardly,' replied Dolly drily. 'Joss Flynn doesn't wear any knickers.'

This provoked a gale of laughter. Jenny coloured up and became minutely interested in the intricacies of sewing up Dolly's black satin shorts. Joss Flynn's "startling revelations" had been all over the *Daily Sketch*, and even she – little Jenny Fisher – had merited a passing but vitriolic mention.

How exactly had Joss put it? She didn't really want to remember, but the words would keep drifting back into her head: '. . . and as for young Henry, well, he spends all his time with a common little gold-digger – Jenny Fisher is her name. Calls herself a singer, but she's really just a shop-girl with her eye on Henry's money . . .'

She could just imagine Joss smiling and pouting as she poured out her poor, wounded heart to the oh-so-understanding newspaper man. Evil bitch, thought Jenny, savagely biting off a length of thread. If you were here now I'd take that smug smile and stuff it right down your throat.

Dolly screwed round her head and looked at Jenny.

'You've gone quiet,' she commented. 'What's up – nervous about tonight?'

'It's that article in the *Sketch*,' said Bella. 'Still brooding about it, aren't you, Jen?'

'At least *you* didn't get your picture in the paper,' pointed out Phoebe. She giggled. 'Where *did* they get that one of Joss and James going into Joss's chalet? They looked three sheets to the wind.'

'You'd have to be dead drunk to want to sleep with Joss,' retorted Phoebe. 'Spiteful cow. D'you know what she called me in that . . . that rag?'

Dolly grinned.

'A "two-farthing trollop with a squint", wasn't it? Cheer up, she didn't actually mention you by *name* . . .'

'Well, I won't forget *that* in a hurry.'

'Nobody's going to forget Joss Flynn,' said Jenny. 'Hand us another pin, would you, Katie? Especially not the Costigerns.'

'Who'd've believed it, eh?' Katie took a pin and gave it to Jenny. 'James Costigern carrying on with Joss . . .'

'. . . and Miranda up the duff . . .' added Dolly.

'. . . *and* it's not James's kid, neither!' said Phoebe with a triumphant flourish of her hairpins. 'There you are, Bella, but don't shake your head about or it'll all come down.'

'Ta very much, Phoebe.' Bella turned round and started doing up the buttons on her black waistcoat. 'Tell you what though, girls, that's the life, eh? More money than you know what to do with, and rumpy-pumpy with anyone you fancy, whenever you damn' well like!'

'I think it's depraved,' sniffed Katie, at sixteen the youngest of the Dukettes. 'Some of the campers are downright scandalised. I heard some of them in the Roman Room, saying they weren't going to come back next year, what with all this scandal.'

Dolly laughed.

'And *I* heard some of 'em in the Caribbean Bar going on about how half their street was planning to come next year, *because* of the scandal! There's nothing like a bit of juicy gossip to get the punters in. I bet Jolly Jimmy's rubbing his hands with glee.'

I doubt it, thought Jenny, recalling Jimmy Costigern's grim-faced expression when she'd walked past him that morning.

'It's Henry I feel sorry for,' she sighed, finishing off the darn and biting off the thread. 'The paper made him look like an idiot.'

Bella winked.

'Still got a soft spot for him, eh? I thought you two had packed it in?'

Just as Jenny was considering her reply, Sid came pushing through the throng.

'Everything all right, girls?'

'Yes, Mr Dukes,' they chorused in unison. Dolly jumped down off the chair, screwed her head round and examined her bottom in the mirror. 'Just about. If this thing holds together.'

'It'd better,' said Bella. 'We don't want any more scandalous revelations, ta very much.'

'Off you go, girls,' said Sid, shooing them away in a fatherly manner. 'Geoff wants a word with you before you go on.'

He and Jenny watched them wiggle off across the dressing room and up the stairs to the wings, their nubile bodies squeezed into tight black shorts and waistcoats, tap shoes and fishnet tights.

'The campers are going to enjoy this,' commented Sid as they followed the girls into the wings. 'Well, the male ones anyway. How're you doing, Jenny? Ready for the number?'

'Just about.' She fiddled with her costume. The satin tailcoat and too-tight, cutaway shorts left very little to the imagination. 'I feel a bit . . . obvious, though. What with that story all over the papers.'

'Don't you worry about that. Just concentrate on the song. Anyway,' he added, 'it's not as if you'll be doing this kind of stuff for much longer.'

Surprised, she stopped wriggling inside her waistcoat and looked at Sid. To her left, Marvo the Memory Man was coming to the end of his act, guessing what colour socks the campers were wearing.

'How's that?'

'Well, you won't be with the band for ever, will you?'

'I don't know, I hadn't really thought about it.' She thought about it now. 'So . . . you want me to leave Geoff and the band?'

Sid shrugged.

'Turnabout is fair play. We'll see. There's the rest of the season to get through first. You'll be all right?'

Jenny nodded. A gale of laughter from the audience was followed by a deafening round of applause.

Geoff appeared in the wings.

'Everything ready?'

'Fine.' Jenny's stomach turned over, the way it always did before something really big. 'I just wish . . .' She glanced across at Mae, but as their eyes met she looked away and started talking to Phoebe and Doris.

'Now, you know how we're playing it? You're doing the number as a solo, with the Dukettes as a chorus-line. It's not how I'd originally planned it, but it should work well enough.'

He clapped his hands.

'Everything in position. Do up that top button, Phoebe, you don't look decent.'

Phoebe winked.

'Thought that was the whole idea, *honeybee.*'

Jenny saw Geoff colour up at the mention of Joss's nickname for him. He too had had his picture in the *Daily Sketch*, and not a very flattering one at that.

'That's enough of that, Phoebe.'

'Is that what you said to Joss Flynn? No wonder she went off with James Costigern.'

'Phoebe,' snarled Geoff. 'Just shut up and get on with your job. There's a show to put on, or have you forgotten?'

Sid laid his hands on Jenny's shoulders and gave her a peck on the cheek.

'Give 'em hell, Jenny. I've just got to have a quick word with Mae.'

Sid went away. Geoff got his temper back and went out on stage to announce the number. Everyone was lost inside their own heads, concentrating frantically on the one thing that they had to do, and not even noticing anything or anybody else. Jenny tried out a few of the dance steps. On her own, without a "shadow" to cover for her, she was sure the audience would notice that she was no dancer.

But that wasn't the way to think. Think positive, that was what Sid always said. Don't dwell on what you can't do, make the most of what you've got.

Give 'em hell, Jenny, she whispered to herself. This is it. If they're not talking about you for the *right* reasons by the end of this show, you might as well go back to cleaning toilets at the Alhambra.

Sid and Jimmy had been right. *Me And My Shadow* was a popular number with the campers, that much was obvious from the way they started swaying and humming along before the band had got halfway through the introduction. Mind you, its popularity might have more to do with the skimpy chorus costumes than with the song itself, thought Jenny, as she pirouetted on to the stage, top hat in one hand and walking cane in the other.

A chorus of wolf-whistles greeted the sight of six chorus-girls in tiny shorts and plunging necklines, fronted by a singer whose slender legs were shown off to perfection by high-heeled tap shoes and black fishnet tights.

Step, turn, tap, step, tap . . . it was going all right, not brilliantly but all right. At least she was remembering the steps to go with the words. It was a bit mechanical though, she'd never been able to dance and sing at the same time without thinking about it.

Making sure not to lose eye-contact with the audience, she mimed strolling down the avenue. Tap, step, tap, turn, *smile*, hat in the air and . . . yes! . . . catch.

So far so good. They were coming towards the chorus, the bit where the shadow was supposed to come on to the stage and start dancing behind her, mirroring her movements. It would have worked so much better with two, she thought, with a sudden twinge of sadness. It would have worked so much better with *Mae*.

Twelve o'clock . . . she went through the motions of yawning, climbing the stairs to an imaginary door. She raised her hand as if to knock, then turned to the audience with a sad shrug of her shoulders.

Nobody there.

But wait a minute; there *was* somebody there. Somebody right behind her, shadowing every movement, matching it, strengthening it, bettering it. Her *shadow*.

For a split second Jenny's heart stopped. She missed a step, swung round, almost fluffed her words. But the shadow missed a step too, matched the movement, made it look as if it had been deliberate. Then . . . then the shadow *smiled*.

'Mae?' mouthed Jenny incredulously, in the four-bar instrumental between the chorus and the second verse.

She just smiled and winked, pirouetted and – at exactly the right moment – threw her hat into the air and caught it on her head.

'Get on with it,' she mouthed, and the smile didn't falter once.

'More!'
  'More!'
  'Encore!'
Cheers, whistles, stamping feet . . . Jenny had never heard so much noise in all her life. She stood there, centre-stage, and felt the sheer weight of the applause buffeting her like a force-ten gale, so strong it almost knocked her off her feet.

Geoff was nodding and smiling, Sid beaming all over his face, Desmond fiddling in his ear with a matchstick . . . but then, that was Desmond for you. Even the band were clapping politely, when more often than not they preferred to pull faces and make rude gestures behind Sid's back.

Jenny bowed a second time, turned towards the chorus and asked the audience to applaud them, too. Then she held out her hand.

'Mae?'

She shook her head, mouthing, 'You're the star, not me.'

Jenny grabbed her hand and dragged her out of the chorus line, right up to the footlights. Then she hugged her, fit to bust, tears of happiness streaming down her face.

The audience loved this even more. Arms waved, feet stamped, whistles of appreciation went on for what seemed like hours. By the time they finally managed to get off the stage, the show was running ten minutes late.

Mae hesitated at the top of the stairs to the dressing room.

'I ought to go . . . there's a quick change before the next number.'

'Wait! Just a minute. I haven't thanked you yet . . .'

'There's no need. Really.'

'You were brilliant, Mae. Really brilliant. With you, the number was ten times as good.'

'Jenny, don't!' But Mae was pink with pleasure.

'Why did you? What made you change your mind? I thought . . . I thought we weren't friends any more?'

Mae smiled.

'I grew up.'

'You . . .?'

'It was Sid who made me realise I've been behaving like a spoilt kid. I suppose deep down . . . deep down I was a little bit jealous of you.'

'I'm sorry, Mae. I should never have gone behind your back, not after everything. I never wanted it to be like this . . .'

Mae took Jenny's hands in hers.

'It's all forgotten.' The smile became a grin. 'Besides, if I didn't make things up with you, who could I ask to be my bridesmaid?'

For a moment, Mae's words didn't really sink in. Then came the shock, the realisation, the delight.

'You're . . .?'

'Getting married, yes!'

'To Sid?'

'Who else!'

'When?'

'Soon . . . here, in the camp chapel.' Mae paused, momentarily uncertain. 'You are pleased, aren't you?'

'Pleased! Oh, Mae, it's wonderful! I'm so happy for you.'

Arms about each other, they danced round and round in the wings, almost knocking over Binky who was hauling his spare snare-drum up the stairs.

'Steady on, girls, you should try taking water with it!'

Jenny just laughed.

'You know something, Mae? This is the best night of my whole life.'

'There'll be even better ones,' she promised as they walked arm in arm down the stairs. 'Just you wait and see.'

Jimmy Costigern laid out the newspapers on his desk, face-up, so that the headlines were painfully visible. His gaze fell first on his daughter-in-law, then his son.

'Well, James?' he said acidly.

James junior tore his gaze away from the lurid account of his exploits.

'Father?'

'Are they true?'

James junior shuffled his feet.

'Yes.'

'I see.' Jimmy turned his attention to Miranda, jabbing his finger at the second paragraph on page one. 'And *this*?'

Miranda was trying to be her usual hard-faced self, but it wasn't easy.

'If you mean, am I pregnant,' she said, 'then yes. Yes, I am.'

Jimmy's already ruddy complexion deepened to an apoplectic purple. For a moment he looked as though he might explode; then he turned away and looked out of the office window. It was dark outside, but the chalet lights were still on and in the distance he could hear the sounds of the campers enjoying themselves at the late-night variety show.

'Worse than I thought then,' he muttered. 'Not just some lying little tart on the make.' He swung round to face James and Miranda.

'This . . . baby.'

'What about it?' demanded Miranda.

'It's James's.'

'No . . .'

'I said, it's *James's*. Is that quite clear?'

Miranda responded with a curt nod. Jimmy fixed his son with a steely glare.

'As for you, James . . . yes, it's true that you've been seeing this . . . *girl*.' He spoke the words with evident distaste. 'But only for simple, innocent companionship. Nothing more. Understand?'

'Yes, Father. Sir.'

'Miranda has only been staying in Greece because she was taken ill and needed a change of climate.' Before she had a chance to open her mouth and make some sarcastic comment, he snapped: 'Miranda, call your father and get him off my back. Now.'

Jimmy drummed his fingers on the desktop.

'As far as this Flynn girl is concerned, I understand she's willing to accept money to change her story. Pay her well enough and she'll say she made the whole thing up because she was bitter about getting the sack. In a week this whole thing'll be over.' He looked daggers at his son and daughter-in-law. 'Except for the time, money and reputation this bloody mess has cost me.'

'Surely, Father . . .'

'Don't you "surely" me, James Costigern. Billy Butlin'll be laughing all the way to the bank.' Jimmy snatched the newspapers, screwed them up and threw them into the wastepaper bin. 'Any more trouble from you, *either* of you . . .'

'There won't be,' said his son hastily.

'No. There damn' well won't,' growled Jimmy, and leaving the office he slammed the door so hard that it shook in its frame.

Miranda glared after him, as though simple loathing might stop him in his tracks and turn him to dust.

'Are you just going to stand there and let him treat us like this?'

'What choice do I have?'

'What *choice*! God, James Costigern, you're forty-five years old and you're still afraid of your father!'

'I didn't notice *you* standing up to him.'

Miranda and James stood facing each other, the old bitterness rekindling.

'Oh, so you need your wife to protect you now, do you?'

'If it hadn't been for you . . .'

'And if it hadn't been for you and that cheap trollop . . .'

Outside the door, Jimmy Costigern listened to James and Miranda, fighting like cat and dog, lashing each other with the full force of their own unhappiness. So much for the reconciliation. Still, so long as they did what they were told and Henry kept his hands off chorus-girls, things would be all right. The Costigerns would soon be one big happy family again.

Constable Harries sat down at Dot's kitchen table.

'How're you feeling then, Mrs Price?'

'How d'you think?' replied Dot, glancing up at John Corlett who was standing protectively behind her chair. Her face was a mass of bumps and bruises, and three long cuts extended from her forehead up into her scalp.

'Yes . . . er, sorry. Stupid question.' The policeman flicked through the pages of his notebook, looking for the right page.

'So, have you caught him yet then?' demanded John impatiently.

'Not yet, no. But I want you to know we're taking this business very seriously.'

John Corlett, normally a patient man, snorted in derision.

'I suppose that means you'll do nothing and hope it goes away?'

Dot levered herself wearily out of her chair.

'I'll put kettle on,' she said.

'You rest. I'll do it.' John went across to the stove and put the kettle on the gas.

'No,' said Constable Harries with evident irritation. 'It

does *not* mean we're doing nothing. As a matter of fact, we've found out one or two very interesting things about Mr Ivan Price.'

John came back to the table.

'What things? He's a villain, what else is there to find out?'

Constable Harries looked from Dot to John and back again.

'Precisely what is this gentleman's relationship to your family, Mrs Price?'

Dot looked up at John, took his hand and laid it on her shoulder.

'A friend,' she said. 'Whatever you tell me, you can tell 'im too.'

'Very well. There's one thing you'll be glad about, at any rate.'

'What's that?'

'You're not married to Ivan Price.'

Dot peered at the policeman.

'I'm not with you. *Not married?* How does he mean, John?'

'Don't talk daft, boy,' said John Corlett. 'I was at the wedding myself, not three years ago.'

The constable cleared his throat.

'I don't doubt it, sir, only the marriage wasn't legal, see. Ivan Price is already married.'

Dot clapped her hand to her mouth.

'No! No . . . 'e can't be!'

'So you didn't know he was married then?' Constable Harries scribbled in his notebook.

'You think I'd 'ave owt to do with 'im if I did? Who . . .?'

'Seems he has a wife and three kiddies back in South Wales. Left her in an even worse state than he's left you, apparently.'

Shocked to the core, Dot shook her head from side to side, slowly, disbelievingly.

'John . . .' she whispered.

'It's all right, Dot, it's all right.'

'That poor woman . . .'

'I know.'

'Anyhow,' went on the policeman, 'chances are that's the last you'll see of Ivan Price – things are a bit hot for him round here now, see.' He got up from the table, tucking his notebook into his top pocket. 'I'll be off now.'

'You'll let me know if . . .'

'Directly we find him. Afternoon, Mrs . . . Fisher, Mr Corlett.'

The door closed behind Constable Harries. Dot sank into her chair.

'Is it really true, John?'

'I reckon it is.'

She wept. He fished a clean hanky out of his pocket and unfolded it.

'Don't upset yourself, shall I get the salts?'

Dot laughed through her tears.

'Upset? I'm not upset, John, it's . . . it's the relief. We're free of 'im, he's gone, he's not my 'usband any more, he never was.'

She dabbed her eyes and blew her nose.

'You're all right then, Dot?'

She nodded.

'When I'm feelin' better, can I use your telephone to ring our Jenny?'

'Of course you can. Or shall I ring her for you? After all, it was her Ivan was looking for, perhaps we should warn her . . .'

Dot shook her head.

'I want to talk to her myself. Besides, no need. He searched the 'ouse but he found nowt, see – nowt that'd tell him where she was. Our Jenny's safe, John, Ivan'll never find her. Thank God for that.'

'Thank God,' echoed John. 'Now, why don't I make us that nice cup of tea?'

Chapter 32

'Give me another.'

The barman looked doubtful.

'Don't you think you've had enough already, mate?'

'Give me *another.*'

Ivan pushed his money across the bar-top and the barman reluctantly pulled him another pint. Ivan turned round, glass in hand.

So this was the Caribbean Bar. What a dump! A plaster galleon and a few parrots in cages. Folk must need their heads examining if they paid good money to come to a place like this. He drank half his pint in one draught and wiped the froth from his mouth with the back of his hand. It wasn't the decor he'd come to see, it was the entertainment.

Two nights a week, there was a late-night show in the bar; a couple of speciality turns, a band for dancing . . . and a singer. Well, well, who'd have thought it, eh? Little Jenny Fisher singing in a bar, flaunting herself for anyone who cared to look. That white evening dress was so tight he could see every curve of her body as the material moulded itself to her small, hard breasts. He imagined that same body naked and vulnerable, at his mercy. This time she wouldn't get away.

Bitch. Sly, cheating, teasing bitch. Anger melded with lust and Ivan licked his lips. He'd obviously been right about the girl all along, she was nothing but a cheap tart. Fight him off, would she? Spit and claw like a wild-cat, and all the time pretending she was some shy little virgin. He'd punish her for what she'd done to him. Setting the police on him, turning the world against him . . .

If she liked it rough, that's just how he'd give it to her.

'Bitch,' he hissed under his breath. The man next to him looked up and peered at him through bleary, drink-sodden eyes.

'Wassat, mate?'

Ivan nodded towards Jenny, singing her heart out on the stage.

'See 'er?' he said. 'Flauntin' 'erself on that stage?'

'Her? That girl singer?'

'That's right.' Ivan smiled grimly. 'I'm goin' to get 'er.'

'Well, that's that then,' said Clive the stand-in pianist, clearing the beer glasses off the Steinway. 'Thank God. I hate these Thursday night dos, they're all too pissed to care what goes on on stage.'

Slowly the Caribbean Bar emptied, leaving only a few stragglers, making the most of drinking-up time. Lindsey packed away the last of Marvo's props and walked across to where Jenny was standing, staring out into the empty, half-lit bar.

'Penny for 'em.'

She started at the touch of Lindsey's hand.

'What! Oh, nothing in particular. I just had this really weird feeling tonight.'

'Weird? What sort of weird?'

'Like . . . like I was being watched.'

Lindsey chuckled.

'We all were, kid – leastwise, I hope so.'

'No, something different. Anyhow, it's gone now.' Jenny picked up her cardigan and slipped it round her shoulders, banishing the faint chill which lingered on her skin. 'Shall we walk back together?'

'As soon as Marvo's sorted himself out.'

'Why, what's the matter with him?'

'He's climbing the walls. Literally. Come on, I'll show you.'

Behind the stage there was a smallish store-room which served as a makeshift dressing room for the artistes. Marvo

– still in his turban and black tuxedo – was balancing precariously on a beer-crate, trying to reach something up in the rafters. Jenny and Lindsey stared up at him.

'What's he *doing*?' asked Jenny.

'It's one of me blinkin' doves,' panted Marvo, jumping down off the crate. 'It won't go back in the box – and now it's playing silly buggers and I can't catch it.'

'I'm not surprised it won't come near you,' said Lindsey. 'You're frightening the life out of it.'

'Don't you believe it, that bird's laughing at me.'

'I still think if you sneaked up on it *slowly* . . .'

'All right, *you* catch it then,' suggested Marvo, sidestepping a small grey-white blob which was heading straight for his right lapel.

'And get myself pecked to death? No fear.'

'I'll get it, if you like,' volunteered Jenny. 'Dad used to keep pigeons when I was a kid.'

She made herself a stack of crates and eased her way, very slowly, towards the dove, making little cooing and chucking noises. Marvo watched her with respect as she stretched out her hand and – very, very gently – curled it around the unsuspecting bird.

'You're a woman of many talents, Jenny Fisher.'

'Trouble with Marvo is, he hasn't got the patience,' said Lindsey, helping Jenny down and popping the dove into its basket. 'I've told him before, all you have to do is stalk them. They're that daft, they don't even realise what you're up to – it works like magic every time.'

Jenny, Marvo and Lindsey walked back through the camp towards the chalet lines, Marvo carrying the basket of doves and Lindsey festooned with bags of stage props. It was a very dark and cloudless night, with a sprinkling of needle-point stars around a huge, waxy yellow moon.

'See that up there?' Marvo jabbed a finger at a cluster of stars.

'The thing just above the belltower?' yawned Lindsey.

'That's right, that's the Great Bear.'

'Bear? It looks more like a saucepan.'

355

'Some people call it the Plough.'

'But it looks like . . .'

'Yes, yes, I know – look, I don't make up the names, do I? Try those three stars over there, the really bright ones. That's Orion's belt.'

'Can't see it myself,' shrugged Lindsey. 'What do you think then, Jenny?'

Jenny huddled into her cardigan, walking along in silence, half a step behind the other two. She looked up as Lindsey nudged her arm.

'What?'

'The stars. Do you think that looks like a bear or a saucepan?'

'Dunno. Sorry, I wasn't really listening.'

Lindsey let Marvo get a few paces ahead.

'You've been funny all night. Something *is* the matter, isn't it? You're not ill, are you? You're all shivery.'

'Not ill, nothing like that.' Jenny hesitated. She liked Lindsey and Marvo, but she didn't know them very well, not like Mae. On the other hand, Mae had gone off to the "bright lights" of Rhyl with Bella and Dolly and there was nobody else to talk to. 'Just a few family problems.'

Lindsey wasn't about to let her get off the hook that easily.

'What sort of problems?'

To her surprise, Jenny found it a relief to open up.

'I heard from Mam today. My stepfather . . .' She swallowed, the acrid taste of bile in her mouth. 'He came back to the house and gave her a terrible hiding.'

Lindsey's eyes grew round with horror.

'Oh, Jenny, no! Was she badly hurt?'

'She's all right . . . I think. Geoff says I can go and see her as soon as he lines somebody up to stand in for me.' She halted, wanting to say more, wanting to tell Lindsey everything yet not knowing if she ever could.

'There's more, isn't there?' said Lindsey quietly. Jenny nodded.

'My sister . . . Nancy.'

'He hurt her too?'

Hurt Nancy? thought Jenny. He's more than hurt her.

'Sort of,' she said. 'He did something . . . something very bad to her.' She felt the beginnings of a cold shiver and forced herself to be strong. 'The police are sorting it out, they'll catch him soon.'

They came up to Jenny's chalet, the lights out and the curtains still open, revealing only darkness within. She wished Mae and the others were back, tonight she didn't want to be alone.

'I'd best go in,' she said, fumbling in her pocket for the key. 'Thanks for walking me back.'

'You'll be all right?' asked Lindsey. 'You could come back with us . . .'

'No, no, I'll be fine, honestly.' She caught the look of concern on Marvo's face, the same puzzled look that Tom always wore when he was worried but not sure what he should be worrying about. 'You get yourselves off to bed, it's been a long day.'

''Night then, Jenny.'

''Night.'

She waited for them to round the corner, then contemplated her darkened front door. No sense in hanging around out here. She slipped the key into the lock and turned it.

As she turned on the light, she caught the reflection of a swift movement in the mirror above the sink. No! No, no, no . . . She was already running as Ivan caught her, seized her, forced her down on the narrow iron bed.

'Missed your da, 'ave you, girl?' The eyes were glazed with hatred, the breath beery and rank.

She tried to cry out, but one of Ivan's huge, dinner-plate hands was over her mouth, almost preventing her from breathing, whilst the other was clawing and tearing at her clothes. And all the time he was ranting on at her, shouting and snarling.

'Bitch, filthy whore, I'll teach you . . . I'll teach you some respect.'

His knee was in her belly, holding her down, but she struggled and fought back with all her strength. Whatever he was going to do to her, whatever vileness, she would fight him every inch of the way. Her nails scratched and tore at his face, and she felt the wetness of his blood on her fingertips as they gouged into the flesh.

'Bitch. Bitch. Bitch.'

Ivan's anger and his lust turned to blind, murderous rage. The next thing Jenny knew, his hands were round her throat, squeezing, compressing, tightening. Jenny struggled for breath, but only the tiniest gasp entered her lungs. She could feel herself weakening, knew that there was no way she could resist Ivan's superior strength. In a few moments she would lose consciousness, and it would be too late.

His face was right above hers, spittle dripping in threads from his parted lips, the nose still bulbous and crooked from the beating Tom had given him. But it was only the eyes that Jenny saw; the black, evil diamonds that glittered with the anticipation of triumph.

Something — she knew not what — made her stretch out her right arm. Her hand made contact with something cool and hard. As her fingers tightened about it, Jenny knew that this was her only chance.

She took it.

Jimmy Costigern believed in making things to last, and the table-lamp was heavy, practically a solid lump of hardwood. With all her strength, Jenny brought it down on the side of Ivan's head. He cursed, and for a split second Jenny felt his grip slacken. It was just long enough to drag a single, painful breath into her lungs, just long enough to gain enough strength to club him a second time.

This time the blow was harder and more precise. It dazed him, and one hand slipped from her throat. She didn't give him the chance to get his wits back. The anger wasn't just inside him now, it was inside her too. It was mad and strong and all-consuming. She hit him again, again, again.

He slumped and rolled sideways, cursing and moaning in Welsh. Something at the back of Jenny's mind told her that all she needed to do was get away, run fast, find help. But she wasn't done with him yet, not by a long, long chalk.

The lamp was still in her hand, sturdy and unbroken.

'You. Bastard. You. Dirty. Filthy. Evil. Bastard.'

Every word was punctuated by a blow from the lamp. Jenny knelt astride Ivan, letting her anger and her pain guide her, unaware of anything but the raging agony inside her, and the need to be cleansed of it for ever.

'Mam.' She hit him. 'Nancy. Poor Nancy. Billy . . . Daisy . . . Tom . . . Ivan, you bastard. You *bastard*. I hate you, I hate you, I hate you . . .'

Jenny scarcely knew what was happening any more, only that she must go on hitting Ivan until the pain went away. But other hands were grabbing at her now.

'Jesus. No!'

She tried to shake the hands off, but they were strong and the voice that accompanied them was calm and familiar.

'Jenny. No more, Jenny. That's enough.'

'M-Marvo?' She looked at him, momentarily unable to comprehend. Her body was shaking violently. Marvo held her close and eased her away from the bed. She tried to look round at Ivan, but Marvo held her head fast. 'Don't look.' She heard him call out: 'Lindsey! Lindsey, for God's sake get help, some maniac's attacked Jenny.'

It was only then that the truth began to sink in, and the tears came; great wrenching sobs, the sounds of a helpless child. Marvo held her close to him, murmuring to her as if she was a baby.

And slowly, very slowly, her fingers relaxed, sending the broken lamp falling with a dull thud to the chalet floor.

'Here, drink this.'

Mae took Jenny's hands and curled them around the cup of hot, sweet tea.

'But I don't . . .'

'*Drink it.* Doctor's orders, remember? You've had a terrible shock, this'll do you good.'

Jenny tried to take a sip of tea, but it was almost impossible to swallow. She coughed, suddenly and painfully. Mae was instantly at her side, fussing like a mother hen.

'Jenny! Are you all right?'

Jenny nodded. She fingered her throat. It was swollen and very sore.

'Does it look . . . terrible?'

Mae smiled.

'Not terrible. It'll be a bit bruised in the morning, mind. Still, the police surgeon said you'll be singing again in no time. And you can wear a scarf till it's better, nobody'll notice.'

I will, thought Jenny. I'll remember this night for the rest of my life. She forced herself to take another sip of tea. This time it went down more easily, though the cup shook and slopped tea into the saucer as she set it down on the bedside table.

'Ivan . . .' she whispered. 'Where is he?'

Mae put her arm round Jenny's shoulders.

'He can't harm you any more.'

'The police . . . have they taken him away?'

Mae and Marvo exchanged looks. Marvo cleared his throat.

'Not the police, the ambulance. That was quite a number you did on him back there.'

'Oh God, no. He's not . . .?'

Mae glared at Marvo, who looked sheepish.

'The doctor said he'll be fine in a week or two,' she assured Jenny. 'Worse luck.'

Jenny put her head in her hands.

'I can't believe I did that to him . . .'

'It was you or him,' said Mae gently. 'I think you were very brave.'

'But . . .' Jenny looked up, her eyes searching Mae's for reassurance. 'Doesn't that make me as bad as him?'

'Don't talk daft,' cut in Lindsey. 'That low-life deserves everything he gets.'

'And more,' said Marvo. 'I just wish I'd got to him first.' He paused. 'I didn't like to say before, Jen, only . . . there's a copper outside, he wants a word.'

Mae rolled up her sleeves, ready to do battle.

'Well, tell him he can't,' she said. 'Can't you see Jenny's not up to it?'

360

Marvo was about to go out and do just that when Jenny stopped him.

'It's all right, let him come in.'

'You're sure?'

She nodded.

'I want to get it over with.'

The constable who stepped into Marvo's chalet was in his late-forties, very Welsh, with a soup-strainer moustache. He took off his helmet and placed it on the table.

'Miss Fisher?'

'Yes.'

Jenny watched the policeman flip through the pages of his notebook, waiting for the words she knew must surely come: 'I'm arresting you in connection with . . .'

'It seems a serious crime has been committed here tonight.'

Jenny felt drained of all strength. All she could do was watch and listen.

'I'll need a statement from you,' continued the police constable, 'but it can wait until you're feeling better.' Much to her surprise, he patted her on the shoulder. 'I'd get some rest if I were you, miss.'

'Aren't you . . . aren't you going to arrest me?'

'Arrest you? Not unless Ivan Price thinks of something we haven't, and if you ask me, he's in enough trouble already.'

'See?' said Mae, giving Jenny a triumphant hug. 'I told you it would be all right.'

Jenny stared unblinkingly at the constable.

'You mean . . . you're not charging me?'

'Nothing to charge you with, miss,' he replied with a kindly smile. 'Far as I'm concerned, you've done nothing wrong.'

Chapter 33

'It was good of Jolly Jimmy,' said Mae, 'springing for a week's holiday for your folks.' She took a critical look at herself in the mirror. 'Do you think this dress'll do? It's not a bit fancy?'

Jenny stood beside her and took a peep in the mirror.

'You look lovely. Sid'll think he's marrying Greta Garbo. Your dad insisted on paying for himself, didn't he?'

Mae pulled a face.

'You know Dad with his Manx pride, always wants to pay his way. He'd have paid for your mam too, only she wouldn't let him!'

'Really?'

'Really.' Mae winked. 'I reckon he's sweet on her, you know.'

'He never is!'

'Who knows? We might end up as sisters yet. This dress isn't too tight round the bum, is it? All these cream teas . . .'

'It looks grand, honest it does. If I were you I'd get changed before Sid gets back – you don't want him seeing it before the wedding, do you?'

Mae suppressed a giggle.

'Why not? He's seen everything else!'

Jenny tried not to look at herself too closely in the mirror. The gauzy scarf around her neck looked quite stylish, but she and Mae both knew what it concealed. And the memory of Ivan Price's violence would linger with her long after the bruises had faded.

She looked out across the camp. Hundreds of people

enjoying themselves in the August sunshine; ordinary, unremarkable people. How many of them had stories every bit as dramatic as that of the Fishers?

'I'm just going out for a few minutes,' she said. 'You don't mind, do you?'

'Going to talk to Nancy?'

'I have to sometime. I've left it too long already.'

Jenny knew where she'd find Nancy; sitting on the same bench, overlooking the sea, that she'd sat on every day since she came to Costigern's. She felt ashamed of herself for avoiding her sister for so long, but what in the world were they going to say to each other?

'Hello, Nancy.'

Silence.

'Mind if I sit here?'

Nancy didn't bother turning round.

'Please yourself.'

Jenny sat down. Beneath them, gaily coloured chalets stretched down towards the beach, the sands almost obscured by holidaymakers. She supposed they must have their dramas too, their joys and tragedies, their own preoccupations. At any rate, not one of them seemed to care much about the Costigerns, or the Czechoslovakian crisis, or Nancy and Jenny Fisher. She shaded her eyes. Along the shoreline, towards the point, a small boy and girl were playing French cricket with a beachball and a length of wood.

'Where's Billy and Daisy?'

'Tom took them to that farm thing. To see the pigs.'

'Oh.' Out of the corner of her eye, Jenny stole a look at Nancy. Her pregnancy was too obvious to hide now, even under that loose summer dress. A needle-sharp dart of helpless sorrow made Jenny's heart contract in sudden pain. 'How are you, Nancy?'

At this, she swung round to look at Jenny.

'How d'you think, after what he did to me?' Her eyes lingered on the scarf round Jenny's neck, and the accusing look faded. The eyes grew wide, staring, unable to look away.

'What's wrong, Nancy?'

'He . . . he hurt you too, didn't he?'

For the first time, Jenny felt the beginnings of an understanding between them. Was it too much to hope that in time it might grow?

'Yes.'

'Show me.'

Startled, Jenny began unwinding the scarf from her throat, very gingerly because the flesh underneath was still bruised and swollen. She slid away the scarf and bared her throat.

Nancy looked at it wonderingly, her eyes devouring the bruised and scabby flesh.

'He . . . did that to you?'

Jenny nodded.

'Can I touch?' Without waiting for Jenny's reply, Nancy reached out trembling fingertips. Jenny winced at the touch of crudely probing fingers, and they drew back. 'I'm sorry.'

'It's all right.'

'I just wanted . . . to see . . .'

Jenny laid her hand on Nancy's.

'To see if it was real?'

Nancy looked shamefaced. Her eyes dropped and her voice was very small.

'Yes.'

'Bad things happen to a lot of people, Nancy. Not just to you, and not just to me.'

Nancy's resentment quickened again.

'But it's not *fair*.' Her hand clutched at the swelling in her belly. 'Don't you see? All you have are the bruises, they'll go away. But this . . . this *thing* . . .'

'I know.'

'You can't know, how can you know?'

Jenny got slowly to her feet, her hand stroking Nancy's long, dark hair. The love inside her was so strong it almost hurt.

'He almost killed me, Nancy. Don't let him do the same to you.'

★ ★ ★

She found Tom with Billy and Daisy at the model farm, feeding lettuce leaves to the rabbits.

'I like it here, Jenny,' declared Daisy, giving her big sister a hug. 'Mam likes it too, she said so. Can we come again?'

'We'll see. If we can save up enough money.'

'That one's havin' babies, Jenny,' announced Billy, pointing at a very fat white rabbit with pink eyes.

'That's nice,' said Jenny.

'Mam says Nancy's havin' a baby,' added Daisy. 'Only we're not to talk about it 'cause it makes her cry. Why does Nancy cry all the time, Jenny?'

She ruffled Daisy's hair.

'People sometimes get like that when they're having a baby,' she said, and drew Tom over to one side, out of earshot of the kids. 'Tom, I'm worried.'

'Ivan won't bother us again, Jen. He'll go to jail, I'm sure.'

'Not about him, about Nancy. I think she still hates me.'

Tom shook his head.

'Nay, she dun't hate you, she just hates what's 'appened to her.'

'Can you blame her? She's only a kid, and now she's having one herself – and Ivan's kid at that. To be honest,' Jenny added in a low voice, 'I didn't think she would be having it, if you know what I mean.'

'She wanted rid of it,' said Tom. 'Only Mam wouldn't 'ear of it – said it's not the kid's fault, it's Ivan's.'

Jenny began to understand.

'Is Mam going to look after the baby herself then?'

'I reckon so.'

So Mam would have the baby she was still grieving over – and Nancy? Nancy could pretend it had never happened. Or at least, she could try. It would take a lot of trying, thought Jenny; a lot of trying and a lot of love.

Jenny took Tom by the arm.

'Look after Nancy, she thinks she's grown up but she's not.'

'Don't you worry, lass. I'll take care of 'em all.'

366

The night before the wedding, the Dukettes insisted on holding a hen-party for Mae in the Caribbean Bar. Naturally word got round the camp that the bar was serving free beer, and by nine o'clock it was chock-full of dancers, singers, Stripeys and campers, all intent on having the time of their lives – on the cheap.

'I thought this was supposed to be a small do!' protested Mae as another port and lemon was forced into her hand.

'Make the most of it,' said Dolly, downing hers in one. 'Get you another one, Jenny?'

'Er . . . no, thanks, maybe later.' She was scanning the bar for a sight of Mam. After a great deal of coaxing, Mae had managed to persuade Dot to come to the party, but she'd been sitting at a table all evening in silence, and now – to Jenny's consternation – she had disappeared altogether. Jenny touched Mae on the shoulder. 'Back in a mo.'

Jenny's hunch led her to the Ladies' Powder Room. Dot was sitting in her new dress on a pink velvet pouffe, her elbows resting on the edge of the sink. She was gazing into the mirror, her eyes red and swollen from crying.

'Oh, Mam.' Jenny wished she knew the right words to say. Talking had always been so difficult between them, not like it had been between her and Dad.

She drew up a gilded wooden chair and sat next to Dot, plucked her hanky from her sleeve and handed it to her.

'You all right, Mam?'

Dot nodded, blowing her nose and wiping it clean. She offered the handkerchief back to Jenny, but she shook her head.

'No, you keep it.'

'I'm all right, Jenny, you go back to your friends.'

'Not till I know what's wrong.'

Dot gazed into the mirror, her fingertips following the fine tracery of lines which time and care had etched at the corners of her eyes.

'Your dad would've loved this place,' she said softly. 'He were always talkin' about holidays, only we never 'ad money, see.'

Dot's words were a revelation to Jenny. It was the first

time she had spoken kindly of Dad in more years than Jenny could remember. Not, perhaps, since the day he died.

'I wish . . .' said Dot, then stopped.

'What, Mam?'

Her eyes met Jenny's in the mirror.

'He were a good man, were Dan Fisher. I couldn't 'ave married better. The day he died . . .'

Jenny could feel her mother's pain, the old bitterness melting away and turning to simple sorrow: the grief which had lain unresolved within her, for so many years.

'It's over now,' said Jenny gently. 'In the past.'

'I'll never forget him, you know.'

'I know.'

Dot's fingers stretched out tentatively to touch her daughter's. After a long moment's hesitation, they interlaced.

'I loved him, Jenny. I loved him so much . . .'

'Oh, Mam, Mam, I loved him too.'

Jenny and Dot held each other close, not weeping, but sharing their silent memories of Dan Fisher. Memories which were strong and clear and pure, which nothing could ever sully. At last, Dot drew away.

'I don't deserve a daughter like you.'

'Don't say that . . .'

'Nay, Jenny, it's true.' Dot squeezed her hand. 'You're a good lass, and I've brought you nowt but trouble.'

'If there's anything you need . . . or the kids . . . You know, don't you?'

'I know.'

'I'll send every spare penny I've got . . . and I'll come and see you, often as I can.'

Dot half-smiled. It was a start, thought Jenny. A better start than she could have hoped for. All at once, she thought of Mr Corlett. Good, steady, honest John Corlett, who'd hardly left Dot's side since they'd arrived at Costigern's; never fussing, never intruding, simply being there. And she thought of how Dot looked when she was with him; how the dark shadows seemed to fade from her face, making her look years younger.

'Mam,' she whispered.

'What, lass?'

'He'd want you to be happy . . . Dad. You know that, don't you?'

Dot looked down, but the smile did not go away.

'He were a lovely man, your dad.'

'But he's gone now, and he'd want you to be happy.' Jenny kissed her mother on the cheek. 'And that's what I want for you, too.'

You could say it was an unconventional sort of wedding, thought Jenny. The bride wore shocking pink, the bride's father was younger than the bridegroom, and the Sid Dukes Band played *Here Comes The Bride* as if it were a New Orleans jazz riff.

The chapel at Costigern's Camp was packed to overflowing as Mae Corlett and Sid Dukes took their vows. Glancing behind her, Jenny made out a sea of faces, some familiar, some not, all bright as the August sunshine which flooded in through the windows. There might be rumours of war on the other side of the English Channel, but here in Llandew nothing mattered beyond today.

Sid looked like a frightened rabbit, thought Jenny. Mae nudged him in the ribs as the chaplain spoke the opening lines of the marriage service.

'Buck up, love, it's supposed to be the happiest day of your life!'

Sid offered a nervous grin and patted Mae's hand.

'It's just . . . I've never done this before,' he said feebly.

'And you'll not be doing it again!' retorted Mae. 'Not if I've got anything to do with it.'

'You look grand,' Sid whispered, suddenly serious. 'I'm the luckiest man in the world.'

Mae winked.

'I know.'

Jenny caught the look that passed between them, the look of love that needed no words to express it. For a brief instant, she felt a twinge of jealousy, then it was gone. One day she'd know that kind of overwhelming love, too. For now, it was enough just to be happy and free.

Afterwards, at the reception in the Roman Room, Jenny sat with the Dukettes and ate cold roast beef and sherry trifle. Desmond and Binky spent most of the second course banging their spoons on the table, shouting 'Speech, speech!' and 'Give her a kiss then, Sid!'

The speeches came soon enough. Sid's was sentimental and loving, Geoff's polite and slightly formal. Desmond followed this up with a stream of bawdy anecdotes, before he was shut up by Dolly, who pushed Jenny to her feet.

'Go on then,' hissed Dolly.

'Go on then what?'

'Make a speech.'

'Who, me?'

'You're the chief bridesmaid, you *have* to, it's traditional.'

Jenny found herself standing up, looking down on a sea of expectant faces. She couldn't have been more alarmed if she'd suddenly woken up to find herself naked on the stage of the Theatre Royal.

Desmond, Duncan, Binky and the Dukettes were all stamping their feet and clapping.

'Speech, speech, speech!'

Marvo's voice rang out above the rest.

'Let's have a bit of hush then, the girl can't hear herself think.'

Jenny cleared her throat. She looked at Henry, who pulled a face and grinned. Mae was giggling and hugging Sid very tight.

'Ladies and gentlemen . . .' Jenny began.

'None of them 'ere,' commented a wit from the back of the hall.

'Dry up, Desmond,' said Jenny. To her surprise, he did. 'Ladies and gentlemen . . . this is supposed to be the happiest day of Mae and Sid's life.' She looked at the newlyweds, such an ill-matched pair, and so obviously happy. 'But I hope every day they have together will be happier than the last. In fact, I know it will.' She raised her glass. 'To Sid and Mae.'

'Sid and Mae!' echoed the wedding guests, to the sound of clinking glasses.

With a grateful sigh, Jenny flopped into her chair.

'Glad that's over,' she commented. 'How was it?'

'Very nice,' said Bella.

'Nice and *short*,' added Dolly with fervour.

Jimmy Costigern was the last to make a speech. He hauled himself to his feet to the accompaniment of assorted groans and quips.

'I'd just like to say a few short words . . .' he began.

'A few?' scoffed Dolly. 'That'll be the day. The only short thing about him is his temper.'

'Shush,' giggled Bella. 'He'll hear you.'

'Good. Then p'raps he'll take the hint.'

Thumbs in his waistcoat pockets, Jimmy launched into a list of pointed comments about the sanctity of marriage, never once taking his eyes off James and Miranda. Much to everybody's relief, he moved on to the story of how he'd met Sid and started him off on his musical career. Ten minutes later he was still talking, and would probably have gone on past tea-time if the Chief Stripey hadn't reminded him about the Grand Final of the kiddies' pitch and putt.

Things lightened up considerably after Jolly Jimmy left. Binky, Desmond and a few of the others set up a scratch band, and persuaded Sid and Geoff to duet on *The Sheikh of Araby*. Jenny was laughing and clapping with the rest when Henry approached with two glasses of wine. He held one out to her.

'Thought you might be thirsty.'

'Thanks.' She accepted it, and their fingers touched briefly yet lingeringly.

'I haven't seen you much since . . .' Henry's eyes were drawn to the high neckline of Jenny's dress.

'No.'

'Are you . . . I mean . . .?'

'I'm fine.' She looked into his eyes and smiled. 'Really I am. He can't hurt any of us now.'

Henry fiddled with the stem of his glass.

'There's something I've been meaning to tell you,' he

began. 'You remember I told you there were things I wanted to do before . . . you know . . . settling down?'

She nodded.

'Well, one of them is to be something useful.'

'*Useful?*'

'The thing is, I'll never be a society lawyer like my dad wants me to be, and maybe I'll go into the family business one day like Grandpa expects, but I'm not ready just yet.'

'So what *are* you going to do?'

'I'm going to be a teacher.'

'Oh.' Jenny took the idea in. It wasn't too difficult to imagine Henry in cap and gown, standing before row upon row of nicely washed prep-school boys. 'At your old school?'

Henry laughed.

'Not quite. A friend of mine runs a ragged school in Salford.'

'Salford!' Jenny stared at him, open-mouthed. 'But that's . . .'

'Not a very nice place? Don't worry, I know. The first time I went there it really knocked the stuffing out of me, I can tell you. But they need an assistant teacher and I'm game to give it a try.'

Jenny drank the rest of the wine in her glass. She needed it.

'What on earth does your dad say about this? And Jolly Jimmy?'

'Actually . . . you're the first person I've told.'

'No! Your grandfather . . . he'll . . .'

'Blow his top? Yes, I rather think he will.'

'You don't mind?'

Henry shrugged.

'He'll get over it. Besides, I've made up my mind – and I'm sick of Grandpa trying to run my life when he can't even sort out his own.' He bent forward and kissed her on the brow. It felt good. 'How about you? What are you going to do?'

'I'll stay with the band for the time being . . . but Sid thinks he can get me and Mae into a panto at Christmas.'

'So you and she are going to be a double act?'

'Looks that way.' Jenny smiled. 'Actually, we've been that way for years.'

'Can I come and see you? When you do the panto?'

'I'll send you a ticket.'

She might have said more, much more, only at that moment Mae came haring across the Roman Room with her skirt hitched up and a hatpin between her teeth.

'Come on, kid,' she gasped breathlessly, seizing Jenny's arm.

'Wh-what? Why?'

'Geoff's been looking for you all over the place! Get a move on Jenny, it's curtain up in fifteen minutes' time!'

Encore

One Year Later
The posters outside the theatre foyer proclaimed their message in jaunty pillar-box red:

GAIETY THEATRE, DOUGLAS, ISLE OF MAN
Sid Dukes Entertainments proudly present . . .
HOLIDAY FOLLIES OF 1939

Across each poster two words were emblazoned in large black capitals: SOLD OUT.

The old Victorian opera-house was sturdily built, but despite its foot-thick walls you could hear the applause halfway along the Loch Promenade. There was no doubt about it, 'Holiday Follies of 1939' was a roaring success.

Jenny Fisher and Mae Corlett – the Gaiety's very own Lancashire Lovelies – stood centre-stage and took another bow. The whole of the first ten rows was already on its feet applauding, the people in the dress circle leaning over and pelting them with a multi-coloured rain of toffee papers.

Mae turned to Jenny and grinned.

'I told you we'd be a success one day.'

'We're still only third on the bill,' pointed out Jenny, but she couldn't conceal her delight as a bouquet of red roses was thrust into her arms.

'Sid says if it keeps on like this, we'll be second turn by next week.'

They linked hands and took a final bow, then skipped off the stage to wait for the inevitable encore.

Jenny was exhausted, yet happiness and excitement lifted

her and she wanted to go on singing and dancing all night.

'We did it!' she laughed, hugging Mae. 'Sid was right, we really did it.'

'I told you he'd make you a star.'

'Not me. Us.'

'I can see it now,' enthused Mae. ' "Holiday Follies of 1940 – starring Jenny and Mae, the Lancashire Lovelies".'

'Perhaps . . .' said Jenny. 'But if Churchill's right and . . .'

But there was no time for doubts, because Mae was dragging her back on stage, to begin the whole intoxicating process all over again.

A selection of bestsellers from Headline

LAND OF YOUR POSSESSION	Wendy Robertson	£5.99 ☐
DANGEROUS LADY	Martina Cole	£5.99 ☐
SEASONS OF HER LIFE	Fern Michaels	£5.99 ☐
GINGERBREAD AND GUILT	Peta Tayler	£5.99 ☐
HER HUNGRY HEART	Roberta Latow	£5.99 ☐
GOING TOO FAR	Catherine Alliott	£5.99 ☐
HANNAH OF HOPE STREET	Dee Williams	£4.99 ☐
THE WILLOW GIRLS	Pamela Evans	£5.99 ☐
A LITTLE BADNESS	Josephine Cox	£5.99 ☐
FOR MY DAUGHTERS	Barbara Delinsky	£4.99 ☐
SPLASH	Val Corbett, Joyce Hopkirk, Eve Pollard	£5.99 ☐
THEA'S PARROT	Marcia Willett	£5.99 ☐
QUEENIE	Harry Cole	£5.99 ☐
FARRANS OF FELLMONGER STREET	Harry Bowling	£5.99 ☐

All Headline books are available at your local bookshop or newsagent, or can be ordered direct from the publisher. Just tick the titles you want and fill in the form below. Prices and availability subject to change without notice.

Headline Book Publishing, Cash Sales Department, Bookpoint, 39 Milton Park, Abingdon, OXON, OX14 4TD, UK. If you have a credit card you may order by telephone – 01235 400400.

Please enclose a cheque or postal order made payable to Bookpoint Ltd to the value of the cover price and allow the following for postage and packing:

UK & BFPO: £1.00 for the first book, 50p for the second book and 30p for each additional book ordered up to a maximum charge of £3.00.
OVERSEAS & EIRE: £2.00 for the first book, £1.00 for the second book and 50p for each additional book.

Name ....

Address ....

....

....

If you would prefer to pay by credit card, please complete:
Please debit my Visa/Access/Diner's Card/American Express (delete as applicable) card no:

Signature .... Expiry Date ....